ISAAC ASIMOV, one of Ar... has by now written more than 330 books. other writer in history has published so much on such a wide variety of subjects, which range from science fiction and murder novels to books on history, the physical sciences, and Shakespeare. Born in the Soviet Union and raised in Brooklyn, he lives in New York City with his wife, electric typewriter, and word processor.

MARTIN H. GREENBERG, who has been called 'the king of anthologists', now has some 130 to his credit. He is also co-editor, with Bill Pronzini, of The Mammoth Book of Short Crime Novels and The Mammoth Book of Short Spy Novels. Greenberg is professor of regional analysis and political science at the University of Wisconsin – Green Bay, USA, where he also teaches a course in the history of science fiction.

CHARLES G. WAUGH, a professor of psychology and mass communications at the University of Maine at Augusta, USA, is a leading authority on science fiction and fantasy who has collaborated on more than 80 anthologies and single-author collections with Isaac Asimov, Martin H. Greenberg, and assorted colleagues.

Also available in
ISAAC ASIMOV'S MAGICAL WORLD OF
FANTASY

**COSMIC KNIGHTS**

**GIANTS**

Also edited by Isaac Asimov,
Martin H. Greenberg and Charles G.
Waugh

**THE MAMMOTH BOOK OF
SHORT SCIENCE FICTION NOVELS**

**THE MAMMOTH BOOK OF
CLASSICAL SCIENCE FICTION**

**INTERGALACTIC EMPIRES**

**SUPERMEN**

# Isaac Asimov's Magical World of Fantasy

# MYTHIC BEASTS

### Edited by Isaac Asimov, Martin H. Greenberg and Charles G. Waugh

Robinson Publishing
London

Robinson Publishing
11 Shepherd House
Shepherd Street
London W1Y 7LD

First published in the UK by Robinson Publishing in 1988.

Printed by Wm. Collins & Sons Ltd., Glasgow

# CONTENTS

# ACKNOWLEDGMENTS

Grateful acknowledgment for permission to reprint material is hereby given to the following:

'Centaur Fielder for the Yankees', by Edward D. Hoch. Copyright © 1986 by Edward D. Hoch; an original story published with the permission of the author.

'The Ice Dragon', by George R. R. Martin. Copyright © 1980 by George R. R. Martin. From DRAGONS OF LIGHT. Reprinted by permission of the author.

'The Gorgon', by Tanith Lee. Copyright © 1983 by Tanith Lee. Reprinted by permission of the author.

'The Kragen', by Jack Vance. Copyright © 1964 by Ziff-Davis Publishing Company. Reprinted by permission of Kirby McCauley, Ltd.

'Letters from Laura', by Mildred Clingerman. Copyright © 1954; renewed © 1982 by Mildred Clingerman. Reprinted by permission of the author.

'The Triumph of Pegasus', by F. A. Javor. Copyright © 1964 by Mercury Press, Inc. From THE MAGAZINE OF FANTASY AND SCIENCE FICTION. Reprinted by permission of the Scott Meredith Literary Agency, Inc., 845 Third Avenue, New York, NY 10022.

'Caution! Inflammable!' by Thomas N. Scortia. Copyright © 1954; © 1975 by E.S.T. International, Ltd. First published as 'The End of the Line.'

'The Pyramid Project', by Robert F. Young. Copyright © 1961 by Ziff-Davis Publishing Company. Reprinted by permission of the Scott Meredith Literary Agency, Inc., 845 Third Avenue, New York, NY 10022.

'The Silken Swift', by Theodore Sturgeon. Copyright © 1953; renewed © 1979 by Theodore Sturgeon. Reprinted by permission of Kirby McCauley, Ltd.

'Mood Wendigo', by Thomas A. Easton. Copyright © 1980 by Davis Publications, Inc. Reprinted by permission of the author.

# CENTAUR

The horse was tamed about 2000 B.C. by the nomads of the Central Asian steppes, and when it drew a light chariot bearing a driver and an armed warrior, it proved a fearsome weapon. The horsemen conquered the entire civilized world from India to Egypt, and held their rule until the dominated people learned the use of the horse themselves.

By 800 B.C., the Medes of western Asia had bred horses large enough to carry men on their backs, and that combination was even more fearsome. To farmers who encountered horsemen for the first time this combination of men and animals must have seemed monstrous.

The early Greeks were not horsepeople, for their mountainous terrain and narrow valleys were not conducive to either the breeding or the use of horses. In northern Greece, however, there was the plain of Thessaly, and there horses and horsemen made their appearance.

The fearful Greeks must have first seen them as horse-human combinations, and so was born the myth of the "centaur," finally portrayed in Greek art as a creature with the head and torso of a human being replacing the head and neck of a horse. For the most part, the Greeks pictured the centaurs as barbarians—crude, wild, lawless, easily made drunk, and, in that state, prone to be lascivious. Perhaps that is how they saw the real Thessalian horsemen.

At least one centaur, however, named Chiron, was wise,

*noble, and learned. He was the tutor of Hercules and Achilles, among others.*

*The centaur of the story that follows falls between these two extremes.*

# CENTAUR FIELDER FOR THE YANKEES

*Edward D. Hoch*

Let me tell you, there was a time not so long ago when a centaur would have been kept in a zoo or a circus. He certainly wouldn't have been allowed to play major league baseball. But times have changed, and we're more tolerant of people who are different. I suppose that's why Mark Eques ended up playing baseball for the New York Yankees.

But I'd better tell it from the beginning.

The idea of centaurs—creatures having the head, trunk and arms of a man and the body and legs of a horse—had been around since Ovid's *Metamorphoses* and Homer's *Iliad*. It was Lucretius who declared that the creature must be mythical because horses reach maturity before humans, and are full-grown at three years of age. The horse would die fifty years before the man. All this is true enough, but when Professor Hagger of Columbia University returned from the Greek island of Antikythira with a young living centaur early in the 22nd century, a great many preconceptions changed.

Like most everyone else in America, I'd equated centaurs with unicorns and other mythical beasts. Seeing one live on the evening news took some getting used to. Hagger christened the young creature Mark Eques, and set about educating him. It was quite a story for a month or two, during the slow news days of summer, but by fall Professor Hagger and his discovery had faded from view. Mark Eques was living on a farm in upstate New York, staying pretty much out of the public eye.

A few years passed before we heard about him again, and this time it was an announcement by Professor Hagger that Mark was about to enter Columbia University, having passed the traditional college entrance examinations. He was even entitled to special consideration by the university, since the government had ruled that Mark was a handicapped human being and not any sort of monster.

Mark found college to be difficult, and by the end of his first year it appeared he was ready to drop out. That was when Roscoe Greene, a scout for the New York Yankees baseball team, contacted Mark, and when I had my first meeting with the boy centaur.

I was a sportswriter on a Boston paper at the time, and I became interested in Mark when he attempted to run in the Boston marathon. They couldn't officially bar him from it, but they did the next best thing. They set up a special category for centaurs. Since he was the only known centaur on earth, he had no one to compete against but himself. There was no point in running at all, and on Patriots' Day he didn't even bother to appear.

But baseball was a different story.

Mark Eques had been ruled a handicapped person, and under federal regulations in those early years of the 22nd century, handicapped persons were allowed to play professional sports, so long as their handicap did not prevent them from performing their duties. I had to hand it to Roscoe Greene for coming up with that one.

An old girl friend in the Yankee front office tipped me off to what was happening, and I drove all night to reach the Dutchess County farm where Mark was living with Professor Hagger after completing his first year at Columbia. It was horse country, with the roads bordered on either side by neat white fences that extended back over the rolling hills as far as the eye could see.

As I pulled into the Hagger farm shortly after nine in the morning I saw that Roscoe Greene had arrived first. He stood at the fence speaking with Mark Eques. When he saw me he cursed, not too softly. "What in hell are you doing here, Danny? Go back to Boston where you belong!"

"Hello, Roscoe. Glad to see you too. Is it true the Yankees are about to sign Mark here to a position in center field?"

Mark Eques, his hairy chest bare to the morning sun, grinned boyishly and pawed the grass with his front hoof. "I'm gonna play in the big leagues," he announced proudly.

"What does Hagger say about all this?" I wanted to know.

"Why don't you ask him?" Greene answered smugly.

Professor Hagger must have observed my arrival, because he came out of the farmhouse to join us. When Greene introduced me, he said, "So the press is onto this already! You don't waste any time."

"Danny's a go-getter," Green confirmed. "One of these days he'll cover a story before it happens."

"Has he ever played ball?" I asked the professor. "Is he any good at it?"

"His family apparently played a version of baseball," Hagger responded. "He remembers it as a child."

"I'm good," Mark Eques answered for himself. "They wouldn't let me run in the marathon but they can't stop me now."

"He has tremendous speed in the outfield," Professor Hagger confirmed. "Virtually nothing gets by him. His base-running is superb too. We're still working on his hitting."

"What do you think, Roscoe?" I asked Greene.

"I think he has unlimited potential. Young, clean-cut— people will flock to the games just to see him play."

"The other managers will never allow it," I predicted.

"We've already got the courts behind us. Let the other clubs go out and hire their own centaur."

Mine was the first exclusive interview with Mark Eques on his signing with the Yankees, and for a week or two it was quite a story. The other major league clubs grumbled, of course, until New York agreed to share with them the additional revenues Mark's appearance was expected to generate. So, after a month of hoopla and further training, the centaur took the field for a July 4th doubleheader against the Boston Red Sox. I was there, of course, covering Boston on the road as I usually did, but so was just about every sportswriter in the country, along with all the TV and satellite people. It's a wonder there was any space left in the Yankees' new domed stadium for just plain fans.

Mark Eques galloped onto the field wearing his Yankee shirt and the crowd went wild. He removed his hat while the National Anthem was played, and then continued on into center field. The first inning was a disappointment for the fans and television cameras, with not a single ball making it out of the infield. But in the top of the second Mark showed his stuff, charging across center field to nab a well-hit grounder and peg it to first base for the out. The crowd went wild for the second time.

He could hit too. He ended the day's doubleheader with two doubles and a single, which wasn't bad. The Yankees won the first game 5–3, and only dropped the nightcap 2–1 as a result of a ninth-inning Boston homer. Even a centaur in the outfield couldn't protect against home runs.

The following week's games showed that his biggest strengths were in fielding and baserunning. Once he got the hang of it, Mark proved a whiz at stolen bases. The sight of him galloping into second at a full charge was enough to intimidate most any second baseman in the league. By the end of July, the Yankees had climbed into a tie with Boston for first place in the American League East.

That was when I was approached by Lippy Lewis.

Lippy was a gambler who specialized in sports betting of any kind. He'd bet big money on Boston as an early-season favorite to take both the pennant and the World Series, and he wasn't about to lose it. "Tell me something, Danny," he said one afternoon in August after the Yankees had extended a midseason winning streak to seven games. "Do you think that Eques guy could be bought off?"

"Lippy, you always did have a big mouth," I told him. "I guess that's how you got your name. Do you want me to run what you just said in tomorrow's edition? I could probably even get your picture in. What were you thinking of offering him—oats?"

Lippy shrugged. "Money. Women. He must have some weakness."

"Stay away from him, Lippy, or I will print that."

"Hell, you're a Boston guy! The Sox are your meal ticket too."

"Mark Eques is my meal ticket this year. He's the greatest thing that's happened to baseball in two decades. Stay away from him, Lippy, or you'll be in big trouble."

But I knew Lippy Lewis would do as he pleased, and I wasn't surprised the following week to see him chatting with Mark after a game, standing by the horse trailer that Professor Hagger used to make the run to and from his farm. The trailer was even used for games on the road, though it had to be transported by air between distant cities. I stood off to one side, waiting until Lippy departed, and then strolled up to Mark.

"Lippy's got a bad reputation," I said casually. "You shouldn't be seen talking to him too much."

"That guy? He doesn't bother me. He offered me money and girls to miss a few fly balls." Mark seemed to find the idea amusing.

"What did you say?"

"I told him I had enough money. As for girls, it's wrong to mate outside your species. Professor Hagger taught me that."

"But there are no female centaurs, are there?"

"Oh sure," he replied offhandedly. "They're just shy, that's all. They live in the caves and the mazes and no one ever sees them."

"I thought mazes were for Minotaurs."

Mark looked disgusted. "No one believes in them anymore."

Professor Hagger always attended the games, of course, transporting Mark back and forth in the trailer. I caught up with him at the next home appearance, with the Yankees now firmly in first place. "Has there been any more trouble with Lippy Lewis?" I asked.

Hagger looked surprised. "We haven't had any trouble with Lippy that I know about."

"I think he tried to bribe Mark to relax a bit. There's big money riding on the pennant and the World Series."

"Mark wouldn't take a bribe."

"I'm sure he wouldn't. But if you have any trouble with Lippy, let me know. A few mentions in my column would cool him off."

Hagger nodded. "We appreciate everything you've done for Mark already. Some of the press still treat him like a freak. Your stories make him seem like a human being."

"I've always considered Mark to be a human being."

Hagger smiled slightly. "Well, he's still a centaur. Nothing can change that."

Mark Eques hit two home runs in that evening's game, and ran the bases like a stallion. His fielding was better than ever—so good, in fact, that the opposing manager raised the point in a post-game press conference that Mark should be banned from organized baseball. "He's not human, after all," Bunty Simmons grumbled.

I fought my way through the throng to the front row of questioners. "Back in July you all went along with it," I reminded him. "The gates would increase and everyone would share in the wealth."

"Well, sure," he admitted. "We knew people would pay to see a centaur playing ball. What we didn't know was—"

"—that he'd be so good," I finished for him.

Through all of this, Roscoe Greene, the scout who'd first signed Mark with the Yankees, was riding high. I heard through the grapevine that he'd gotten a big raise, with a bonus promised if Mark Eques came through strong in the World Series. Greene and I had never really been friends, and I was surprised when he phoned me in Boston the day the Yankees clinched the pennant in the American League East.

"Have you heard the news?" he asked without preamble.

"About what?"

"Mark Eques."

The panic in his voice was catching. "He's not hurt?"

"Worse than that."

"What—?"

"It just came over the radio. An expedition on that Greek island has discovered a female centaur!"

"Then he wasn't kidding me. He said there were females. That's great news, Roscoe."

"It's terrible news."

"How come?"

"The expedition is financed by Lewis Enterprises, the video people. In case you didn't know, that's Lippy Lewis's brother."

"My God!"

"I know Lippy's been trying to bribe Mark. Now he's got his weapon. Mark may not be tempted by regular women, but a female centaur is something else again!"

Well, this latest development really stirred up the press. About the only thing they like better than a bribery scandal is a sex scandal. Although the whereabouts of the newly discovered female centaur was a carefully guarded secret, the papers were full of rumors of a secret tryst with Mark Eques. I phoned Professor Hagger nearly every day in late September, but he assured me there'd been no word from Lippy and no sign of a female centaur.

I spoke with Mark too, of course. The playoffs began in early October, and I covered all the games. The Yankees made short work of the Las Vegas Wheels, capturing four straight behind some good pitching and Mark's fleet-footed fielding. There was a general feeling that the only team to present a real challenge to the Yankees might be the St. Louis Cardinals, and when the Cards clinched the National League pennant to move on to the World Series, there was talk of the greatest Series since '75.

I interviewed Mark Eques on the eve of the first game at St. Louis. "What about it, Mark?" I asked. "You seem a little bit troubled and off your feed. Has Lippy Lewis been after you again?"

"Yeah," the young centaur admitted. "He talked to me."

"About the newly discovered female?"

Mark nodded. "He showed me pictures."

"And asked you to throw the game?"

"Either that or not play at all."

"You were tempted?"

"By the pictures? No."

"Why not?"

"She's my sister, Carza."

"Your—"

"I told you there were females down in the caves. Carza was never as shy as the rest. I should have known she'd be the one to come outside and get caught."

"If she's your sister, I'd think you'd be happy at the prospect of seeing her again. Why are you so glum?"

"I guess because I don't know what Lippy will try next. There's something about Carza they might discover—"

"What's that?"

Mark Eques hung his shoulders. "She's a better ball player than I am."

We learned the following day that Lewis and his people had indeed discovered it. Carza took the field wearing a Cardinals shirt and started warming up with the rest of the team. She was a lovely young woman, frisky and smiling, and she captured the hearts of almost everyone at once. The Yankee owners were not quite so enchanted, and they could be seen huddling with the baseball commissioner in his box. Certainly no one could object to a centaur playing baseball, nor to a woman, since Iris Schultz had pitched a full season for the Dodgers. But this was a new player, joining the team just in time for the Series!

The game was delayed an hour while they argued the point, disrupting television schedules around the world, but the commissioner finally ruled that she could play. The teams took the field. It would be centaur against centaur.

For the first few innings the crowd went wild each time Mark or his sister took the field. But it soon became obvious that each of them was so skilled in playing the outfield that nothing less than a home run would make it onto the scoreboard that day. Mark was the better hitter, probably because he'd been playing since July, but he only succeeded in hitting two high flies that Carza caught without any trouble. The crowd wanted hits, but all they were getting was a demonstration of some remarkable fielding.

As the ninth inning ended in a scoreless tie I spotted Lippy Lewis at a refreshment stand by the back of the stadium. "How's it going, Lippy? I see you switched your allegiance from the Sox to the Cards."

"You gotta go with the smart money, Danny," he said, squeezing some mustard onto a hot dog.

"The smart money used to say you should never bet against the Yankees."

"Yeah? Well, we got our own centaur now."

The tenth inning had begun while we chatted, and suddenly there came a groan of anguish from the St. Louis fans. Lippy and I hurried to see what had happened, and I think we were equally horrified to see Carza lying on the field in obvious pain. She'd tripped while chasing a hard-hit grounder to center, and the ball had rolled all the way to the outfield fence for a triple.

Mark hurried to her side as she was carried off the field. "Marque," she murmured. "Take me home. I want to go home."

"Will they have to shoot her?" Lippy asked me.

"No. She's not a horse."

The Yankees won it, 1-0, and went on to win the Series, but that was the last game Mark Eques and his sister played. Professor Hagger accompanied them back to the Greek island where he'd first found Mark. During their winter meeting the baseball managers voted to bar any players having more than two legs, whatever their species. The day of the centaur was over, as quickly as it had begun.

It was sort of a sad ending to the story, and that was one reason I decided to fly over to Antikythira the following spring, to see how Mark and his sister were doing. I feared I'd have difficulty finding them, imagining that they'd retreated deep into their caves after their brush with fame, but I was wrong. Mark was running a messenger service—a sort of Centaur Express—and Carza had fully recovered from her injury.

"She's too old for the game," Mark explained. "I remember her playing ball when I was only a child."

"Will you ever play again?" I asked.

"Not in America. I heard they'd banned centaurs. But Carza and I are talking about starting a league over here. An all-centaur league. We think there are enough good players, and it would make a great tourist attraction. We hope to get started by next year."

When I told Lippy Lewis about it, back in the States, he was interested. "Might be some betting action there," he decided, "once they get organized. But I'm sorry he didn't stay in this country and let me handle him."

"There are no more centaurs in baseball, Lippy," I reminded him.

"Who's talking baseball? I wanted to run him in the Kentucky Derby!"

# DRAGON

*The concept of the dragon was originally built up out of
the fears of early human beings for the largest and most
threatening reptiles with which they came in contact, the
largest snakes and crocodiles. The very word comes from
the Greek* drakon, *meaning a large snake.*

*Like the crocodile, the dragon was thick-bodied and had
small legs. From the snake, some of which (though not the
largest) were poisonous, it developed a fiery breath. (The
poison, we can well imagine, might burn like fire when
one is bitten by a snake.) Also because the snake moves
unseen through the underbrush and comes upon you unaware, the notion of rapid movement, hence flight, was
sometimes applied to the dragon, and it developed wings.
(In the nineteenth century, scientists discovered the fossils
of flying reptiles remarkably like dragons in some ways,
but they had all died out 65 million years ago and the
similarity to the legend is purely coincidence.)*

*Size, wings, fiery breath—so mighty, in imagination,
did the dragons become that they began to represent elemental forces of nature, cruel and malevolent. Finally,
they were viewed as the embodiment of the drive toward
chaos, toward the destruction of the order built by the
creative gods. In the Greek myths, the world could not be
reconstructed after a universal flood till Apollo had slain a
monstrous dragon called Python. (Large snakes are still
called pythons today.) Similarly, in the Babylonian myths,
the gods could not create the world till they had slain the*

dragon Tiamat, and there are rather obscure references in the Bible to God slaying Leviathan, who is pictured as the dragon of chaos.

In the following story, a dragon is pictured as a personification of cold, not common in legend, and as not entirely malevolent.

# THE ICE DRAGON

## *George R. R. Martin*

Adara liked the winter best of all, for when the world grew cold the ice dragon came.

She was never quite sure whether it was the cold that brought the ice dragon or the ice dragon that brought the cold. That was the sort of question that often troubled her brother Geoff, who was two years older than her and insatiably curious, but Adara did not care about such things. So long as the cold and the snow and the ice dragon all arrived on schedule, she was happy.

She always knew when they were due because of her birthday. Adara was a winter child, born during the worst freeze that anyone could remember, even Old Laura, who lived on the next farm and remembered things that had happened before anyone else was born. People still talked about that freeze. Adara often heard them.

They talked about other things as well. They said it was the chill of that terrible freeze that had killed her mother, stealing in during her long night of labor past the great fire that Adara's father had built, and creeping under the layers of blankets that covered the birthing bed. And they said that the cold had entered Adara in the womb, that her skin had been pale blue and icy to the touch when she came forth, and that she had never warmed in all the years since. The winter had touched her, left its mark upon her, and made her its own.

It was true that Adara was always a child apart. She was a very serious little girl who seldom cared to play with the others. She was beautiful, people said, but in a strange,

15

distant sort of way, with her pale skin and blond hair and wide clear blue eyes. She smiled, but not often. No one had ever seen her cry. Once when she was five she had stepped upon a nail imbedded in a board that lay concealed beneath a snowbank, and it had gone clear through her foot, but Adara had not wept or screamed even then. She had pulled her foot loose and walked back to the house, leaving a trail of blood in the snow, and when she had gotten there she had said only, "Father, I hurt myself." The sulks and tempers and tears of ordinary childhood were not for her.

Even her family knew that Adara was different. Her father was a huge, gruff bear of a man who had little use for people in general, but a smile always broke across his face when Geoff pestered him with questions, and he was full of hugs and laughter for Teri, Adara's older sister, who was golden and freckled, and flirted shamelessly with all the local boys. Every so often he would hug Adara as well, especially when he was drunk, which was frequent during the long winters. But there would be no smiles then. He would only wrap his arms around her, and pull her small body tight against him with all his massive strength, sob deep in his chest, and fat wet tears would run down his ruddy cheeks. He never hugged her at all during the summers. During the summers he was too busy.

Everyone was busy during the summers except for Adara. Geoff would work with his father in the fields and ask endless questions about this and that, learning everything a farmer had to know. When he was not working he would run with his friends to the river, and have adventures. Teri ran the house and did the cooking, and worked a bit at the inn by the crossroads during the busy season. The innkeeper's daughter was her friend, and his youngest son was more than a friend, and she would always come back giggly and full of gossip and news from travelers and soldiers and king's messengers. For Teri and Geoff the summers were the best time, and both of them were too busy for Adara.

Their father was the busiest of all. A thousand things needed to be done each day, and he did them, and found a thousand more. He worked from dawn to dusk. His muscles grew hard and lean in summer, and he stank from sweat each night when he came in from the fields, but he always came in smiling. After supper he would sit with Geoff and tell him stories and answer his questions, or teach Teri things she did not know about cooking, or stroll down to the inn. He was a summer man, truly.

He never drank in summer, except for a cup of wine now and again to celebrate his brother's visits.

That was another reason why Teri and Geoff loved the summers, when the world was green and hot and bursting with life. It was only in summer that Uncle Hal, their father's younger brother, came to call. Hal was a dragonrider in service to the king, a tall slender man with a face like a noble. Dragons cannot stand the cold, so when winter fell Hal and his wing would fly south. But each summer he returned, brilliant in the king's green-and-gold uniform, en route to the battlegrounds to the north and west of them. The war had been going on for all of Adara's life.

Whenever Hal came north, he would bring presents; toys from the king's city, crystal and gold jewelry, candies, and always a bottle of some expensive wine that he and his brother could share. He would grin at Teri and make her blush with his compliments, and entertain Geoff with tales of war and castles and dragons. As for Adara, he often tried to coax a smile out of her, with gifts and jests and hugs. He seldom succeeded.

For all his good nature, Adara did not like Hal; when Hal was there, it meant that winter was far away.

Besides, there had been a night when she was only four, and they thought her long asleep, that she overheard them talking over wine. "A solemn little thing," Hal said. "You ought to be kinder to her, John. You cannot blame *her* for what happened."

"Can't I?" her father replied, his voice thick with wine. "No, I suppose not. But it is hard. She looks like Beth, but she has none of Beth's warmth. The winter is in her, you know. Whenever I touch her I feel the chill, and I remember that it was for her that Beth had to die."

"You are cold to her. You do not love her as you do the others."

Adara remembered the way her father laughed then. "Love her? Ah, Hal. I loved her best of all, my little winter child. But she has never loved back. There is nothing in her for me, or you, any of us. She is such a cold little girl." And then he began to weep, even though it was summer and Hal was with him. In her bed, Adara listened and wished that Hal would fly away. She did not quite understand all that she had heard, not then, but she remembered it, and the understanding came later.

She did not cry; not at four, when she heard, or six, when she finally understood. Hal left a few days later, and Geoff and Teri waved to him excitedly when his wing passed overhead, thirty great dragons in proud formation against the summer sky. Adara watched with her small hands by her sides.

There were other visits in other summers, but Hal never made her smile, no matter what he brought her.

Adara's smiles were a secret store, and she spent of them only in winter. She could hardly wait for her birthday to come, and with it the cold. For in winter she was a special child.

She had known it since she was very little, playing with the others in the snow. The cold had never bothered her the way it did Geoff and Teri and their friends. Often Adara stayed outside alone for hours after the others had fled in search of warmth, or run off to Old Laura's to eat the hot vegetable soup she liked to make for the children. Adara would find a secret place in the far corner of the fields, a different place each winter, and there she would build a tall white castle, patting the snow in place with small bare hands, shaping it into towers and battlements like those Hal often talked about on the king's castle in the city. She would snap icicles off from the lower branches of trees, and use them for spires and spikes and guardposts, ranging them all about her castle. And often in the dead of winter would come a brief thaw and a sudden freeze, and overnight her snow castle would turn to ice, as hard and strong as she imagined real castles to be. All through the winters she would build on her castle, and no one ever knew. But always the spring would come, and a thaw not followed by a freeze; then all the ramparts and walls would melt away, and Adara would begin to count the days until her birthday came again.

Her winter castles were seldom empty. At the first frost each year, the ice lizards would come wriggling out of their burrows, and the fields would be overrun with the tiny blue creatures, darting this way and that, hardly seeming to touch the snow as they skimmed across it. All the children played with the ice lizards. But the others were clumsy and cruel, and they would snap the fragile little animals in two, breaking them between their fingers as they might break an icicle hanging from a roof. Even Geoff, who was too kind ever to do something like that, sometimes grew curious, and held the lizards too long in his efforts to examine them, and the heat of his hands would make them melt and burn and finally die.

Adara's hands were cool and gentle, and she could hold the lizards as long as she liked without harming them, which always made Geoff pout and ask angry questions. Sometimes she would lie in the cold, damp snow and let the lizards crawl all over her, delighting in the light touch of their feet as they skittered across her face. Sometimes she would wear ice lizards hidden in her hair as she went about her chores, though she took care never to take them inside where the heat of the fires would kill them. Always she would gather up scraps after the family ate, and bring them to the secret place where her castle was a-building, and there she would scatter them. So the castles she erected were full of kings and courtiers every winter; small furry creatures that snuck out from the woods, winter birds with pale white plumage, and hundreds and hundreds of squirming, struggling ice lizards, cold and quick and fat. Adara liked the ice lizards better than any of the pets the family had kept over the years.

But it was the ice dragon that she loved.

She did not know when she had first seen it. It seemed to her that it had always been a part of her life, a vision glimpsed during the deep of winter, sweeping across the frigid sky on wings serene and blue. Ice dragons were rare, even in those days, and whenever it was seen the children would all point and wonder, while the old folks muttered and shook their heads. It was a sign of a long and bitter winter when ice dragons were abroad in the land. An ice dragon had been seen flying across the face of the moon on the night Adara had been born, people said, and each winter since it had been seen again, and those winters had been very bad indeed, the spring coming later each year. So the people would set fires and pray and hope to keep the ice dragon away, and Adara would fill with fear.

But it never worked. Every year the ice dragon returned. Adara knew it came for her.

The ice dragon was large, half again the size of the scaled green war dragons that Hal and his fellows flew. Adara had heard legends of wild dragons larger than mountains, but she had never seen any. Hal's dragon was big enough, to be sure, five times the size of a horse, but it was small compared to the ice dragon, and ugly besides.

The ice dragon was a crystalline white, that shade of white that is so hard and cold that it is almost blue. It was covered with hoarfrost, so when it moved its skin broke and crackled as the crust on the snow crackles beneath a man's boots, and flakes of rime fell off.

Its eyes were clear and deep and icy.

Its wings were vast and batlike, colored all a faint translucent blue. Adara could see the clouds through them, and oftentimes the moon and stars, when the beast wheeled in frozen circles through the skies.

Its teeth were icicles, a triple row of them, jagged spears of unequal length, white against its deep blue maw.

When the ice dragon beat its wings, the cold winds blew and the snow swirled and scurried and the world seemed to shrink and shiver. Sometimes when a door flew open in the cold of winter, driven by a sudden gust of wind, the householder would run to bolt it and say, "An ice dragon flies nearby."

And when the ice dragon opened its great mouth, and exhaled, it was not fire that came streaming out, the burning sulfurous stink of lesser dragons.

The ice dragon breathed cold.

Ice formed when it breathed. Warmth fled. Fires guttered and went out, shriven by the chill. Trees froze through to their slow secret souls, and their limbs turned brittle and cracked from their own weight. Animals turned blue and whimpered and died, their eyes bulging and their skin covered over with frost.

The ice dragon breathed death into the world; death and quiet and *cold*. But Adara was not afraid. She was a winter child, and the ice dragon was her secret.

She had seen it in the sky a thousand times. When she was four, she saw it on the ground.

She was out building on her snow castle, and it came and landed close to her, in the emptiness of the snow-covered fields. All the ice lizards ran away. Adara simply stood. The ice dragon looked at her for ten long heartbeats, before it took to the air again. The wind shrieked around her and through her as it beat its wings to rise, but Adara felt strangely exalted.

Later that winter it returned, and Adara touched it. Its skin was very cold. She took off her glove nonetheless. It would not be right otherwise. She was half afraid it would burn and melt at her touch, but it did not. It was much more sensitive to heat than even the ice lizards, Adara knew somehow. But she was special, the winter child, cool. She stroked it, and finally gave its wing a kiss that hurt her lips. That was the winter of her fourth birthday, the year she touched the ice dragon.

The winter of her fifth birthday was the year she rode upon it for the first time.

It found her again, working on a different castle at a different place in the fields, alone as ever. She watched it come, and ran to it when it landed, and pressed herself against it. That had been the summer when she had heard her father talking to Hal.

They stood together for long minutes until finally Adara, remembering Hal, reached out and tugged at the dragon's wing with a small hand. And the dragon beat its great wings once, and then extended them flat against the snow, and

Adara scrambled up to wrap her arms about its cold white neck.

Together, for the first time, they flew.

She had no harness or whip, as the king's dragonriders use. At times the beating of the wings threatened to shake her loose from where she clung, and the coldness of the dragon's flesh crept through her clothing and bit and numbed her child's flesh. But Adara was not afraid.

They flew over her father's farm, and she saw Geoff looking very small below, startled and afraid, and knew he could not see her. It made her laugh an icy, tinkling laugh, a laugh as bright and crisp as the winter air.

They flew over the crossroads inn, where crowds of people came out to watch them pass.

They flew above the forest, all white and green and silent.

They flew high into the sky, so high that Adara could not even see the ground below, and she thought she glimpsed another ice dragon, way off in the distance, but it was not half so grand as *hers*.

They flew for most of the day, and finally the dragon swept around in a great circle, and spiraled down, gliding on its stiff and glittering wings. It let her off in the field where it had found her, just after dusk.

Her father found her there, and wept to see her, and hugged her savagely. Adara did not understand that, nor why he beat her after he had gotten her back to the house. But when she and Geoff had been put to sleep, she heard him slide out of his own bed and come padding over to her. "You missed it all," he said. "There was an ice dragon, and it scared everybody. Father was afraid it had eaten you."

Adara smiled to herself in the darkness, but said nothing.

She flew on the ice dragon four more times that winter, and every winter after that. Each year she flew farther and more often than the year before, and the ice dragon was seen more frequently in the skies above their farm.

Each winter was longer and colder than the one before.

Each year the thaw came later.

And sometimes there were patches of land, where the ice

dragon had lain to rest, that never seemed to thaw properly at all.

There was much talk in the village during her sixth year, and a message was sent to the king. No answer ever came.

"A bad business, ice dragons," Hal said that summer when he visited the farm. "They're not like real dragons, you know. You can't break them or train them. We have tales of those that tried, found frozen with their whip and harness in hand. I've heard about people that have lost hands or fingers just by touching one of them. Frostbite. Yes, a bad business."

"Then why doesn't the king do something?" her father demanded. "We sent a message. Unless we can kill the beast or drive it away, in a year or two we won't have any planting season at all."

Hal smiled grimly. "The king has other concerns. The war is going badly, you know. They advance every summer, and they have twice as many dragonriders as we do. I tell you, John, it's hell up there. Some year I'm going to come back. The king can hardly spare men to go chasing an ice dragon." He laughed. "Besides, I don't think anybody's ever killed one of the things. Maybe we should just let the enemy take this whole province. Then it'd be *his* ice dragon."

But it wouldn't be, Adara thought as she listened. No matter what king ruled the land, it would always be *her* ice dragon.

Hal departed and summer waxed and waned. Adara counted the days until her birthday. Hal passed through again before the first chill, taking his ugly dragon south for the winter. His wing seemed smaller when it came flying over the forest that fall, though, and his visit was briefer than usual, and ended with a loud quarrel between him and her father.

"They won't move during the winter," Hal said. "The winter terrain is too treacherous, and they won't risk an advance without dragonriders to cover them from above. But come spring, we aren't going to be able to hold them. The king may not even try. Sell the farm now, while you can still get a good price. You can buy another piece of land in the south."

"*This* is my land," her father said. "I was born here. You

too, though you seem to have forgotten. Our parents were buried here. And Beth too. I want to lie beside her when I go."

"You'll go a lot sooner than you'd like if you don't listen to me," Hal said angrily. "Don't be stupid, John. I know what the land means to you, but it isn't worth your life." He went on and on, but her father would not be moved. They ended the evening swearing at each other, and Hal left in the dead of night, slamming the door behind him as he went.

Adara, listening, had made a decision. It did not matter what her father did or did not do. She would stay. If she moved, the ice dragon would not know where to find her when winter came, and if she went too far south it would never be able to come to her at all.

It did come to her, though, just after her seventh birthday. The winter was the coldest one of all. She flew so often and so far that she scarcely had time to work on her ice castle.

Hal came again in the spring. There were only a dozen dragons in his wing, and he brought no presents that year. He and her father argued once again. Hal raged and pleaded and threatened, but her father was stone. Finally Hal left, off to the battlefields.

That was the year the king's line broke, up north near some town with a long name that Adara could not pronounce.

Teri heard about it first. She returned from the inn one night flushed and excited. "A messenger came through, on his way to the king," she told them. "The enemy won some big battle, and he's to ask for reinforcements. He said our army is returning."

Their father frowned, and worry lines creased his brow. "Did he say anything of the king's dragonriders?" Arguments or no, Hal was family.

"I asked," Teri said. "He said the dragonriders are the rear guard. They're supposed to raid and burn, delay the enemy while our army pulls back safely. Oh, I hope Uncle Hal is safe!"

"Hal will show them," Geoff said. "Him and Brimstone will burn 'em all up."

Their father smiled. "Hal could always take care of himself. At any rate, there is nothing we can do. Teri, if any more messengers come through, ask them how it goes."

She nodded, her concern not quite covering her excitement. It was all quite thrilling.

In the weeks that followed, the thrill wore off, as the people of the area began to comprehend the magnitude of the disaster. The king's highway grew busier and busier, and all the traffic flowed from north to south, and all the travelers wore green-and-gold. At first the soldiers marched in disciplined columns, led by officers wearing plumed golden helmets, but even then they were less than stirring. The columns marched wearily, and the uniforms were filthy and torn, and the swords and pikes and axes the soldiers carried were nicked and oftimes stained. Some men had lost their weapons; they limped along blindly, empty-handed. And the trains of wounded that followed the columns were often longer than the columns themselves. Adara stood in the grass by the side of the road and watched them pass. She saw a man with no eyes supporting a man with only one leg, as the two of them walked together. She saw men with no legs, or no arms, or both. She saw a man with his head split open by an axe, and many men covered with caked blood and filth, men who moaned low in their throats as they walked. She *smelled* men with bodies that were horribly greenish and puffed-up. One of them died and was left abandoned by the side of the road. Adara told her father and he and some of the men from the village came out and buried him.

Most of all, Adara saw the burned men. There were dozens of them in every column that passed, men whose skin was black and seared and falling off, who had lost an arm or a leg or half of a face to the hot breath of a dragon. Teri told them what the officers said, when they stopped at the inn to drink or rest; the enemy had many, many dragons.

For almost a month the columns flowed past, more every day. Even Old Laura admitted that she had never seen so much traffic on the road. From time to time a lone messenger on horseback rode against the tide, galloping towards the north, but always alone. After a time everyone knew there would be no reinforcements.

An officer in one of the last columns advised the people of the area to pack up whatever they could carry, and move south. "They are coming," he warned. A few listened to him, and indeed for a week the road was full of refugees from towns farther north. Some of them told frightful stories. When they left, more of the local people went with them.

But most stayed. They were people like her father, and the land was in their blood.

The last organized force to come down the road was a ragged troop of cavalry, men as gaunt as skeletons riding horses with skin pulled tight around their ribs. They thundered past in the night, their mounts heaving and foaming, and the only one to pause was a pale young officer, who reined his mount up briefly and shouted, "Go, go. They are burning everything!" Then he was off after his men.

The few soldiers who came after were alone or in small groups. They did not always use the road, and they did not pay for the things they took. One swordsman killed a farmer on the other side of town, raped his wife, stole his money, and ran. His rags were green-and-gold.

Then no one came at all. The road was deserted.

The innkeeper claimed he could smell ashes when the wind blew from the north. He packed up his family and went south. Teri was distraught. Geoff was wide-eyed and anxious and only a bit frightened. He asked a thousand questions about the enemy, and practiced at being a warrior. Their father went about his labors, busy as ever. War or no war, he had crops in the field. He smiled less than usual, however, and he began to drink, and Adara often saw him glacing up at the sky while he worked.

Adara wandered the fields above, played by herself in the damp summer heat, and tried to think of where she would hide if her father tried to take them away.

Last of all, the king's dragonriders came, and with them Hal.

There were only four of them. Adara saw the first one, and went and told her father, and he put his hand on her shoulder and together they watched it pass, a solitary green dragon with a vaguely tattered look. It did not pause for them.

Two days later, three dragons flying together came into view, and one of them detached itself from the others and circled down to their farm while the other two headed south.

Uncle Hal was thin and grim and sallow-looking. His dragon looked sick. Its eyes ran, and one of its wings had been partially burned, so it flew in an awkward, heavy manner, with much difficulty. "Now will you go?" Hal said to his brother, in front of all the children.

"No. Nothing has changed."

Hal swore. "They will be here within three days," he said. "Their dragonriders may be here even sooner."

"Father, I'm scared," Teri said.

He looked at her, saw her fear, hesitated, and finally turned back to his brother. "I am staying. But if you would, I would have you take the children."

Now it was Hal's turn to pause. He thought for a moment, and finally shook his head. "I can't, John. I would, willingly, joyfully, if it were possible. But it isn't. Brimstone is wounded. He can barely carry me. If I took on any extra weight, we might never make it."

Teri began to weep.

"I'm sorry, love," Hal said to her. "Truly I am." His fists clenched helplessly.

"Teri is almost full-grown," their father said. "If her weight is too much, then take one of the others."

Brother looked at brother, with despair in their eyes. Hal trembled. "Adara," he said finally. "She's small and light." He forced a laugh. "She hardly weighs anything at all. I'll take Adara. The rest of you take horses, or a wagon, or go on foot. But go, damn you, *go*."

"We will see," their father said noncommittally. "You take Adara, and keep her safe for us."

"Yes," Hal agreed. He turned and smiled at her. "Come, child. Uncle Hal is going to take you for a ride on Brimstone."

Adara looked at him very seriously. "No," she said. She turned and slipped through the door and began to run.

They came after her, of course, Hal and her father and

even Geoff. But her father wasted time standing in the door, shouting at her to come back, and when he began to run he was ponderous and clumsy, while Adara was indeed small and light and fleet of foot. Hal and Geoff stayed with her longer, but Hal was weak, and Geoff soon winded himself, though he sprinted hard at her heels for a few moments. By the time Adara reached the nearest wheat field, the three of them were well behind her. She quickly lost herself amid the grain, and they searched for hours in vain while she made her way carefully towards the woods.

When dusk fell, they brought out lanterns and torches and continued their search. From time to time she heard her father swearing, or Hal calling out her name. She stayed high in the branches of the oak she had climbed, and smiled down at their lights as they combed back and forth through the fields. Finally she drifted off to sleep, dreaming about the coming of winter and wondering how she would live until her birthday. It was still a long time away.

Dawn woke her, dawn and a noise in the sky.

Adara yawned and blinked, and heard it again. She shinnied to the uppermost limb of the tree, as high as it would bear her, and pushed aside the leaves.

There were dragons in the sky.

She had never seen beasts quite like these. Their scales were dark and sooty, not green like the dragon Hal rode. One was a rust color and one was the shade of dried blood and one was black as coal. All of them had eyes like glowing embers, and steam rose from their nostrils, and their tails flicked back and forth as their dark, leathery wings beat the air. The rust-colored one opened its mouth and roared, and the forest shook to its challenge, and even the branch that held Adara trembled just a little. The black one made a noise too, and when it opened its maw a spear of flame lanced out, all orange and blue, and touched the trees below. Leaves withered and blackened, and smoke began to rise from where the dragon's breath had fallen. The one the color of blood flew close overhead, its wings creaking and straining, its mouth half-open. Between its yellowed teeth Adara saw soot and cinders, and the wind stirred by its passage was fire and sandpaper, raw and chafing against her skin. She cringed.

On the backs of the dragons rode men with whip and lance, in uniforms of black-and-orange, their faces hidden behind dark helmets. The one on the rust dragon gestured with his lance, pointing at the farm buildings across the fields. Adara looked.

Hal came up to meet them.

His green dragon was as large as their own, but somehow it seemed small to Adara as she watched it climb upwards from the farm. With its wings fully extended, it was plain to see how badly injured it was; the right wing tip was charred, and it leaned heavily to one side as it flew. On its back, Hal looked like one of the tiny toy soldiers he had brought them as a present years before.

The enemy dragonriders split up and came at him from three sides. Hal saw what they were doing. He tried to turn, to throw himself at the black dragon head-on, and flee the other two. His whip flailed angrily, desperately. His green dragon opened its mouth, and roared a weak challenge, but its flame was pale and short and did not reach the oncoming enemy.

The others held their fire. Then, on a signal, their dragons all breathed as one. Hal was wreathed in flames.

His dragon made a high wailing noise, and Adara saw that it was burning, *he* was burning, they were all burning, beast and master both. They fell heavily to the ground, and lay smoking amidst her father's wheat.

The air was full of ashes.

Adara craned her head around in the other direction, and saw a column of smoke rising from beyond the forest and the river. That was the farm where Old Laura lived with her grandchildren and *their* children.

When she looked back, the three dark dragons were circling lower and lower above her own farm. One by one they landed. She watched the first of the riders dismount and saunter towards their door.

She was frightened and confused and only seven, after all. And the heavy air of summer was a weight upon her, and it

filled her with a helplessness and thickened all her fears. So
Adara did the only thing she knew, without thinking, a thing
that came naturally to her. She climbed down from her tree
and ran. She ran across the fields and through the woods,
away from the farm and her family and the dragons, away
from it all. She ran until her legs throbbed with pain, down in
the direction of the river. She ran to the coldest place she
knew, to the deep caves underneath the river bluffs, to chill
shelter and darkness and safety.

And there in the cold she hid. Adara was a winter child,
and cold did not bother her. But still, as she hid, she trembled.

Day turned into night. Adara did not leave her cave.

She tried to sleep, but her dreams were full of burning
dragons.

She made herself very small as she lay in the darkness, and
tried to count how many days remained until her birthday.
The caves were nicely cool; Adara could almost imagine that
it was not summer after all, that it was winter, or near to
winter. Soon her ice dragon would come for her, and she
would ride on its back to the land of always-winter, where
great ice castles and cathedrals of snow stood eternally in
endless fields of white, and the stillness and silence were all.

It almost felt like winter as she lay there. The cave grew
colder and colder, it seemed. It made her feel safe. She
napped briefly. When she woke, it was colder still. A white
coating of frost covered the cave walls, and she was sitting on
a bed of ice. Adara jumped to her feet and looked up towards
the mouth of the cave, filled with a wan dawn light. A cold
wind caressed her. But it was coming from outside, from the
world of summer, not from the depths of the cave at all.

She gave a small shout of joy, and climbed and scrambled
up the ice-covered rocks.

Outside, the ice dragon was waiting for her.

It had breathed upon the water, and now the river was
frozen, or at least a part of it was, although she could see that
the ice was fast melting as the summer sun rose. It had
breathed upon the green grass that grew along the banks,
grass as high as Adara, and now the tall blades were white
and brittle, and when the ice dragon moved its wings the

grass cracked in half and tumbled, sheared as clean as if it had been cut down with a scythe.

The dragon's icy eyes met Adara's, and she ran to it and up its wing, and threw her arms about it. She knew she had to hurry. The ice dragon looked smaller than she had ever seen it, and she understood what the heat of summer was doing to it.

"Hurry, dragon," she whispered. "Take me away, take me to the land of always-winter. We'll never come back here, never. I'll build you the best castle of all, and take care of you, and ride you every day. Just take me away, dragon, take me home with you."

The ice dragon heard and understood. Its wide translucent wings unfolded and beat the air, and bitter arctic winds howled through the fields of summer. They rose. Away from the cave. Away from the river. Above the forest. Up and up. The ice dragon swung around to the north. Adara caught a glimpse of her father's farm, but it was very small and growing smaller. They turned their back to it, and soared.

Then a sound came to Adara's ears. An impossible sound, a sound that was too small and too far away for her to ever have heard it, especially above the beating of the ice dragon's wings. But she heard it nonetheless. She heard her father scream.

Hot tears ran down her cheeks, and where they fell upon the ice dragon's back they burned small pockmarks in the frost. Suddenly the cold beneath her hands was biting, and when she pulled one hand away Adara saw the mark that it had made upon the dragon's neck. She was scared, but still she clung. "Turn back," she whispered. "Oh, *please*, dragon. Take me back."

She could not see the ice dragon's eyes, but she knew what they would look like. Its mouth opened and a blue-white plume issued, a long cold streamer that hung in the air. It made no noise; ice dragons are silent. But in her mind Adara heard the wild keening of its grief.

"Please," she whispered once again. "Help me." Her voice was thin and small.

The ice dragon turned.

The three dark dragons were outside of the barn when Adara returned, feasting on the burned and blackened carcasses of her father's stock. One of the dragonriders was standing near them, leaning on his lance and prodding his dragon from time to time.

He looked up when the cold gust of wind came shrieking across the fields, and shouted something, and sprinted for the black dragon. The beast tore a last hunk of meat from her father's horse, swallowed, and rose reluctantly into the air. The rider flailed his whip.

Adara saw the door of the farmhouse burst open. The other two riders rushed out, and ran for their dragons. One of them was struggling into his pants as he ran. He was barechested.

The black dragon roared, and its fire came blazing up at them. Adara felt the searing blast of heat, and a shudder went through the ice dragon as the flame played along its belly. Then it craned its long neck around, and fixed its baleful empty eyes upon the enemy, and opened its frost-rimed jaws. Out from among its icy teeth its breath came streaming, and that breath was pale and cold.

It touched the left wing of the coal-black dragon beneath them, and the dark beast gave a shrill cry of pain, and when it beat its wings again, the frost-covered wing broke in two. Dragon and dragonrider began to fall.

The ice dragon breathed again.

They were frozen and dead before they hit the ground.

The rust-colored dragon was flying at them, and the dragon the color of blood with its barechested rider. Adara's ears were filled with their angry roaring, and she could feel their hot breath around her, and see the air shimmering with heat, and smell the stink of sulfur.

Two long swords of fire crossed in midair, but neither touched the ice dragon, though it shriveled in the heat, and water flew from it like rain whenever it beat its wings.

The blood-colored dragon flew too close, and the breath of the ice dragon blasted the rider. His bare chest turned blue before Adara's eyes, and moisture condensed on him in an instant, covering him with frost. He screamed, and died, and fell from his mount, though his harness hand remained be-

hind, frozen to the neck of his dragon. The ice dragon closed
on it, wings screaming the secret song of winter, and a blast
of flame met a blast of cold. The ice dragon shuddered once
again, and twisted away, dripping. The other dragon died.

But the last dragonrider was behind them now, the enemy
in full armor on the dragon whose scales were the brown of
rust. Adara screamed, and even as she did the fire enveloped
the ice dragon's wing. It was gone in less than an instant, but
the wing was gone with it, melted, destroyed.

The ice dragon's remaining wing beat wildly to slow its
plunge, but it came to earth with an awful crash. Its legs
shattered beneath it, and its wings snapped in two places, and
the impact of the landing threw Adara from its back. She
tumbled to the soft earth of the field, and rolled, and strug-
gled up, bruised but whole.

The ice dragon seemed very small now, and very broken.
Its long neck sank wearily to the ground, and its head rested
amid the wheat.

The enemy dragonrider came swooping in, roaring with
triumph. The dragon's eyes burned. The man flourished his
lance and shouted.

The ice dragon painfully raised its head once more, and
made the only sound that Adara ever heard it make: a terrible
thin cry full of melancholy, like the sound the north wind
makes when it moves around the towers and battlements of
the white castles that stand empty in the land of always-
winter.

When the cry had faded, the ice dragon sent cold into the
world one final time: a long smoking blue-white stream of
cold that was full of snow and stillness and the end of all
living things. The dragonrider flew right into it, still bran-
dishing whip and lance. Adara watched him crash.

Then she was running, away from the fields, back to the
house and her family within, running as fast as she could,
running and panting and crying all the while like a seven-year-
old.

Her father had been nailed to the bedroom wall. They had
wanted him to watch while they took their turns with Teri.
Adara did not know what to do, but she untied Teri, whose

tears had dried by then, and they freed Geoff, and then they got their father down. Teri nursed him and cleaned out his wounds. When his eyes opened and he saw Adara, he smiled. She hugged him very hard, and cried for him.

By night he said he was fit enough to travel. They crept away under cover of darkness, and took the king's road south.

Her family asked no questions then, in those hours of darkness and fear. But later, when they were safe in the south, there were questions endlessly. Adara gave them the best answers she could. But none of them ever believed her, except for Geoff, and he grew out of it when he got older. She was only seven, after all, and she did not understand that ice dragons are never seen in summer, and cannot be tamed nor ridden.

Besides, when they left the house that night, there was no ice dragon to be seen. Only the huge dark corpses of three war dragons, and the smaller bodies of three dragonriders in black-and-orange. And a pond that had never been there before, a small quiet pool where the water was very cold. They had walked around it carefully, headed towards the road.

Their father worked for another farmer for three years in the south. His hands were never as strong as they had been, before the nails had been pounded through them, but he made up for that with the strength of his back and his arms, and his determination. He saved whatever he could, and he seemed happy. "Hal is gone, and my land," he would tell Adara, "and I am sad for that. But it is all right. I have my daughter back." For the winter was gone from her now, and she smiled and laughed and even wept like other little girls.

Three years after they had fled, the king's army routed the enemy in a great battle, and the king's dragons burned the foreign capital. In the peace that followed, the northern provinces changed hands once more. Teri had recaptured her spirit and married a young trader, and she remained in the south. Geoff and Adara returned with their father to the farm.

When the first frost came, all the ice lizards came out, just as they had always done. Adara watched them with a smile on her face, remembering the way it had been. But she did not try to touch them. They were cold and fragile little things, and the warmth of her hands would hurt them.

# FIREDRAKE

*The firedrake is a form of dragon. The second syllable, "drake," does not refer to a male duck, but is a shortened form of the Greek drakon (large snake, or dragon).*

*Where emphasis is placed upon the dragon's fiery breath, it can be called a "fire-dragon" or firedrake. Both Sigurd (Siegfried) and Beowulf killed firedrakes as culminating deeds of heroism.*

*The firedrake is, in the following story, abstracted into a principle of heat. People have, after all, always suffered from excess of heat and cold (depending on the season, altitude, and latitude) and have tended to malevolize them (if I may coin a word).*

*The sun is the obvious principle of heat, but it is difficult to malevolize the sun unless you live in an unusually hot, dry climate. The sun is too obviously a bringer of welcome warmth and light, and is clearly a fructifying force on which life depends. A firedrake must then be converted into the principle of excessive heat. The discovery of fire gave humanity something else that showed this double aspect. It could warm and give life like the sun and could burn and kill like the firedrake.*

*There is no natural principle of cold—for cold is only the absence of heat. It is possible to invent one, however. The Scandinavians in their myths had, among the enemies of the gods, both the fire-giants and the frost-giants. Naturally, considering the Scandinavian climate, it was frost-giants who were emphasized.*

*In the following utterly charming story not only is there a firedrake but also a sort of frost-giant which the author calls the Remora (a name also given to a small fish with a sucker organ on its back that hitches rides on sharks). The Remora, as described, seems even more frightful, though less malevolent, than the firedrake.*

# PRINCE PRIGIO

*Andrew Lang*

## CHAPTER I

## *How the Fairies Were Not Invited to Court*

Once upon a time there reigned in Pantouflia a king and a
queen. With almost everything else to make them happy, they
wanted one thing: they had no children. This vexed the King
even more than the Queen, who was very clever and learned,
and who had hated dolls when she was a child. However, she
too, in spite of all the books she read and all the pictures she
painted, would have been glad enough to be a mother of a
little prince. The King was anxious to consult the fairies, but
the Queen would not hear of such a thing. She did not believe
in fairies: she said that they had never existed; and that she
maintained, though *The History of the Royal Family* was full
of chapters about nothing else.

Well, at long and at last they had a little boy, who was
generally regarded as the finest baby that had ever been
seen. Even Her Majesty herself remarked that, though she
could never believe all the courtiers told her, yet he certainly
was a fine child—a very fine child.

Now the time drew near for the christening party, and the
King and Queen were sitting at breakfast in their summer
parlour talking over it. It was a splendid room, hung with
portraits of the royal ancestors. There was Cinderella, the

grandmother of the reigning monarch, with her little foot in her glass slipper thrust out before her. There was the Marquis de Carabas, who, as everyone knows, was raised to the throne as prince consort after his marriage with the daughter of the king of the period. On the arm of the throne was seated his celebrated cat, wearing boots. There, too, was a portrait of a beautiful lady, sound asleep: this was Madame La Belle au Bois-dormant, also an ancestress of the royal family. Many other pictures of celebrated persons were hanging on the walls.

"You have asked all the right people, my dear?" said the King.

"Everyone who should be asked," answered the Queen.

"People are so touchy on these occasions," said His Majesty. "You have not forgotten any of our aunts?"

"No; the old cats!" replied the Queen; for the King's aunts were old-fashioned, and did not approve of her, and she knew it.

"They are very kind old ladies in their way," said the King, "and were nice to me when I was a boy."

Then he waited a little, and remarked: "The fairies, of course, you have invited? It has always been usual in our family, on an occasion like this; and I think we have neglected them a little of late."

"How *can* you be so *absurd*?" cried the Queen. "How often must I tell you that there are *no* fairies? And even if there were—but, no matter; pray let us drop the subject."

"They are very old friends of our family, my dear, that's all," said the King timidly. "Often and often they have been godmothers to us. One, in particular, was most kind and most serviceable to Cinderella I, my own grandmother."

"Your grandmother!" interrupted Her Majesty. "Fiddle-dee-dee! If anyone puts such nonsense into the head of my little Prigio—"

But here the baby was brought in by the nurse, and the Queen almost devoured it with kisses. And so the fairies were not invited! It was an extraordinary thing, but none of the nobles could come to the christening party when they learned that the fairies had not been asked. Some were abroad; several were ill; a few were in prison among the Saracens; others were captives in the dens of ogres. The end of it was that the King and Queen had to sit down alone, one at each end of a very long table, arrayed with plates and glasses for a hundred guests—for a hundred guests who never came!

"Any soup, my dear?" shouted the King, through a speaking-trumpet; when suddenly the air was filled with a sound like the rustling of the wings of birds.

*Flitter, flitter, flutter,* went the noise; and when the Queen looked up, lo and behold! on every seat was a lovely fairy, dressed in green, each with *a most interesting-looking parcel* in her hand. Don't you like opening parcels? The King did, and he was most friendly and polite to the fairies. But the Queen, though she saw them distinctly, took no notice of them. You see, she did not believe in fairies, nor in her own eyes, when she saw them. So she talked across the fairies to the King, just as if they had not been there; but the King behaved as politely as if they were *real*—which, of course, they were.

When dinner was over, and when the nurse had brought in the baby, all the fairies gave him the most magnificent presents. One offered a purse which could never be empty; and one a pair of seven-league boots; and another a cap of darkness, that nobody might see the Prince when he put it on; and another a wishing-cap; and another a carpet, on which, when he sat, he was carried wherever he wished to find himself. Another made him beautiful forever; and another, brave; and another, lucky; but the last fairy of all, a cross old thing, crept up and said: "My child, you shall be *too* clever!"

This fairy's gift would have pleased the Queen, if she had believed in it, more than anything else, because she was so clever herself. But she took no notice at all; and the fairies went each to her own country, and none of them stayed there at the palace, where nobody believed in them, except the King, a little. But the Queen tossed all their nice boots and caps, carpets, purses, swords and all away into a dark lumber room; for, of course, she thought that they were *all nonsense*, and merely old rubbish out of books or whatever.

## CHAPTER II

## *Prince Prigio and His Family*

Well, the little prince grew up. I think I've told you that his name was Prigio—did I not? Well, that *was* his name. You cannot think how clever he was. He argued with his nurse as soon as he could speak, which was very soon. He argued that he did not like to be washed because the soap got into his eyes. However, when he was told all about the *pores of the skin,* and how they could not be healthy if he was not washed, he at once ceased to resist, for he was very reasonable. He argued with his father that he did not see why there should be kings who were rich while beggars were poor; and why the King—who was a little greedy—should have poached eggs and plumcake at afternoon tea while many other persons went without dinner. The King was so surprised and hurt at these remarks that he boxed the Prince's ears, saying: "I'll teach you to be too clever, my lad." Then he remembered the awful curse of the oldest fairy, and was sorry for the rudeness of the Queen. And when the Prince, after having his ears boxed, said that "force was no argument," the King went away in a rage.

Indeed, I cannot tell you how the Prince was hated by all! He would go down into the kitchen and show the cook how to make soup. He would visit the poor people's cottages and teach them how to make the beds, and how to make plumpudding out of turnip-tops and venison cutlets out of rusty bacon. He showed the fencing-master how to fence, and the professional cricketer how to bowl, and instructed the rat-catcher in breeding terriers. He sent sums to the Chancellor of the Exchequer, and assured the Astronomer Royal that the sun does not go round the earth—which, for my part, I believe it does. The young ladies of the Court disliked dancing with him, in spite of his good looks, because he was always asking: "Have you read this?" and "Have you read that?"—and when they said they hadn't, he sneered; and when they said they *had,* he found them out.

He found out all his tutors and masters in the same horrid way; correcting the accent of his French teacher, and trying to get his German tutor not to eat peas with his knife. He also endeavoured to teach the Queen-dowager, his grandmother, an art with which she had long been perfectly familiar! In fact, he knew everything better than anybody else; and the worst of it was that he *did;* and he never was in the wrong, and he always said: "Didn't I tell you so?" And, what was more, he *had*!

As time went on, Prince Prigio had two younger brothers, whom everybody liked. They were not a bit clever, but jolly. Prince Alphonso, the third son, was round, fat, good-humoured, and as brave as a lion. Prince Enrico, the second, was tall, thin, and a little sad, but *never* too clever. Both were in love with two of their own cousins (with the approval of their dear parents); and all the world said: "What nice, unaffected princes they are!" But Prigio nearly got the country into several wars by being too clever for the foreign ambassadors. Now, as Pantouflia was a rich, lazy country, which hated fighting, this was very unpleasant, and did not make people love Prince Prigio any better.

# CHAPTER III

## *About the Firedrake*

Of all the people who did not like Prigio, his own dear papa, King Grognio, disliked him most. For the King knew he was not clever himself. When he was in the counting-house, counting out his money, and when he happened to say:

"Sixteen shillings and fourteen and twopence are three pounds, fifteen," it made him wild to hear Prigio whisper: "One pound, ten, and twopence"—which of course it *is*. And the King was afraid that Prigio would conspire, and get made king himself—which was the last thing Prigio really wanted. He much preferred to idle about, and know everything without seeming to take any trouble.

Well, the King thought and thought. How was he to get Prigio out of the way, and make Enrico or Alphonso his successor? He read in books about it; and all the books showed that, if a king sent his three sons to do anything, it was always the youngest who did it and got the crown. And he wished he had the chance. Well, it arrived at last.

There was a very hot summer! It began to be hot in March. All the rivers were dried up. The grass did not grow. The corn did not grow. The thermometers exploded with heat. The barometers stood at SET FAIR. The people were much distressed, and came and broke the palace windows—as they usually do when things go wrong in Pantouflia.

The King consulted the learned men about the Court, who told him that probably a FIREDRAKE was in the neighborhood.

Now the Firedrake is a beast, or bird, about the bigness of an elephant. Its body is made of iron, and it is always red hot. A more terrible and cruel beast cannot be imagined; for, if you go near it, you are at once broiled by the Firedrake.

But the King was not ill-pleased: "for," thought he, "of course my three sons must go after the brute, the eldest first, and, as usual, it will kill the first two and be beaten by the youngest. It is a little hard on Enrico, poor boy; but *anything* to get rid of that Prigio!"

Then the King went to Prigio, and said that his country was in danger, and that he was determined to leave the crown to whichever of them would bring him the horns (for it has horns) and tail of the Firedrake.

"It is an awkward brute to tackle," the King said, "but you are the oldest, my lad; go where glory waits you! Put on your armour and be off with you!"

This the King said, hoping that either the Firedrake would roast Prince Prigio alive (which he could easily do, as I have said; for he is all over as hot as a red-hot poker), or that, if the Prince succeeded, at least his country would be freed from the monster.

But the Prince, who was lying on the sofa doing sums in compound division, for fun, said in the politest way:

"Thanks to the education Your Majesty has given me, I have learned that the Firedrake, like the siren, the fairy, and so forth, is a fabulous animal which does not exist. But even granting, for the sake of argument, that there is a Firedrake, Your Majesty is well aware that there is no kind of use in sending *me*. It is always the eldest son who goes out first, and comes to grief on these occasions, and it is always the third son that succeeds. Send Alphonso" (this was the youngest brother), "and *he* will do the trick at once. At least, if he fails, it will be most unusual, and Enrico can try his luck."

Then he went back to his arithmetic and his slate, and the King had to send for Prince Alphonso and Prince Enrico. They both came in very warm; for they had been whipping tops, and the day was unusually hot.

"Look here," said the King, "just you two younger ones look at Prigio! You see how hot it is, and how coolly he takes it, and the country suffering; and all on account of a Firedrake, you know, which has apparently built his nest not far off. Well, I have asked that lout of a brother of yours to kill it, and he says—"

"That he does not believe in Firedrakes," interrupted Prigio. "The weather's warm enough without going out hunting!"

"Not believe in Firedrakes!" cried Alphonso. "I wonder what you *do* believe in! Just let me get at the creature!" For he was as brave as a lion. "Hi! page, my chain-armour, helmet, lance, and buckler! *A Molinda! A Molinda!*" (which was his *war cry*).

The page ran to get the armour, but it was *so uncommonly hot* that he dropped it, and put his fingers to his mouth, crying!

"You had better put on flannels, Alphonso, for this kind of work," said Prigio. "And if I were you I'd take a light garden engine, full of water, to squirt at the enemy."

"Happy thought!" said Alphonso. "I will!" And off he

went, kissed his dear Molinda, bade her keep a lot of dances for him (there was to be a dance when he had killed the Firedrake), and then he rushed to the field!

But he never came back any more!

Everyone wept bitterly—everyone but Prince Prigio; for he thought it was a practical joke, and said that Alphonso had taken the opportunity to start off on his travels and see the world.

"There is some dreadful mistake, sir," said Prigio to the King. "You know as well as I do that the youngest son has always succeeded up to now. But I entertain great hopes for Enrico!"

And he grinned; for he fancied it was all *nonsense*, and that there were no Firedrakes.

Enrico was present when Prigio was consoling the King in this unfeeling way.

"Enrico, my boy," said His Majesty, "the task awaits you and the honour. When *you* come back with the horns and tail of the Firedrake you shall be crown prince; and Prigio shall be made an usher at the grammar school—it is all he is fit for."

Enrico was not quite so confident as Alphonso had been. He insisted on making his will; and he wrote a poem about the pleasures and advantages of dying young. This is part of it:

> The violet is a blossom sweet,
>     That droops before the day is done—
> Slain by thine overpowering heat,
>         O Sun!
>
> And I, like that sweet purple flower,
>     May roast, or boil, or broil, or bake,
> If burned by thy terrific power,
>         Firedrake!

This poem comforted Enrico more or less, and he showed it to Prigio. But the Prince only laughed, and said that the second line of the last verse was not very good, for violets do not "roast, or boil, or broil, or bake."

Enrico tried to improve it but could not. So he read it to his cousin, Lady Kathleena, just as it was; and she cried over it (though I don't think she understood it); and Enrico cried a little too.

However, next day he started, with a spear, a portable refrigerator, and a lot of bottles people throw at fires to put them out.

But *he* never came back again!

After shedding torrents of tears the King summoned Prince Prigio to his presence.

"Dastard!" he said. "Poltroon! *Your* turn, which should have come first, has arrived at last. *You* must fetch me the horns and the tail of the Firedrake. Probably you will be grilled, thank goodness; but who will give me back Enrico and Alphonso?"

"Indeed, Your Majesty," said Prigio, "you must permit me to correct your policy. Your only reason for dispatching your sons in pursuit of this dangerous but I believe *fabulous* animal was to ascertain which of us would most worthily succeed to your throne, at the date—long may it be deferred!—of your lamented decease. Now, there can be no further question about the matter. I, unworthy as I am, represent the sole hope of the royal family. Therefore to send me after the Firedrake were* both dangerous and unnecessary. Dangerous, because, if he treats me as you say he did my brothers—my unhappy brothers—the throne of Pantouflia will want an heir. But if I do come back alive—why, I cannot be more the true heir than I am at present; now *can* I? Ask the Lord Chief Justice, if you don't believe *me*."

These arguments were so clearly and undeniably correct that the King, unable to answer them, withdrew into a solitary place where he could express himself with freedom and give rein to his passions.

*Subjunctive mood. He was a great grammarian!

## CHAPTER IV

# How Prince Prigio Was Deserted by Everybody

Meanwhile Prince Prigio had to suffer many unpleasant things. Though he was the crown prince (and though his arguments were unanswerable) everybody shunned him for a coward. The Queen, who did not believe in Firedrakes, alone took his side. He was not only avoided by all, but he had most disagreeable scenes with his own cousins, Lady Molinda and Lady Kathleena. In the garden Lady Molinda met him walking alone, and did not bow to him.

"Dear Molly," said the Prince, who liked her, "how have I been so unfortunate as to offend you?"

"My name, sir, is Lady Molinda," she said very proudly; "and you have sent your own brother to his grave!"

"Oh, excuse me," said the Prince, "I am certain he has merely gone off on his travels. He'll come back when he is tired: there *are* no Firedrakes; a French writer says they are *purement fabuleux*, purely fabulous, you know."

"Prince Alphonso has gone on his travels, and will come back when he is tired! And was he then—tired—of *me*?" cried poor Molinda, bursting into tears, and forgetting her dignity.

"Oh! I beg your pardon, I never noticed; I'm sure I'm very sorry," cried the Prince, who, never having been in love himself, never thought of other people. And he tried to take Molinda's hand, but she snatched it from him and ran away through the garden to the palace, leaving Prince Prigio to feel foolish for once, and ashamed.

As for Lady Kathleena, she swept past him like a queen, without a word. So the Prince, for all his cleverness, was not happy.

After several days had gone by the King returned from the solitary place where he had been speaking his mind. He now felt calmer and better; and so at last he came back to the palace. But on seeing Prince Prigio, who was lolling in a hammock, translating Egyptian hieroglyphs into French poetry for his mother, the King broke out afresh, and made use of the most cruel and impolite expressions.

At last he gave orders that all the Court should pack up and move to a distant city; and that Prince Prigio should be left alone in the palace by himself. For he was quite unendurable, the King said, and he could not trust his own temper when he thought of him. And he grew so fierce that even the Queen was afraid of him now.

The poor Queen cried a good deal; Prigio being her favourite son, on account of his acknowledged ability and talent. But the rest of the courtiers were delighted at leaving Prince Prigio behind. For his part, he, very good-naturedly, showed them the best and shortest road to Falkenstein, the city where they were going; and easily proved that neither the Chief Secretary for Geography nor the General of the Army knew anything about the matter—which, indeed, they did not.

The ungrateful courtiers left Prigio with hoots and yells, for they disliked him so much that they forgot he would be king one day. He therefore reminded them of this little fact in future history, which made them feel uncomfortable enough, and then lay down in his hammock and went asleep.

When he wakened the air was cold and the day was beginning to grow dark. Prince Prigio thought he would go down and dine at a tavern in the town, for no servants had been left with him. But what was his annoyance when he found that his boots, his sword, his cap, his cloak—all his clothes, in fact, except those he wore—had been taken away by the courtiers, merely to spite him! His wardrobe had been ransacked, and everything that had not been carried off had been cut up, burned, and destroyed. Never was there such a spectacle of wicked mischief. It was as if hay had been made of everything he possessed. What was worse, he had not a penny in his pocket to buy new things; and his father had stopped his allowance of £50,000 a month.

Can you imagine anything more cruel and *unjust* than this conduct? For it was not the Prince's fault that he was so clever. The cruel fairy had made him so. But even if the Prince had been born clever (as may have happened to you), was he to be blamed for that? The other people were just as much at fault for being born so stupid; but the world, my dear children, can never be induced to remember this. If you are clever, you will find it best not to let people know it—if you want them to like you.

Well, here was the Prince in a pretty plight. Not a pound in his pocket, not a pair of boots to wear, not even a cap to cover his head from the rain; nothing but cold meat to eat, and never a servant to answer the bell.

# CHAPTER V

## *What Prince Prigio Found in the Garret*

The Prince walked from room to room of the palace, but, unless he wrapped himself up in a curtain, there was nothing for him to wear when he went out in the rain. At last he climbed up a turret stair in the very oldest part of the castle, where he had never been before; and at the very top was a lttle round room, a kind of garret. The Prince pushed in the door with some difficulty—not that it was locked, but the handle was rusty, and the wood had swollen with the damp. The room was very dark; only the last grey light of the rainy evening came through a slit of a window, one of those narrow windows that they used to fire arrows out of in old times.

But in the dusk the Prince saw a heap of all sorts of things lying on the floor and on the table. There were two caps; he put one on—an old, grey, ugly cap it was, made of felt. There was a pair of boots; and he kicked off his slippers, and got into *them*. They were a good deal worn, but fitted as if they had been made for him. On the table was a purse with just three gold coins—old ones too—in it; and this, as you may fancy, the Prince was very well pleased to put in his pocket. A sword, with a sword-belt, he buckled about his waist; and the rest of the articles, a regular collection of odds and ends, he left just where they were lying. Then he ran downstairs and walked out of the hall door.

## CHAPTER VI

## What Happened to Prince Prigio in Town

By this time the Prince was very hungry. The town was just three miles off; but he had such a royal appetite that he did not like to waste it on bad cookery, and the people of the royal town were bad cooks.

"I wish I were in the Bear, at Gluckstein," said he to himself; for he remembered that there was a very good cook there. But then the town was twenty-one leagues away—sixty-three long miles!

No sooner had the Prince said this, and taken just three steps, than he found himself at the door of the Bear Inn at Gluckstein!

"This is the most extraordinary dream," said he to himself; for he was far too clever of course to believe in seven-league boots. Yet he had a pair on at that very moment, and it was they which had carried him in three strides from the palace to Gluckstein!

The truth is that the Prince, in looking about the palace for clothes, had found his way into the very old lumber room where the magical gifts of the fairies had been thrown by his clever mother, who did not believe in them. But this of course the Prince did not know.

Now you should be told that seven-league boots only take those prodigious steps when you say you *want* to go a long distance. Otherwise they would be very inconvenient—when you only want to cross the room, for example. Perhaps this has not been explained to you by someone?

Well, the Prince walked into the Bear, and it seemed odd to him that nobody took any notice of him. And yet his face was as well known as that of any man in Pantouflia; for everybody had seen it, at least in pictures. He was so puzzled by not being attended to as usual that *he quite forgot to take off his cap*. He sat down at a table, however, and shouted "Kellner!" at which all the waiters jumped, and looked round in every direction, but nobody came to him. At first he thought they were too busy, but presently another explanation occurred to him.

"The King," said he to himself, "has threatened to execute anybody who speaks to me, or helps me in any way. Well, I don't mean to starve in the midst of plenty, anyhow; here goes!"

The Prince rose and went to the table in the midst of the room, where a huge roast turkey had just been placed. He helped himself to half the breast, some sausages, chestnut stuffing, bread sauce, potatoes, and a bottle of red wine— Burgundy. He then went back to a table in a corner, where he dined very well, nobody taking any notice of him. When he had finished, he sat watching the other people dining, and smoking his cigarette. As he was sitting thus, a very tall man, an officer in the uniform of the Guards, came in, and, walking straight to the Prince's table, said: "Kellner, clean this table, and bring in the bill of fare."

With these words, the officer sat down suddenly in the Prince's lap, as if he did not see him at all. He was a heavy man, and the Prince, enraged at the insult, pushed him away and jumped to his feet. As he did so, *his cap dropped off*. The officer fell on his knees at once, crying: "Pardon, my Prince, pardon! I never saw you!"

This was more than the Prince could be expected to believe.

"Nonsense! Count Frederick von Matterhorn," he said, "you must be intoxicated. Sir! you have insulted your Prince and your superior officer. Consider yourself under arrest! You shall be sent to a prison tomorrow!"

On this, the poor officer appealed piteously to everybody in the tavern. They all declared that they had not seen the Prince, nor even had an idea that he was doing them the honour of being in the neighbourhood of their town.

More and more offended, and convinced that there was a conspiracy to annoy and insult him, the Prince shouted for the landlord, called for his bill, threw down his three pieces of gold without asking for change, and went into the street.

"It is a disgraceful conspiracy," he said. "The King shall answer for this! I shall write to the newspapers at once!"

He was not put in a better temper by the way in which people hustled him in the street. They ran against him exactly as if they did not see him, and then staggered back in the greatest surprise, looking in every direction for the person they had jostled. In one of these encounters, the Prince pushed so hard against a poor old beggar woman that she fell down. As he was usually most kind and polite, he pulled off his cap to beg her pardon, when, behold, the beggar woman gave one dreadful scream, and fainted! A crowd was collecting, and the Prince, forgetting that he had thrown down all his money in the tavern, pulled out his purse. Then he remembered what he had done, and expected to find it empty; but, lo, there were three pieces of gold in it! Overcome with surprise, he thrust the money into the woman's hand, and put on his cap again. In a moment the crowd, which had been staring at him, rushed away in every direction, with cries of terror, declaring that there was a magician in the town, and a fellow who could appear and disappear at pleasure!

By this time, you or I, or anyone who was not so extremely clever as Prince Prigio, would have understood what was the matter. He had put on, without knowing it, not only the seven-league boots, but the cap of darkness, and had taken Fortunatus's purse, which could never be empty, however often you took all the money out. All those and many other delightful wares the fairies had given him at his christening, and the Prince had found them in the dark garret. But the Prince was so extremely wise, and learned, and scientific, that he did not believe in fairies nor in fairy gifts.

"It is indigestion," he said to himself. "Those sausages were not of the best; and that Burgundy was extremely strong. Things are not as they appear."

Here, as he was arguing with himself, he was nearly run over by a splendid carriage and six, the driver of which never took the slightest notice of him. Annoyed at this, the Prince leaped up behind, threw down the two footmen, who made no resistance, and so was carried to the door of a magnificent palace. He was determined to challenge the gentleman who was in the carriage; but noticing that he had a very beautiful young lady with him, whom he had never seen before, he followed them into the house, not wishing to alarm the girl, and meaning to speak to the gentleman when he found him alone.

A great ball was going on; but, as usual, nobody took notice of the Prince. He walked among the guests, being careful not to jostle them, and listening to their conversation.

It was all about himself! Everyone had heard of his disgrace, and almost everyonce cried, "Serve him right!" They said that the airs he gave himself were quite unendurable—that nothing was more rude than to be always in the right—that cleverness might be carried far too far—that it was better even to be born stupid ("Like the rest of you," thought the Prince); and, in fact, nobody had a good word for him.

Yes, one had! It was the pretty lady of the carriage. I never could tell you how pretty she was. She was tall, with cheeks like white roses blushing, she had dark hair, and very large dark-grey eyes, and her face was the kindest in the world! The Prince first thought how nice and good she looked, even before he thought how pretty she looked. *She* stood up for Prince Prigio when her partner would speak ill of him. She had never seen the Prince, for she was but newly come to Pantouflia; but she declared that it was his *misfortune*, not his fault, to be so clever. "And then, think how hard they made him work at school! Besides," said this kind young lady, "I hear he is extremely handsome, and very brave; and he has a good heart, for he was kind. I have heard, to a poor boy, and did all his examination papers for him, so that the boy passed first in *everything*. And now he is Minister of Education, though he can't do a line of Greek prose!''

The Prince blushed at this, for he knew his conduct had not been honourable. But he at once fell over head and ears in love with the young lady, a thing he had never done in his life before, because—he said—''women are so stupid!'' You see he was so clever!

Now, at this very moment—when the Prince, all of a sudden, was as deep in love as if he had been the stupidest officer in the room—an extraordinary thing happened! Something seemed to give a *whirr!* in his brain, and in one instant *he knew all about it!* He believed in fairies and fairy gifts, and understood that his cap was the cap of darkness, and his shoes the seven-league boots, and his purse the purse of Fortunatus! He had read about those things in historical books: but now he believed in them.

# CHAPTER VII

## *The Prince Falls in Love*

He understood all this, and burst out laughing, which nearly frightened an old lady near him out of her wits. Ah! how he wished he were only in evening dress, that he might dance with the charming young lady. But there he was, dressed just as if he were going out to hunt, if anyone could have seen him. So, even if he took off his cap of darkness and became visible, he was no figure for a ball. Once he would not have cared, but now he cared very much indeed.

But the Prince was not clever for nothing. He thought for a moment, then went out of the room, and in three steps of the seven-league boots was at his empty, dark, cold palace again. He struck a light with a flint and steel, lit a torch, and ran upstairs to the garret. The flaring light of the torch fell on the pile of "rubbish," as the Queen would have called it, which he turned over with eager hands. Was there—yes, there was another cap! There it lay, a handsome green one with a red feather. The Prince pulled off the cap of darkness, put on the other, and said: *"I wish I were dressed in my best suit of white and gold, with the royal Pantouflia diamonds!"*

In one moment there he was in white and gold, the greatest and most magnificent dandy in the whole world, and the handsomest man!

"How about my boots, I wonder," said the Prince; for his seven-league boots were stout riding-boots, not good to dance in, whereas now he was in elegant shoes of silk and gold.

He threw down the wishing cap, put on the other—the cap of darkness—and made three strides in the direction of Gluckstein. But he was only three steps nearer it than he had been, and the seven-league boots were standing beside him on the floor!

"No," said the Prince, "no man can be in two different pairs of boots at one and the same time! That's mathematics!"

He then hunted about in the lumber room again till he found a small, shabby, old Persian carpet, the size of a hearthrug. He went to his own room, took a portmanteau in his hand, sat down on the carpet, and said: "I wish I were in Gluckstein!"

In a moment there he found himself; for this was that famous carpet which Prince Hussein bought long ago, in the market at Bisnagar, and which the fairies had brought with the other presents to the christening of Prince Prigio.

When he arrived at the house where the ball was going on, he put the magical carpet in the portmanteau, and left it in the cloakroom, receiving a numbered ticket in exchange. Then he marched in all his glory (and of course without the cap of darkness) into the room where they were dancing. Everybody made place for him, bowing down to the ground, and the loyal band struck up *The Prince's March:*

Heaven bless our Prince Prigio!
What is there he doesn't know?
Greek, Swiss, German (High and Low),
And the names of the mountains in Mexico,
Heaven bless the Prince!

He used to be very fond of this march, and the words—some people said he had made them himself. But now, somehow, he didn't much like it. He went straight to the Duke of Stumpfelbahn, the Hereditary Master of the Ceremonies, and asked to be introduced to the beautiful young lady. She was the daughter of the new English Ambassador, and her name was Lady Rosalind. But she nearly fainted when she heard who it was that wished to dance with her, for she was not at all particularly clever; and the Prince had such a bad character for snubbing girls, and asking them difficult questions. However, it was impossible to refuse, and so she danced with the Prince, and he danced very well. Then they sat out in the conservatory, among the flowers, where nobody came near them; and then they danced again, and then the Prince took her down to supper. And all the time he never once said: "Have you read *this*?" or "Have you read *that?*" or "What! you never heard of Alexander the Great?" or Julius Caesar, or Michelangelo, or whoever it might be—horrid, difficult questions he used to ask. That was the way he *used* to go on: but now he only talked to the young lady about *herself;* and she quite left off being shy or frightened, and asked him all about his own country, and about the Firedrake shooting, and said how fond she was of hunting herself. And the Prince said: "Oh, if *you* wish it, you shall have the horns and tail of a Firedrake to hang up in your hall, tomorrow evening!"

Then she asked if it was not very dangerous work, Firedrake hunting; and he said it was nothing, when you knew the trick of it; and he asked her if she would not give him a rose out of her bouquet; and, in short, he made himself so agreeable and *unaffected* that she thought him very nice indeed.

For even a clever person can be nice when he likes—above all when he is not thinking about himself. And now the Prince was thinking of nothing in the world but the daughter of the English Ambassador, and how to please her. He got introduced to her father too, and quite won his heart; and at last he was invited to dine next day at the embassy.

In Pantouflia, it is the custom that a ball must not end while one of the royal family goes on dancing. *This* ball lasted till the light came in, and the birds were singing out of doors, and all the mothers present were sound asleep. Then nothing would satisfy the Prince but that they all should go home singing through the streets: in fact, there never had been so merry a dance in all Pantouflia. The Prince had made a point of dancing with almost every girl there; and he had suddenly become the most beloved of the royal family. But everything must end at last; and the Prince, putting on the cap of darkness and sitting on the famous carpet, flew back to his lonely castle.

## CHAPTER VIII

### *The Prince Is Puzzled*

Prince Prigio did not go to bed. It was bright daylight, and he had promised to bring the horns and tail of a Firedrake as a present to a pretty lady. He had said it was easy to do this; but now, as he sat and thought it over, he did not feel so victorious.

"First," he said, "where is the Firedrake?"

He reflected for a little, and then ran upstairs to the garret.

"It *should* be here!" he cried, tossing the fairies' gifts about, "and, by George, here it is!"

Indeed, he had found the spy-glass of carved ivory which Prince Ali, in the *Arabian Nights,* bought in the bazaar in Schiraz. Now this glass was made so that by looking through it you could see anybody or anything you wished, however far away. Prigio's first idea was to look at his lady. "But she does not expect to be looked at," he thought, "and I *won't*!" On the other hand, he determined to look at the Firedrake; for of course he had no delicacy about spying on *him*, the brute.

The Prince clapped the glass to his eye, stared out of the window, and there, sure enough, he saw the Firedrake. He was floating about in a sea of molten lava, on the top of a volcano. There he was, swimming and diving for pleasure, tossing up the flaming waves, and blowing fountains of fire out of his nostrils, like a whale spouting!

The Prince did not like the looks of him.

"With all my cap of darkness, and my shoes of swiftness, and my sword of sharpness, I never could get near that beast," he said; "and if I *did* stalk him, I could not hurt him. Poor little Alphonso! poor Enrico! what plucky fellows they were! I fancied that there was no such thing as a Firedrake: he's not in the Natural History books; and I thought the boys were only making fun, and would be back soon, safe and sound. How horrid being too clever makes one! And now, what *am* I to do?"

What was he to do indeed? And what would you have done? Bring the horns and tail he must, or perish in the adventure. Otherwise, how could he meet his lady?—why, she would think him a mere braggart.

The Prince sat down and thought and thought; and the day went on, and it was now high noon.

At last he jumped up and rushed into the library, a room where nobody ever went except himself and the Queen. There he turned the books upside down, in his haste, till he found an old one by a French gentleman, Monsieur Cyrano de Bergerac. It was an account of a voyage to the moon, in which there is a great deal of information about matters not generally known; for few travellers have been to the moon. In that book, Prince Prigio fancied he would find something he half-remembered, and that would be of use to him. And he did! So you see that cleverness, and minding your book, have some advantages, after all. For here the Prince learned that there is a very rare beast called a Remora, which is at least as cold as the Firedrake is hot!

"Now," thought he, "*if I can only make these two fight*, why, the Remora may kill the Firedrake, or take the heat out of him, at least, so that I may have a chance."

Then he seized the ivory glass, clapped it to his eye, and looked for the Remora. Just the tip of his nose, as white as snow and as smooth as ice, was sticking out of a chink in a frozen mountain, not far from the burning mountain of the Firedrake.

"Hooray!" said the Prince softly to himself; and he jumped like mad into the winged shoes of swiftness, stuck on the cap of darkness, girdled himself with the sword of sharpness, and put a good slice of bread, with some cold tongue, in a wallet, which he slung on his back. Never you fight, if you can help it, except with plenty of food to keep you going and in good heart. Then off he flew, and soon he reached the volcano of the Firedrake.

# CHAPTER IX

## *The Prince and the Firedrake*

It was dreadfully hot, even high up in the air, where the Prince hung invisible. Great burning stones were tossed up by the volcano, and nearly hit him several times. Moreover, the steam and smoke, and the flames which the Firedrake spouted like foam from his nostrils, would have daunted even the bravest man. The sides of the hill too were covered with the blackened ashes of his victims, whom he had roasted when they came out to kill him. The garden engine of poor little Alphonso was lying in the valley, all broken and useless. But the Firedrake, as happy as a wild duck on a lonely loch, was rolling and diving in the liquid flame, all red-hot and full of frolic.

"Hi!" shouted the Prince.

The Firedrake rose to the surface, his horns as red as a red crescent moon, only bigger, and lashing the fire with his hooves and his blazing tail.

"Who's there?" he said in a hoarse, angry voice. "Just let me get at you!"

"It's me," answered the Prince. It was the first time he had forgotten his grammar, but he was terribly excited.

"What do you want?" grunted the beast. "I wish I could see you"; and, horrible to relate, he rose on a pair of wide, flaming wings, and came right at the Prince, guided by the sound of his voice.

Now the Prince had never heard that Firedrakes could fly; indeed, he had never believed in them at all, till the night before. For a moment he was numb with terror; then he flew down like a stone to the very bottom of the hill and shouted: "Hi!"

"Well," grunted the Firedrake, "what's the matter? Why can't you give a civil answer to a civil question?"

"Will you go back to your hole and swear, on your honour as a Firedrake, to listen quietly?"

"On my sacred word of honour," said the beast, casually scorching an eagle that flew by into ashes. The cinders fell, jingling and crackling, round the Prince in a little shower.

Then the Firedrake dived back, with an awful splash of flame, and the mountain roared round him.

The Prince now flew high above him, and cried: "A message from the Remora. He says you are afraid to fight him."

"Don't know him," grunted the Firedrake.

"He sends you his glove," said Prince Prigio, "as a challenge to mortal combat, till death do you part!"

Then he dropped his own glove into the fiery lake.

"Does he?" yelled the Firedrake. "Just let me get at him!" and he scrambled out, all red-hot as he was.

"I'll go and tell him you're coming," said the Prince; and with two strides he was over the frozen mountain of the Remora.

# CHAPTER X

## *The Prince and the Remora*

If he had been too warm before, the Prince was too cold now.
The hill of the Remora was one solid mass of frozen steel,
and the cold rushed out of it like the breath of some icy beast,
which indeed it *was*. All around were things like marble
statues of men in armour: they were the dead bodies of the
knights, horses and all, who had gone out of old to fight the
Remora, and who had been frosted up by him. The Prince felt
his blood stand still, and he grew faint; but he took heart, for
there was no time to waste. Yet he could nowhere see the
Remora.

"Hi!" shouted the Prince.

Then, from a narrow chink at the bottom of the smooth,
black hill—a chink no deeper than that under a door, but a
mile wide—stole out a hideous head!

It was as flat as the head of a skate-fish, it was deathly
pale, and two chill-blue eyes, dead-coloured like stones,
looked out of it.

Then there came a whisper, like the breath of the bitter east
wind on a wintry day: "Where are you, and how can I come
to you?"

"Here I am!" said the Prince from the top of the hill.

Then the flat, white head set itself against the edge of the
chink from which it had peeped, and slowly, like the movement of a sheet of ice, it slipped upwards and curled upwards, and up, and up! There seemed no end to it at all; and
it moved horribly, without feet, holding on by its own frost to
the slippery side of the frozen hill. Now all the lower part of
the black hill was covered with the horrid white thing coiled
about it in smooth, flat, shiny coils; and still the head was

higher than the rest; and still the icy cold came nearer and nearer, like Death.

The Prince almost fainted; everything seemed to swim; and in one moment more he would have fallen stiff on the mountain-top, and the white head would have crawled over him, and the cold coils would have slipped over him and turned him to stone. And still the thing slipped up from the chink under the mountain.

But the Prince made a great effort; he moved, and in two steps he was far away, down in the valley where it was not so very cold.

"Hi!" he shouted, as soon as his tongue could move within his chattering teeth.

There came a clear, hissing answer, like frozen words dropping round him: "Wait till I come down. What do you want?"

Then the white folds began to slide, like melting ice, from the black hill.

Prince Prigio felt the air getting warmer behind him, and colder in front of him.

He looked round, and there were the trees beginning to blacken in the heat, and the grass looking like a sea of fire along the plains; for the Firedrake was coming!

The Prince just took time to shout: "The Firedrake is going to pay you a visit!" and then soared to the top of a neighbouring hill, and looked on at what followed.

## CHAPTER XI

## *The Battle*

It was an awful sight to behold! When the Remora heard the name of the Firedrake, his hated enemy, he slipped with wonderful speed from the cleft of the mountain into the valley. On and on and on he poured over rock and tree, as if a frozen river could slide downhill; on and on, till there were miles of him stretching along the valley—miles of the smooth-ribbed, icy creature, crawling and slipping forwards. The green trees dropped their leaves as he advanced; the birds fell down dead from the sky, slain by his frosty breath! But, fast as the Remora stole forward, the Firedrake came quicker yet, flying and clashing his fiery wings. At last they were within striking distance; and the Firedrake, stooping from the air, dashed with his burning horns and flaming feet slap into the body of the Remora.

Then there rose a steam so dreadful, such a white yet fiery vapour of heat, that no one who had not the Prince's magic glass could have seen what happened. With horrible grunts and roars the Firedrake tried to burn his way right through the flat body of the Remora, and to chase him to his cleft in the rock. But the Remora, hissing terribly and visibly melting away in places, yet held his ground; and the Prince could see his cold white folds climbing slowly up the hooves of the Firedrake—up and up till they reached his knees, and the great burning beast roared like a hundred bulls with the pain. Then up the Firedrake leaped, and hovering on his fiery wings he lighted in the midst of the Remora's back, and dashed into it with his horns. But the flat, cruel head writhed backwards, and, slowly bending over on itself, the wounded Remora slid greedily to fasten again on the limbs of the Firedrake.

Meanwhile, the Prince, safe on his hill, was lunching on the loaf and the cold tongue he had brought with him.

"Go to it, Remora! Go to it, Firedrake! You're gaining. Give it to him, Remora!" he shouted in the wildest excitement.

Nobody had ever seen such a battle; he had it all to himself, and he never enjoyed anything more. He hated the Remora so much, that he almost wished the Firedrake could beat it; for the Firedrake was the more natural beast of the pair. Still, he was alarmed when he saw the vast flat body of the Remora was now slowly coiling backwards, backwards, into the cleft below the hill; while a thick wet mist showed how cruelly it had suffered. But the Firedrake too was in an unhappy way; for his legs were now cold and black, his horns were black also, though his body, especially near the heart, glowed still like red-hot iron.

"Go to it, Remora!" cried the Prince, "his legs are giving way; he's groggy on his pins! One more effort, and he won't be able to move!"

Encouraged by this advice, the white slippery Remora streamed out of his cavern again, more and more of him uncoiling as if the mountain were quite full of him. He had lost strength no doubt: for the steam and mist went up from him in clouds, and the hissing of his angry voice grew fainter; but so did the roars of the Firedrake. Presently they sounded more like groans; and at last the Remora slipped up his legs above the knees, and fastened on his very heart of fire. Then the Firedrake stood groaning like a black bull, knee-deep in snow; and still the Remora climbed and climbed.

"Go to it now, Firedrake!" shouted the Prince; for he knew that if the Remora won, it would be too cold for him to draw near the place and cut off the Firedrake's head and tail.

"Go to it, Drake! he's slackening!" cried the Prince again; and the brave Firedrake made one last furious effort, and rising on his wings, dropped just on the spine of his enemy.

The wounded Remora curled back his head again on himself, and again crawled, steaming terribly, towards his enemy. But the struggle was too much for the gallant Remora. The flat, cruel head moved slower; the steam from his thousand wounds grew fiercer; and he gently breathed his last just as the Firedrake too fell over and lay exhausted. With one final roar, like the breath of a thousand furnaces, the Firedrake expired.

The Prince, watching from the hill-top, could scarcely believe that these two *awful scourges of Nature*, which had so long devastated his country, were actually dead. But when he had looked on for half an hour, and only a river ran where the Remora had been, while the body of the Firedrake lay stark and cold, he hurried to the spot.

Drawing the sword of sharpness he hacked off, at two blows, the iron head and the tail of the Firedrake. They were a weary weight to carry; but in a few strides of the shoes of swiftness he was at his castle, where he threw down his burden and nearly fainted with excitement and fatigue.

But the castle clock struck half past seven; dinner was at eight, and the poor Prince crawled on hands and knees to the garret. Here he put on the wishing-cap; wished for a pint of champagne, a hot bath, and his best black velvet and diamond suit. In a moment these were provided; he bathed, dressed, drank a glass of wine, packed up the head and tail of the Firedrake, sat down on the flying carpet, and knocked at the door of the English Ambassador as the clocks were striking eight in Gluckstein.

*Punctuality is the politeness of princes;* and a prince is polite when he is in love!

The Prince was received at the door by a stout porter and led into the hall, where *several* butlers met him, and he laid the mortal remains of the Firedrake under the cover of the flying carpet.

Then he was led upstairs, and he made his bow to the pretty lady, who, of course, made him a magnificent curtsy. She seemed prettier and kinder than ever. The Prince was so happy that he never noticed how something went wrong about the dinner. The ambassador looked about, and seemed to miss someone, and spoke in a low voice to one of the servants, who answered also in a low voice, and what he said seemed to displease the ambassador. But the Prince was so busy in talking to his lady, and in eating his dinner too, that he never observed anything unusual. He had *never* been at such a pleasant dinner!

## CHAPTER XII

## A Terrible Misfortune

When the ladies left, and the Prince and the other gentlemen were alone, the ambassador appeared more gloomy than ever. At last he took the Prince into a corner on pretense of showing him a rare statue.

"Does Your Royal Highness not know," he asked, "that you are in considerable danger?"

"Still?" said the Prince, thinking of the Firedrake.

The ambassador did not know what he meant, for *he* had never heard of the fight, but he answered gravely: "Never more than now."

Then he showed the Prince two proclamations, which had been posted all about the town.

Here is the first:

## TO ALL LOYAL SUBJECTS

*Whereas,*

Our eldest son, Prince Prigio, hath of late been guilty of several crimes and misdemeanours.

First: By abandoning the post of danger against the Firedrake, whereby our beloved sons, Prince Alphonso and Prince Enrico, have perished, and been overdone by that monster.

Secondly: By attending an unseemly revel in the town of Gluckstein, where he brawled in the streets.

Thirdly: By trying to seduce away the hearts of our loyal subjects in that city, and to blow up a party against our crown and our peace.

*This is to give warning,*

That whoever consorts with, comforts, aids or abets the said Prince Prigio, is thereby a partner in his treason; and

That a reward of FIVE THOUSAND PURSES will be given to whosoever brings the said prince, alive, to our Castle of Falkenstein.

GROGNIO R.

And here is the second proclamation:

## REWARD
## THE FIREDRAKE

*Whereas,*

Our dominions have lately been devastated by a Firedrake (the *Salamander Furiosus* of Buffon);

*This is to advise all,*

That whosoever brings the horns and tail of the said Fire-drake to our Castle of Falkenstein, shall receive FIVE THOUSAND PURSES, the position of Crown Prince, with the usual perquisites, and the hand of the King's niece, the Lady Molinda.

GROGNIO R.

"H'm," said the Prince, "I did not think His Majesty wrote so well," and he would have *liked* to say: "Don't you think we might join the ladies?"

"But, sir," said the ambassador, "the streets are lined with soldiers; and I know not how you have escaped them. *Here*, under my roof, you are safe for the moment; but a prolonged stay—excuse my inhospitality—could not but strain the harmonious relations which prevail between the Government of Pantouflia and that which I have the honour to represent."

"We don't want to fight; and no more, I think, do you," said the Prince, smiling.

"Then how does Your Royal Highness mean to treat the proclamations?"

"Why, by winning these ten thousand purses. I can tell you £1,000,000 is worth having," said the Prince. "I'll deliver up the said prince, alive, at Falkenstein this very night; also the horns and tail of the said Firedrake. But I don't want to marry my Cousin Molly."

"May I remind Your Royal Highness that Falkenstein is three hundred miles away? Moreover, my head butler, Benson, disappeared from the house before dinner, and I fear he went to warn Captain Kopzoffski that you are *here*!"

"That is nothing," said the Prince, "but, my dear Lord Kelso, may I not have the pleasure of presenting Lady Rosalind with a little gift, the forfeit of a game which I lost to her last night, merely the head and tail of a Firedrake which I stalked this morning?"

The ambassador was so very astonished that he ran straight upstairs, forgetting his manners, and crying: "Linda! Linda! come down at once; here's a surprise for you!"

Lady Rosalind came sweeping down, with a smile on her

kind face. *She* guessed what it was, though the Prince had said nothing about it at dinner.

"Lead the way, Your Royal Highness!" cried the ambassador; and the Prince, offering Lady Rosalind his arm, went out into the hall, where he saw neither his carpet nor the horns and tail of the Firedrake!

He turned quite pale, and said: "Will you kindly ask the servants where the little Persian prayer-rug and the parcel which I brought with me have been placed?"

Lord Kelso rang the bell, and in came all the servants, with William, the under-butler, at their head.

"William," said his lordship, "where have you put His Royal Highness's parcel and his carpet?"

"Please, your lordship," said William, "we think Benson have took them away with him."

"And where is Benson?"

"We don't know, your lordship. We think he have been come for!"

"Come for—by whom?"

William stammered, and seemed at a loss for a reply.

"Quick! Answer! What do you know about it?"

William said at last, rather as if he were making a speech: "Your Royaliness, and my lords and ladies, it was like this. His Royaliness comed in with a rug over his arm and summat under it. And he lays it down on that there seat, and Thomas shows him into the droring room. Then Benson says: 'Dinner'll be ready in five minutes; how tired I do feel!' Then he takes the libbuty of sitting hisself down on His Royaliness's rug, and he says, asking your pardon, 'I've had about enough of service here, I'm about tired, and I thinks of bettering myself. I wish I was at the King's court, and butler.' But before the words was out of his mouth, off he flies like a shot through the open door, and His Royaliness's parcel with him. I run to the door, and there he was flying right hover the town, in a northerly direction. And that's all I know; for I would not tell a lie, not if it was never so. And me, and Thomas—as didn't see it—and cook, we thinks as how Benson was come for. And cook says as she don't wonder at it, neither; for a grumblinger, more ill-conditioneder—''

"Thank you, William," said Lord Kelso, "that will do; you can go, for the present."

# CHAPTER XIII

## *Surprises*

The Prince said nothing, the ambassador said nothing, Lady Rosalind said never a word till they were in the drawing room. It was a lovely warm evening, and the French windows were wide open on the balcony, which looked over the town and away north to the hills. Below them flowed by the clear, green water of the Gluckthal. And still nobody said a word.

At last the Prince spoke: "This is a very strange story, Lord Kelso!"

"Very, sir!" said the ambassador.

"But true," added the Prince, "at least, there is no reason in the nature of things why it shouldn't be true."

"I can hardly believe, sir, that the conduct of Benson, whom I always found a most respectable man, deserved—"

"That he should be 'come for,' " said the Prince. "Oh no; it was a mere accident, and might have happened to any of us who chanced to sit down on my carpet."

And then the Prince told them, shortly, all about it: how the carpet was one of a number of fairy properties which had been given him at his christening; and how, probably, the carpet had carried the butler where he had said he wanted to go—namely, to the King's Court at Falkenstein.

"It would not matter so much," added the Prince, "only I had relied on making my peace with His Majesty, my father, by aid of those horns and that tail. He was set on getting them; and if the Lady Rosalind had not expressed a wish for them, they would today have been in his possession.''

"Oh, sir, you honour us too highly," murmured Lady Rosalind; and the Prince blushed and said: "Not at all! Impossible!''

Then, of course, the ambassador became quite certain that his daughter was admired by the Crown Prince, who was on bad terms with the King of the country; and a more uncomfortable position for an ambassador—however, they are used to them.

"What on earth am I to do with the young man?" he thought. "He can't stay here forever; and without his carpet he can't get away, for the soldiers have orders to seize him as soon as he appears in the street. And in the meantime Benson will be pretending that *he* killed the Firedrake—for he must have got to Falkenstein by now—and they will be for marrying him to the King's niece, and making my butler crown prince to the kingdom of Pantouflia! It is dreadful!''

Now all this time the Prince was on the balcony telling Lady Rosalind all about how he got the Firedrake done for, in the most modest way; for, as he said: "*I* didn't kill him: and it is really the Remora, poor fellow, who should marry Molly; but he's dead.''

At this very moment there was a *whizz* in the air; something shot past them, and, through the open window, the King, the Queen, Benson, and the mortal remains of the Firedrake were shot into the ambassador's drawing room!

# CHAPTER XIV

## *The King Explains*

The first who recovered his voice and presence of mind was Benson.

"Did your lordship ring for coffee?" he asked quietly; and when he was told "Yes," he bowed and withdrew, with majestic composure.

When he had gone, the Prince threw himself at the King's feet, crying: "Pardon, pardon, my liege!"

"Don't speak to me, sir!" answered the King very angrily; and the poor Prince threw himself at the feet of the Queen.

But she took no notice of him whatever, no more than if he had been a fairy; and the Prince heard her murmur, as she pinched her royal arms: "I shall waken presently; this is nothing out of the way for a dream. Dr. Rumpfino ascribes it to imperfect nutrition."

All this time the Lady Rosalind, as pale as a marble statue, was leaning against the side of the open window. The Prince thought he could do nothing wiser than go and comfort her, so he induced her to sit down on a chair on the balcony—for he felt that he was not wanted in the drawing room; and soon they were talking happily about the stars, which had begun to appear in the summer night.

Meanwhile the ambassador had induced the King to take a seat; but there was no use in talking to the Queen.

"It would be a miracle," she said to herself, "and miracles do not happen; therefore this has not happened. Presently, I shall wake up in my own bed at Falkenstein."

Now, Benson, William, and Thomas brought in the coffee, but the Queen took no notice. When they went away the rest of the company slipped off quietly, and the King was left alone with the ambassador; for the Queen could hardly be said to count.

"You want to know all about it, I suppose?" said His Majesty in a sulky voice. "Well, you have a right to it, and I shall tell you. We were just sitting down to dinner at Falkenstein, rather late—hours get later every year, I think—when I heard a row in the premises, and the Captain of the Guard, Colonel McDougal, came and told us that a man had arrived with the horns and tail of the Firedrake, and was claiming the reward. Her Majesty and I rose and went into the outer court, where we found, sitting on that carpet with a glass of beer in his hand, a respectable-looking upper-servant, whom I recognized as your butler. He informed us that he had just killed the beast, and showed us the horns and tail, sure enough; there they are! The tail is like the iron handle of a pump, but the horns are genuine. A pair were thrown up by a volcano, in my great-grandfather's time, Giglio I.* Excellent coffee this, of yours!"

The ambassador bowed.

"Well, we asked him *where* he killed the Firedrake, and he said in a garden near Gluckstein. Then he began to speak about the reward, and the 'perkisits,' as he called them, which it seems he had read about in my proclamation. Rather a neat thing; drew it up myself," added His Majesty.

"Very much to the point," said the ambassador, wondering what the King was coming to.

"Glad you like it," said the King, much pleased. "Well, where was I? Oh yes; your man said he had killed the creature in a garden, quite near Gluckstein. I didn't much like the whole affair: he is an alien, you see; and then there was my niece, Molinda—poor girl, *she* was certain to give trouble. Her heart is buried, if I may say so, with poor Alphonso. But the Queen is a very remarkable woman—very remarkable—"

"Very!" said the ambassador, with perfect truth.

*The history of this prince may be read in a treatise called *The Rose and the Ring* by W.M. Thackeray [now published by the Pierpont Morgan Library—Ed.].

" 'Caitiff!' she cried to your butler," His Majesty went on; " 'perjured knave, thou liest in thy throat! Gluckstein is a hundred leagues from here, and how sayest thou that thou slewest the monster, and camest hither in a few hours' space?' This had not occurred to me—I am a plain king, but I at once saw the force of Her Majesty's argument. 'Yes,' said I; 'how did you manage it?' But he—your man, I mean—was not a bit put out. 'Why, Your Majesty,' says he, 'I just sat down on that there bit of carpet, wished I was here, and here I ham. And I'd be glad, having had the trouble—and my time not being my own—to see the colour of them perkisits, according to the proclamation.' On this Her Majesty grew more indignant, if possible. 'Nonsense!' she cried, 'a story out of the *Arabian Nights* is not suited for a modern public and fails to win aesthetic credence.' These were her very words."

"Her Majesty's expressions are ever choice and appropriate," said the ambassador.

" 'Sit down there, on the carpet, knave,' she went on, 'ourself and consort'—meaning *me*—'will take our places by thy side, and I shall wish us in Gluckstein, at thy master's! When the experiment has failed, thy head shall from thy shoulders be shorn!' So your man merely said: 'Very well, mum—Your Majesty, I mean,' and sat down. The Queen took her place at the edge of the carpet; I sat between her and the butler, and she said: 'I wish I were in Gluckstein!' Then we rose, flew through the air at an astonishing pace, and here we are! So I suppose the rest of the butler's tale is true, which I regret; but a king's word is sacred, and he shall take the place of that sneak, Prigio. But as we left home before dinner, and as yours is over, may I request your lordship to believe that I should be delighted to take something cold?"

The ambassador at once ordered a sumptuous collation, to which the King did full justice; and His Majesty was shown to the royal chamber, as he complained of fatigue. The Queen accompanied him, remarking that she was sound asleep, but would waken presently. Neither of them said "Good night" to the Prince. Indeed, they did not see him again, for he was on the balcony with Lady Rosalind. They found a great deal to say to each other, and at last the Prince asked her to be his wife; and she said that if the King and her father gave their permission—why, then she would! After this she went to bed; and the Prince, who had not slept at all the night before, felt very sleepy also. But he knew that first he had something that must be done. So he went into the drawing room, took his carpet, and wished to be—now where do you suppose? Beside the dead body of the Firedrake! There he was in a moment; and dreadful the body looked, lying stark and cold in the white moonshine. Then the Prince cut off its four hooves, put them in his wallet, and with these he flew back in a second, and met the ambassador just as he came from ushering the King to bed. Then the Prince was shown to his own room, where he locked up the hooves, the carpet, the cap of darkness, and his other things in an iron box; and so he went to bed and dreamed of his Lady Rosalind.

# CHAPTER XV

## *The King's Cheque*

When they all awakened next morning, their first ideas were confused. It is often confusing to wake in a strange bed, much more so when you have flown through the air, like the King, the Queen, and Benson the butler. For her part, the Queen was the most perplexed of all; for she did undeniably wake, and yet she was not at home, where she had expected to be. However, she was a determined woman, and stood to it that nothing unusual was occurring. The butler made up his mind to claim the crown princeship and the hand of the Lady Molinda; because, as he justly remarked to William, here was such a chance to better himself as might not soon come in his way again. As for the King, he was only anxious to get back to Falkenstein, and have the whole business settled in a constitutional manner. The ambassador was not sorry to get rid of the royal party; and it was proposed that they should all sit down on the flying carpet and wish themselves at home again. But the Queen would not hear of it: she said it was childish and impossible; so the carriage was got ready for her, and she started without saying a word of goodbye to anyone. The King, Benson, and the Prince were not so particular, and they simply flew back to Falkenstein in the usual way, arriving there at 11:35—a week before Her Majesty.

The King at once held a Court; the horns and tail of the monster were exhibited amidst general interest, and Benson and the Prince were invited to state their claims.

Benson's evidence was taken first. He declined to say exactly where or how he killed the Firedrake. There might be more of them left, he remarked—young ones, that would take a lot of killing—and he refused to part with his secret. Only he claimed the reward, which was offered, if you remember, *not* to the man who killed the beast, but to him who brought its horns and tail. This was allowed by the lawyers present to be very sound law; and Benson was cheered by the courtiers, who decidedly preferred him to Prigio, and who, besides, thought he was going to be crown prince. As for Lady Molinda, she was torn by the most painful feelings; for, much as she hated Prigio, she could not bear the idea of marrying Benson. Yet one or the other choice seemed certain.

Unhappy lady! Perhaps no girl was ever more strangely beset by misfortune!

Prince Prigio was now called on to speak. He admitted that the reward was offered for bringing the horns and tail, not for killing the monster. But were the King's *intentions* to go for nothing? When a subject only *meant* well, of course he had to suffer; but when a king said one thing, was he not to be supposed to have meant another? Any fellow with a wagon could *bring* the horns and tail; the difficult thing was to kill the monster. If Benson's claim was allowed, the royal prerogative of saying one thing and meaning something else was in danger.

On hearing this argument the King so far forgot himself as to cry: "Bravo, well said!" and to clap his hands, whereon all the courtiers shouted and threw up their hats.

The Prince then said that whoever had killed the monster could of course tell where to find him, and could bring his hooves. He was ready to do this himself. Was Mr. Benson equally ready? On this being interpreted to him—for he did not speak Pantouflian—Benson grew pale with horror, but fell back on the proclamation. He had brought the horns and tail, and so he must have the perquisites, and the Lady Molinda!

The King's mind was so much confused by this time that he determined to leave it to the Lady Molinda herself.

"Which of them will you have, my dear?" he asked, in a kind voice.

But poor Molinda merely cried. Then His Majesty was almost *driven* to say that he would give the reward to whoever produced the hooves by that day of the following week. But no sooner had he said this than the Prince brought them out of his wallet, and displayed them in open Court. This ended the case; and Benson, after being entertained with sherry and sandwiches in the steward's room, was sent back to his master. And I regret to say that his temper was not at all improved by his failure to better himself. On the contrary, he was unusually cross and disagreeable for several days; but we must perhaps make some allowance for his disappointment.

But if Benson was irritated, and suffered from the remarks of his fellow servants, I do not think we can envy Prince Prigio. Here he was, restored to his position indeed, but by no means to *the royal favour*. For the King disliked him as much as ever, and was as angry as ever about the deaths of Enrico and Alphonso. Nay, he was even *more* angry; and, perhaps, not without reason. He called up Prigio before the whole Court, and thereon the courtiers cheered like anything, but the King cried:

"Silence! McDougal, drag the first man that shouts to the serpent-house in the zoological gardens, and lock him up with the rattlesnakes!"

After that the courtiers were very quiet.

"Prince," said the King, as Prigio bowed before the throne, "you are restored to your position, because I cannot break my promise. But your base and malevolent nature is even more conspicuously manifest in your selfish success than in your previous dastardly contempt of duty. Why, confound you!'' cried the King, dropping the high style in which he had been speaking, and becoming the father, not the *monarch*, "why, if you *could* kill the Firedrake, did you let your poor little brothers go and be b-b-b-broiled? Eh! what do you say, you sneak? You didn't believe there *were* any Firedrakes? That just comes of your eternal conceit and arrogance! If you were clever enough to kill the creature—and I admit that— you were clever enough to know that what everybody said must be true. You have not generally found it so? Well, you *have* this time, and let it be a lesson to you; not that there is much comfort in that, for it is not likely you will have another chance"—exactly the idea that had occurred to Benson.

Here the King wept, among the tears of the Lord Chief Justice, the Poet Laureate (who had been awfully frightened when he heard of the rattlesnakes), the maids of honour, the Chaplain Royal, and everyone but Colonel McDougal, a Scottish soldier of fortune, who maintained a military reserve.

When His Majesty had recovered, he said to Prigio (who had not been crying, being too much absorbed): "A king's word is his bond. Bring me a pen, somebody, and my cheque-book."

The royal cheque-book, bound in red morocco, was brought in by eight pages, with ink and a pen. His Majesty then filled up and signed the following satisfactory document:

No. VV8 961047     Falkenstein  July 10, 1718

**The Bank of Pantouflia**

FALKENSTEIN BRANCH

**Pay to**  Prince Prigio                    **on Order**
Ten Thousand Purses

£ 1,000,000                    Grognio R.

"There!" said His Majesty, crossing his cheque and throwing sand over it, for blotting paper had not yet been invented. "There, take that, and be off with you!"

Prince Prigio was respectfully but rapidly obeying his royal command, for he thought he had better cash the royal cheque as soon as possible, when His Majesty yelled: "Hi, there! Come back! I forgot something; you've got to marry Molinda!"

# CHAPTER XVI

## *A Melancholy Chapter*

The Prince had gone some way when the King called after him. How he wished he had the seven-league boots on, or that he had the cap of darkness in his pocket! If he had been so lucky, he would now have got back to Gluckstein, and crossed the border with Lady Rosalind. A million of money may not seem much, but a pair of young people who really love each other could live happily on less than the cheque he had in his pocket. However, the King shouted very loud, as he always did when he meant to be obeyed, and the Prince sauntered slowly back again.

"Prigio!" said His Majesty, "where were you off to? Don't you remember that this is your wedding day? My proclamation offered not only the money (which you have), but the hand of the Lady Molinda, which the Court chaplain will presently make your own. I congratulate you, sir; Molinda is a dear girl."

"I have the highest affection and esteem for my cousin, sir," said the Prince, "but—"

"I'll never marry him!" cried poor Molinda, kneeling at the throne, where her streaming eyes and hair made a pretty and touching picture. "Never! I despise him!"

"I was about to say, sir," the Prince went on, "that I cannot possibly have the pleasure of wedding my cousin."

"The family gallows, I presume, is in good working order?" asked the King of the family executioner, a tall gaunt man in black and scarlet, who was only employed in the case of members of the blood royal.

"Never better, sire," said the man, bowing with more courtliness than his profession indicated.

"Very well," said the King. "Prince Prigio, you have your choice. *There* is the gallows, *here* is Lady Molinda. My duty is painful, but clear. A king's word cannot be broken. Molly, or be hanged!"

The Prince bowed respectfully to Lady Molinda.

"Madam, my cousin," said he, "your clemency will excuse my answer, and you will not misinterpret the apparent discourtesy of my conduct. I am compelled, most unwillingly, to slight your charms, and to select the Extreme Rigour of the Law. Executioner, lead on! Do your duty; for me, *Prigio est prêt!*"—for this was his motto, and meant that he was ready.

Poor Lady Molinda could not but be hurt by the Prince's preference for death over marriage to her, little as she liked him. "Is life then so worthless? and is Molinda so terrible a person, that you prefer *those* arms," and she pointed to the gallows, "to *these*?"—here she held out her own, which were very white, round, and pretty; for Molinda was a good-hearted girl, she could not bear to see Prigio put to death; and then, perhaps, she reflected that there are worse positions than the queenship of Pantouflia. For Alphonso was gone— crying would not bring him back.

"Ah, madam!" said the Prince, "you are forgiving—"

"For *you* are brave!" said Molinda, feeling quite a respect for him.

"But neither your heart nor mine is ours to give. Since mine is another's, I understand too well this feeling of *yours*! Do not let us buy life at the price of happiness and honour."

Then, turning to the King, the Prince said: "Sir, is there no way but by death or marriage? You say you cannot keep half only of your promise; and that if I accept the reward I must also unite myself with my unwilling cousin. Cannot the whole proclamation be annulled, and will you consider the bargain void if I tear up this flimsy scroll?''

And here the Prince fluttered in the air the cheque for £1,000,000.

For a moment the King was tempted; but then he said to himself: "Never mind, it's only an extra penny on the income-tax." Then: "Keep your dross," he shouted, meaning the million; "but let *me* keep my promise. To chapel at once, or—" and he pointed to the executioner. "The word of a king of Pantouflia is sacred."

"And so is that of a crown prince," answered Prigio, "and *mine* is pledged to a lady."

"She shall be a mourning bride," cried the King savagely, "unless"—here he paused for a moment—"unless you bring me back Alphonso and Enrico, safe and well!"

The Prince thought for the space of a flash of lightning. "I accept the alternative," he said, "if Your Majesty will grant me my conditions."

"Name them!" said the King.

"Let me be transported to Gluckstein, left there unguarded, and if, in three days, I do not return with my brothers safe and well, Your Majesty shall be spared a cruel duty. Prigio of Pantouflia will perish by his own hand."

The King, whose mind did not work very quickly, took some minutes to think it over. Then he saw that by granting the Prince's conditions, he would either recover his dear sons, or, at least, get rid of Prigio, without the unpleasantness of having him executed. For, though some kings have put their eldest sons to death, and most have wished to do so, they have never been better loved by the people for their Roman virtue.

"Honour bright?" said the King at last.

"Honour bright!" answered the Prince, and for the first time in many months, the royal father and son shook hands.

"For you, madam," said Prigio in a stately way to Lady Molinda, "in less than a week I trust we shall be taking our vows at the same altar, and that the close of the ceremony which finds us cousins will leave us brother and sister."

Poor Molinda merely stared; for she could not imagine what he meant. In a moment he was gone; and having taken, by the King's permission, the flying carpet, he was back at the ambassador's house in Gluckstein.

## CHAPTER XVII

## *The Black Cat and the Brethren*

Who was glad to see the Prince, if it was not Lady Rosalind? The white roses of her cheeks turned to red roses in a moment, and then back to white again, they were so alarmed at the change. So the two went into the gardens together, and talked about a number of things; but at last the Prince told her that, before three days were over, all would be well, or all would be over with him. For either he would have brought his brothers back, sound and well, to Falkenstein, or he would not survive his dishonour.

"It is no more than right," he said, "for had I gone first, neither of them would have been sent to meet the monster after I had fallen. And I *should* have fallen, dear Rosalind, if I had faced the Firedrake before I knew *you*."

Then when she asked him why, and what good she had done him, he told her all the story; and how, before he fell in love with her, he didn't believe in fairies, or Firedrakes, or caps of darkness, or anything nice and impossible, but only in horrid useless facts, and chemistry, and geology, and arithmetic, and mathematics, and even political economy. And the Firedrake would have made a mouthful of him then.

So she was delighted when she heard this, almost as much delighted as she was afraid that he might fail in the most difficult adventure. For it was one thing to egg on a Remora to kill a Firedrake, and quite another to find the princes if they were alive, and restore them if they were dead!

But the Prince said he had his plan, and he stayed that night at the ambassador's. Next morning he rose very early, before anyone else was up, that he might not have to say "Goodbye" to Lady Rosalind. Then he flew in a moment to the old lonely castle, where nobody went for fear of ghosts, ever since the Court retired to Falkenstein.

How still it was, how deserted; not a sign of life, and yet the Prince was looking everywhere *for some living thing*. He hunted through the castle in vain, and then went out to the stable yard; but all the dogs of course had been taken away, and the neighbouring farmers had offered homes to the poultry. At last, stretched at full length in a sunny place, the Prince found a very old, half-blind, miserable cat. The poor creature was lean, and its fur had fallen off in patches; it could no longer catch birds, nor even mice, and there was nobody to give milk to it. But cats do not look far into the future; and this old black cat—Frank was his name—had got a breakfast somehow, and was happy in the sun. The Prince stood and looked at him pityingly, and he thought that even a sick old cat was, in some ways, happier than most men.

"Well," said the Prince at last, "he could not live long anyway, and it must be done. He will feel nothing."

Then he drew the sword of sharpness, and with one turn of his wrist cut the cat's head clean off.

It did not at once change into a beautiful young lady, as perhaps you expect; no, that was improbable and, as the Prince was in love already, would have been vastly inconvenient. The dead cat lay there, like any common cat.

Then the Prince built up a heap of straw, with wood on it; and there he laid poor puss, and set fire to the pile. Very soon there was nothing of old black Frank left but ashes!

Then the Prince ran upstairs to the fairy cupboard, his heart beating loudly with excitement. The sun was shining through the arrow-shot window; all the yellow motes were dancing in its rays. The light fell on the strange heaps of fairy things— talismans and spells. The Prince hunted about here and there, and at last he discovered six ancient water vessels of black leather, each with a silver plate on it, and on the plate letters engraved. This was what was written on the plates:

## AQVA. DE. FONTE. LEONUM.*

"Thank Heaven!" said the Prince. "I thought they were sure to have brought it!"

Then he took one of the old black leather bottles, and ran downstairs again to the place where he had burned the body of the poor old sick cat.

He opened the bottle and poured a few drops of the water on the ashes and the dying embers.

Up there sprang a tall, white flame of fire, waving like a tongue of light; and forth from the heap jumped the most beautiful, strong, furry black cat that ever was seen!

It was Frank as he had been in the vigour of his youth; and he knew the Prince at once, and rubbed himself against him and purred.

The Prince lifted up Frank and kissed his nose for joy; and a bright tear rolled down on Frank's face, and made him rub his nose with his paw in the most comical manner.

Then the Prince set him down, and he ran round and round after his tail; and, lastly, cocked his tail up, and marched proudly after the Prince into the castle.

"Oh, Frank!" said Prince Prigio, "no cat since the time of Puss in Boots was ever so well taken care of as you shall be. For if the fairy water from the Fountain of Lions can bring *you* back to life—why, there is a chance for Alphonso and Enrico!"

Then Prigio bustled about, got ready a cold luncheon from the storeroom, took all his fairy things that he was likely to need, sat down with them on the flying carpet, and wished himself at the mountain of the Firedrake.

Off he flew; and there he was in a second, just beside poor Alphonso's garden engine. Then Prigio, seeing a little heap of grey ashes beside the engine, watered them with the fairy water; and up jumped Alphonso, as jolly as ever, his sword in his hand.

*Water from the Fountain of Lions.

"Hallo, Prigio!" cried he. "Are you come after the monster too? I've been asleep, and I had a kind of dream that he beat me. But the pair of us will tackle him. How is Molinda?"

"Prettier than ever," said Prigio, "but very anxious about you. However, the Firedrake's dead and done for; so never mind him. But I left Enrico somewhere about. Just you sit down and wait a minute, till I fetch him." The Prince said this because he did not wish Alphonso to know that he and Enrico had not had quite the best of it in the affair with the monster.

"All right, old fellow," says Alphonso, "but have you any luncheon with you? Never was I so hungry in my life!"

Prince Prigio had thought of this, and he brought out some cold sausage (to which Alphonso was partial) and some bread, with which the younger prince expressed himself satisfied. Then Prigio went up the hill some way, first warning Alphonso *not* to sit on his carpet for fear of *accidents* like that which happened to Benson. In a hollow of the hill, sure enough there was the sword of Enrico, the diamonds of the hilt gleaming in the sun. And there was a little heap of grey ashes.

The Prince poured a few drops of the water from the Fountain of Lions on them and up of course jumped Enrico, just as Alphonso had done.

"Sleepy old chap you are, Enrico," said the Prince; "but come on, Alphonso will have finished the grub unless we look smart."

So back they came in time to get their share of what was going; and they drank to the Remora's very good health, when Prigio told them about the fight. But neither of them ever knew that they had been dead and done for; because Prigio invented a story that the mountain was enchanted, and that, as long as the Firedrake lived, everyone who came there fell asleep. He did tell them about the flying carpet, however, which of course did not much surprise them, because they had read all about it in the *Arabian Nights* and other historical works.

"And now I'll show you fun!" said Prigio; and he asked them both to take their seats on the carpet, and wished to be in the valley of the Remora.

There they were in a moment, among the old knights whom, if you remember, the Remora had frozen into stone. There were quite a troop of them, in all sorts of armour— Greek and Roman, and Knights Templar like Front de Bœuf and Brian du Bois Gilbert—all the brave warriors that had tried to fight the Remora since the world began.

Then Prigio gave each of his brothers some of the water in their caps, and told them to go round pouring a drop or two on each frozen knight. And as they did it, lo and behold! each knight came alive, with his horse, and lifted his sword and shouted:

### "LONG LIVE PRINCE PRIGIO!"

in Greek, Latin, Egyptian, German, and Spanish—all of which the Prince perfectly understood, and spoke like a native.

So he marshalled them in order, and sent them off to ride to Falkenstein and cry: "Prince Prigio is coming!"

Off they went, the horses' hooves clattering, banners flying, sunshine glittering on the spear points. Off they rode to Falkenstein; and when the King saw them come galloping in, I can tell you he had no more notion of hanging Prigio.

## CHAPTER XVIII

# The Very Last

The Princes returned to Gluckstein on the carpet, and went to the best inn, where they dined together and slept. Next morning they, and the ambassador, who had been told all the story, and Lady Rosalind, floated comfortably on the carpet, back to Falkenstein, where the King wept like anything on the shoulders of Alphonso and Enrico. They could not make out why he cried so, nor why Lady Molinda and Lady Kathleena cried; but soon they were all laughing and happy again. But then—would you believe he could be so mean?—he refused to keep his royal promise, and restore Prigio to his crown princeship! Kings are like that.

But Prigio, very quietly asking for the head of the Firedrake, said he'd pour the magic water on *that*, and bring the Firedrake back to life again, unless His Majesty behaved rightly. This threat properly frightened King Grognio, and he apologized. Then the King shook hands with Prigio in public, and thanked him, and said he was proud of him. As to Lady Rosalind, the old gentleman quite fell in love with her, and he sent at once to the Chaplain Royal to get into his surplice, and marry all the young people off at once, without waiting for wedding cakes and milliners and all the rest of it.

Now, just as they were forming a procession to march into church, who should appear but the Queen! Her Majesty had been travelling by post all the time, and, luckily, had heard of none of the doings since Prigio, Benson, and the King left Gluckstein. I say *luckily* because if she *had* heard of them, she would not have believed a word of them. But when she saw Alphonso and Enrico, she was much pleased, and said: "Naughty boys! Where have you been hiding? The King had some absurd story about your having been killed by a fabulous monster. Bah! don't tell *me*. I always said you would come back after a little trip—didn't I, Prigio?"

"Certainly, madam," said Prigio, "and I said so too. Didn't I say so?" And all the courtiers cried: "Yes, you did"; but some added, to themselves, "He *always* says, 'Didn't I say so?' "

Then the Queen was introduced to Lady Rosalind, and she said it was "rather a short engagement, but she supposed young people understood their own affairs best." And they do! So the three pairs were married, with the utmost rejoicings; and Her Majesty never, her whole life long, could be got to believe that anything unusual had occurred.

The honeymoon of Prince Prigio and the Crown Princess Rosalind was passed at the castle, where the Prince had been deserted by the Court. But now it was delightfully fitted up;

and Master Frank marched about the house with his tail in the air, as if the place belonged to him.

Now, on the second day of their honeymoon, the Prince and Princess were sitting in the garden together, and the Prince said: "Are you *quite* happy, my dear?" and Rosalind said: "Yes; *quite*."

But the Prince did not like the tone of her voice, and he said: "No, there's something; do tell me what it is."

"Well," said Rosalind, putting her head on his shoulder, and speaking very low, "I want everybody to love you as much as I do. No, not quite so very much—but I want them to like you. Now they *can't*, because they are afraid of you; for you are so awfully clever. Now, couldn't you take the wishing cap, and wish to be no cleverer than other people? Then everybody would like you!"

The Prince thought a minute, then he said: "Your will is law, my dear; anything to please you. Just wait a minute!"

Then he ran upstairs, for the last time, to the fairy garret, and he put on the wishing cap.

"No," thought he to himself, "I won't wish *that*. Every man has one secret from his wife, and this shall be mine."

Then he said aloud: "I WISH TO SEEM NO CLEVERER THAN OTHER PEOPLE."

Then he ran downstairs again, and the Princess noticed a great difference in him (though of course there was really none at all), and so did everyone. For the Prince remained as clever as ever he had been; but, as nobody observed it, he became the most popular prince, and finally the best beloved king who had ever sat on the throne of Pantouflia.

But occasionally Rosalind would say: "I do believe, my dear, that you are really as clever as ever!"

And he *was!*

# GORGON

The gorgons appear in the Greek myths as terrifying monsters. The very word is from the Greek *gorgos*, meaning "terrifying." In some of the myths there are three gorgons, but the one that is usually the only one dealt with is the one named Medusa.

The most frightening aspect of the gorgon is its hair, which is pictured as consisting of living snakes. The notion of snakes coiling and uncoiling on the head of a woman, usually pictured as beautiful in a ghastly way, is indeed unnerving, but it is an easy thing to imagine. You have only to see a sea anemone or an octopus and you will find a creature that seems to have living snakes as part of itself. In fact, I have always thought the gorgons and other snake-haired monsters to be inspired by the octopus.

The gorgon is pictured as so terrifying that people who unwittingly glance at the gorgon face turn into stone.

But, then, it is an instinct in some young animals to freeze when danger looms, for many predators will not see their prey if it does not move. Some animals will even feign death, if frightened, since some predators will not touch dead bodies. And we freeze, too, temporarily, when frightened, and it is an easy leap from that to suppose that if the fright were great and intense enough, we would freeze permanently.

The gorgon may also symbolize the nightmare. A very common nightmare is to have to catch someone or something, or to be pursued, and despite all possible efforts to be unable to move. *I have always thought this to be a natural reaction to entanglement in the bedclothes. The inability to move, in reality, is shifted to the dream, which becomes a nightmare. So the nightmare-freezing becomes the Gorgon-freezing. —But see what the author in the following story does with the legend.*

# THE GORGON

## Tanith Lee

The small island, which lay off the larger island of Daphaeu, obviously contained a secret of some sort, and day by day, and particularly night by night, began to exert an influence on me, so that I must find it out.

Daphaeu itself (or more correctly herself, for she was a female country, voluptuous and cruel by turns in the true antique fashion of the Goddess) was hardly enormous. A couple of roads, a tangle of sheep tracks, a precarious, escalating village, rocks and hillsides thatched by blistered grass. All of which overhung an extraordinary sea, unlike any sea which I have encountered elsewhere in Greece. Water which might be mistaken for blueness from a distance, but which, from the harbour, or the multitude of caves and coves that undermined the island, revealed itself a clear and succulent green, like milky limes, or the bottle glass of certain spirits.

On my first morning, having come on to the natural terrace, the only recommendation of the hovel-like accommodation, to look over this strange green ocean, I saw the smaller island, lying like a little boat of land moored just wide of Daphaeu's three hills. The day was clear, the water frilled with white where it hit the fangs in the interstices below the terrace. About the smaller island, barely a ruffle showed. It seemed to glide up from the sea, smooth as a mirror. The little island was verdant, also. Unlike Daphaeu's limited stands of stone-pine, cypress and cedar, the smaller sister was clouded by a still, lambent haze of foliage, that looked to be woods. Visions of groves, springs, a ruined temple, a statue of Pan playing the panpipes forever in some glade—where only yesterday, it might seem, a thin column of aromatic smoke had gone up—these images were enough fancifully to draw me into inquiries about how the small island might be reached. And when my inquiries met first with a polite bevy of excuses, next with a refusal, lastly with a blank wall of silence, as if whomever I mentioned the little island to had gone temporarily deaf or mad, I became, of course determined to get to it, to find out what odd superstitious thing kept these people away. Naturally, the Daphaeui were not friendly to me at any time, beyond the false friendship one anticipates extended to a man of another nationality and clime, who can be relied on to pay his bills, perhaps allow himself to be overcharged, even made a downright monkey of in order to preserve goodwill. In the normal run of things, I could have had anything I wanted, in exchange for a pack of local lies, a broad local smile, and a broader local price. That I could not get to the little island puzzled me. I tried money, and I tried barter. I even, in a reckless moment, probably knowing I would not succeed, offered Pitos, one of the younger fishermen, the gold and onyx ring he coveted. My sister had made it for me, the faithful copy of an intaglio belonging to the house of Borgia, no less. Generally, Pitos could not pass the time of day with me without mentioning the ring, adding something in the nature of: "If ever you want a great service, any great service, I will do it for that ring." I half believe he would have stolen or murdered for it, certainly shared the bed with me. But he would not, apparently, even for the Borgia ring, take me to the little island.

"You think too much of foolish things," he said to me. "For a big writer, that is not good."

I ignored the humorous aspect of "big," equally inappropriate in the sense of height, girth or fame. Pitos' English was fine, and when he slipped into mild inaccuracies, it was likely to be a decoy.

"You're wrong, Pitos. That island has a story in it somewhere, I'd take a bet on it."

"No fish today," said Pitos. "Why you think that is?"

I refrained from inventing a tale for him that I had seen

giant swordfish leaping from the shallows by the smaller island.

I found I was prowling Daphaeu, but only on the one side, the side where I would get a view, or views, of the small island. I would climb down into the welter of coves and smashed emerald water, to look across at the small island. I would climb up and stand, leaning on the sunblasted walls of a crumbling church, and look at the small island. At night, cruched over a bottle of wine, a scatter of manuscript, moths falling like rain in the oil lamp, my stare stayed fixed on the small island, which, as the moon came up, would seem turned to silver, or to some older metal, Nemean metal perhaps, sloughed from the moon herself.

Curiosity accounts for much of this, and contra-suggestive-ness. But the influence I presently began to feel, that I cannot account for exactly. Maybe it was only the writer's desire to fantasize rather than to work. But every time I reached for the manuscript I would experience a sort of distraction, a sort of calling, uncanny, poignant, like nostalgia, though for a place I had never visited.

I am very bad at recollecting my dreams, but once or twice, just before sunrise, I had a suspicion I had dreamed of the island. Of walking there, hearing its inner waters, the leaves brushing my hands and face.

Two weeks went by, and precious little had been done in the line of work. And I had come to Daphaeu with the sole intention of working. The year before, I had accomplished so much in a month of similar islands—or had they been similar? —that I had looked for results of some magnitude. In all of fourteen days I must have squeezed out two thousand words, and most of those dreary enough that the only covers they would ever get between would be those of the trash can. And yet, it was not that I could not produce work, it was that I knew, with blind and damnable certainty, that the work I needed to be doing sprang from that spoonful of island.

The first day of the third week I had been swimming in the calm stretch of sea west of the harbour, and had emerged to sun myself and smoke on the parched hot shore. Presently Pitos appeared, having scented cigarettes. Surgical and gov-

ernment health warnings have not yet penetrated to spots like
Daphaeu, where filtered tobacco continues to symbolize Hollywood, or some other amorphous, anachronistic surrealism
still hankered after and long vanished from the world beyond.
Once Pitos had acquired his cigarette, he sprawled down on
the dry grass, grinned, indicated the Borgia ring, and mentioned a beautiful cousin of his, whether male or female I
cannot be sure. After this had been cleared out of the way, I
said to him,

"You know how the currents run. I was thinking of a
slightly more adventurous swim. But I'd like your advice."

Pitos glanced at me warily. I had had the plan as I lazed in
the velvet water. Pitos was already starting to guess it.

"Currents are very dangerous. Not to be trusted, except by
harbour."

"How about between Daphaeu and the other island? It
can't be more than a quarter mile. The sea looks smooth
enough, once you break away from the shoreline here."

"No," said Pitos. I waited for him to say there were no
fish, or a lot of fish, or that his brother had got a broken
thumb, or something of the sort. But Pitos did not resort to
this. Troubled and angry, he stabbed my cigarette into the
turf half-smoked. "Why do you want to go to the island so
much?"

"Why does nobody else want me to go there?"

He looked up then, and into my eyes. His own were very
black, sensuous, carnal, earthbound eyes, full of orthodox
sins, and extremely young in a sense that had nothing to do
with physical age, but with race, I suppose, the youngness of
ancient things, like Pan himself, quite possibly.

"Well," I said at last, "are you going to tell me, or not?
Because believe me, I intend to swim over there, today or
tomorrow."

"No," he said again. And then: "You should not go. On
the island there is a—" and he said a word in some tongue
neither Greek nor Turkish, not even the corrupt Spanish that
sometimes peregrinates from Malta.

"A *what?*"

Pitos shrugged helplessly. He gazed out to sea, safe sea

without islands. He seemed to be putting something together in his mind, and I let him do it, very curious now, pleasantly unnerved by this waft of the occult I had already suspected to be the root cause of the ban.

Eventually he turned back to me, treated me once more to the primordial innocence of his stare, and announced:

"The cunning one."

"Ah," I said. Both irked and amused, I found myself smiling. At this, Pitos' face grew savage with pure rage, an expression I had never witnessed before—the facade kept for foreigners had well and truly come down.

"Pitos," I said, "I don't understand."

*"Meda,"* he said then, the Greek word, old Greek.

"Wait," I said. I caught at the name, which was wrong, trying to fit it to a memory. Then the list came back to me, actually from Graves, the names which meant "the cunning" —Meda, Medea, Medusa.

"Oh," I said. I hardly wanted to offend him further by bursting into loud mirth. At the same time, even while I was trying not to laugh, I was aware of the hair standing up on my scalp and neck. "You're telling me there is a gorgon on the island."

Pitos grumbled unintelligibly, stabbing the dead cigarette over and over into the ground.

"I'm sorry, Pitos, but it can't be Medusa. Someone cut her head off quite a few years ago. A guy called Perseus."

His face erupted into the awful expression again, mouth in a rictus, tongue starting to protrude, eyes flaring at me—quite abruptly I realized he wasn't raging, but imitating the visual panic-contortions of a man turning inexorably to stone. Since that is what the gorgon is credited with, literally petrifying men by the sheer horror of her countenance, it now seemed almost pragmatic of Pitos to be demonstrating. It was, too, a creditable facsimile of the sculpted gorgon's face sometimes used to seal ovens and jars. I wondered where he had seen one to copy it so well.

"All right," I said. "O.K., Pitos, fine." I fished in my shirt, which was lying on the ground, and took out some money to give him, but he recoiled. "I'm sorry," I said, "I don't think it merits the ring. Unless you'd care to row me over there after all.''

The boy rose. He looked at me with utter contempt, and without another word, before striding off up the shore. The mashed cigarette protruded from the grass, and I lay and watched it, the tiny strands of tobacco slowly crisping in the heat of the sun, as I plotted my route from Daphaeu.

Dawn seemed an amiable hour. No one in particular about on that side of the island, the water chill but flushing quickly with warmth as the sun reached over it. And the tide in the right place to navigate the rocks. . . .

Yes, dawn would be an excellent time to swim out to the gorgon's island.

The gods were on my side, I concluded, as I eased myself out into the open sea the following morning. Getting clear of the rocks was no problem, their channels only half filled by the returning tide. While just beyond Daphaeu's coast I picked up one of those contrary currents that lace the island's edges and which, tide or no, would funnel me away from shore.

The swim was ideal, the sea limpid and no longer any more than cool. Sunlight filled in the waves and touched Daphaeu's retreating face with gold. Barely altered in a thousand years, either rock or sea or sun. And yet one knew that against all the claims of romantic fiction, this place did not look now as once it had. Some element in the air, or in time itself, changes things. A young man of the Bronze Age, falling asleep at sunset in his own era, waking at sunrise in mine, looking about him, would not have known where he was. I would swear to that.

Some thoughts I had leisure for in my facile swim across to the wooded island moored off Daphaeu.

As I had detected, the approach was smooth, virtually inviting. I cruised in as if sliding on butter. A rowboat would have had no more difficulty. The shallows were clear, empty of rocks, and if anything greener than the water off Daphaeu.

I had not looked much at Medusa's Island (i had begun jokingly to call it this), as I crossed, knowing I would have all the space on my arrival. So I found myself wading in on a seamless beach of rare glycerine sand, and looking up, saw the mass of trees spilling from the sky.

The effect was incredibly lush, so much heavy green, and seemingly quite impenetrable, although the sun struck in glistening shafts, lodging like arrows in the foliage, which reminded me very intensely of huge clusters of grapes on a vine. Anything might lie behind such a barricade.

It was already beginning to be hot. Dry, I put on the loose cotton shirt, and ate breakfast packed in the same waterproof wrapper, standing on the beach impatient to get on.

As I moved forward, a bird shrilled somewhere in its cage of boughs, sounding an alarm of invasion. But surely the birds, too, would be stone, on Medusa's Island, if the legends were correct? And when I stumbled across the remarkable stone carving of a man in the forest, I would pause in shocked amazement at its verisimilitude to the life. . . .

Five minutes into the thickets of the wood, I did indeed stumble on a carving, but it was of a moss-grown little faun. My pleasure in the discovery was considerably lessened, however, when investigation told me it was scarcely classical in origin. Circa 1920 would be nearer the mark.

A further minute and I had put the faun from my mind. The riot of waterfalling plants through which I had been picking my way broke open suddenly on an inner vista much wider than I had anticipated, while the focal point of the vista threw me completely. I cannot say what I had really been expecting. The grey-white stalks of pillars, some temple shrine, the spring with its votary of greenish rotted bronze, none of these would have surprised me. On the other hand, to find a house before me took me completely by surprise. I stood and looked at it in abject dismay, cursing its wretched normalcy, until I gradually began to see the house was not normal, in the accepted sense.

It had been erected probably at the turn of the century, when such things were done. An eccentric two-storeyed building, intransigently European, that is, the Europe of the North, with its dark walls and arched roofing. Long windows, smothered by the proximity of the wood, received and refracted no light. The one unique and startling feature—startling because of its beauty—was the parade of columns that ran along the terrace, in form and choreography for all the world like the columns of Knossos, differing only in colour. For these stems of the gloomy house were of a luminous sea-green marble, and shone as the windows did not.

Before the house was a stretch of rough-cut lawn, tamarisk, and one lost dying olive tree. As I was staring, an apparition seemed to manifest out of the centre of the tree. For a second we peered at each other, before he came from the bushes with a clashing of gnarled brown forearms. He might have been an elderly satyr; I, patently, was only a swimmer, with my pale foreigner's tan, my bathing trunks, the loose shirt. It occurred to me at last that I was conceivably trespassing. I wished my Greek were better.

He planted himself before me and shouted intolerantly, and anyone's Greek was good enough to get his drift. "Go! Go!" He was ranting, and he began to wave a knife with which, presumably, he had been pruning or mutilating something. "Go, you *go!*"

I said I had been unaware anybody lived on the island. He took no notice. He went on waving the knife, and his attitude provoked me. I told him sternly to put the knife down, that I would leave when I was ready, that I had seen no notice to the effect that the island was private property. Generally I would never take a chance like this with someone so obviously qualified to be a lunatic, but my position was so vulnerable, so ludicrous, so entirely indefensible, that I felt bound to act firmly. Besides which, having reached the magic grotto and found it was not as I had visualized, I was still very reluctant to abscond with only a memory of dark windows and sea-green columns to brood upon.

The maniac was by now quite literally foaming, due most likely to a shortage of teeth, but the effect was alarming, not to mention unaesthetic. As I was deciding which fresh course to take and if there might be one, a woman's figure came out on to the terrace. I had the impression of a white frock,

before an odd, muffled voice called out a rapid—too rapid for
my translation—stream of peculiarly accented Greek. The old
man swung around, gazed at the figure, raised his arms, and
bawled another foaming torrent to the effect that I was a
bandit, or some other kind of malcontent. While he did so,
agitated as I was becoming, I nevertheless took in what I
could of the woman standing between the columns. She was
mostly in shadow, just the faded white dress, with a white
scarf at the neck, marking her position. And then there was an
abrupt flash of warmer pallor that was her hair. A blonde Greek,
or maybe just a peroxided Greek. At any rate, no snakes.

The drama went on, from his side, from hers. I finally got
tired of it, went by him and walked toward the terrace,
pondering, rather too late, if I might not be awarded the knife
in my back. But almost as soon as I started to move, she
leaned foward a little, and she called another phrase to him,
which this time I made out, telling him to let me come on.

When I reached the foot of the terrace steps, I halted,
really involuntarily, struck by something strange about her.
Just as the strangeness of the house had begun to strike me,
not its evident strangeness, the ill-marriage to location, the
green pillars, but a strangeness of atmosphere, items the
unconscious eye notices, where the physical eye is blind, and
will not explain. And so with her. What was it? Still in
shadow, I had the impression she might be in her early
thirties, from her figure, her movements, but she had turned
away as I approached, adjusting some papers on a wicker
table.

"Excuse me," I said. I stopped, and spoke in English. For
some reason I guessed she would be familiar with the language, perhaps only since it was current on Daphaeu. "Excuse me. I had no idea the island was private. No one gave
me the slightest hint—"

"You are English," she broke in, in the vernacular, prov-
ing the guess to be correct.

"Near enough. I find it easier to handle than Greek, I
confess."

"Your Greek is very good," she said, with the indifferent
patronage of one who is multi-lingual. I stood there under the

steps, already fascinated. Her voice was the weirdest I had ever heard, muffled, almost unattractive, and with the most incredible accent, not Greek at all. The nearest approximation I could come up with was Russian, but I could not be sure.

"Well," I said. I glanced over my shoulder and registered that the frothy satyr had retired into his shrubbery; the knife glinted as it slashed tamarisk in lieu of me. "Well, I suppose I should retreat to Daphaeu. Or am I permitted to stay?"

"Go, stay," she said. "I do not care at all."

She turned then, abruptly, and my heart slammed into the base of my throat. A childish silly reaction, yet I was quite unnverved, for now I saw what it was that had seemed vaguely peculiar from a distance. The lady on Medusa's island was masked.

She remained totally still, and let me have my reaction, neither helping nor hindering me.

It was an unusual mask, or usual—I am unfamiliar with the norm of such things. It was made of some matte light substance that toned well with the skin of her arms and hands, possibly not so well with that of her neck, where the scarf provided camouflage. Besides which, the chin of the mask, this certainly an extra to any mask I had ever seen, continued under her own. The mask's physiognomy was bland, nondescriptly pretty in a way that was somehow grossly insulting to her. Before confronting the mask, if I had tried to judge the sort of face she would have, I would have suspected a coarse, rather heavy beauty, probably redeemed by one chiseled feature, a small slender nose, perhaps. The mask, however, was vacuous. It did not suit her, was not true to her. Even after three minutes I could tell as much, or thought I could, which amounts to the same thing.

The blonde hair, seeming natural as the mask was not, cascaded down, lush as the foliage of the island. A blonde Greek, then, like the golden Greeks of Homer's time, when gods walked the earth in disguise.

In the end, without any help or hindrance from her, as I have said, I pulled myself together. As she had mentioned no aspect of her state, neither did I. I simply repeated what I had said before: "Am I permitted to stay?"

The mask went on looking at me. The astonishing voice said:

"You wish to stay so much; what do you mean to do here?"

Talk to you, oblique lady, and wonder what lies behind the painted veil.

"Look at the island, if you'll let me. I found the statue of a faun near the beach," elaboration implied I should lie: "Someone told me there was an old shrine here."

"Ah!" She barked. It was apparently a laugh. "No one," she said, "*told* you anything about this place."

I was at a loss. Did she know what she said? "Frankly then, I romantically hoped there might be."

"Unromantically, there is not. No shrine. No temple. My father bought the faun in a shop, in Athens. A tourist shop. He had vulgar tastes, but he knew it, and that has a certain charm, does it not?"

"Yes, I suppose it does. Your father—"

She cut me short again.

"The woods cover all the island. Except for an area behind the house. We grow things there, and we keep goats and chickens. We are very domesticated. Very sufficient for ourselves. There is a spring of fresh water, but no votary. No *genius loci*. I am *so* sorry to dash your dreams to pieces."

It suggested itself to me, from her tone of amusement, from little inflections in her shoulders, that she might be enjoying this, enjoying, if you like, putting me down as an idiot. Presumably visitors were rare. Perhaps it was even fun for her to talk to a man, youngish and unknown, though admittedly never likely to qualify for anyone's centrefold.

"But you have no objections to my being here," I pursued. "And your father?"

"My parents are dead," she informed me. "When I employed the plural, I referred to him," she gestured, a broad sweep of her hand, to the monster on the lawn, "and a woman who attends to the house. My servants, my unpaid servants. I have no money anymore. Do you see this dress? It is my mother's dress. How lucky I am the same fitting as my mother, do you not think?"

"Yes. . . ."

I was put in mind, suddenly, of myself as an ambassador at the court of some notorious female potentate, Cleopatra, say, or Catherine de Medici.

"You are very polite," she said, as if telepathically privy to my fantasies.

"I have every reason to be."

"What reason?"

"I'm trespassing. You treat me like a guest."

"And how," she said, vainglorious all at once, "do you rate my English?"

"It's wonderful."

"I speak eleven languages fluently," she said, with off-handed boastfulness. "Three more I can read very well."

I liked her. This display, touching and magnificent at once, her angular theatrical gesturings, which now came more and more often, her hair, her flat-waisted figure in its 1940's dress, her large, well-made hands, and her challenging me with the mask, saying nothing to explain it, all this hypnotised me.

I said something to express admiration, and she barked again, throwing back her blonde head and irresistibly, though only for a moment, conjuring Garbo's Queen Christina.

Then she walked down the steps, straight to me, demonstrating something else I had deduced, that she was only about an inch shorter than I.

"I," she said, "will show you the island. Come."

She showed me the island. Unsurprisingly, it was small. To go directly round it would maybe have taken less than thirty minutes. But we lingered, over a particular tree, a view, and once we sat down on the ground near the gushing milk-white spring. The basin under the spring, she informed me, had been added in 1910. A little bronze nymph presided over the spot, dating from the same year, which you could tell in any case from the way her classical costume and her filletted hair had been adapted to the fashions of hobble skirt and Edwardian coiffeur. Each age imposes its own overlay on the past.

Behind the house was a scatter of the meagre white dwellings that make up such places as the village on Daphaeu, now plainly unoccupied and put to other uses. Sheltered from the sun by a colossal cypress, six goats played about in the grass. Chickens, and an assortment of other fowl, strutted up and down, while a pig, or pigs, grunted somewhere out of sight. Things grew in strips and patches, and fruit trees and vines ended the miniature plantation before the woods resumed. Self-sufficiency of a tolerable kind, I suppose. But there seemed, from what she said, no contact maintained with any other area, as if the world did not exist. Postulate that a blight, or harsh weather, intervened, what then? And the old satyr, how long would he last to tend the plots? He looked two hundred now, which on the islands probably meant sixty. I did not ask her what contingency plans she had for these emergencies and inevitabilities. What good, after all, are most plans? We could be invaded from Andromeda tomorrow, and what help for us all then? Either it is in your nature to survive, somehow, anyhow, or it is not.

She had well and truly hooked me, of course. If I had met her in Athens, some sun-baked afternoon, I would have felt decidedly out of my depth, taken her for cocktails, and foundered before we had even reached the dinner hour. But here, in this pulsing green bubble of light and leaves straight out of one's most irrational visions of the glades of Arcadia, conversation, however erratic, communication, however eccentric, was happening. The most inexplicable thing of all was that the mask had ceased, almost immediately, to bother me. I cannot, as I look back, properly account for this, for to spend a morning, a noon, an afternoon, allowing yourself to become fundamentally engaged by a woman whose face you have not seen, whose face you are actively being prevented from seeing, seems now incongruous, to the point of perversity. But there it is. We discussed Ibsen, Dickens, Euripides and Jung. I remembered trawling anecdotes of a grandfather, mentioned my sister's jewellery store in St. Louis, listened to an astonishing description of wild birds flying in across a desert from a sea. I assisted her over rocky turf, flirted with her, felt excited by and familiar with her, all this with her masked face before me. As if the mask, rather than being a part of her, meant no more than the frock she had elected to wear, or the narrow-heeled vanilla shoes she had chosen to put on. As if I knew her face totally and had no need to be shown it, the face of her movements and her ridiculous voice.

But in fact, I could not even make out her eyes, only the shine in them when they caught the light, flecks of luminescence but not colour, for the eyeholes of the mask were long-lidded and rather small. I must have noticed, too, that there was no aperture in the lips, and this may have informed me that the mask must be removed for purposes of eating or drinking. I really do not know. I can neither excuse nor quite understand myself, seen in the distance there, with her, on her island. Hartley tells us that the past is another country. Perhaps we also were other people, strangers, yesterday. But when I think of this, I remember, too, the sense of drawing I had had, of being magnetised to that shore, those trees, the nostalgia for a place I had never been to. For she, it may be true to say, was a figment of her nostalgia, as if I had known her and come back to her. Some enchantment, then. Not Medusa's island, but Circe's.

The afternoon, even through the dapple *L'Après-midi d'un Faune* effect of the leaves, was a viridian furnace, when we regained the house. I sat in one of the wicker chairs on the terrace, and woke with a start of embarrassment to hear her laughing at me.

"You are tired and hungry. I must go into the house for a while. I will send Kleia to you with some wine and food."

It made a bleary sense, and when I woke again it was to find an old fat woman in the ubiquitous Grecian island black— demonstrably Kleia—setting down a tray of pale red wine, amber cheese and dark bread.

"Where is—" I realized I did not know the enchantress's name.

In any event, the woman only shook her head, saying brusquely in Greek: "No English. No English."

And when I attempted to ask again in Greek where my hostess had got to, Kleia waddled away leaving me unanswered. So I ate the food, which was passable, and drank the wine, which was very good, imagining her faun-buying father putting down an enormous patrician cellar, then fell asleep again, sprawled in the chair.

When I wakened, the sun was setting and the clearing was swimming in red light and rusty violet shadows. The columns burned as if they were internally on fire, holding the core of the sunset, it appeared, some while after the sky had cooled and the stars became visible, a trick of architectural positioning that won my awe and envy. I was making a mental note to ask her who had been responsible for the columns, and jumped when she spoke to me, softly and hoarsely, almost seductively, from just behind my chair—thereby promptly making me forget to ask any such thing.

"Come into the house, now. We will dine soon."

I got up, saying something lame about imposing on her, though we were far beyond that stage.

"Always," she said to me, "you apologise. There is no imposition. You will be gone tomorrow."

How do you know? I nearly inquired, but prevented myself. What guarantee? Even if the magic food did not change me into a swine, perhaps my poisoned dead body would be carried from the feast and cast into the sea, gone, well and truly, to Poseidon's fishes. You see, I did not trust her, even though I was somewhat in love with her. The element of her danger—for she *was* dangerous in some obscure way—may well have contributed to her attraction.

We went into the house, which in itself alerted me. I had forgotten a great curiosity I had had to look inside it. There was a shadowy unlit entrance hall, a sort of Roman atrium of a thing. Then we passed, she leading, into a small salon that took my breath away. It was lined, all over, floor, ceiling, walls, with the sea-green marble the columns were made of. Whether in good taste or bad I am not qualified to say, but the effect, instantaneous and utter, was of being beneath the sea. Smoky oil lamps of a very beautiful Art Nouveau design hung from the profundity of the green ceiling, lighting the dreamlike swirls and oceanic variations of the marble, so they seemed to breathe, definitely to move, like nothing else but waves. Shoes on that floor would have squeaked or clattered unbearably, but I was barefoot, and now so was she.

A mahogany table, with a modest placing for eight, stood centrally. Only one place was laid.

I looked at it, and she said,

"I do not dine, but that will not prevent you."

An order. I considered vampires, idly, but mainly I was subject to an infantile annoyance. I had looked for the subtraction of the mask when she ate, without quite realizing it, and now this made me very conscious of the mask for the first time since I had orginally seen it.

We seated ourselves, she two places away from me. And I began to feel nervous. To eat this meal while she watched me did not appeal. And now the idea of the mask, unconsidered all morning, all afternoon, stole over me like an incoming tide.

Inevitably, I had not dressed for dinner, having no means, but she had changed her clothes, and was now wearing a high-collared long grey gown, her mother's again, no doubt. It had the fragile look of age, but was very feminine and appealing for all that. Above it, the mask now reared, stuck out like the proverbial sore thumb.

The mask. What on earth was I going to do, leered at by the myopic soulless face which had suddenly assumed such disastrous importance.

Kleia waddled in with the dishes. I cannot recall the meal, save that it was spicey, and mostly vegetable. The wine came too, and I drank it. As I drank the wine, I began to consider seriously, for the first time (which seems very curious indeed to me now), the reason for the mask. What did it hide? A scar, a birthmark? I drank her wine, and I saw myself snatch off the mask, take in the disfigurement, unquelled, and behold the painful gratitude in her eyes as she watched me. I would inform her of the genius of surgeons. She would repeat, she had no money. I would promise to pay for the operation.

Suddenly she startled me by saying: "Do you believe that we have lived before?"

I looked in my glass, that fount of wisdom and possibility,

and said, "It seems as sensible a proposition as any of the others I've ever heard."

I fancied she smiled to herself, and do not know why I thought that; I know now I was wrong.

Her accent had thickened and distorted further when she said,

"I rather hope that I have lived before. I could wish to think I may live again."

"To compensate for this life?" I said brutishly. I had not needed to be so obvious when already I had been given the implication on a salver.

"Yes. To compensate for this."

I downed all the wisdom and possibility left in my glass, swallowed an extra couple of times, and said, "Are you going to tell me why you wear a mask?"

As soon as I said it, I grasped that I was drunk. Nor was it a pleasant drunkenness. I did not like the demanding tone I had taken with her, but I was angry at having allowed the game to go on for so long. I had no knowledge of the rules, or pretended I had not. And I could not stop myself. When she did not reply, I added on a note of ghastly banter, "Or shall I guess?"

She was still, seeming very composed. Had this scene been enacted before? Finally she said, "I would suppose you do guess it is to conceal something that I wear it."

"Something you imagine worth concealing, which, perhaps, isn't."

That was the stilted fanfare of bravado. I had braced myself, flushed with such stupid confidence.

"Why not," I said, and I grow cold when I remember how I spoke to her, "take the damn thing off. Take off the mask, and drink a glass of wine with me."

A pause. Then, "No," she said.

Her voice was level and calm. There was neither eagerness nor fear in it.

"Go on," I said, the drunk not getting his way, aware (oh God) he could get it by the power of his intention alone, "please. You're an astounding woman. You're like this island. A fascinating mystery. But I've seen the island. Let me see you.''

"No," she said.

I started to feel, even through the wine, that I had made an indecent suggestion to her, and this, along with the awful clichés, I was bringing out, increased my anger and my discomfort.

"For Heaven's sake," I said. "Do you know what they call you on Daphaeu?"

"Yes."

"This is absurd. You're frightened—"

"No. I am not afraid."

"Afraid. Afraid to let me see. But maybe I can help you."

"No. You cannot help me."

"How can you be sure?"

She turned in her chair, and all the way to face me with the mask. Behind her, everywhere about her, the green marble dazzled.

"If you know," she said, "what I am called on Daphaeu, are you not uneasy as to what you may see?"

"Jesus. Mythology and superstition and ignorance. I assure you, I won't turn to stone."

"It is I," she said quietly, "who have done that."

Something about the phrase, the way in which she said it, chilled me. I put down my glass, and in that instant, her hands went to the sides of the mask and her fingers worked at some complicated strap arrangement which her hair had covered.

"Good," I said, "good. I'm glad—"

But I faltered over it. The cold night sea seemed to fill my veins where the warm red wine had been. I had been heroic and sure and bold, the stuff of celluloid. But now I had my way, with hardly any preliminary, what *would* I see? And then she drew the plastic away and I saw.

I sat there, and then I stood up. The reflex was violent, and the chair scraped over the marble with an unbearable noise. There are occasions, though rare, when the human mind grows blank of all thought. I had no thought as I looked at her. Even now, I can evoke those long, long empty seconds, that lapse of time. I recollect only the briefest confusion, when I believe she still played some kind of hideous game, that what I witnessed was a product of her decision and her will, a gesture—

After all, Pitos had done this very thing to illustrate and endorse his argument, produced this very expression, the eyes bursting from the head, the jaw rigidly outthrust, the tendons in the neck straining, the mouth in the grimace of a frozen, agonised scream, the teeth visible, the tongue slightly protruding. The gorgon's face on the jar or the oven. The face so ugly, so demented, so terrible, it could petrify.

The awful mouth writhed.

"You have seen," she said. Somehow the stretched and distorted lips brought out these words. There was even that nuance of humour I had heard before, the smile, although physically, a smile would have been out of the question. "You have seen."

She picked up the mask again, gently, and put it on, easing the underpart of the plastic beneath her chin, to hide the convulsed tendons in her throat. I stood there, motionless. Childishly, I informed myself that now I comprehended the reason for her peculiar accent, which was caused, not by some exotic foreign extraction, but by the atrocious malformation of jaw, tongue and lips, which somehow must be fought against for every sound she made.

I went on standing there, and now the mask was back in place.

"When I was very young," she said, "I suffered, without warning, from a form of fit, or stroke. Various nerve centres were paralysed. My father took me to the very best of surgeons, you may comfort yourself with that. Unfortunately, any effort to correct the damage entailed a penetration of my brain so uncompromisingly delicate that it was reckoned impossible, for it would surely render me an idiot. Since my senses, faculties and intelligence were otherwise unaffected, it was decided not to risk this dire surgery, and my doctors resorted instead to alternative therapies, which, patently, were unsuccessful. As the months passed, my body adjusted to the unnatural physical tensions resulting from my facial paralysis. The pain of the rictus faded, or grew acceptable. I learned both how to eat, and how to converse, although the former activity is not attractive, and I attend to it in private. The mask was made for me in Athens. I am quite fond of it. The man who designed it had worked a great many years in the theatre, and could have made me a face of enormous beauty or character, but this seemed pointless, even wasteful."

There was a silence, and I realized her explanation was finished.

Not once had she stumbled. There was neither hurt nor madness in her inflexion. There *was* something . . . at the time, I missed it, though it came to me after. Then I knew only that she was far beyond my pity or my anguish, far away indeed from my terror.

"And now," she said, rising gracefully, "I will leave you to eat your meal in peace. Good night."

I wanted, or rather I felt impelled, to stay her with actions or sentences, but I was incapable of either. She walked out of the green marble room, and left me there. It is a fact that for a considerable space of time, I did not move.

I did not engage the swim back to Daphaeu that night, I judged myself too drunk, and slept on the beach at the edge of the trees, where at sunrise the tidal water woke me with a strange low hissing. Green sea, green sunlight through leaves. I swam away and found my course through the warming ocean and fetched up, exhausted and swearing, bruising myself on Daphaeu's fangs that had not harmed me when I left her. I did not see Pitos anywhere about, and that evening I caught the boat which would take me to the mainland.

There is a curious thing which can happen with human beings. It is the ability to perform for days or weeks like balanced and cheerful automata, when some substratum, something upon which our codes or our hopes had firmly rested, has given way. Men who lose their wives or their God are quite capable of behaving in this manner, for an indefinite season. After which the collapse is brilliant and total. Something of this sort had happened to me. Yet, to fathom what I had lost, what she had deprived me of, is hard to say. I found its symptoms, but not the sickness which it was.

Medusa (I must call her that, she has no other name I know), struck by the extraordinary arrow of her misfortune, condemned to her relentless, uncanny, horrible isolation, her tragedy most deeply rooted in the fact that she was not a myth, not a fabulous and glamorous monster . . . For it came to me one night in a bar in Corinth, to consider if the first Medusa might have been also such a victim, felled by some awesome fit, not petrifying but petrified, so appalling to the eyes, and, more significantly, to the brooding aesthetic spirit that lives in man, that she too was shunned and hated, and slain by a murderer who would observe her only in a polished surface.

I spent some while in bars that summer. And later, much later, when the cold climate of the year's end closed the prospect of travel and adventure, I became afraid for myself, that dreadful writer's fear which has to do with the death of the idea, with the inertia of hand and heart and mind. Like one of the broken leaves, the summer's withered plants, I had dried. My block was sheer. I had expected a multitude of pages from the island, but instead I saw those unborn pages die on the horizon, where the beach met the sea.

And this, merely a record of marble, water, a plastic shell strapped across a woman's face, this is the last thing, it seems, which I shall commit to paper. Why? Perhaps only because she was to me such a lesson in the futility of things, the waiting fist of chance, the random despair we name the World.

And yet, now and then, I hear that voice of hers, I hear the way she spoke to me. I know now what I heard in her voice, which had neither pain nor shame in it, nor pleading, nor whining, nor even a hint of the tragedy, the Greek tragedy, of her life. And what I heard was not dignity, either, or acceptance, or nobleness. It was *contempt*. She despised me. She despised all of us who live without her odds, who struggle with our small struggles, incomparable to hers. "Your Greek is very good," she said to me, with the patronage of one who is multi-lingual. And in that same disdain she says, over and over to me: "that you live is very good." Compared to her life, her existence, her multi-lingual endurance, what are my life or my ambitions worth? Or anything.

It did not occur immediately, but still it occurred. In its way, the myth is perfectly accurate. I see it in myself, scent it, taste it, like the onset of inescapable disease. What they say about the gorgon is true. She has turned me to stone.

# GRIFFIN

*"Griffin" can also be spelled "griffon" or, more correctly, though this spelling is not often used, "gryphon." The word is from the Greek* gryps, *meaning "having a hooked nose," for reasons that will soon be plain.*

*The griffin is a composite creature, like the centaur, and such composites are common in mythology. In early periods of history, it was common to deify the animals on which a hunting society lives. Perhaps, as people grow more sophisticated, they become embarrassed at having their gods in the form of animals, and they compromise by making those gods human, but with animal heads. Thus the Egyptians had human gods with the head of a hawk, or an ibis; the Indians had human gods with the head of a monkey or an elephant, and so on.*

*One could also make a composite of a monster, so that one could combine the characteristics of several dangerous creatures into one. The most familiar such composite is the chimera, from a Greek word for "goat," since it had the body of a goat. However, it had the head of a lion and its tail was a serpent. (Sometimes it was pictured as a creature with three heads, one of a lion, one of a goat, and one of a serpent). It was slain by the Greek hero Bellerophon. Nowadays, plants and animals made up of mixtures of material from different species, through human manipulation, are called chimeras.*

*The griffin has the body of a lion, but the head and wings of an eagle, and, sometimes, a serpent tail. It is a* kind of dragon in its functioning, and may be viewed as breathing fire. It is usually pictured as guarding treasures, as dragons are commonly represented as doing, and, in modern times, it is frequently represented in grotesque carvings as in the story you are about to read.

It is the curved beak of an eagle, by the way, that is the ''hooked nose'' that gives it its name.

# THE GRIFFIN AND THE MINOR CANON

*Frank R. Stockton*

Over the great door of an old, old church, which stood in a quiet town of a faraway land, there was carved in stone the figure of a large griffin. The old-time sculptor had done his work with great care, but the image he had made was not a pleasant one to look at. It had a large head, with enormous open mouth and savage teeth. From its back arose great wings, armed with sharp hooks and prongs. It had stout legs in front, with projecting claws, but there were no legs behind, the body running out into a long and powerful tail, finished off at the end with a barbed point. This tail was coiled up under him, the end sticking up just back of his wings.

The sculptor, or the people who had ordered this stone figure, had evidently been very much pleased with it, for little copies of it, also in stone, had been placed here and there along the sides of the church, not very far from the ground, so that people could easily look at them and ponder on their curious forms. There were a great many other sculptures on the outside of this church—saints, martyrs, grotesque heads of men, beasts, and birds, as well as those of other creatures which cannot be named, because nobody knows exactly what they were. But none were so curious and interesting as the great griffin over the door and the little griffins on the sides of the church.

A long, long distance from the town, in the midst of dreadful wilds scarcely known to man, there dwelt the Griffin whose image had been put up over the church door. In some way or other the old-time sculptor had seen him, and afterwards, to the best of his memory, had copied his figure in stone. The Griffin had never known this until, hundreds of years afterwards, he heard from a bird, from a wild animal, or in some manner which is not easy to find out, that there was a likeness of him on the old church in the distant town.

Now, this Griffin had no idea whatever how he looked. He had never seen a mirror, and the streams where he lived were so turbulent and violent that a quiet piece of water, which would reflect the image of anything looking into it, could not be found. Being, as far as could be ascertained, the very last of his race, he had never seen another griffin. Therefore it was that, when he heard of this stone image of himself, he became very anxious to know what he looked like, and at last he determined to go to the old church and see for himself what manner of being he was. So he started off from the dreadful wilds, and flew on and on until he came to the countries inhabited by men, where his appearance in the air created great consternation. But he alighted nowhere, keeping up a steady flight until he reached the suburbs of the town which had his image on its church. Here, late in the afternoon, he alighted in a green meadow by the side of a brook, and stretched himself on the grass to rest. His great wings were tired, for he had not made such a long flight in a century or more.

The news of his coming spread quickly over the town, and the people, frightened nearly out of their wits by the arrival of so extraordinary a visitor, fled into their houses and shut themselves up. The Griffin called loudly for some one to come to him; but the more he called, the more afraid the people were to show themselves. At length he saw two laborers hurrying to their homes through the fields, and in a terrible voice he commanded them to stop. Not daring to disobey, the men stood, trembling.

"What is the matter with you all?" cried the Griffin. "Is there not a man in your town who is brave enough to speak to me?"

"I think," said one of the laborers, his voice shaking so that his words could hardly be understood, "that—perhaps—the Minor Canon—would come."

"Go, call him, then!" said the Griffin. "I want to see him."

The Minor Canon, who filled a subordinate position in the old church, had just finished the afternoon service, and was coming out of a side door, with three aged women who had formed the week-day congregation. He was a young man of a kind disposition, and very anxious to do good to the people of the town. Apart from his duties in the church, where he conducted services every week-day, he visited the sick and the poor; counselled and assisted persons who were in trouble, and taught a school composed entirely of the bad children in the town, with whom nobody else would have anything to do. Whenever the people wanted something difficult done for them, they always went to the Minor Canon. Thus it was that the laborer thought of the young priest when he found that some one must come and speak to the Griffin.

The Minor Canon had not heard of the strange event, which was known to the whole town except himself and the three old women, and when he was informed of it, and was told that the Griffin had asked to see him, he was greatly amazed and frightened.

"Me!" he exclaimed. "He has never heard of me! What should he want with *me?*"

"Oh, you must go instantly!" cried the two men. "He is very angry now because he has been kept waiting so long, and nobody knows what may happen if you don't hurry to him."

The poor Minor Canon would rather have had his hand cut off than go out to meet an angry griffin; but he felt that it was his duty to go, for it would be a woeful thing if injury should come to the people of the town because he was not brave enough to obey the summons of the Griffin; so, pale and frightened, he started off.

"Well," said the Griffin, as soon as the young man came near, "I am glad to see that there is someone who has the courage to come to me."

The Minor Canon did not feel very courageous, but he bowed his head.

"Is this the town," said the Griffin, "where there is a church with a likeness of myself over one of the doors?"

The Minor Canon looked at the frightful creature before him, and saw that it was, without doubt, exactly like the stone image on the church. "Yes," he said, "you are right."

"Well, then," said the Grifin, "will you take me to it? I wish very much to see it."

The Minor Canon instantly thought that if the Griffin entered the town without the people knowing what he came for, some of them would probably be frightened to death, and so he sought to gain time to prepare their minds.

"It is growing dark now," he said, very much afraid, as he spoke, that his words might enrage the Griffin, "and objects on the front of the church cannot be seen clearly. It will be better to wait until morning, if you wish to get a good view of the stone image of yourself."

"That will suit me very well," said the Griffin. "I see you are a man of good sense. I am tired, and I will take a nap here on this soft grass, while I cool my tail in the little stream that runs near me. The end of my tail gets red-hot when I am angry or excited, and it is quite warm now. So you may go; but be sure and come early tomorrow morning, and show me the way to the church."

The Minor Canon was glad enough to take his leave, and hurried into the town. In front of the church he found a great many people assembled to hear his report of his interview with the Griffin. When they found that he had not come to spread ruin and devastation, but simply to see his stony likeness on the church, they showed neither relief nor gratification, but began to upbraid the Minor Canon for consenting to conduct the creature into the town.

"What could I do?" cried the young man. "If I should not bring him he would come himself, and perhaps end by setting fire to the town with his red-hot tail."

Still the people were not satisfied, and a great many plans were proposed to prevent the Griffin from coming into the town. Some elderly persons urged that the young men should go out and kill him. But the young men scoffed at such a ridiculous idea. Then some one said it would be a good thing to destroy the stone image, so that the Griffin would have no excuse for entering the town. This proposal was received with such favor that many of the people ran for hammers, chisels, and crowbars with which to tear down and break up the stone griffin. But the Minor Canon resisted this plan with all the strength of his mind and body. He assured the people that this action would be impossible to conceal from him that his image had been destroyed during the night.

But they were so determined to break up the stone griffin that the Minor Canon saw that there was nothing for him to do but stay there and protect it. All night he walked up and down in front of the church door, keeping away the men who brought ladders by which they might mount to the great stone griffin and knock it to pieces with their hammers and crowbars. After many hours the people were obliged to give up their attempts, and went home to sleep. But the Minor Canon remained at his post till early morning, and then he hurried away to the field where he had left the Griffin.

The monster had just awakened, and rising to his forelegs and shaking himself, he said that he was ready to go into the town. The Minor Canon, therefore, walked back, the Griffin flying slowly through the air at a short distance above the head of his guide. Not a person was to be seen in the streets, and they proceeded directly to the front of the church, where the Minor Canon pointed out the stone griffin.

The real Griffin settled down in the little square before the church and gazed earnestly at his sculptured likeness. For a long time he looked at it. First he put his head on one side, and then he put it on the other. Then he shut his right eye and gazed with his left, after which he shut his left eye and gazed with his right. Then he moved a little to one side and looked at the image, then he moved the other way. After a while he said to the Minor Canon, who had been standing by all this time:

"It is, it must be, an excellent likeness! That breadth between the eyes, that expansive forehead, those massive jaws! I feel that it must resemble me. If there is any fault to find with it, it is that the neck seems a little stiff. But that is nothing. It is an admirable likeness—admirable!"

The Griffin sat looking at his image all the morning and all the afternoon. The Minor Canon had been afraid to go away and leave him, and had hoped all through the day that he would soon be satisfied with his inspection and fly away home. But by evening the poor young man was utterly exhausted, and felt that he must eat and sleep. He frankly admitted this fact to the Griffin, and asked him if he would not like something to eat. He said this because he felt obliged in politeness to do so; but as soon as he had spoken the words, he was seized with dread lest the monster should demand half a dozen babies, or some tempting repast of that kind.

"Oh, no," said the Griffin, "I never eat between the equinoxes. At the vernal and at the autumnal equinox I take a good meal, and that lasts me for half a year. I am extremely regular in my habits, and do not think it healthful to eat at odd times. But if you need food, go and get it, and I will return to the soft grass where I slept last night, and take another nap."

The next day the Griffin came again to the little square before the church, and remained there until evening, steadfastly regarding the stone griffin over the door. The Minor Canon came once or twice to look at him, and the Griffin seemed very glad to see him. But the young clergyman could not stay as he had done before, for he had many duties to perform. Nobody went to the church, but the people came to the Minor Canon's house, and anxiously asked him how long the Griffin was going to stay.

"I do not know," he answered, "but I think he will soon be satisfied with looking at his stone likeness, and then he will go away."

But the Griffin did not go away. Morning after morning he went to the church, but after a time he did not stay there all day. He seemed to have taken a great fancy to Minor Canon, and followed him about as he pursued his various avocations. He would wait for him at the side door of the church, for the Minor Canon held services every day, morning and evening, though nobody came now. "If any one should come," he said to himself, "I must be found at my post." When the young man came out, the Griffin would accompany him in his visits to the sick and the poor, and would often look into the windows of the school-house where the Minor Canon was teaching his unruly scholars. All the other schools were closed, but the parents of the Minor Canon's scholars forced them to go to school, because they were so bad they could not endure them all day at home—griffin or no griffin. But it must be said they generally behaved very well when that great monster sat up on his tail and looked in at the school-room window.

When it was perceived that the Griffin showed no sign of going away, all the people who were able to do so left the town. The canons and the higher officers of the church had fled away during the first day of the Griffin's visit, leaving behind only the Minor Canon and some of the men who opened the doors and swept the church. All the citizens who could afford it shut up their houses and travelled to distant parts, and only the working-people and the poor were left behind. After some days these ventured to go about and attend to their business, for if they did not work they would starve. They were getting a little used to seeing the Griffin, and having been told that he did not eat between equinoxes, they did not feel so much afraid of him as before.

Day by day the Griffin became more and more attached to the Minor Canon. He kept near him a great part of the time, and often spent the night in front of the little house where the young clergyman lived alone. This strange companionship was often burdensome to the Minor Canon. But, on the other hand, he could not deny that he derived a great deal of benefit and instruction from it. The Griffin had lived for hundreds of years, and had seen much, and he told the Minor Canon many wonderful things.

"It is like reading an old book," said the young clergyman to himself. "But how many books I would have had to read before I would have found out what the Griffin has told me about the earth, the air, the water, about minerals, and metals, and growing things, and all the wonders of the world!"

Thus the summer went on, and drew toward its close. And now the people of the town began to be very much troubled again.

"It will not be long," they said, "before the autumnal equinox is here, and then that monster will want to eat. He will be dreadfully hungry, for he has taken so much exercise since his last meal. He will devour our children. Without doubt, he will eat them all. What is to be done?"

To this question no one could give an answer, but all agreed that the Griffin must not be allowed to remain until the approaching equinox. After talking over the matter a great deal, a crowd of the people went to the Minor Canon, at a time when the Griffin was not with him.

"It is all your fault," they said, "that that monster is among us. You brought him here, and you ought to see that he goes away. It is only on your account that he stays here at all, for, although he visits his image every day, he is with you the greater part of the time. If you were not here he would not stay. It is your duty to go away, and then he will follow you, and we shall be free from the dreadful danger which hangs over us."

"Go away!" cried the Minor Canon, greatly grieved at being spoken to in such a way. "Where shall I go? If I go to some other town, shall I not take this trouble there? Have I a right to do that?"

"No," said the people, "you must not go to any other town. There is no town far enough away. You must go to the dreadful wilds where the Griffin lives, and then he will follow you and stay there."

They did not say whether or not they expected the Minor Canon to stay there also, and he did not ask them anything about it. He bowed his head, and went into his house to think. The more he thought, the more clear it became to his mind that it was his duty to go away, and thus free the town from the presence of the Griffin.

That evening he packed a leather bag full of bread and meat, and early the next morning he set out on his journey to the dreadful wilds. It was a long, weary, and doleful journey, especially after he had gone beyond the habitations of men; but the Minor Canon kept on bravely, and never faltered. The way was longer than he had expected, and his provisions soon grew so scanty that he was obliged to eat but a little every day; but he kept up his courage, and pressed on, and after many days of toilsome travel he reached the dreadful wilds.

When the Griffin found that the Minor Canon had left the town, he seemed sorry, but showed no disposition to go and look for him. After a few days had passed, he became much annoyed, and asked some of the people where the Minor Canon had gone. But although the citizens had been so anxious that the young clergyman should go to the dreadful wilds, thinking that the Griffin would immediately follow him, they were now afraid to mention the Minor Canon's destination, for the monster seemed angry already, and if he should suspect their trick, he would doubtless become very much enraged. So every one said he did not know, and the Griffin wandered about disconsolate. One morning he looked into the Minor Canon's school-house, which was always empty now, and thought that it was a shame that everything should suffer on account of the young man's absence.

"It does not matter so much about the church," he said, "for nobody went there. But it is a pity about the school. I think I will teach it myself until he returns."

It was the hour for opening the school, and the Griffin went inside and pulled the rope which rang the school bell. Some of the children who heard the bell ran in to see what was the matter, supposing it to be a joke of one of their companions. But when they saw the Griffin they stood astonished and scared.

"Go tell the other scholars," said the monster, "that school is about to open, and that if they are not all here in ten minutes I shall come after them."

In seven minutes every scholar was in place.

Never was seen such an orderly school. Not a boy or girl moved or uttered a whisper. The Griffin climbed into the master's seat, his wide wings spread on each side of him, because he could not lean back in his chair while they stuck out behind, and his great tail coiled around in front of the desk, the barbed end sticking up, ready to tap any boy or girl who might misbehave. The Griffin now addressed the scholars, telling them that he intended to teach them while their master was away. In speaking he endeavored to imitate, as far as possible, the mild and gentle tones of the Minor Canon, but it must be admitted that in this he was not very successful. He had paid a good deal of attention to the studies of the school, and he determined not to attempt to teach them anything new, but to review them in what they had been studying. So he called up the various classes, and questioned them upon their previous lessons. The children racked their brains to remember what they had learned. They were so afraid of the Griffin's displeasure that they recited as they had never recited before. One of the boys, far down in his class, answered so well that the Griffin was astonished.

"I should think you would be at the head," said he. "I am sure you have never been in the habit of reciting so well. "Why is this?"

"Because I did not choose to take the trouble," said the boy, trembling in his boots. He felt obliged to speak the truth, for all the children thought that the great eyes of the Griffin could see right through them, and that he would know when they told a falsehood.

"You ought to be ashamed of yourself," said the Griffin. "Go down to the very tail of the class, and if you are not at the head in two days, I shall know the reason why."

The next afternoon this boy was number one.

It was astonishing how much these children now learned of what they had been studying. It was as if they had been educated over again. The Griffin used no severity toward them, but there was a look about him which made them unwilling to go to bed until they were sure they knew their lessons for the next day.

The Griffin now thought that he ought to visit the sick and the poor, and he began to go about the town for this purpose. The effect upon the sick was miraculous. All, except those who were very ill indeed, jumped from their beds when they heard he was coming, and declared themselves quite well. To those who could not get up he gave herbs and roots, which none of them had ever before thought of as medicines, but which the Griffin had seen used in various parts of the world, and most of them recovered. But, for all that, they afterwards said that no matter what happened to them, they hoped that they should never again have such a doctor coming to their bedsides, feeling their pulses and looking at their tongues.

As for the poor, they seemed to have utterly disappeared. All those who had depended upon charity for their daily bread were now at work in some way or other, many of them offering to do odd jobs for their neighbors just for the sake of their meals—a thing which before had been seldom heard of in the town. The Griffin could find no one who needed his assistance.

The summer now passed, and the autumnal equinox was rapidly approaching. The citizens were in a state of great alarm and anxiety. The Griffin showed no signs of going away, but seemed to have settled himself permanently among them. In a short time the day for his semi-annual meal would arrive, and then what would happen? The monster would certainly be very hungry, and would devour all their children.

Now they greatly regretted and lamented that they had sent away the Minor Canon. He was the only one on whom they could have depended in this trouble, for he could talk freely with the Griffin, and so find out what could be done. But it would not do to be inactive. Some step must be taken immediately. A meeting of the citizens was called, and two old men were appointed to go and talk to the Griffin. They were instructed to offer to prepare a splendid dinner for him on equinox day—one which would entirely satisfy his hunger. They would offer him the fattest mutton, the most tender beef, fish and game of various sorts, and anything of the kind he might fancy. If none of these suited, they were to mention that there was an orphan asylum in the next town.

"Anything would be better," said the citizens, "than to have our dear children devoured."

The old men went to the Griffin, but their propositions were not received with favor.

"From what I have seen of the people of this town," said the monster, "I do not think I could relish anything which was prepared by them. They appear to be all cowards, and, therefore, mean and selfish. As for eating one of them, old or young, I could not think of it for a moment. In fact, there was only one creature in the whole place for whom I could have had any appetite, and that is the Minor Canon, who has gone away. He was brave, and good, and honest, and I think I should have relished him.''

"Ah!" said one of the old men, very politely, "in that case I wish we had not sent him to the dreadful wilds!''

"What!" cried the Griffin. "What do you mean? Explain instantly what you are talking about?''

The old man, terribly frightened at what he had said, was obliged to tell how the Minor Canon had been sent away by the people, in the hope that the Griffin might be induced to follow him.

When the monster heard this he became furiously angry. He dashed away from the old men and, spreading his wings, flew backward and forward over the town. He was so much excited that his tail became red-hot, and glowed like a meteor against the evening sky. When at last he settled down in the little field where he usually rested, and thrust his tail into the brook, the steam arose like a cloud, and the water of the stream ran hot through the town. The citizens were greatly frightened, and bitterly blamed the old man for telling about the Minor Canon.

"It is plain," they said, "that the Griffin intended at last to go and look for him, and we should have been saved. Now who can tell what misery you have brought upon us?''

The Griffin did not remain long in the little field. As soon as his tail was cool he flew to the town hall and rang the bell. The citizens knew that they were expected to come there, and although they were afraid to go, they were still more afraid to stay away, and they crowded into the hall. The Griffin was on the platform at one end, flapping his wings and walking up and down, and the end of his tail was still so warm that it slightly scorched the boards as he dragged it after him.

When everybody who was able to come was there, the Griffin stood still and addressed the meeting.

"I have had a contemptible opinion of you," he said, "ever since I discovered what cowards you are, but I had no idea that you were so ungrateful, selfish, and cruel as I now find you to be. Here was your Minor Canon, who labored day and night for your good, and thought of nothing else but how he might benefit you and make you happy; and as soon as you imagine yourselves threatened with danger—for well I know you are dreadfully afraid of me—you send him off, caring not whether he returns or perishes, hoping thereby to save yourselves. Now, I had conceived a great liking for that young man, and had intended, in a day or two, to go and look him up. But I have changed my mind about him. I shall go and find him, but I shall send him back here to live among you, and I intend that he shall enjoy the reward of his labor and his sacrifices. Go, some of you, to the officers of the church, who so cowardly ran away when I first came here, and tell them never to return to this town under penalty of death. And if, when your Minor Canon comes back to you, you do not bow yourselves before him, put him in the highest place among you, and serve and honor him all his life, beware of my terrible vengeance! There were only two good things in this town: the Minor Canon and the stone image of myself over your church door. One of these you have sent away, and the other I shall carry away myself.''

With these words he dismissed the meeting; and it was time, for the end of his tail had become so hot that there was danger of its setting fire to the building.

The next morning the Griffin came to the church, and tearing the stone image of himself from its fastenings over the great door, he grasped it with his powerful forelegs and flew up into the air. Then, after hovering over the town for a moment, he gave his tail an angry shake, and took up his flight to the dreadful wilds. When he reached this desolate region, he set the stone griffin upon a ledge of a rock which rose in front of the dismal cave he called his home. There the image occupied a position somewhat similar to that it had had over the church door; and the Griffin, panting with the exertion of carrying such an enormous load to so great a distance, lay down upon the ground, and regarded it with much satisfaction. When he felt somewhat rested he went to look for the Minor Canon. He found the young man, weak and half starved, lying under the shadow of a rock. After picking him up and carrying him to his cave, the Griffin flew away to a distant marsh, where he procured some roots and herbs which he well knew were strengthening and beneficial to man, though he had never tasted them himself. After eating these the Minor Canon was greatly revived, and sat up and listened while the Griffin told him what had happened in the town.

"Do you know," said the monster, when he had finished, "that I have had, and still have, a great liking for you?"

"I am very glad to hear it," said the Minor Canon, with his usual politeness.

"I am not at all sure that you would be," said the Griffin, "if you thoroughly understood the state of the case, but we will not consider that now. If some things were different, other things would be otherwise. I have been so enraged by discovering the manner in which you have been treated that I have determined that you shall at last enjoy the rewards and honors to which you are entitled. Lie down and have a good sleep, and then I will take you back to the town."

As he heard the words, a look of trouble came over the young man's face.

"You need not give yourself any anxiety," said the Griffin, "about my return to the town. I shall not remain there. Now that I have that admirable likeness of myself in front of my cave, where I can sit at my leisure and gaze upon its noble features and magnificent proportions, I have no wish to see that abode of cowardly and selfish people."

The Minor Canon, relieved from his fears, lay back, and dropped into a doze; and when he was sound asleep, the Griffin took him up and carried him back to the town. He arrived just before daybreak, and putting the young man gently on the grass in the little field where he himself used to rest, the monster, without having been seen by any of the people, flew back to his home.

When the Minor Canon made his appearance in the morning among the citizens, the enthusiasm and cordiality with which he was received were truly wonderful. He was taken to a house which had been occupied by one of the banished high officers of the place, and every one was anxious to do all that could be done for his health and comfort. The people crowded into the church when he held services, so that the three old women who used to be his week-day congregation could not get the best seats, which they had always been in the habit of taking; and the parents of the bad children determined to reform them at home, in order that he might be spared the trouble of keeping up his former school. The Minor Canon was appointed to the highest office of the old church, and before he died he became a bishop.

During the first years after his return from the dreadful wilds, the people of the town looked up to him as a man to whom they were bound to do honor and reverence. But they often, also, looked up to the sky to see if there were any signs of the Griffin coming back. However, in the course of time they learned to honor and reverence their former Minor Canon without the fear of being punished if they did not do so.

But they need never have been afraid of the Griffin. The autumnal equinox day came round, and the monster ate nothing. If he could not have the Minor Canon, he did not care for anything. So, lying down with his eyes fixed upon the great stone griffin, he gradually declined, and died. It was a good thing for some of the people of the town that they did not know this.

If you should ever visit the old town, you would still see the little griffins on the sides of the church, but the great stone griffin that was over the door is gone.

# KRAGEN

*The sea is a natural repository of enormous beasts, since the buoyancy of water largely neutralizes gravity. The blue whale with a top mark of 150 tons is far larger than any land creature that ever lived; larger even than the largest dinosaurs.*

*Furthermore, water, in depths greater than a few yards, is opaque, so who knows what might be hidden in the deep. Even today, the relatively small Loch Ness in Scotland is thought to harbor a "monster," while the ocean itself is supposed to contain "sea serpents" of all kinds.*

*The Norwegians had legends of an enormous sea monster they called the kraken (is this another form of the Greek* drakon? *I wonder). It was pictured as an enormous round creature, possibly a mile and a half in circumference. To its rim were attached long tentacles, with which it could seize and pull under even the largest ships. When it submerged suddenly, it left a whirlpool in its wake, and sometimes whirlpools themselves were referred to as krakens.*

*In 1752, a Norwegian bishop, Erik Pontoppidan, published a* Natural History of Norway *in which the kraken was popularized.*

*There may be a germ of truth in even the wildest legend, however. The kraken sounds like a large and monstrous octopus, and, indeed, in recent times the "giant squid" had been discovered. It does not normally come to the surface but it is the preferred food of the sperm whale, and* dying squid that have had a fight with a sperm whale come to the surface on occasion. They are far, far smaller than the kraken, but one must allow for the exaggerations of legend.

In the following story, we have a large sea monster. It is not a giant squid. It is, rather, extraterrestrial, but the author indicates its conceptual origin in its name, which is almost *kraken*.

# THE KRAGEN

*Jack Vance*

## CHAPTER I

Among the people of the Floats caste distinctions were fast losing their old-time importance. The Anarchists and Procurers had disappeared altogether; intercaste marriages were by no means uncommon, especially when they involved castes of approximately the same social status. Society of course was not falling into chaos; the Bezzlers and the Incendiaries still maintained their traditional aloofness; the Advertisermen still could not evade a subtle but nonetheless general disesteem, and where the castes were associated with a craft or trade, they functioned with undiminished effectivesness. The Swindlers comprised the vast majority of those who fished from coracles; Blackguards constructed all the sponge-arbors in every lagoon; the Hoodwinks completely monopolized the field of hood-winking. This last relationship always excited the curiosity of the young, who would inquire, "Which first: the Hoodwinks or hood-winking?" To which the elders customarily replied, "When the Ship of Space discharged our ancestors upon these blessed floats, there were four Hoodwinks among the Eighty-three. Later, when the towers were built and the lamps established, there were hoods to wink, and it seemed nothing less than apposite that the Hoodwinks should occupy themselves at the trade. It may well be that matters stood so in the Outer Wildness, before the Escape. It seems likely. There were undoubtedly lamps to be flashed and hoods to be winked. Of course there is much we do not know, much concerning which the dicta are silent.''

Whether or not the Hoodwinks had been drawn to the trade by virtue of ancient use, it was now the rare Hoodwink who did not in some measure find his vocation upon the towers, either as a rigger, a lamp-tender, or as full-fledged hoodwink.

Another caste, the Larceners, constructed the towers, which customarily stood sixty to ninety feet high at the center of the float, directly above the primary stalk of the sea-plant; there were usually four legs of woven withe, which passed through holes in the pad to join a stout stalk twenty or thirty feet below the surface. At the top of the tower was a cupola, with walls of split withe, a roof of gummed and laminated pad-skin. Yard-arms extending to either side supported lattices, each carrying nine lamps arranged in a square, three to the side, together with the hoods and trip-mechanisms. Within the cupola, windows afforded a view across the water to the neighboring floats—as much as two miles or as little as a quarter-mile distant. The Master Hoodwink sat at a panel. At his left hand were nine tap-rods, cross-coupled to lamp-hoods on the lattice to his right. Similarly the tap-rods at his right hand controlled the hoods to his left. By this means the configurations he formed and those he received, from his point of view, were of identical aspect and caused him no confusion. During the day time, the lamps were not lit and white targets served the same function. The hoodwink set his configuration with quick strokes of right and left hands, kicked the release, which thereupon flicked the hoods or shutters at the respective lamps or targets. Each configuration signified a word; the mastery of a lexicon and a sometimes remarkable dexterity where the Master Hoodwink's stock in trade. All could send at speeds approximating that of speech; all knew at least four thousand, and some six, seven or even nine thousand configurations. The folk of the floats could in varying degrees read the configurations, which were also employed in the keeping of the archives, and other communications, memoranda and messages.*

On Tranque Float, at the extreme east of the group, the Master Hoodwink was one Chaezy Zander, a rigorous and exacting old man with a mastery of over eight thousand configurations. His first assistant, Sklar Hast, had well over five thousand configurations at his disposal. There were two further assistants, as well as three apprentices, two riggers, a lamp-tender and a maintenance witheweaver, this latter a Larcener. Chaezy Zander tended the tower from dusk until middle evening: the busy hours during which gossip, announcements, news and notifications regarding King Kragen flickered up and down the fifty-mile-line of the floats.

Sklar Hast winked hoods during the afternoon; then, when Chaezy Zander appeared in the cupola, he looked to maintenance and supervised the apprentices. A relatively young man, Sklar Hast had achieved his status by working in accordance with a simple and uncomplicated policy: without compromise and with great tenacity he strove for excellence, and sought to instill the same standards into the apprentices. He was an almost brutally direct man, without affability, know-

---

*The orthography had been adopted in the earliest days and was highly systematic. The cluster at the left indicated the genus of the idea, the cluster at the right denoted the specific. In such a fashion . . . at the left, signified *color*, and hence:

•
•••

White      •                       •
              •••

Black      •
              •••                •
              •••

Red        •
              •••                ••
              •••

Pink      •                      ••
              •••                •

Dark     •••
Red       •                      ••
              •••                •

and so forth.

ing nothing of either malice, guile, tact or patience. The apprentices disliked but respected him; Chaezy Zander considered him overpragmatic and deficient in reverence for his betters, notably himself. Sklar Hast cared nothing one way or the other. Chaezy Zander must soon retire; in due course Sklar Hast would become Master Hoodwink. He was in no hurry; on this placid, limpid, changeless world, time drifted rather than throbbed. In the meantime, life was easy and for the most part pleasant. Sklar Hast owned a small pad of which he was the sole occupant. The pad, a leaf of spongy tissue a hundred feet in diameter braced by tough woody radial ribs, floated in the lagoon, separated from the main float by twenty feet of water. Sklar Hast's hut was of standard construction: sea-plant withe bent and lashed, then sheathed with sheets of pad-skin, the tough near-transparent membrane peeled from the bottom of the sea-plant pad. All was then coated with well-aged varnish, prepared by boiling sea-plant sap until the water was driven off and the resins amalgamated.

On the pad grew other vegetation: shrubs rooted in the spongy tissue, a thicket of bamboolike rods yielding a good-quality withe, epiphytes hanging from the central spike of the sea-plant—this rising twenty or thirty feet to terminate in a coarse white spore-producing organ. Most of the plants of the pad yielded produce of benefit to man: fruit, fiber, dye, drug or decorative foliage. On other pads the plants might be ordered according to aesthetic theory; Sklar Hast had small taste in these matters, and the center of his pad was little more than an untidy copse of various stalks, fronds, tendrils and leaves, in various shades of black, green and rusty orange.

Sklar Hast reckoned himself a lucky man. As a Hoodwink by caste and assistant Master Hoodwink by trade he enjoyed a not inconsiderable prestige. Standing before his hut, Sklar Hast watched the gold and lavender dusk and its dark pastel reflection in the ocean. The afternoon rain had freshened and cooled the air; now the evening breeze arose to rustle the foliage and brush susurrations across the water . . . Chaezy Zander was growing old. Sklar Hast wondered how long the old man would persist in fulfilling the rigorous exactitude of his duties. True, he showed no lapse whatever in precision or flexibility of usage, but almost insensibly his speed was falling off. Sklar Hast could outwink him without difficulty should he choose to do so; a capability which Sklar Hast, for all his bluntness, had so far not demonstrated. Useless folly to irritate the old man! Sklar Hast suspected that even now he delayed his retirement mainly out of jealousy and antipathy toward Sklar Hast.

There was no hurry. Life seemed to extend ahead of him as wide and lucid as the dreaming expanse of water and sky which filled his vision. On this water-world, which had no name, there were no seasons, no tides, no storms, no change, very little anxiety regarding time. Sklar Hast was currently testing five or six girls of orthodox Hoodwink background for marital suitability. In due course, he would make a choice, and enlarge his hut. And forever abandon privacy, Sklar Hast reflected wistfully. There was definitely no need for haste. He would continue to test such girls as were eligible, and perhaps a few others as well. Meanwhile, life was good. In the lagoon hung arbors on which grew the succulent spongelike organisms which when cleaned, plucked and boiled formed the staple food of the Float-folk. The lagoon teemed likewise with other edible fish, separated from the predators of the ocean by the enormous net which hung in a great hemisphere from various buoys, pads and the main float—this a complex of ancient pads, compressed, wadded and interlocked to create an unbroken surface five acres in area and varying from two feet to six feet in thickness. There was much other food available: spores from the sea-plant fruiting organ, from which a crusty bread could be baked. There were in addition other flowers, tendrils and bulbs, as well as the prized flesh of the gray-fish to take which the Swindlers must fare forth in their coracles and cunningly swindle from the ocean, which horizon to horizon, pole to pole, enveloped the entire surface of the world.

Sklar Hast turned his eyes up to the skies, where the constellations already blazed with magnificent ardor. To the south, half up the sky, hung a cluster of twenty-five middle-bright stars, from which, so tradition asserted, his ancestors had fled in the Ship of Space, finally to reach the world of water. Eighty-three persons, of various castes, managed to disembark before the ship foundered and sank; the eighty-three had become twenty thousand, scattered east and west along fifty miles of floating sea-plant. The castes so jealously differentiated during the first few generations, with the Bezzlers at the top and the Advertisermen at the bottom, had now accommodated themselves to one another and were even intermingling. There was little to disturb the easy flow of life; nothing harsh nor unpleasant—except, perhaps, King Kragen.

Sklar Hast made a sour face and examined those three of his arbors which only two days before had been plucked clean by King Kragen, whose appetite as well as his bulk grew by the year. Sklar Hast scowled westward across the ocean, in the direction from which King Kragen customarily appeared, moving with long strokes of his four propulsive vanes, in a manner to suggest some vast, distorted, grotesquely ugly anthropoid form swimming by means of the breaststroke. There, of course, the resemblance to man ended. King Kragen's body was tough black cartilage, a cylinder on a rectangle, from the corners of which extended the vanes. The cylinder comprising King Kragen's main bulk opened forward in a maw fringed with four mandibles and eight palps, and aft in an anus. Atop this cylinder, somewhat to the front, rose a turret from which the four eyes protruded: two peering forward, two aft. During Sklar Hast's lifetime King Kragen had grown perceptibly, and now measured perhaps sixty feet in length. King Kragen was a terrible force for destruction, but luckily could be placated. King Kragen enjoyed copious quantities of sponges and when his appetite was appeased he injured no one and did no damage; indeed he kept the area clear of other marauding kragen, which either he killed or sent flapping and skipping in a panic across the ocean.

Sklar Hast's attention was attracted by a dark swirl in the water at the edge of the net: a black bulk surrounded by glistening cusps and festoons of starlit water. Sklar Hast ran forward to the edge of the pad, peered. No question about it! A lesser kragen was attempting to break the net that it might plunder the lagoon!

Sklar Hast shouted a curse, shook his fist, turned, ran at

full speed across the pad. He jumped into his coracle, crossed the twenty feet of water to the central float. He delayed only long enough to tie the coracle to a stake formed of a human femur, then ran at top speed to the hoodwink tower.

A mile to the west the tower on Thrasneck Float flickered its lamps, the configurations coming with the characteristic style of Durdan Farr, the Thrasneck Master Hoodwink: ". . . *thirteen . . . bushels . . . of . . . salt . . . lost . . . when . . . a . . . barge . . . took . . . water . . . between . . . Sumber . . . and . . . Adelvine . . .*"

Sklar Hast climbed the ladder, burst into the cupola. He pointed to the lagoon. "A rogue, breaking the nets. I just saw him. Call King Kragen!"

Chaezy Zander instantly flashed the cut-in signal. His fingers jammed down rods, he kicked the release. *"Call . . . King . . . Kragen!"* he signaled. *"Rogue . . . in . . . Tranque . . . Lagoon!"*

On Thrasneck Float Durden Farr relayed the message to the tower on Bickle Float, and so along the line of floats to Sciona at the far west, who thereupon returned the signal: *"King . . . Kragen . . . is . . . nowhere . . . at . . . hand."*

Back down the line of towers flickered the message, returning to Tranque Float in something short of sixty seconds. Sklar Hast read the message as it left the Bickle Tower, before reaching Thrasneck, and rushed over to the side of the cupola, to peer down into the lagoon.

Others had now discovered the rogue kragen and set up a shout to the tower: "Call King Kragen!" Sklar Hast shouted in return, "He can't be found!" Chaezy Zander, tight-lipped, was already dispatching another message: *"To . . . the . . . various . . . intercessors . . . along . . . the . . . line. Kindly . . . summon . . . King . . . Kragen . . . and . . . direct . . . him . . . to . . . Tranque . . . Float."*

Sklar Hast pointed and bellowed, "Look! The beast has broken the net! Where is Voidenvo?"

He swung down the ladder, ran to the edge of the lagoon. The kragen, a beast perhaps fifteen feet in length, was surging easily through the water, a caricature of a man performing the breaststroke. Starlight danced and darted along the disturbed water, and so outlined the gliding black bulk. Sklar Hast cried out in fury: the brute was headed for his arbors, so recently devastated by the appetite of King Kragen! It could not be borne! He ran to his coracle, returned to his pad. Already the kragen had extended its palps and was feeling for sponges. Sklar Hast sought for an implement which might serve as a weapon; there was nothing to hand: a few articles fashioned from human bones and fish cartilage. Leaning against the hut was a boat-hook, a stalk ten feet long, carefully straightened, scraped, and seasoned, to which a hook-shaped human rib had been lashed. He took it up and now from the central pad came a cry of remonstrance. "Sklar Hast! What do you do?" This was the voice of Semon Voidenvo the Intercessor. Sklar Hast paid him no heed. He ran to the edge of the pad, jabbed the boat-hook at the kragen's turret. It scraped uselessly along resilient cartilage. The kragen swung up one of its vanes, knocked the pole aside. Sklar Hast jabbed the pole with all his strength at what he considered the kragen's most vulnerable area: a soft pad of receptor-endings directly above the maw. Behind him he heard Semon Voidenvo's outraged protest: "This is not to be done! This is not to be done! Desist!"

The kragen quivered at the blow, twisted its massive turret to gaze at Sklar Hast. Again it swung up its fore-vane, smashing the pole, slashing at Sklar Hast, who leapt back with inches to spare. From the central pad Semon Voidenvo bawled, "By no means molest the kragen; it is a matter for the King! We must respect the King's perquisites."

Sklar Hast stood back in fury as the kragen resumed its feeding. As if to punish Sklar Hast for his assault, it passed close beside the arbors, worked its vanes, and the arbors, sea-plant stalk lashed with fiber, collapsed. Sklar Hast groaned. "No more than you deserve," called out Semon Voidenvo with odious complacence. "You interfered with the duties of King Kragen; now your arbors are destroyed. This is justice."

" 'Justice'? Bah!" bellowed Sklar Hast. "Where is King Kragen? You, Voidenvo the Intercessor! Why don't you summon the great gluttonous beast?"

"Come, come," admonished Semon Voidenvo. "This is not the tone in which to speak of King Kragen."

Sklar Hast thrust himself and his coracle back to the central float, where now stood several hundred folk of Tranque Float. He pointed. "Look. See that vile beast of the sea. He is plundering us of our goods. I say, kill him. I say that we need not suffer such molestation."

Semon Voidenvo emitted a high-pitched croak. "Are you insane? Someone, pour water on this maniac Hoodwink, who has too long focused his eyes on flashing lights."

In the lagoon the kragen moved to the arbors of the Belrod family, deep-divers for stalk and withe, of the Advertiserman caste and prone to a rude and surly vulgarity. The Belrod elder, Poe, a squat large-featured man, still resilient and vehement despite his years, emitted a series of hoots, intended to distract the kragen, which instead tore voraciously at the choicest Belrod sponges.

"I say, kill the beast!" cried Sklar Hast. "The King despoils us; must we likewise feed all the kragen of the ocean?"

"Kill the beast!" echoed the younger Belrods.

Semon Voidenvo gesticulated in vast excitement, but Poe Belrod shoved him roughly aside. "Quiet, let us listen to the Hoodwink. How would we kill the kragen?"

"Come! I will show you how!"

Thirty or forty men followed him, mostly Swindlers, Advertisermen, Blackguards and Extorters. The remainder hung dubiously back. Sklar Hast led the way to a pile of poles intended for the construction of a storehouse. Each pole, fabricated from withes laid lengthwise and bound in glue, was twenty feet long by eight inches in diameter, and combined great strength with lightness.

Sklar Hast found rope, worked with vicious energy. "Now—lift! Across to my pad!"

Excited by his urgency, the men shouldered the pole, carried it to the lagoon, floated it across to Sklar Hast's pad. Then, crossing in coracles, they dragged the pole up on the pad and carried it across to the edge of the lagoon. At Sklar Hast's direction, they set it down with one end resting on the hard fiber of a rib. "Now," said Sklar Hast. "Now we kill the kragen." He made a noose in the end of a light hawser, advanced toward the kragen, which watched him through the rear-pointing eyes of its turret. Sklar Hast moved slowly, so as not to alarm the creature, which continued to pluck sponges with a contemptuous disregard.

Sklar Hast, crouching, approached the edge of the pad. "Beast!" he called. "Ocean brute! Come closer. Come." He bent, splashed water at the kragen. Provoked, it surged toward him. Sklar Hast waited, and just before it swung its vane, he tossed the noose over its turret. He signaled his men. "Now!" They heaved on the line dragged the thrashing kragen through the water. Sklar Hast guided the line to the end of the pole. The kragen surged suddenly forward; in the confusion and the dark the men heaving on the rope fell backward. Sklar Hast seized the slack, and dodging a murderous slash of the kragen's fore-vane he flung a hitch around the end of the pole. He danced back. "Now!" he called. "Pull, pull! Both lines! The beast is as good as dead!"

On each of a pair of lines tied to the head of the pole fifteen men heaved. The pole rose up on its base; the line tautened around the kragen's turret, the men dug in their heels, the base of the pole bit into the hard rib. The pole rose, braced by the angle of the ropes. With majestic deliberation the thrashing kragen was lifted from the water and swung up into the air. From those watching on the central pad came a murmurous moan of fascination and dread.

The kragen made gulping noises, reached its vanes this way and that, to no avail. Sklar Hast surveyed the creature, somewhat at a loss as how to proceed. The project thus far had gone with facility: what next? The men were looking at the kragen in awe, uncomfortable at their own daring, and already were stealing furtive glances out over the ocean. Perfectly calm, it glistened with the reflections of the blazing constellations. Sklar Hast thought to divert their attention. "The nets!" he called out to those on the float. "Where are the Extorters? Repair the nets before we lose all our fish! Are you helpless?"

Certain net-makers, a trade dominated by the Extorter caste, detached themselves from the group, went out in coracles to repair the broken net.

Sklar Hast returned to a consideration of the dangling kragen. At his orders the ropes supporting the tilted pole were made fast to ribs on the surface of the pad; the men now gathered gingerly about the dangling kragen, and speculated as to the best means to kill the creature. Perhaps it was already dead? Someone posed the question; a lad of the Belrods prodded the kragen with a length of stalk and suffered a broken collarbone from a quick blow of the fore-vane.

Sklar Hast stood somewhat apart, studying the creature. Its hide was tough; its cartilaginous tissue even tougher. He sent one man for a boat-hook, another for a sharp femur-stake, and from the two fashioned a spear.

The kragen hung limp, the vanes swaying, occasionally twitching. Sklar Hast moved forward cautiously, touched the point of the spear to the side of the turret, thrust with all his weight. The point entered the tough hide perhaps half an inch, then broke. The kragen jerked, snorted, a vane slashed out. Sklar Hast sensed the dark flicker of motion, dodged and felt the air move beside his face. The spear shaft hurtled out over the pond; the vane struck the pole on which the kragen hung, bruising the fibers.

"What a quarrelsome beast!" declared Sklar Hast. "Bring more rope; we must prevent any further such demonstrations."

From the main float came a harsh command: "You are madmen; who do you risk the displeasure of King Kragen? I decree that you desist from your rash acts!"

This was the voice of Ixon Myrex, the Tranque Arbiter, a Bezzler of great physical power and moral conviction, a man with recognized powers and large prestige. Sklar Hast could not ignore Ixon Myrex as he had Semon Voidenvo. He considered the dangling kragen, looked about at the dubious faces of his comrades. They were hesitating; Ixon Myrex was not a man to be trifled with. Sklar Hast walked truculently to the edge of the pad, peered across the intervening water to the shape of Ixon Myrex.

"The kragen is destroying our arbors, Arbiter Myrex. The King is slothful about his duties, hence—"

Ixon Myrex's voice shook with wrath. "That is no way to speak! You violate the spirit of our relationship with King Kragen!"

Sklar Hast said in a reasonable voice, "King Kragen is nowhere to be seen. The Intercessors who claim such large power run back and forth in futility. We must act for ourselves. Cross the water to my pad. Join us in killing this ravenous beast."

Ixon Myrex held up his hands, which trembled in indignation. "Return the kragen to the lagoon, that thereby—"

"That thereby it may destroy more arbors?" demanded Sklar Hast. "This is not the result I hope for." He took a deep breath and made his decision. "Where is the rope?"

Arbiter Myrex called out in his sternest tones, "You men on the pad! This is how I interpret the customs of Tranque Float: the kragen must be restored to the water, with all haste. No other course is consistent with custom."

Sklar Hast waited. There was an uneasy stirring among the men. He said nothing, but taking up the rope, formed a noose. He crawled forward, flipped up the noose to catch a dangling vane, then crawling back and rising to his feet he circled the creature, binding the dangling vanes. The kragen's motions became increasingly constricted and finally were reduced to spasmodic shudders. Sklar Hast approached the creature from the rear, careful to remain out of reach of mandibles and palps, and made the bonds secure. "Now—the vile beast can only squirm. Lower it to the pad and we will find a means to make its end." The guy ropes were shifted, the pole tilted and swung; the kragen fell to the surface of the pad, where it lay passive, palps and mandibles moving slightly in and out. It showed no agitation, nor discomfort; perhaps it felt none: the exact degree of the kragen's sensitivity and ratiocinative powers had never been determined.

In the east the sky was lightening where the cluster of flaring blue and white suns known as Phocan's Cauldron began to rise. The ocean glimmered with a leaden sheen, and the folk who stood on the central pad began to glance furtively along the obscure horizon, muttering and complaining. Some few called out encouragement to Sklar Hast, recommending the most violent measures against the kragen. Between these and certain others furious arguments raged. Chaezy Zander had descended from the tower, to join Semon Voidenvo and Ixon Myrex, obviously in disapprovel of Sklar Hast's activity. Of the Caste Elders only Elmar Pronave, Jackleg and Master Witheweaver, defended Sklar Hast and his unconventional acts.

Sklar Hast ignored all. He sat watching the black hulk with vast distaste, furious with himself for having become involved in so perilous a project. What had been gained? The kragen had broken his arbors; he had revenged himself and prevented more destruction. On the other hand he had incurred the ill-will of the most influential folk of the Float, including Ixon Myrex and Chaezy Zander: no small matter. He likewise had involved those others who had trusted him and looked to him for leadership, and toward whom he now felt responsibility.

He rose to his feet. There was no help for it; the sooner the beast was disposed of, the more quickly life would return to normal. He approached the kragen, examined it gingerly. The mandibles quivered in their anxiety to sever his torso; Sklar Hast stayed warily to the side. How to kill the beast?

Elmar Pronave crossed over from the main float the better to examine the kragen. He was a tall man with a high-bridged broken nose and black hair worn in the two ear-plumes of the old Procurer Caste, now no longer in existence save for a few aggressively unique individuals scattered through the floats, who used the caste-marks to emphasize their emotional detachment.

Pronave circled the hulk, kicked at the rear vane, bent to peer into one of the staring eyes. "If we could cut it up, its parts might be of some use."

"The hide is too tough for our knives," growled Sklar Hast. "There's no neck to be strangled."

"There are other ways to kill."

Sklar Hast nodded. "We could sink the beast into the

depths of the ocean—but what to use for weight? Bones? Far too valuable. We could load bags with ash, but there is not that much ash to hand. We could burn every hut on the float as well as the hoodwink tower, and still not secure sufficient. To burn the kragen would require a like mountain of fuel.''

A young Larcener who had worked with great enthusiasm during the trapping of the kragen spoke forth: "Poison exists! Find me poison, I will fix a capsule to a stick and push it into the creature's maw!''

Elmar Pronave gave a sardonic bark of laughter. "Agreed; poisons exist, hundreds of them, derived from various sea-plants and animals—but which are sufficiently acrid to destroy this beast? And where is it to be had? I doubt if there is that much poison nearer than Sankeston Float.''

Sklar Hast went again to survey the black hulk, and now Phocan's Cauldron, rising into the sky, revealed the kragen in fuller detail. Sklar Hast examined the four blind-seeming eyes in the turret, the intricate construction of the mandibles and tentacles at the maw. He touched the turret, peered at the dome-shaped cap of chitin which covered it. The turret itself seemed laminated, as if constructed of stacked rings of cartilage, the eyes protruding fore and aft in inflexible tubes of a rugose harsh substance. Others in the group began to crowd close; Sklar Hast jumped forward, thrust at a young Felon boat-builder, but too late. The kragen flung out a palp, seized the youth around the neck. Sklar Hast cursed, heaved, tore; the clenched palp was unyielding. Another curled out for his leg; Sklar Hast kicked, danced back, still heaving upon the Felon's writhing form. The kragen drew the Felon slowly forward, hoping, so Sklar Hast realized, to pull him within easier reach. He loosed his grip, but the kragen allowed its palp to sway back to encourage Sklar Hast, who once more tore at the constricting palp. Again the kragen craftily drew its captive and Sklar Hast forward; the second palp snapped out once more and this time coiled around Sklar Hast's leg. Sklar Hast dropped to the ground, twisted himself around and broke the hold, though losing skin. The kragen petulantly jerked the Felon to within reach of its mandible, neatly snipped off the young man's head, tossed body and head aside. A horrified gasp came from the watching crowd. Ixon Myrex bellowed, "Sklar Hast, a man's life is gone, due to your savage obstinacy! You have much to answer for! Woe to you!"

Sklar Hast ignored the imprecation. He ran to his hut, found chisels and a mallet with a head of dense sea-plant stem, brought up from a depth of two hundred feet.* The chisels had blades of pelvic bone ground sharp against a board gritted with the silica husks of foraminifera. Sklar Hast returned to the kragen, put the chisel against the pale lamellum between the chitin dome and the foliations of the turret. He tapped; the chisel penetrated; this, the substance of a new layer being added to the turret, was relatively soft, the consistency of cooked gristle. Sklar Hast struck again; the chisel cut deep. The kragen squirmed.

Sklar Hast worked the chisel back out, made a new incision beside the first, then another and another, working around the periphery of the chitin dome, which was approximately two feet in diameter. The kragen squirmed and shuddered, whether in pain or apprehension it alone knew. As Sklar Hast worked around to the front, the palps groped back for him, but he shielded himself behind the turret, and finally gouged out the lamellum completely around the circumference of the turret.

His followers watched in awe and silence; from the main float came somber mutters, and occasional whimpers of superstitious dread from the children.

The channel was cut; Sklar handed chisel and mallet back to Elmar Pronave. He mounted the body of the kragen, bent his knees, hooked fingers under the edge of the chitin dome, heaved. The dome ripped up and off, almost unbalancing Sklar Hast. The dome rolled down to the pad, the turret stood like an open-topped cylinder; within were coils and loops of

---

*The Avertiserman takes below a pulley which he attaches to a sea-plant stalk. By means of ropes, buckets of air are pulled down, allowing him to remain under water as long as he chooses. Using two such systems, alternately lowered, the diver can descend to a depth of two hundred feet, where the sea-plant stalks grow dense and rigid.

something like dirty gray string. There were knots here, nodes there, on each side a pair of kinks, to the front a great tangle of kinks and loops.

Sklar Hast looked down in interest. He was joined by Elmar Pronave. "The creature's brain, evidently," said Sklar Hast. "Here the ganglions terminate. Or perhaps they are merely the termini of muscles."

Elmar Pronave took the mallet and with the handle prodded at a node. The kragen gave a furious jerk. "Well, well," said Pronave. "Interesting indeed." He prodded further: here, there. Every time he touched the exposed ganglions the kragen jerked. Sklar Hast suddenly put out his hand to halt him. "Notice. On the right, those two long loops; likewise on the left. When you touched this one here, the fore-vane jerked." He took the mallet, prodded each of the loops in turn; and in turn each of the vanes jerked.

"Aha!" declared Elmar Pronave. "Should we persist, we could teach the kragen to jig."

"Best we should kill the beast," said Sklar Hast. "Day is approaching and who knows but what . . ." From the float sounded a sudden low wail, quickly cut off as by the constriction of breath. The group around the kragen stirred; someone vented a deep sound of dismay. Sklar Hast jumped up on the kragen, looked around. The population on the float were staring to sea; he looked likewise, to see King Kragen. He floated under the surface, only his turret above water. The eyes stared forward, each a foot across; lenses of tough crystal behind which flickered milky films and pale blue sheen. King Kragen had either drifted close down the trail of Phocan's Cauldron on the water, or approached subsurface.

Fifty feet from the lagoon nets he let his bulk come to the surface; first the whole of his turret, then the black cylinder housing the maw and the digestive process, finally the great flat sub-body: this, five feet thick, thirty feet wide, sixty feet long. To the sides protruded the propulsive vanes, thick as the girth of three men. Viewed from dead ahead King Kragen appeared a deformed ogre swimming the breaststroke. His forward eyes, in their horn tubes, were turned toward the float of Sklar Hast, and seemed fixed upon the hulk of the

mutilated kragen. The men stared back, muscles stiff as
sea-plant stalk. The kragen which they had captured, once so
huge and formidable, now seemed a miniature, a doll, a toy.
Through its after-eyes it saw King Kragen, and gave a fluting
whistle, a sound completely lost and desolate.

Sklar Hast suddenly found his tongue. He spoke in a husky
urgent tone. "Back. To the back of the pad. Swim to the
float."

From the main float rose the voice of Semon Voidenvo the
Intercessor. In quavering tones he called out across the water:
"Behold, King Kragen, the men of Tranque Float! Now we
denounce the presumptuous bravado of these few heretics!
Behold, this pleasant lagoon, with its succulent sponges,
devoted to the well-being of the magnanimous King Kragen—"
The reedy voice faltered as King Kragen twitched his great
vanes and eased forward. The great eyes stared without dis-
cernible expression, but behind there seemed to be a leaping
and shifting of pale pink and pale blue lights. The folk on the
float drew back as King Kragen breasted close to the net.
With a twitch of his vanes, he ripped the net; two more
twitches shredded it. From the folk on the float came a moan
of dread; King Kragen had not been mollified.

King Kragen eased into the lagoon, approached Sklar Hast's
pad, which now was deserted except for the helpless kragen.
The bound beast thrashed feebly, sounded its fluting whistle.
King Kragen reached forth a palp, seized it, lifted it into the
air, where it dangled helplessly. King Kragen drew it con-
temptuously close to his great mandibles, chopped it quickly
into slices of gray and black gristle. These he tossed away,
out into the ocean. He paused to drift a moment, to consider.
Then he surged on Sklar Hast's pad. One blow of his fore-
vane demolished the hut, another cut a great gouge in the
pad. The after-vanes thrashed among the arbors; water, debris, broken sponges boiled up from below. King Kragen
thrust again, wallowed completely up on the pad, which
slowly crumpled and sank beneath his weight.

King Kragen pulled himself back into the lagoon, cruised
back and forth destroying arbors, shredding the net, smashing

the huts of all the pads of the lagoon. Then he turned his attention to the main float, breasting up to the edge. For a moment he eyed the population, which started to set up a terrified keening sound, then thrust himself forward, wallowed up on the float, and the keening became a series of hoarse cries and screams. The folk ran back and forth with jerky scurrying steps.

King Kragen bulked on the float like a toad on a lilypad. He struck with his vanes; the float split. The hoodwink tower, the great structure so cunningly woven, so carefully contrived, tottered. King Kragen lunged again, the tower toppled, falling into the huts along the north edge of the float.

King Kragen floundered across the float. He destroyed the granary, the bushels of yellow meal laboriously scraped from sea-plant pistils streamed into the water. He crushed the racks where stalk, withe and fiber were stretched and flexed; he dealt likewise with the ropewalk. Then, as if suddenly in a hurry, he swung about, heaved himself to the southern edge of the float. A number of huts and thirty-two of the folk, mostly aged and very young, were crushed or thrust into the water and drowned.

King Kragen regained the open sea. He floated quietly a moment or two, palps twitching in the expression of some unknowable emotion. Then he moved his vanes and slid off across the calm ocean.

Tranque Float was a devastation, a tangle, a scene of wrath and grief. The lagoon had returned to the ocean, with the arbors reduced to rubbish and the shoals of food-fish scattered. Many huts had been crushed. The hoodwink tower lay toppled. Of a population of four hundred and eighty, forty-three were dead, and as many more injured. The survivors stood blank-eyed and limp, unable to comprehend the full extent of the disaster which had come upon them.

Presently they roused themselves, and gathered at the far western edge where the damage had been the least. Ixon Myrex sought through the faces, eventually spied Sklar Hast sitting on a fragment of the fallen hoodwink tower. He raised his hand slowly, pointed. "Sklar Hast! I denounce you. The evil you have done to Tranque Float cannot be uttered in words. Your arrogance, your callous indifference to our pleas, your cruel and audacious villainy—how can you hope to expiate them?"

Sklar Hast looked off across the sea.

"In my capacity as Arbiter of Tranque Float, I now declare you to be a criminal of the basest sort, together with all those who served you as accomplices, and most noteworthy Elmar Pronave! Elmar Pronave, show your shameful face! Where do you hide?"

But Elmar Pronave had been drowned and did not answer.

Chaezy Zander limped across the area to stand beside Ixon Myrex. "I likewise denounce Sklar Hast and declare him Assistant Master Hoodwink no longer. He has disgraced his caste and his calling: I hereby eject him from the fellowship of both!"

Semon Voidenvo the Intercessor rose to speak. "Denunciations are not enough. King Kragen, in wreaking his terrible but just vengeance, intended that the primes of the deed should die. I now declare the will of King Kragen to be death, by either strangulation or bludgeoning, of Sklar Hast and all his accomplices."

"Not so fast," said Sklar Hast at last. "It appears to me that a certain confusion is upon us. Two kragen, a large one and small one, have injured us. I, Sklar Hast, and my friends, are those who hoped to protect the float from depredation. We failed. We are not criminals; we are simply not as strong nor as wicked as King Kragen."

"You are aware," Semon Voidenvo persisted, "that King Kragen reserves to himself the duty of guarding us from the lesser kragen? You are aware that in assaulting the kragen, you in effect assaulted King Kragen?"

Sklar Hast considered. "We will need more powerful tools than ropes and chisels to kill King Kragen."

Semon Voidenvo turned away speechless. The people looked apathetically toward Sklar Hast. Few seemed to share the indignation of the elders.

Ixon Myrex sensed the general feeling of misery and fatigue. "This is no time for recrimination. There is work to be done, vast work; all our structures to be rebuilt, our tower rendered operative, our net rewoven. But Sklar Hast's crime must not go without appropriate punishment. I therefore propose a Grand Convocation to take place one week from today, on Apprise Float. The fate of Sklar Hast and his gang will be inexorably decided by a Council of Elders."

# CHAPTER II

The ocean had never been plumbed. At two hundred feet, the maximum depth attempted by stalk-cutters and pod-gatherers, the sea-plant stems were still a tangle. One Waller Murven, a man half-daredevil, half-maniac, had descended to three hundred feet, and in the indigo gloom noted the stalks merging to disappear into the murk as a single great trunk. But attempts to sound the bottom, by means of a line weighted with a bag of bone chippings, were unsuccessful. How then had the sea-plants managed to anchor themselves? Some supposed that the plants were of great antiquity, and had developed during a time when the water was much lower. Others conjectured a sinking of the ocean bottom; still others were content to ascribe the feat to an innate tendency of the sea-plants.

Of all the floats Apprise was the largest and one of the first to be settled. The central agglomeration was perhaps seven acres in extent; the lagoon was bounded by thirty or forty smaller pads. Apprise Float was the traditional site of the convocations, which occurred at approximately yearly intervals and which were attended by the active and responsible adults of the system. Drama and excitement attended the holding of the convocations. The folk of the floats seldom ventured far from home, since it was widely believed that King Kragen disapproved of travel. He ignored the coracles of swindlers, and also the rafts of withe or stalk which occasionally passed back and forth between the floats; but on various occasions he had demolished boats or coracles which seemed to have no ostensible business or purpose. Coracles conveying folk to a convocation had never been molested, however, even though King Kragen always seemed aware that a convocation was in progress, and often watched proceedings from a distance of a half-mile or so. How King Kragen gained his knowledge was a matter of great mystery: some asserted that on every float lived a man who was a man in semblance only: who inwardly was a manifestation of King Kragen. It was through this man, according to the superstition, that King Kragen knew what transpired on the floats.

For three days preceding the convocation there was incessant flickering along the line of the hoodwink towers; the destruction of Tranque Float was reported in full detail, together with Ixon Myrex's denunciation of Sklar Hast and Sklar Hast's rebuttal. On each of the floats there was intense discussion and a certain degree of debate. But since, in most cases, the Arbiter and the Intercessor of each float inveighed against Sklar Hast, there was little organized sentiment in his favor.

On the morning of the convocation, early, before the morning sky showed blue, coracles full of folk moved between the floats. The survivors of the Tranque Float disaster, who for the most part had sought refuge on Thrasneck and Bickle, were among the first underway, as were the folk from Almack and Sciona, to the far west.

All morning the coracles shuttled back and forth between the floats; shortly before noon the first groups began to arrive on Apprise. Each group wore the distinctive emblems of its float; and those who felt caste distinction important likewise wore the traditional hair-stylings, forehead plaques and dorsal ribbons; otherwise all dressed in much the same fashion: shirts and pantlets of coarse linen woven from sea-plant fiber; sandals of rug-fish leather, ceremonial gauntlets and epaulettes of sequins cut from the kernels of a certain half-animal, half-vegetable mollusc.

As the folk arrived they trooped to the famous old Apprise

Inn, where they refreshed themselves at a table on which was set forth a collation of beer, pod-cakes and pickled fingerlings; after which the newcomers separated to various quarters of the float, in accordance with traditional caste distinctions.

In the center of the float was a rostrum and on benches surrounding the notables took their places: craft-masters, caste-chiefs, Arbiters and Intercessors. The rostrum was at all times open to any who wished to speak, so long as they gained the sponsorship of one of the notables. The first speakers at the convocations customarily were elders intent on exhorting the younger folk to excellence and virtue; so it was today. An hour after the sun had reached the zenith the first speaker made his way to the rostrum; a portly old Incendiary from Maudelinda Float who had in just such a fashion opened the speaking at the last five convocations. He sought and was perfunctorily granted sponsorship—by now his speeches were regarded as a necessary evil; he mounted the rostrum and began to speak. His voice was rich, throbbing, voluminous; his periods were long, his sentiments well-used, his illuminations unremarkable:

"We meet again; I am pleased to see so many of the faces which over the years have become familiar and well-beloved; and alas there are certain faces no more to be seen, those who have slipped away to the Bourne, many untimely, as those who suffered punishment only these few days past before the wrath of King Kragen, of which we all stand in awe. A dreadful circumstance thus to provoke the majesty of this Elemental Reality; it should never have occurred; it would never have occurred if all abided by the ancient disciplines. Why must we scorn the wisdom of our ancestors? Those noble and most heroic of man who dared to revolt against the tyranny of the mindless helots, seize the Ship of Space which was taking them to brutal confinement, and seek a haven here on this blessed world! Our ancestors knew the benefits of order and rigor: they designated the castes and set them to tasks for which they presumably had received training on the Home World. In such a fashion the Swindlers were assigned the task of swindling fish; the Hoodwinks were set to winking hoods; the Incendiaries, among whom I am proud to number myself, wove ropes; while the Bezzler gave us the Intercessors who have procured the favor and benevolent guardianship of King Kragen.

"Like begets like; characteristics persist and distill: why then are the castes crumbling and giving way to helter-skelter disorder? I appeal to the young of today: read the old books: the Dicta. Study the artifacts in the Museum, renew your dedication to the system formulated by our forefathers: you have no heritage more precious than your caste identity!"

The old Incendiary spoke on in such a vein for several minutes further, and was succeeded by another old man, a former Hoodwink of good reputation, who worked until films upon his eyes gave one configuration much the look of another. Like the old Incendiary he too urged a more fervent dedication to the old-time values. "I deplore the sloth and pudicity of today's youth! We are becoming a race of sluggards! It is sheer good fortune that King Kragen protects us from the gluttony of the lesser kragen. And what if the tyrants of out-space discovered our haven and sought once more to enslave us? How would we defend ourselves? By hurling fishheads? By diving under the floats in the hope that our adversaries would follow and drown themselves? I propose that each float form a militia, well-trained and equipped with darts and spears, fashioned from the most durable stalk obtainable!"

The old Hoodwink was followed by the Sumber Float Intercessor, who courteously suggested that should the out-space tyrants appear, King Kragen would be sure to visit upon them the most poignant punishments, the most absolute of rebuffs, so that the tyrants would flee in terror never to return. "King Kragen is mighty, King Kragen is wise and benevolent, unless his dignity is impugned, as in the detestable incident at Tranque Float, where the wilfulness of a bigoted free-thinker caused agony to many." Now he modestly turned down his head. "It is neither my place nor my privilege to propose a punishment suitable to so heinous an offense as the one under discussion. But I would go beyond this particular crime to dwell upon the underlying causes; namely the bravado of certain folk, who ordain themselves equal or superior to the accepted ways of life which have served us so well so long . . ."

Presently he descended to the float. His place was taken by a somber man of stalwart physique, wearing the plainest of garments. "My name is Sklar Hast," he said. "I am that so-called 'bigoted free-thinker' just referred to. I have much to say, but I hardly know how to say it. I will be blunt. King Kragen is not the wise beneficent guardian the Intercessors like to pretend. King Kragen is a gluttonous beast who every year becomes more enormous and more gluttonous. I sought to kill a lesser kragen which I found destroying my arbors; by some means King Kragen learned of this attempt and reacted with insane malice."

"Hist! Hist!" cried the Intercessors from below. "Shame! Outrage!"

"Why does King Kragen resent my effort? After all, he kills any lesser kragen he discovers in the vicinity. It is simple and self-evident. King Kragen does not want men to think about killing kragen for fear they will attempt to kill him. I propose that this is what we do. Let us put aside this ignoble servility, this groveling to a sea-beast, let us turn our best efforts to the destruction of King Kragen."

"Irresponsible maniac!" "Fool!" "Vile-minded ingrate!" called the Intercessors in wrath.

Sklar Hast waited, but the invective increased in volume. Finally Phyral Berwick the Apprise Arbiter mounted the rostrum and held up his hands. "Quiet! Let Sklar Hast speak! He stands on the rostrum; it is his privilege to say what he wishes."

"Must we listen to garbage and filth?" called Semon Voidenvo. "This man has destroyed Tranque Float; now he urges his frantic lunacy upon the rest of us."

"Let him urge," declared Phyral Berwick. "You are under no obligation to comply."

Sklar Hast said, "The Intercessors naturally resist these ideas; they are bound closely to King Kragen, and claim to have some means of communicating with him. Possibly this is so. Why else should King Kragen arrive so opportunely at Tranque Float? Now here is a very cogent point: if we can agree to liberate ourselves from King Kragen, we must prevent the Intercessors from making known our plans to him, otherwise we shall suffer more than necessary. Most of you know in your hearts that I speak truth. King Kragen is a crafty beast with an insatiable appetite and we are his slaves. You know this truth but you fear to acknowledge it. Those who spoke before me have mentioned our forefathers: the men who captured a ship from the tyrants who sought to immure them on a penal planet. What would our forefathers have done? Would they have submitted to this gluttonous ogre? Of course not.

"How can we kill King Kragen? The plans must wait upon agreement, upon the concerted will to act, and in any event must not be told before the Intercessors. If there are any here who believe as I do, now is the time for them to make themselves heard."

He stepped down from the rostrum. Across the float was silence. Men's faces were frozen. Sklar Hast looked to right and to left. No one met his eye.

Semon Voidenvo mounted the rostrum. "You have listened to the shameless murderer. On Tranque Float we condemned him to death for his malevolent acts. According to custom he demanded the right to speak before a convocation; now he has done so. Has he confessed his great crime; has he wept for the evil he has visited upon Tranque Float? No; he gibbers his plans for further enormities; he outrages decency by mentioning our ancestors in the same breath with his foul proposals. Let the convocation endorse the verdict of Tranque Float; let all those who respect King Kragen and benefit from his ceaseless vigilance, raise now their hands in the clenched fist of death!"

"Death!" roared the Intercessors and raised their fists. But elsewhere through the crowd there was hesitation and uneasiness. Eyes shifted backwards and forwards; there were furtive glances out to sea. Semon Voidenvo once more called for a signal, and now a few fists were raised.

Phyral Berwick, the Apprise Monitor, rose to his feet. "I remind Semon Voidenvo that he has now called twice for the death of Sklar Hast. If he calls once more and fails to achieve an affirmative vote Sklar Hast is vindicated."

Semon Voidenvo's face sagged. He looked uncertainly over the crowd, and without further statement descended.

The rostrum was empty. No one sought to speak. Finally Phyral Berwick himself mounted the steps. He was a stocky square-faced man with gray hair, ice-blue eyes, a short gray beard. He spoke slowly. "You have heard Sklar Hast, who calls for the death of King Kragen. You have heard Semon Voidenvo, who calls for the death of Sklar Hast. I will tell you my feelings. I have great fear in the first case and great disinclination in the second. I have no clear sense of what I should do."

From the audience a man called "Question!" Phyral Berwick nodded. "State your name, caste and craft, and propound your question."

"I am Meth Cagno; I am by blood a Larcener, although I no longer follow caste custom; my craft is that of Scrivener. My question has this background: Sklar Hast has voiced a conjecture which I think deserves an answer: namely, that Semon Voidenvo, the Tranque Intercessor, called King Kragen to Tranque Float. This is a subtle question, because much depends upon not only *if* Semon Voidenvo issued the call, but precisely *when*. If he did so when the rogue kragen was first discovered, well and good. But—if he called after Sklar Hast made his attempt to kill the rogue, Semon Voidenvo is more guilty of the Tranque disaster than Sklar Hast. My question then: what is the true state of affairs? Do the Intercessors, secretly communicate with King Kragen? Specifically, did Semon Voidenvo call King Kragen to Tranque Float in order that Sklar Hast should be punished?"

Phyral Berwick deliberated. "I cannot answer your question. But I think it deserves an answer. Semon Voidenvo, what do you say?"

"I say nothing."

"Come," said Phyral Berwick reasonably. "Your craft is Intercessor; your responsibility is to the men whom you represent, not to King Kragen, no matter how fervent your respect. Any evasion or secrecy can only arouse our misgivings."

"It is to be understood," said Semon Voidenvo tartly,

"that if I did indeed summon King Kragen, my motives were of the highest order."

"Well, then did you do so?"

Semon Voidenvo cast about for a means to escape from his dilemma, and found none. Finally he said, "There is a means by which the Intercessors are able to summon King Kragen in the event that a rogue kragen appears. This occurred; I so summoned King Kragen."

"Indeed." Phyral Berwick drummed his fingers on the rail of the rostrum. "Are these the only occasions that you summon King Kragen?"

"Why do you question me?" demanded Semon Voidenvo. "I am Intercessor; the criminal is Sklar Hast."

"Easy, then; the questions illuminate the extent of the alleged crime. For instance, let me ask this: do you ever summon King Kragen to feed from your lagoon in order to visit a punishment upon the folk of your float?"

Semon Voidenvo blinked. "The wisdom of King Kragen is inordinate. He can detect delinquencies, he makes his presence known—"

"Specifically then, you summoned King Kragen to Tranque Float when Sklar Hast sought to kill the lesser kragen?"

"My acts are not in the balance. I see no reason to answer the question."

Phyral Berwick spoke to the crowd in a troubled voice. "There seems no way to determine exactly when Semon Voidenvo called King Kragen. If he did so after Sklar Hast had begun his attack upon the rogue, then in my opinion, Semon Voidenvo the Intercessor is more immediately responsible for the Tranque disaster than Sklar Hast. Thereupon it becomes a travesty to visit any sort of penalty upon Sklar Hast. Unfortunately there seems no way of settling this question."

The Apprise Intercessor, Barquan Blasdel, rose slowly to his feet. "Arbiter Berwick, I fear that you are seriously confused. Sklar Hast and his gang committed an act knowingly proscribed both by the Tranque Monitor Ixon Myrex and by the Tranque Intercessor Semon Voidenvo. The consequences stemmed from this act; hence Sklar Hast is guilty."

"Barquen Blasdel," said Phyral Berwick, "you are Apprise Intercessor. Have you ever summoned King Kragen to Apprise Float?"

"As Semon Voidenvo pointed out, Sklar Hast is the criminal at the bar, not the conscientious Intercessors of the various floats. By no means may Sklar Hast be allowed to evade his punishment. King Kragen is not lightly to be defied. Even though the convocation will not raise their collective fist to smite Sklar Hast, I say that he must die."

Phyral Berwick fixed his pale blue eyes upon Barquan Blasdel. "If the convocation gives Sklar Hast his life, he will not die unless I die before him."

Meth Cagno came forward. "And I likewise."

The men of Tranque Float who had joined Sklar Hast in the killing of the rogue kragen came toward the rostrum, shouting their intention of joining Sklar Hast either in life or death, and with them came others, from various floats.

Barquan Blasdel climbed onto the rostrum, held his hands wide. "Before others declare themselves—look out to sea. King Kragen watches, attentive to learn who is loyal and who is faithless."

The crowd swung about as if one individual. A hundred yards off the float the water swirled lazily around King Kragen's great turret. The crystal eyes pointed like telescopes toward Apprise Float. Presently the turret sank beneath the surface. The blue water roiled, then flowed smooth and featureless.

Sklar Hast went to the ladder, started to mount to the rostrum. Barquen Blasdel the Intercessor halted him. "The rostrum must not become a shouting-place. Stay till you are summoned!" But Sklar Hast pushed him aside, went to face the crowd. He pointed toward the smooth ocean. "There you have seen the vile beast, our enemy! Why should we deceive ourselves? Intercessors, arbiters, all of us—let us forget our differences, let us join our crafts and our resources! If we do so, we can evolve a method to kill King Kragen! So now—decide!"

Barquan Blasdel threw back his head aghast. He took a

step toward Sklar Hast, as if to seize him, then turned to the audience. "You have heard this madman—twice you have heard him. You have also observed the vigilance of King Kragen, whose force is known to all. You can choose therefore either to obey the exhortations of a twitching lunatic, or be guided by your ancient trust in the benevolence of mighty King Kragen. In one manner only does Sklar Hast speak truth: there must be a definite resolution to this matter. We can have no half-measures! Sklar Hast must die! So now hold high your fists—each and all! Silence the frantic screamings of Sklar Hast! King Kragen is near at hand! Death to Sklar Hast!" He thrust his fist high into the air.

The Intercessors followed suit. "Death to Sklar Hast!"

Hesitantly, indecisively, other fists raised, then others and others. Some changed their minds and drew down their fists; others submitted to arguments and either drew down their fists or thrust them high; some raised their fists only to have others pull them down. Altercations sprang up across the float; the hoarse sound of contention began to make itself heard. Barquan Blasdel leaned forward in sudden concern, calling for calm. Sklar Hast likewise started to speak, but he desisted—because suddenly words were of no avail. In a bewildering, almost magical, shift the placid convocation had become a melee. Men and women tore savagely at each other, screaming, cursing, raging, squealing. Emotion accumulated from childhood, stored and constrained, had suddenly exploded; and the identical fear and hate had prompted opposite reactions. Across the float the tide of battle surged, out into the water where staid Bezzlers and responsible Larceners sought to drown each other. Few weapons were available: clubs of stalk, a bone axe or two, a half-dozen stakes, as many knives. While the struggle was at its most intense King Kragen once more surfaceed, this time a quarter-mile to the north from whence he turned his vast incurious gaze upon the float.

The fighting slowed and dwindled, from sheer exhaustion. The combatants drew apart into panting bleeding groups. In the lagoon floated half a dozen corpses; on the float lay as many more. Now for the first time it could be seen that those who stood by Sklar Hast were considerably outnumbered, by almost two to one, and also that this group included for the most part the most vigorous and able of the craftsmen, though few of the Masters: about half of the Hoodwinks, two-thirds of the Scriveners, relatively few from the Jacklegs, Advertisermen, Nigglers and other low castes, fewer still of the Arbiters and no Intercessors whatever.

Barquan Blasdel, still on the rostrum, cried out, "This is a sorry day indeed; a sorry day! Sklar Hast, see the anguish you have brought to the floats! There can be no mercy for you now!"

Sklar Hast came forward, pale and flaming-eyed. Blood coursed down his face from the slash of knife. Ignoring Blasdel, he mounted the rostrum, and addressed the two groups:

"As Blasdel the Intercessor has said, there is no turning back now. So be it. Let those who want to serve King Kragen remain. Let those who want free lives go forth across the sea. There are floats to north and south, to east and west, floats as kind and hospitable as these, where we will soon have homes as rich and modern—perhaps more so."

Barquan Blasdel stroked forward. "Go then! All you faithless, you irreverent ones—get hence and good riddance! Go where you will, and never seek to return when the teeming kragen, unchided by the great King, devour your sponges, tear your nets, crush your coracles!"

"The many cannot be as rapacious as the one," said Sklar Hast. "You who will go then, return to your floats, load tools and cordage, all your utile goods into your coracles. In two days we depart. Our destination and other details must remain secret. I need not explain why." He cast an ironic look toward Barquan Blasdel.

"You need not fear our interference," said Blasdel. "You may depart at will; indeed we will facilitate your going."

"On the morning of the third day hence, then, when the wind blows fair, we depart."

## CHAPTER III

Barquan Blasdel the Apprise Intercessor, with his spouse and six daughters, occupied a pad to the north of the main float, somewhat isolated and apart. It was perhaps the choicest and most pleasant pad of the Apprise complex, situated where Blasdel could read the hoodwink towers of Apprise, of Quatrefoil and the Bandings to the east, of Granolt to the west. The pad was delightfully overgrown with a hundred different plants and vines: some yielding resinous pods, others capsules of fragrant sap, others crisp tendrils and shoots. Certain shrubs produced stains and pigment; a purple-leaved epiphyte yielded a rich-flavored pith. Other growths were entirely ornamental—a situation not too usual along the floats, where space was at a premium and every growing object weighed for its utility. Along the entire line of floats few pads could compare to that of Barquan Blasdel for beauty, variety of plantings, isolation and calm.

In late afternoon of the second day after the turbulent convocation, Barquan Blasdel returned to his pad. He dropped the painter of his coracle over a stake of carved bone, gazed appreciatively into the west. The sun had only just departed the sky, which now glowed with effulgent greens, blues, and, at the zenith, a purple of exquisite purity. The ocean, shuddering to the first whispers of the evening breeze, reflected the sky. Blasdel felt surrounded, immersed in color. He turned away, marched to his house, whistling a complacent tune between his teeth. On the morrow the most troublesome elements of all the floats would depart on the morning breeze, and no more would be heard from them ever. And Blasdel's whistling became slow and thoughtful. Although life flowed smoothly and without contention, over the years a certain uneasiness and dissatisfaction had begun to make itself felt. Dissident elements had begun to question the established order. The sudden outbreak of violence at the convocation perhaps had been inevitable: an explosion of suppressed or even unconscious tensions. But all was working out for the best. The affair could not have resolved itself more smoothly if he had personally arranged the entire sequence of events. At one stroke all the skeptics, grumblers, ne'er-do-wells, the covertly insolent, the obstinate hardheads—at one stroke, all would disappear, never again to trouble the easy and orthodox way of life.

Almost jauntily Barquan Blasdel ambled up the path to his residence: a group of five semidetached huts, screened by the garden from the main float, and so providing a maximum of privacy for Blasdel, his spouse and his six daughters. Blasdel halted. On a bench beside the door sat a man. Twilight murk concealed his face. Blasdel frowned, peered. Intruders upon his private pad were not welcome. Blasdel marched forward. The man rose from the bench and bowed: it was Phyral Berwick, the Apprise Arbiter. "Good evening," said Berwick. "I trust I did not startle you."

"By no means," said Blasdel shortly. With rank equal to his own Berwick could not be ignored, although after his unconventional actions at the convocation Blasdel could not bring himself to display more than a minimum of formal courtesy. He said, "Unfortunately I was not expecting callers and can offer you no refreshment."

"A circumstance of no moment," declared Berwick. "I desire neither food nor drink." He waved his hand around the pad. "You live on a pad of surpassing beauty, Barquan Blasdel. There are many who might envy you."

Blasdel shrugged. "Since my conduct is orthodox, I am armored against adverse opinion. But what urgency brings you here? I fear that I must be less than ceremonious; I am shortly due at the hoodwink tower to participate in a coded all-float conference."

Berwick made a gesture of polite acquiescence. "My business is of small moment. But I would not keep you standing out here in the dusk. Shall we enter?"

Blasdel grunted, opened the door, allowed Berwick to enter. From a cupboard he brought luminant fiber, which he set aglow and arranged in a holder. Turning a quick side glance toward Berwick he said, "In all candor I am somewhat surprised to see you. Apparently you were among the most vehement of those dissidents who planned to depart."

"I may well have given that impression," Berwick agreed. "But you must realize that declarations uttered in the heat of emotion are occasionally amended in the light of sober reason."

Blasdel nodded curtly. "True enough. I suspect that many of the ingrates will think twice before joining this harebrained expedition."

"This is partly the reason for my presence here," said Berwick. He looked around the room. "An interesting chamber. You own dozens of valuable artifacts. But where are the others of your family?"

"In the domestic area. This is my sanctum, my workroom, my place of meditation."

"Indeed." Berwick inspected the walls. "Indeed, indeed! I believe I notice certain relics of the forefathers!"

"True," said Blasdel. "This small flat object is of the substance called 'metal,' and is extremely hard. The best bone knife will not scratch it. The purpose of this particular object I cannot conjecture. It is an heirloom. These books are exact copies of the Dicta in the Hall of Archives, and present the memoirs of the Forefathers. Alas! I find them beyond my comprehension. There is nothing more of any great interest. On the shelf—my ceremonial headdresses; you have seen them before. Here is my telescope. It is old; the case is warped, the gum of the lenses has bulged and cracked. It was poor gum, to begin with. But I have little need for a better instrument. My possessions are few. Unlike many Intercessors and certain Arbiters," here he cast a meaningful eye at Phyral Berwick, "I do not choose to surround myself with sybaritical cushions and baskets of sweetmeats."

Berwick laughed ruefully. "You have touched upon my weaknesses. Perhaps the fear of deprivation has occasioned second thoughts in me."

"Ha hah!" Blasdel became jovial. "I begin to understand. The scalawags who set off to wild new floats can expect nothing but hardship: wild fish, horny sponges, new varnish with little more body than water; in short they will be returning to the life of savages. They must expect to suffer the depredations of lesser kragen, who will swiftly gather. Perhaps in time . . ." His voice dwindled, his face took on a thoughtful look.

"What was it you were about to say?" prompted Phyral Bewick.

Blasdel gave a noncommittal laugh. "An amusing, if farfetched, conceit crossed my mind. Perhaps in time one of these lesser kragen will vanquish the others, and drive them away. When this occurs, those who flee King Kragen will have a king of their own, who may eventually . . ." Again his voice paused.

"Who may eventually rival King Kragen in size and force?" Berwick supplied. "The concept is not unreasonable—although King Kragen is already enormous from long feasting, and shows no signs of halting his growth." An almost imperceptible tremor moved the floor of the hut. Blasdel went to look out the door. "I thought I felt the arrival of a coracle."

"Conceivably a gust of wind," said Berwick. "Well, to my errand. As you have guessed I did not come to examine your relics or comment upon the comfort of your cottage. My business is this. I feel a certain sympathy for those who are leaving and I feel that no one, not even the most violently fanatic Intercessor, would wish this group to meet King Kragen upon the ocean. King Kragen, as you are aware, disapproves of exploration, and becomes petulant, even wrathful, when he finds men venturing out upon the ocean. Perhaps he fears the possibility of the second King Kragen concerning which we speculated. Hence I came to inquire the whereabouts of King Kragen. In the morning the wind blows east, and the optimum location for King Kragen would be to the far west at Tranque or Thrasneck."

Blasdel nodded sagely. "The emigrants are putting their luck to the test. Should King Kragen chance to be waiting in the east tomorrow morning and should he spy the flotilla, his wrath might well be excited, to the detriment of the expedition."

"And where," inquired Berwick, "was King Kragen at last notification?"

Barquan Blasdel knit his brows. "I believe I noted a hoodwink message to the effect that he was seen cruising in a westerly direction to the south of Maudelinda Float, toward Bickle. I might well have misread the flicker, I only noted the configuration from the corner of my eye—but such was my understanding."

"Excellent," declared Berwick. "This is good news. The emigrants should make their departure safely and without interference."

"So we hope," said Blasdel. "King Kragen of course is subject to unpredictable whims and quirks."

Berwick made a confidential sign. "Sometimes—so it is rumored—he responds to signals transmitted in some mysterious manner by the Intercessors. Tell me, Barquan Blasdel, is this the case? We are both notables and together share responsibility for the welfare of Apprise Float. Is it true then that the Intercessors communicate with King Kragen, as has been alleged?"

"Now then, Arbiter Berwick," said Blasdel, "this is hardly a pertinent question. Should I answer yes, then I would be divulging a craft secret. Should I answer no, then it would seem that we Intercessors boast of nonexistent capabilities. So you must satisfy yourself with those hypotheses which seem the most profitable."

"Fairly answered," said Phyral Berwick. "However—and in the strictest confidence—I will report to you an amusing circumstance. As you know, at the convocation I declared myself for the party of Sklar Hast. Subsequently I was accepted into their most intimate counsels. I can inform you with authority—but first, you will assure me of your silence? As under no circumstances would I betray Sklar Hast or compromise the expedition."

"Certainly, indeed; my lips are sealed as with fourteen-year-old varnish."

"Well then, I accept you at your word. This is Sklar Hast's amusing tactic: he has arranged that a group of influential Intercessors shall accompany the group. If all goes well, the

Intercessors live. If not, like all the rest, they are crushed in the mandibles of King Kragen." And Phyral Berwick, standing back, watched Barquan Blasdel with an attentive gaze. "What do you make of that?"

Blasdel stood rigid, fingering his fringe of black beard. He darted a quick glance toward Berwick. "Which Intercessors are to be kidnapped?"

"Aha," said Berwick. "That, like the response of the question I put to you, is in the nature of a craft secret. I doubt if lesser men will be troubled, but if I were Intercessor for Aumerge, or Sumber, or Quatrefoil, or even Apprise, I believe that I might have cause for caution."

Blasdel stared at Berwick with mingled suspicion and uneasiness. "Do you take this means to warn me? If so, I would thank you to speak less ambiguously. Personally I fear no such attack. Within a hundred feet are three stalwarts, testing my daughters for marriage. A loud call would bring instant help from the float, which is scarcely a stone's throw beyond the garden."

Berwick nodded sagely. "It seems then that you are utterly secure."

"Still, I must hurry to the float," said Blasdel. "I am expected at a conference, and the evening grows no younger."

Berwick bowed and stood aside. "You will naturally remember to reveal nothing of what I told you, to vouchsafe no oblique warning, to hint nothing of the matter—in fact to make no reference to it whatever."

Blasdel considered. "I will say nothing beyond my original intention, to the effect that the villain Sklar Hast obviously knows no moderation, and that it behooves all notables and craft masters to guard themsleves against some form of final vegeance."

Berwick paused. "I hardly think you need go quite so far. Perhaps you could phrase it somewhat differently. In this wise: Sklar Hast and his sturdy band take their leave in the morning; now is the last chance for persons so inclined to cast in their lot with the group; however, you hope that all Intercessors will remain at their posts."

"Pah," cried Barquan Blasdel indignantly. "That conveys

no sense of imminence. I will say, Sklar Hast is desperate; should he decide to take hostages, his diseased mind would select Intercessors as the most appropriate persons.''

Berwick made a firm dissent. ''This, I believe, transcends the line I have drawn. My honor is at stake and I can agree to no announcement which baldly states the certainty as a probability.If you choose to make a jocular reference, or perhaps urge that not too many Intercessors join the expedition, then all is well: a subtle germ of suspicion has been planted, you have done your duty and my honor has not been compromised.''

''Yes, yes,'' cried Blasdel, ''I agree to anything. But I must hurry to the hoodwink tower. While we quibble Sklar Hast and his bandits are kidnaping Intercessors.''

''And what is the harm there?'' inquired Berwick mildly. ''You state that King Kragen has been observed from Maudelinda Float proceeding to the west; hence the Intercessors are in no danger, and presumably will be allowed to return once Sklar Hast is assured that King Kragen is no longer a danger. Conversely, if the Intercessors have betrayed Sklar Hast and given information to King Kragen so that he waits off Sciona Float, then they deserve to die with the rest. It is justice of the most precise and exquisite balance.''

''That is the difficulty,'' muttered Blasdel, trying to push past Berwick to the door. ''I cannot answer for the silence of the other Intercessors. Suppose one among them has notified King Kragen? Then a great tragedy ensues.''

''Interesting! So you can indeed summon King Kragen when you so desire?''

''Yes, yes, but, mind you, this is a secret. And now—''

''It follows then that you always know the whereabouts of King Kragen. How do you achieve this?''

''There is no time to explain; suffice it to say that a means is at hand.''

''Right here? In your workroom?''

''Yes indeed. Now stand aside. After I have broadcast the warning I will make all clear. Stand aside then!''

Berwick shrugged and allowed Blasdel to run from the cottage, through the garden to the edge of the pad.

Blasdel stopped short at the water's edge. The coracle had disappeared. Where previously Apprise Float had raised its foliage and its great hoodwink tower against the dusk, there was now only blank water and blank sky. The pad floated free; urged by the west wind of evening it already had left Apprise Float behind.

Blasdel gave an inarticulate cry of fury and woe. He turned to find Berwick standing behind him. "What has happened?"

"It seems that while we talked, divers cut through the stem of your pad. At least this is my presumption."

"Yes, yes," grated Blasdel. "So much is obvious. What else?"

Berwick shrugged. "It appears that willy-nilly, whether we like it or not, we are part of the great emigration. Now that such is the case I am relieved to know that you have a means to determine the whereabouts of King Kragen. Come. Let us make use of this device and reassure ourselves."

Blasdel made a guttural sound deep in his throat. He crouched and for a moment appeared on the point of hurling himself at Phyral Berwick. From the shadows of the verdure appeared another man. Berwick pointed. "I believe Sklar Hast himself is at hand."

"You tricked me," groaned Barquan Blasdel between clenched teeth. "You have performed an infamous act, which you shall regret."

"I have done no such deed, although it appears that you may well have misunderstood my position. Still, the time for recrimination is over. We share a similar problem, which is how to escape the malevolence of King Kragen. I suggest that you now proceed to locate him."

Without a word Blasdel turned, proceeded to his cottage. He entered the main room, with Berwick and Sklar Hast close behind. He crossed to the wall, lifted a panel to reveal an inner room. He brought more lights; all entered. A hole had been cut in the floor, and through the pad, the spongy tissue having been painted with a black varnish to prevent its growing together. A tube fashioned from fine yellow stalk perhaps four inches in diameter led down into the water. "At the bottom," said Blasdel curtly, "is a carefully devised horn, of exact shape and quality. The end is four feet in diameter and covered with a diaphragm of seasoned and varnished pad-skin. King Kragen emits a sound to which this horn is sensitive." He went to the tube, put down his ear, listened, slowly turned the tube around a vertical axis. He shook his head. "I hear nothing. This means that King Kragen is at least ten miles distant. If he is closer I can detect him. He passed to the east early today; presumably he swims somewhere near Sumber, or Adelvine."

Sklar Hast laughed quietly. "Urged there by the Intercessors?"

Blasdel shrugged sourly. "As to that I have nothing to say."

"How then do you summon King Kragen?"

Blasdel pointed to a rod rising from the floor, the top of which terminated in a crank. "In the water below is a drum. Inside this drum fits a wheel. When the crank is turned, the wheel, working in resin, rubs against the drum and emits a signal. King Kragen can sense this sound from a great distance—once again about ten miles. When he is needed, at say Bickle Float, the Intercessor at Aumerge calls him, until the horn reveals him to be four or five miles distant, whereupon the Intercessor at Paisley calls him a few miles, then the Maudelinda Intercessor, and so forth until he is within range of the Intercessor at Bickle Float."

Sklar Hast nodded. "I see. In this fashion Semon Voidenvo called King Kragen to Tranque. Whereupon King Kragen destroyed Tranque Float and killed forty-three persons."

"That is the case."

Sklar Hast turned away. Phyral Berwick told Blasdel, "I believe that Semon Voidenvo is one of the Intercessors who are accompanying the emigration. His lot may not be a happy one."

"This is unreasonable," Barquan Blasdel declared heatedly." He was as faithful to his convictions as Sklar Hast is to his own. After all, Voidenvo did not enjoy the devastation of Tranque Float. It is his home. Many of those killed were his friends. But he gives his faith and trust to King Kragen."

Sklar Hast swung around. "And you?"

Blasdel shook his head. "Not with such wholeheartedness."

Sklar Hast looked toward Berwick. "What should we do with this apparatus? Destroy it? Or preserve it?"

Berwick considered. "We might on some occasion wish to listen for King Kragen. I doubt if we ever will desire to summon him."

Sklar Hast gave a sardonic jerk of the head. "Who knows? To his death perhaps." He turned to Blasdel. "What persons are aboard the pad in addition to us?"

"My spouse—in the cottage two roofs along. Three young daughters who weave ornaments for the Star-cursing Festival. Three older daughters are attempting to prove themselves to three stalwarts who test them for wives. All are unaware that their home floats out on the deep ocean. None wish to become emigrants to a strange line of floats."

Sklar Hast said, "No more were any of the rest of us—until we were forced to choose. I feel no pity for them, or for you. Undoubtedly there will be ample work for all hands. Indeed, we may formulate a new guild: the Kragen-killers. If rumor is accurate, they infest the ocean."

He left the room, went out into the night. Blasdel cast a wry look at Phyral Berwick, went to listen once more at the detecting horn. Then he likewise left the room. Berwick followed, and lowered the panel. Both joined Sklar Hast at the edge of the pad, where now several coracles were tied. A dozen men stood in the garden. Sklar Hast turned to Blasdel. "Summon your spouse, your daughters and those who test them. Explain the circumstances, and gather your belongings. The evening breeze will soon die and we cannot tow the pad."

Blasdel departed, accompanied by Berwick. Sklar Hast and the others entered the workroom, carried everything of value or utility to the coracles, including the small metal relict, the Books of Dicta, the listening horn and the summoning drum. Then all embarked in the coracles, and Barquan Blasdel's beautiful pad was left to drift solitary upon the ocean.

# CHAPTER IV

Morning came to the ocean and with it the breeze from the west. The floats could no longer be seen; the ocean was a blue mirror in all directions. Sklar Hast lowered Blasdel's horn into the water, listened. Nothing could be heard. Barquan Blasdel did the same and agreed that King Kragen was nowhere near.

There were perhaps six hundred coracles in the flotilla, each carrying from four to eight persons, with as much gear, household equipment and tools as possible, together with sacks of food and water.

Late in the afternoon they noted a few medium-sized floats to the north, but made no attempt to land. King Kragen was yet too near at hand.

The late afternoon breeze arose. Rude sails were rigged and the oarsmen rested. At dusk Sklar Hast ordered all the coracles connected by lines to minimize the risk of separation. When the breeze died and seas reflected the dazzling stars, the sails were brought down and all slept.

The following day was like the first, and also the day after. On the morning of the fourth day a line of splendid floats appeared ahead, easily as large and as rich of foliage as those they had left. Sklar Hast would have preferred to sail on another week, but the folk among the coracles were fervent in their rejoicing, and he clearly would have encountered near-unanimous opposition. So the flotilla landed upon three closely adjoining floats, drove stakes into the pad surface, tethered the coracles.

Sklar Hast called an informal convocation. "In a year or two," he said, "we can live lives as comfortable as those we left behind us. But this is not enough. We left our homes because of King Kragen, who is now our deadly enemy. We shall never rest secure until we find a means to make ourselves supreme over all the kragen. To this purpose we must live different lives than we did in the old days—until King Kragen is killed. How to kill King Kragen? I wish I knew. He is a monster, impregnable to any weapon we now can use against him. So this must be our primary goal: weapons against King Kragen." Sklar Hast paused, looked around the somber group. "This is my personal feeling. I have no authority over any of you, beyond that of the immediate circumstances, which are transient. You have a right to discredit me, to think differently—in which case I will muster those who feel as I do, and sail on to still another float, where we can dedicate ourselves to the killing of King Kragen. If we are all agreed, that our souls are not our own until King Kragen is dead, then we must formalize this feeling. Authority must be given to some person or group of persons. Responsibilities must be delegated; work must be organized. As you see I envision a life different to the old. It will be harder in some respects, easier in others. First of all, we need not feed King Kragen. . . ."

A committee of seven members was chosen, to serve as a temporary governing body until the needs of the new community required a more elaborate system. As a matter of course Sklar Hast was named to the committee, as well as Phyral Berwick, who became the first chairman, and also Meth Cagno the Scrivener. The captured Intercessors sat aside in a sullen group and took no part in the proceedings.

The committee met for an hour, and as its first measure, ordained a census, that each man's caste and craft might be noted.

After the meeting Meth Cagno took Sklar Hast aside. "When you captured Barquan Blasdel, you brought his books."

"True."

"I have been examining these books. They are a set of the Ancient Dicta."

"So I understand."

"This is a source of great satisfaction to me. No one except the Scrivener reads the Dicta nowadays, though everyone professes familiarity. As the generations proceed, the lives of our ancestors and the fantastic environment from which they came seem more like myth than reality.''

"I suppose this is true enough. I am a Hoodwink by trade and only know Hoodwink configurations. The Dicta are written in ancient calligraph, which puzzles me.''

"It is difficult to read, that I grant," said Cagno. "However, a patient examination of the Dicta can be profitable. Each volume represents the knowledge of one of our ancestors, to the extent that he was able to organize it. There is also a great deal of repetition and dullness; our ancestors, whatever their talents, had a few literary skills. Some are vainglorious and devote pages to self-encomium. Others are anxious to explain in voluminous detail the vicissitudes which led to their presence on the Ship of Space. They seem to have been a very mixed group, from various levels of society. There are hints here and there which I, for one, do not understand. Some describe the Home World as a place of maniacs. Others seem to have held respected places in this society until, as they explain it, the persons in authority turned on them and instituted a savage persecution, ending, as we know, in our ancestors seizing control of the Ship of Space and fleeing to this planet.''

"It is all very confusing," said Sklar Hast, "and none of it seems to have much contemporary application. For instance, they do not tell us how they boiled varnish on the Home World, or how they propelled their coracles. Do creatures like the kragen infest the Home World? If so, how do the Home Folk deal with them? Do they kill them or feed them sponges? Our ancestors are silent on these points.''

Meth Cagno shrugged. "Evidently they were not overly concerned, or they would have dealt with these matters at length. But I agree that there is much they fail to make clear. As in our own case, the various castes seemed trained to explicit trades. Especially interesting are the memoirs of James Brunet. His caste, that of Counterfeiter, is now extinct among us. Most of his Dicta are rather conventional exhortations to virtue, but toward the middle of the book he says this.'' Here Cagno opened a book and read:

" 'To those who follow us, to our children and grandchildren, we can leave no tangible objects of value. We brought nothing to the world but ourselves and the wreckage of our lives. We will undoubtedly die here—a fate probably preferable to New Ossining, but by no means the destiny any of us had planned for ourselves. There is no way to escape. Of the entire group I alone have a technical education, most of which I have forgotten. And to what end could I turn it? This is a soft world. It consists of ocean and seaweed. There is land nowhere. To escape—even if we had the craft to build a new ship, which we do not—we need metal and metal there is none. Even to broadcast a radio signal we need metal. None. . . . No clay to make pottery, no silica for glass, no limestone for concrete, no ore from which to smelt metal. Presumably the ocean carries various salts, but how to extract the metal without electricity? There is iron in our blood: how to extract it? A strange helpless sensation to live on this world where the hardest substance is our own bone! We have, during our lives, taken so many things for granted, and now it seems that no one can evoke something from nothing. . . . This is a problem on which I must think. An ingenious man can work wonders, and I, a successful counterfeiter—or, rather, almost successful—am certainly ingenious.' "

Meth Cagno paused in his reading. "This is the end of the chapter."

"He seems to be a man of no great force," mused Sklar Hast. "It is true that metal can be found nowhere." He took the bit of metal from his pocket which had once graced the workroom of Barquan Blasdel. "This is obdurate stuff indeed, and perhaps it is what we need to kill King Kragen."

Meth Cagno returned to the book. "He writes his next chapter after a lapse of months:

" 'I have considered the matter at length. But before I proceed I must provide as best I can a picture of the way the universe works, for it is clear that none of my colleagues are in any position to do so, excellent fellows though they are. Please do not suspect me of whimsy: our personalities and social worth undoubtedly vary with the context in which we live.' "

Here Cagno looked up. "I don't completely understand his

meaning here. But I suppose that the matter is unimportant.'' He turned the pages. "He now goes into an elaborate set of theorizations regarding the nature of the world, which, I confess, I don't understand. There is small consistency to his beliefs. Either he knows nothing, or is confused, or the world essentially is inconsistent. He claims that all matter is composed of less than a hundred 'elements,' joined together in 'compounds.' The elements are constructed of smaller entities: 'electrons,' 'protons,' 'neutrons,' which are not necessarily matter, but forces. depending on your point of view. When electrons move the result is an electric current: a substance or condition—he is not clear here—of great energy and many capabilities. Too much electricity is fatal; in smaller quantities we use it to control our bodies. According to Brunet all sorts of remarkable things can be achieved with electricity.''

"Let us provide ourselves an electric current then,'' said Sklar Hast. "This may become our weapon against the kragen.''

"The matter is not so simple. In the first place the electricity must be channeled through metal wires.''

"Here is metal,'' said Sklar Hast, tossing to Meth Cagno the bit of metal he had taken from Blasdel, "though it is hardly likely to be enough.''

"The electricity must also be generated,'' said Cagno, "which on the Home Planet seems to be a complicated process, requiring a great deal of metal.''

"Then how do we get metal?''

"On other planets there seems to be no problem. Ore is refined and shaped into a great variety of tools. Here we have no ore. In other cases, metals are extracted from the sea, once again using electricity.''

"Hmph,'' said Sklar Hast. "To procure metal, one needs electricity. To obtain the electricity, metal is required. It seems a closed circle, into which we are unable to break.''

Cagno made a dubious face. "It may well be. Brunet mentions various means to generate electricity. There is the 'voltaic cell'—in which two metals are immersed in acid, and he describes a means to generate the acid, using water, brine, and electricity. Then there is thermo-electricity, photoelectricity, chemical electricity, electricity produced by the Rous effect, electricity generated by moving a wire near another wire in which electricity flows. He states that all living creatures produce small quantities of electricity.''

"Electricity seems rather a difficult substance to obtain," mused Sklar Hast. "Are there no simple methods to secure metal?"

"Brunet mentions that blood contains a small quantity of iron. He suggests a method for extracting it, by using a high degree of heat. But he also points out that there is at hand no substance capable of serving as a receptacle under such extremes of heat. He states that on the Home World many plants concentrate metallic compounds, and suggests that certain of the sea-plants might do the same. But again either heat or electricity are needed to secure the pure metal."

Sklar Hast ruminated. "Our first and basic problem, as I see it, is self-protection. In short, we need a weapon to kill King Kragen. It might be a device of metal—or it might be a larger and more savage kragen, if such exist. . . ." He considered. "Perhaps you should make production of metal and electricity your goal, and let no other pursuits distract you. I am sure that the council will agree, and put at your disposal such helpers as you may need."

"I would gladly do my best."

"And I," said Sklar Hast, "I will reflect upon the kragen."

Three days later the first kragen was seen, a beast of not inconsiderable size, perhaps twenty feet in length. It came cruising along the edge of the float, and observing the men, stopped short and for twenty minutes floated placidly, swirling water back and forth with its vanes. Then slowly it swung about and continued along the line of floats.

By this time a large quantity of stalk and withe had been cut, scraped and racked, as well as a heap of root-wisp, to cure during the rigging of a ropewalk. A week later the new rope was being woven into net.

Two large pads were cut from the side of the float, stripped of rib-trussing, upper and lower membrane, then set adrift. The space thus opened would become a lagoon. Over the severed stalks sleeves were fitted with one end above water; the sap presently exuding would be removed, boiled and aged for varnish and glue. Meanwhile arbors were constructed, seeded with sponge-floss, and lowered into the lagoon. When the withe had cured, hut frames were constructed, pad membrane stretched over the mesh and daubed inside and out with varnish.

In a month the community had achieved a rude measure of comfort. On four occasions a kragen had passed by, and the fourth occurrence seemed to be a return visit of the first. On this fourth visit the kragen paused, inspected the lagoon with care. It tentatively nudged the net, backed away and presently floated off.

Sklar Hast watched the occurrence, went to inspect the new-cut stalk, which now was sufficiently cured. He laid out a pattern and work began. First a wide base was built near the mouth of the lagoon, with a substructure extending down to the main stem of the float. On this base was erected an A-frame derrick of glued withe, seventy feet tall, with integral braces, the entire structure whipped tightly with strong line and varnished. Another identical derrick was built to overhang the ocean. Before either of the derricks were completed a small kragen broke through the net to feast upon the yet unripe sponges. Sklar Hast laughed grimly at the incident. "At your next visit, you will not fare so well," he called to the beast. "May the sponges rot in your stomach!"

The kragen swam lazily off down the line of floats, unperturbed by the threat. It returned two days later. This time the derricks were guyed and in place, but not yet fitted with tackle. Again Sklar Hast reviled the beast, which this time ate with greater fastidiousness, plucking only those sponges which like popcorn had overgrown their husks. The men worked far into the night installing the strut which, when the derrick tilted out over the water, thrust high the topping-halyard to provide greater leverage.

On the next day the kragen returned, and entered the lagoon with insulting assurance: a beast somewhat smaller than that which Sklar Hast had captured on Tranque Float, but nonetheless a creature of respectable size. Standing on the float, a stalwart old Swindler flung a noose around the creature's turret, and on the pad a line of fifty men marched away with a heavy rope. The astonished kragen was towed to the outward leaning derrick, swung up and in. The dangling vanes were lashed; it was lowered to the float. As soon as the bulk collapsed the watching folk, crying out in glee, shoved forward, almost dancing into the gnashing mandibles. "Back, fools!" roared Sklar Hast. "Do you want to be cut in half? Back!" He was largely ignored. A dozen chisels hacked at the horny hide; clubs battered at the eyes. "Back!" raged Sklar Hast. "Back! What do you achieve by antics such as this? Back!" Daunted, the vengeful folk moved aside. Sklar Hast took chisel and mallet and as he had done on Tranque Float, cut at the membrane joining dome to turret. He was joined by four others; the channel was swiftly cut and a dozen hands ripped away the dome. Again, with pitiless outcry, the crowd surged forward. Sklar Hast's efforts to halt them were fruitless. The nerves and cords of the creature's ganglionic center were torn from the turret, while the kragen jerked and fluttered and made a buzzing sound with its mandibles. The turret was plucked clean of the wet-string fibers as well as other organs, and the kragen lay limp. Sklar Hast moved away in disgust. Another member of the Seven, Nicklas Rile, stepped forward: "Halt now—no more senseless hacking! If the kragen has bones harder than our own, we will want to preserve them for use. Who knows what use can be made of a kragen's cadaver? The hide is tough; the mandibles are harder than the deepest stalk. Let us proceed intelligently!"

Sklar Hast watched from a little distance as the crowd examined the dead beast. He had no further interest in the kragen. A planned experiment had been foiled almost as soon as the hate-driven mob had rushed forward. But there would be more kragen for his derricks; hopefully they could be noosed by the sea-derrick before they broke into the lagoon. In years to come, strongboats or barges equipped with derricks might even go forth to hunt the kragen. . . . He approached the kragen once again, peered into the empty turret, where now welled a viscous milky blue fluid. James Brunet, in his Dicta, had asserted that the metal iron was a constituent of human blood; conceivably other metals or metallic compounds might be discovered in the blood of a kragen. He found Meth Cagno, who had been watching from a dignified distance, and communicated his hypothesis. Cagno made no dissent. "It may well be the case. Our basic problem, however, remains as before: separating the metal from the dross."

"You have no idea how to proceed?"

Meth Cagno smiled slightly. "I have one or two ideas. In fact, tomorrow, at noon precisely, we will test one of these ideas."

The following day, an hour before noon. Sklar Hast rowed to the isolated pad on which Meth Cagno had established his workshop. Cagno himself was hard at work on an intricate contrivance whose purpose Sklar Hast could not fathom. A rectangular frame of stalk rose ten feet in the air, supporting a six-foot hoop of woven withe in a plane parallel to the surface of the float. To the hoop was glued a rather large sheet of pad-skin, which had been scraped, rubbed and oiled until it was almost transparent. Below Meth Cagno was arranging a box containing ashes. As Sklar Hast watched, he mixed in a quantity of water and some gum, enough to make a gray dough, which he worked with his fingers and knuckles, to leave a saucer-shaped depression.

The sun neared the zenith; Cagno signaled two of his helpers. One climbed up the staging; the other passed up buckets of water. The first poured these upon the transparent membrane, which sagged under the weight.

Sklar Hast watched silently, giving no voice to his perplexity. The membrane, now brimming, seemed to bulge perilously. Meth Cagno, satisfied with his arrangements, joined Sklar Hast. "You are puzzled by this device; nevertheless it is very simple. You own a telescope?"

"I do. An adequately good instrument, though the gum is clouded."

"The purest and most highly refined gum discolors, and even with the most careful craftsmanship, lenses formed of gum yield distorted images, of poor magnification. On the

Home World, according to Brunet, lenses are formed of a material called 'glass.' "

The sun reached the zenith; Sklar Hast's attention was caught by a peculiar occurrence in the box of damp ash. A white-hot spot had appeared; the ash began to hiss and smoke. He drew near in wonderment. "Glass would seem to be a useful material," Meth Cagno was saying. "Brunet describes it as a mixture of substances occuring in ash together with a compound called 'silica' which is found in ash but also occurs in the husks of sea-ooze: 'plankton,' so Brunet calls it. Here I have mixed ash and sea-ooze; I have constructed a water-lens to condense sunlight, I am trying to make glass. . . ." He peered into the box, then lifted it a trifle, bringing the image of the sun to its sharpest focus. The ash glowed red, orange, yellow; suddenly it seemed to slump. With a rod Cagno pushed more ash into the center, until the wooden box gave off smoke, whereupon Cagno pulled it aside, and gazed anxiously at the molten matter in the center. "Something has happened; exactly what we will determine when the stuff is cool." He turned to his bench, brought forward another box, this half-full of powdered charcoal. In a center depression rested a cake of black-brown paste.

"And what do you have there?" asked Sklar Hast, already marveling at Cagno's ingenuity.

"Dried blood. I and my men have drained ourselves pale. Brunet reveals that blood contains iron. Now I will try to burn away the various unstable fluids and oozes, to discover what remains. I hope to find unyielding iron." Cagno thrust the box under the lens. The dried blood smoldered and smoked, then burst into a reeking flame which gave off a nauseous odor. Cagno squinted up at the sun. "The lens burns well only when the sun is overhead, so our time is necessarily limited."

"Rather than water, transparent gum might be used, which then would harden, and the sun could be followed across the sky."

"Unfortunately no gum is so clear as water," said Cagno regretfully. "Candle-plant sap is yellow. Bindlebane seep holds a blue fog."

"What if the two were mixed, so that the blue defeated the yellow? And then the two might be filtered and boiled. Or perhaps water can be coagulated with tincture of bone."

Cagno assented. "Possibly feasible, both."

They turned to watch the blood, now a glowing sponge which tumbled into cinders and then, apparently consumed, vanished upon the surface of the blazing charcoal. Cagno snatched the crucible out from under the lens. "Your blood seems not over-rich," Sklar Hast noted critically. "It might be wise to tap Barquan Blasdel and the other Intercessors; they appear a hearty lot."

Cagno clapped a cover upon the box. "We will know better when the charcoal goes black." He went to his bench, brought back another box. In powdered charcoal stood another tablet, this of black paste. "And what substance is this?" inquired Sklar Hast.

"This," said Meth Cagno, "is kragen blood, which we boiled last night. If man's blood carries iron, what will kragen blood yield? Now we discover." He thrust it under the lens. Like the human blood it began to smolder and burn, discharging a smoke even more vile than before. Gradually the tablet flaked and tumbled to the surface of the charcoal; as before Cagno removed it and covered it with a lid. Going to his first box, he prodded among the cinders with a bit of sharp bone, scooped out a congealed puddle of fused material which he laid on the bench. "Glass. Beware. It is yet hot."

Sklar Hast, using two pieces of bone, lifted the object. "So this is glass. Hmm. It hardly seems suitable for use as a telescope lens. But it may well prove useful otherwise. It seems dense and hard—indeed, almost metallic."

Cagno shook his head in deprecation. "I had hoped for greater transparency. There are probably numerous impurities in the ash and sea-ooze. Perhaps they can be removed by washing the ash or treating it with acid, or something of the sort."

"But to produce acid, electricity is necessary, or so you tell me."

"I merely quote Brunet."

"And electricity is impossible?"

Cagno pursed his lips. "That we will see. I have hopes. One might well think it impossible to generate electricity using only ash, wood, water and sea-stuff—but we shall see. Brunet offers a hint or two. But first, as to our iron. . . ."

The yield was small: a nodule of pitted gray metal half the size of a pea. "That bit represents three flasks of blood." Cagno remarked glumly. "If we bled every vein on the float we might win sufficient iron for a small pot."

"This is not intrinsically an unreasonable proposal," said Sklar Hast. "We can all afford a flask of blood, or two, or even more during the course of months. To think—we have produced metal entirely on our own resources!"

Cagno wryly inspected the iron nodule. "There is no problem to burning the blood under the lens. If every day ten of the folk come to be bled, eventually we will sink the pad under the accumulated weight of iron." He removed the lid from the third box. "But observe here! We have misused our curses! The kragen is by no means a creature to be despised!"

On the charcoal rested a small puddle of reddish-golden metal: three times as large as the iron nodule. "I presume this metal to be copper, or one of its alloys." said Cagno. "Brunet describes copper as a dark red metal, very useful for the purpose of conducting electricity."

Sklar Hast lifted the copper from the coals, tossed it back and forth till it was cool. "Metal everywhere! Nicklas Rile has been hacking apart the kragen for its bones. He is discarding the internal organs, which are black as snuff-flower. Perhaps they should also be burned under the lens."

"Convey them here, I will burn them. And then, after we burn the kragen's liver, or whatever the organ, we might attempt to burn snuff-flowers as well."

The kragen's internal organs yielded further copper. The snuff-flowers produced only a powder of whitish-yellow ash which Meth Cagno conscientiously stored in a tube labeled: *ash of snuff-flower*.

Four days later the largest of the kragen seen so far reappeared. It came swimming in from the west, paralleling the line of floats. A pair of Swindlers, returning to the float with a catch of gray-fish, were the first to spy the great black cylinder surmounted by its four-eyed turret. They bent to their oars, shouting the news ahead. A well-rehearsed plan now went into effect. A team of four young swindlers ran to a lightweight coracle, shoved off, paddled out to intercept the kragen. Behind the coracle trailed two ropes, each controlled by a gang of men. The kragen, lunging easily through the water, approached, swimming fifty yards off the float. The coracle eased forward, with one named Bade Beach going forward to stand on the gunwhales. The kragen halted the motion of its vanes, to drift and eye the coracle and the derricks with flint-eyed suspicion.

The two swindlers yet at the oars eased the coracle closer. Bade Beach stood tensely, twitching a noose, while the fourth man controlled the lines to the float. The kragen, contemptuous of attack, issued a few nonplussed clicks of the mandibles, twitched the tips of its vanes, creating four whirlpools. The coracle eased closer, to within a hundred feet, eighty—sixty feet. Bade Beach bent forward. The kragen decided to punish the men for their provocative actions and thrust sharply forward. When it was but thirty feet distant, Bade Beach tossed a noose toward the turret—and missed. From the float came groans of disappointment; one of the gangs hastily jerked the coracle back. The kragen swerved, turned, made a second furious charge which brought it momentarily to within five feet of the coracle, whereupon Bade Beach dropped the noose over its turret. From the float came a cheer; both gangs hauled on their lines, one snatching the coracle back to safety, the other tightening the noose and pulling the kragen aside, almost as it touched the coracle.

Thrashing and jerking, the kragen was dragged over to the sea-leaning derrick, and hoisted from the water in the same fashion as the first. This was a large beast: the derrick creaked, the float sagged; before the kragen heaved clear from the water sixty-five men were tugging on the end of the lift. The derrick tilted back, the kragen swung in over the float. The vanes were lashed, the beast lowered. Again the onlookers surged forward, laughing, shouting, but no longer exemplifying the fury with which they had attacked the first kragen.

At a distance a group of Intercessors watched with curled lips. They had not reconciled themselves to their new circumstances, and conscious of their status as the lowest of castes worked as little as possible. Chisels and mallets were plied against the kragen turret; the dome was pried loose, the nerve nodes destroyed. Fiber buckets were brought, the body fluids were scooped out and carried off to evaporation trays.

Sklar Hast had watched from the side. This had been a large beast—about the size of King Kragen when first he had approached the Old Floats, a hundred and fifty years previously. Since they had successfully dealt with this creature, they need have small fear of any other—except King Kragen. And Sklar Hast was forced to admit that the answer was not yet known. No derrick could hoist King Kragen from the water. No line could restrain the thrust of his vanes. No float could bear his weight. Compared to King Kragen, his dead hulk now being hacked apart was a pygmy. . . .

From behind came a rush of feet; a woman tugged at his elbow, gasping and gulping in the effort to catch her breath. Sklar Hast, scanning the float in startlement, could see nothing to occasion her distress. Finally she was able to blurt: "Barquan Blasdel has taken to the sea, Barquan Blasdel is gone!"

"What!" cried Sklar Hast.

The woman told her story. For various reasons, including squeamishness and pregnancy, she had absented herself from the killing of the kragen, and kept to her hut at the far side of the float. Seated at her loom she observed a man loading bags into a coracle, but preoccupied with her own concerns she paid him little heed, and presently arose to the preparation of the evening meal. As she kneaded the pulp from which the breadstuff known as pangolay was baked, it came to her that the man's actions had been noticeably furtive. Why had he not participated in the killing of the kragen? The man she had seen was Barquan Blasdel! The implications of the situation stunned her for a moment. Wiping her hands, she went to the hut where Blasdel and his spouse were quartered, to find no one at home. It was still possible that she was mistaken; Blasdel might even now be watching the killing of the kragen.

So she hurried across the float to investigate. But on the way the conviction hardened: the man indeed had been Barquan Blasdel, and she had sought out Sklar Hast with the information.

From the first Barquan Blasdel had made no pretense of satisfaction with his altered circumstances. His former rank counted nothing, in fact aroused antagonism among his float-fellows. Barquan Blasdel grudgingly adapted himself to his new life, building sponge arbors and scraping withe. His spouse, who on Apprise Float had commanded a corps of four maidens and three garden-men, at first rebelled when Blasdel required her to bake pangolay and core sponges "like any low-caste slut," as she put it, but finally she surrendered to the protests of her empty stomach. Her daughters adopted themselves with better grace, and indeed the four youngest participated with great glee at the slaughter of the kragen. The remaining two stayed in the background, eyebrows raised disdainfully at the vulgar fervor of their sisters.

Barquan Blasdel, his spouse, his two older daughters and their lovers were missing, as was a sturdy six-man coracle together with considerable stores. Sklar Hast dispatched four coracles in pursuit, but evening had brought the west wind, and there was no way of determining whether Blasdel had paddled directly east, or had taken refuge in the jungle of floats at the eastern edge of the chain, where he could hide indefinitely.

The coracles returned to report no sign of the fugitives. The Council of Seven gathered to consider the situation. "Our mistake was leniency," complained Robin Magram, a gnarled and weather-beaten old Swindler. "These Intercessors—Barquan Blasdel and all the rest—are our enemies. We should have made a complete job of it, and strangled them. Our qualms have cost us our security."

"Perhaps," said Sklar Hast. "But I for one cannot bring myself to commit murder—even if such murder is in our best interest."

"These other Intercessors now—" Margram jerked his thumb to a group of huts near the central pinion "—what of them? Each wishes us evil. Each is now planning the same despicable act as that undertaken by Barquan Blasdel and his spouse. I feel that they should be killed at once—quietly, without malice, but with finality."

His proposal met no great enthusiasm. Arrel Sincere, a Bezzler of complete conviction and perhaps the most caste-conscious man on the float, said glumly, "What good do we achieve? If Barquan Blasdel returns to the Old Floats, our refuge is known and we must expect inimical actions."

"Not necessarily," contended Meth Cagno. "The folk of the Old Floats gain nothing by attacking us."

Sklar Hast made a pessimistic dissent. "We have escaped King Kragen, we acknowledge no overlord. Misery brings jealousy and resentment. The Intercessors can whip them to a sullen fury." He pitched his voice in a nasal falsetto. " 'Those insolent fugitives! How dare they scamp their responsibility to noble King Kragen? How dare they perform such bestial outrages against the lesser kragen? Everyone aboard the cora-cles! We go to punish the iconoclasts!' "

"Possibly correct," said Meth Cagno. "But the Interces-sors are by no means the most influential folk of the Floats. The Arbiters will hardly agree to any such schemes."

"In essence," said Phyral Berwick, "we have no informa-tion. We speculate in a void. In fact Barquan Blasdel may lose himself on the ocean and never return to the Old Floats. He may be greeted with apathy or with excitement. We talk without knowledge. It seems to me that we should take steps to inform ourselves as to the true state of affairs: in short, that we send spies to derive this information for us."

Phyral Berwick's proposal ultimately became the decision of the Seven. They also ordained that the remaining Intercessors be guarded more carefully, until it was definitely learned whether or not Barquan Blasdel had returned to the Old Floats. If such were the case the location of the New Floats was no longer a secret, and the concensus was that the remaining Intercessors should likewise be allowed to return, should they choose to do so. Nicklas Rile considered the decision soft-headed. "Do you think they would warrant us like treatment in a similar situation? Remember, they planned that King Kragen should waylay us!''

''True enough,'' said Arrel Sincere wearily, ''but what of that? We can either kill them, hold them under guard, or let them go their ways, the last option being the least taxing and the most honorable.''

Nicklas Rile made no further protest, and the council then concerned itself with the details of the projected spy operation. None of the coracles at hand were considered suitable, and it was decided to build a coracle of special design—long, light, low to the water, with two sails of fine weave to catch every whisper of wind. Three men were named to the operation, all originally of Almack Float, a small community far to the east, in fact next to Sconia, the end of the chain. None of the three men had acquaintance on Apprise and so stood minimal chances of being recognized.

The coracle was built at once. A light keel of laminated and glued withe was shaped around pegs; ribs were bent and lashed into place; diagonal ribs were attached to these, then the whole frame was covered with four layers of varnished pad-skin.

At midmorning of the fourth day after Barquan Blasdel's flight, the coracle, which was almost a canoe, departed to the east, riding easily and swiftly over the sunny blue water. For three hours it slid along the line of floats, each an islet bedecked in blue, green and purple verdure, surmounted by the arching fronds of prime plant, each surrounded by its constellation of smaller pads. The coracle reached the final float of the group and struck out east across the water. Water swirled and sparkled behind the long oars; the men in their short-sleeved white smocks working easily. Afternoon waned; the rain clouds formed and came scudding with black brooms hanging below. After the rain came sunset, making a glorious display among the broken clouds. The breeze began to blow from the west; the three men crouched and rowed with only sufficient force to maintain headway. Then came the mauve dusk with the constellations appearing and then night with the stars blazing down on the glossy black water. The men took turns sleeping, and the night passed. Before dawn the favoring wind rose; the sails were set, the coracle bubbled ahead, with a chuckling of bow-wave and wake. The second day was like the first. Just before dawn of the third day the men lowered the horn into the water and listened.

Silence.

The men stood erect, looked into the west. Allowing for the increased speed of their passage, Tranque Float should be near at hand. But nothing could be seen but the blank horizons.

The dawn wind came; the sails were set, the coracle surged west. At noon the men, increasingly dubious, ceased paddling, and once more searched the horizons carefully. As before there was nothing visible save the line dividing dark blue from bright blue. The floats by now should be well within sight. Had they veered too far north or too far south?

The men deliberated, and decided that while their own course had generally been true west, the original direction of flight might have been something south of east: hence the floats in all probability lay behind the northern horizon. They agreed to paddle four hours to the north, then if nothing were seen, to return to the south.

Toward the waning of afternoon, with the rain-clouds piling up, far smudges showed themselves. Now they halted, lowered the horn, to hear *crunch crunch crunch*, with startling loudness. The men twisted the tube, to detect the direction of the sound. It issued from the north. Crouching low they listened, ready to paddle hastily away if the sound grew louder. But it seemed to lessen and the direction veered to the east. Presently it died to near inaudibility, and the men proceeded.

The floats took on substance, extending both east and west; soon the characteristic profiles could be discerned, and then the hoodwink towers. Dead ahead was Aumerge, with Apprise Float yet to the west.

So they paddled up the chain, the floats with familiar and beloved names drifting past, floats where their ancestors had lived and died: Aumerge, Quincunx, Fay, Hastings, Quatrefoil, with its curious cloverleaf configuration, and then the little outer group, the Bandings, and beyond, after a gap of a mile, Apprise Float.

The sun set, the hoodwink towers began to flicker, but the configurations could not be read. The men paddled the coracle toward Apprise. Verdure bulked up into the sky; the sounds and odors of the Old Floats wafted across the water, inflicting nostalgic pangs upon each of the men. They landed in a secluded little cove which had been described to them by Phyral Berwick, covered the coracle with leaves and rubbish. According to the plan, two remained by the coracle, while the third, one Henry Bastaff, moved across the float toward the central common and Apprise Market.

Hundreds of people were abroad on this pleasant evening, but Henry Bastaff thought their mood to be weary and even a trifle grim. He went to the ancient Apprise Inn, which claimed to be the oldest building of the floats: a long shed beamed with twisted oldstalks, reputedly cut at the astounding depth of three hundred feet. Within was a long bar of laminated strips, golden-brown with wax and use; shelves behind displayed jars and tubes of arrack, beer, and spirits of life, while buffets to each end offered various delicacies and sweet-meats. To the front wide eaves thatched with garwort frond and lit by yellow and red lanterns protected several dozen tables and benches where travelers rested and lovers kept rendezvous. Henry Bastaff seated himself where he could watch both the Apprise hoodwink tower and that of Quatre-foil to the east. The serving maid approached; he ordered beer and nut-wafers. As he drank and ate he listened to conversations at nearby tables and read the messages which flickered up and down the line of floats.

The conversations were uninformative; the hoodwink messages were the usual compendium of announcements, messages, banter. Then suddenly in midmessage came a blaze, all eighteen lights together, to signal news of great importance. Henry Bastaff sat up straight on the bench.

*"Important . . . information! This . . . afternoon . . . Apprise . . . Intercessor . . . Barquan Blasdel . . . kidnaped . . . by . . . the . . . rebels . . . returned . . . to . . . the . . .*

*Floats . . . with . . . his . . . spouse . . . and . . . several
. . . dependents. They . . . have . . . a . . . harrowing . . .
tale . . . to . . . tell. The . . . rebels . . . are . . . established
. . . on . . . a . . . float . . . to . . . the . . . east . . . where
. . . they . . . kill . . . kragen . . . with . . . merciless . . .
glee . . . and . . . plan . . . a . .. war . . . of . . . ex-
termination . . . upon . . . the . . . folk . . . of . . . the
. . . old . . . floats. Barquan Blasdel . . . escaped . . . and
. . . after . . . an . . . unnerving . . . voyage . . . across . . .
the . . . uncharted . . . ocean . . . late today . . . landed
. . . on . . . Green Lamp Float. He . . . has . . . called . . .
for . . . an . . . immediate . . . convocation . . . to . . .
consider . . . what . . . measures . . . to . . . take . . .
against . . . the . . . rebels . . . who . . . daily . . . wax . . .
in . . . arrogance.''*

# CHAPTER V

Four days later Henry Bastaff reported to the Seven. "Our
arrival was precarious, for our initial direction took us many
miles to the south of the Old Floats. Nevertheless we arrived.
Apparently Blasdel experienced even worse difficulties, for
he reached Green Lamp Float about the same time that we
landed on Apprise. I sat at the Old Tavern when the news
came, and I saw great excitement. The people seemed more
curious than vindictive, even somewhat wistful. A convocation was called for the following day. Since the folk of
Almack Float would attend, I thought it best that Maible and
Barway remain hidden. I stained my face, shaved eyebrows,
mustache and hair, and at the convocation looked eye to eye
with my Uncle Fodor the withe-peeler, who never gave a
second glance.

"The convocation was vehement and lengthy. Barquan
Blasdel resumed his rank of Apprise Intercessor. In my opin-

ion Vrink Smathe, who had succeeded to the post, found no joy in Blasdel's return.

"With great earnestness Blasdel called for a punitive expedition. He spoke of those who had departed as 'iconoclasts,' 'monsters,' 'vicious scum of the world, which it was the duty of all decent folk to expunge.'

"He aroused only lukewarm attention. No one showed heart for the project. The new Intercessors in particular were less than enthusiastic. Blasdel accused them of coveting their new posts, which they would lose if the old Intercessors returned. The new Intercessors refuted the argument with great dignity. 'Our concern is solely for the lives of men,' they said. 'What avail is there in destroying these folk? They are gone; good riddance. We shall maintain our ancient ways with more dedication because the dissidents have departed.'

"One of the new Intercessors had a crafty thought: 'Of course, if by some means we can direct King Kragen's attention to these fugitives, that is a different story.'

"Barquan Blasdel was forced to be content with this much. 'How can we do this?'

" 'By our usual means for summoning King Kragen: how else?'

"Blasdel agreed. 'It is necessary to hurry. These evil folk kill kragen and smelt metal from the blood. They plan mischief against us, and we must rebuff them with decisive severity.'

"There was further discussion, but no clear resolutions, which exasperated Barquan Blasdel. The convocation dissolved; we caught the evening wind to the east."

The Seven considered Henry Bastaff's report. "At least we are in no immediate peril," ruminated Robin Magram. "It appears that our surest guarantee of security is our custody of the old Intercessors, who would supersede the new officials if rescued. So here is a powerful deterrent against any large-scale attack."

"Still, we always must fear discovery by King Kragen," stated Sklar Hast. "King Kragen is our basic enemy; it is King Kragen whom we must destroy."

After a minute's silence Arrel Sincere said, "That, at the moment, is in the nature of a remote day-dream. In the meantime we must prepare for various contingencies, including demolishment by King Kragen of our new facilities. Also we must maintain a continued source of information: in short, spies must presently return to the Old Floats."

Henry Bastaff looked uncomfortably at his mates. "I will volunteer, for at least one more trip. Much effort and delay could be avoided if it were possible to sail with more assurance of reaching the destination."

Meth Cagno said, "Brunet mentions the 'compass'—an iron needle which points always to the north. The iron is 'magnetized' by wrapping it in a coil of copper strands and passing an electric current through these strands. We have copper, we have iron."

"But no electricity."

"No electricity," agreed Meth Cagno.

"And no means of obtaining electricity."

"As to that—we shall see."

Four days later Meth Cagno summoned the Seven to his workshop. "You will now see electricity produced."

"What? In that device?" Sklar Hast inspected the clumsy apparatus. To one side a tube of hollow stalk five inches in diameter and twenty feet high was supported by a scaffold. The base was contained at one end of a long box holding what appeared to be wet ashes. The far end of the box was closed by a slab of compressed carbon, into which were threaded copper wires. At the opposite end, between the tube and wet ashes was another slab of compressed carbon.

"This is admittedly a crude device, unwieldy to operate and of no great efficiency," said Meth Cagno. "It does however meet our peculiar requirements: which is to say, it produces electricity without metal, through the agency of water pressure. Brunet describes it in his Dicta. He calls it the 'Rous machine.' The tube is filled with water, which is thereby forced through the mud, which is a mixture of ashes and sea-slime. The water carries an electric charge which it communicates to the porous carbon as it seeps through. By this

means a small but steady and quite dependable source of electricity is at our hand. As you may have guessed, I have already tested the device, and so can speak with confidence."
He turned, snapped his fingers, and his helpers mounted the scaffold carrying buckets of water which they poured into the tube. Meth Cagno connected the wires to a coil of several dozen revolutions. He brought forward a dish. On a cork rested a small rod of iron.

"I have already magnetized this iron," said Cagno. "Note how it points to the north? Now—I bring it near the end of the coil. See it jerk! Electricity is flowing in the wire!"

The other members of the Seven were impressed. "And this iron needle will now serve to guide Henry Bastaff?"

"So I believe. But the Rous machine provides an even more dramatic possibility. With electricity we can disassociate seawater to produce, after certain operations, the acid of salt, and a caustic of countering properties as well. The acid can then be used to produce more highly concentrated streams of electricity—if we are able to secure more metal. There is iron in our blood: I ask myself, where does the iron originate? Which of our foods contains the iron? I plan to reduce each of our foods under the lens, as well as any other distinctive substance which might yield a concentration of metal." He turned, went to the table, returned with a glistening object. "Look. A bottle of glass. Bolin Hyse has produced this bottle. He fashioned a tube of copper, fixed it to a longer tube of withe, dipped the copper into molten glass and blew. The result"—Meth Cagno inspected the object critically—"is not beautiful. The glass is gray and streaked with ash. The shape is uncertain. Nevertheless—here is a glass bottle, produced from ash and sea-ooze. Eventually, we will be building devices of great intricacy."

"Subject to the indulgence of King Kragen," muttered Sklar Hast.

Meth Cagno threw up his hands. "King Kragen bah! We shall kill him. When next a kragen is brought to the derrick, allow me to deal with it. There are tests I wish to make."

# CHAPTER VI

On the world which had no name, there were no seasons, no variations of climate except those to be found by traversing the latitudes. Along the equatorial doldrums, where floats of sea-plant grew in chains and clots, each day was like every other, and the passage of a year could be detected only by watching the night sky. Though the folk had small need for accurate temporal distinctions, each day was numbered and each year named for some significant event. A duration of twenty-two years was a "surge," and was also reckoned by number. Hence a given date might be known as the 349th day in the Year of Malvinon's Deep Dive during the Tenth Surge. Time-reckoning was almost exclusively the province of the Scriveners. To most of the folk life seemed as pellucid and effortless as the glassy blue sea at noon.

King Kragen's attack upon Tranque Float occurred toward the year's end, which thereupon became the Year of Tranque's Abasement, and it was generally assumed that the following year would be known as the Year of the Dissenters' Going.

As the days passed and the year approached its midpoint, Barquan Blasdel, Apprise Intercessor, instead of allowing the memory of his kidnapping to grow dim, revived it daily with neverflagging virulence. Each evening saw a memorandum from Barquan Blasdel flicker up and down the chain of floats: "Vigilance is necessary. The dissidents are led by seven men of evil energy. They flout the majesty of King Kragen; they despise the folk who maintain old traditions and most especially the Intercessors. They must be punished and taught humility. Think well on this matter. Ask yourself, how may the dissidents most expeditiously be chastened?"

The other Intercessors, while politely attending Blasdel's urgencies, did little to give them effect. Blasdel daily became more hectic. At a Conclave of Notables his demands that the floats assemble an armada to invade the new floats and destroy the dissidents was vetoed by the Arbiters, Guild Masters and Caste Chiefs, on the grounds of utter infeasibility and pointlessness. "Let them be," growled Emacho Feroxibus, Chief of the Quatrefoil Bezzlers. "So long as they do not molest us, why should we molest them? I for one don't care to risk drowning for so dismal a cause."

Barquan Blasdel, containing his temper, explained carefully, "The matter is more complex than this. Here is a group who have fled in order to avoid paying their due to King Kragen. If they are allowed to prosper, to make profit of their defection, then other folk may be tempted to wonder, why do we not do likewise? If the sin of kragen-killing becomes vulgar recreation, where is reverence? Where is continuity? Where is obedience to High Authority?"

"This may be true," stated Providence Dringle, Chief Hoodwink for the Populous Equity Float. "Nonetheless in my opinion the cure is worse than the complaint. And to risk a heretical opinion, I must say the benefits we derive from High Authority no longer seem commensurate with the price we pay."

Blasdel swung about in shock, as did the other Intercessors. "May I ask your meaning?" Blasdel inquired icily.

"I mean that King Kragen consumes six to seven bushels of choice sponges daily. He maintains his rule in the waters surrounding the floats, true, but what do we need fear from the lesser kragen? By your own testimony the dissidents have developed a method to kill the kragen with facility."

Blasdel said with frigid menace, "I can not overlook the fact that your remarks are identical to the preposterous ravings of the dissidents, who so rightly shall be obliterated."

"Do not rely on my help," said Providence Dringle.

"Nor mine," said Emacho Feroxibus.


The conclave had divided into two antagonistic camps, the Intercessors and certain others supporting Barquan Blasdel, though few favored the more extreme of his propositions.

From the foliage which surrounded the scene of the conclave came a crash and a muttered exclamation. A number of men sprang into the shrubbery. There was a confused scuffle, the sound of blows and exclamations, and presently a man was dragged out into the lamplight. His skin was dark, his face was bland and bare of hair.

Barquan Blasdel marched forward. "Who are you? Why do you lurk in these forbidden precincts?"

The man staggered and blinked foolishly. "Is this the tavern? Pour out the arrack, pour for all! I am a stranger on Apprise, I would know the quality of your food and drink."

Emacho Feroxibus snorted, "The fool is drunk. Turn him off the float."

"No!" roared Blasdel, jerking forward in excitement. "This is a dissident, this is a spy! I know him well! He has shaved his head and his face, but never can he defeat my acuity! He is here to learn our secrets!"

The group turned their attention upon the man, who blinked even more vehemently. "A spy? Not I. I came to find the Old Tavern."

Blasdel sniffed the air in front of the captive's face. "There is no odor: neither beer nor arrack nor spirits of life. Come! All must satisfy themselves as to this so that there will be no subsequent contradictions and vacillations."

"What is your name?" demanded Vogel Womack, the Parnassus Arbiter. "Your float and your caste?"

The captive took a deep breath, cast off his pretense of drunkenness. "I am Henry Bastaff. I am a dissident. I am here to learn if you plan evil against us. That is my sole purpose."

"A spy!" cried Barquan Blasdel in a voice of horror. "A self-confessed spy!"

"It is a serious matter," said Emacho Feroxibus, "but the truth of the matter is undoubtedly as he has averred."

The Intercessors set up a chorus of indignant hoots and jibes. Barquan Blasdel said, "He is guilty of at least a double offense: first, the various illegalities entering into his dissidence; and second, his insolent attempt to conspire against us, the staunch and the faithful. The crime has occurred on Apprise Float, and affects our relations with King Kragen. Hence, I, Barquan Blasdel, am compelled to demand an extreme penalty. Parler Denk, the new Apprise Arbiter, in such instance, can implement such a penalty by simple executive command, without consultation with the council. Arbiter Denk, what is your response?"

"Be not hasty," warned Vogel Womack. "Tomorrow the man's deed will not appear so grave."

Barquan Blasdel ignored him. "Parler Denk, what is your response?"

"I agree, in all respects. The man is a vile dissident, an agent of turmoil and a spy. He must suffer an extreme penalty. To this declaration there will be allowed no appeal."

On the following day a significant alteration was made in the method by which King Kragen was tendered his customary oblation. Previously, when King Kragen approached a lagoon with the obvious intent of feasting, arbors overgrown with sponges were floated to the edge of the net, for King Kragen to pluck with his palps. Now the sponges were plucked, heaped upon a great tray and floated forth between a pair of coracles. When the tray was in place, Barquan Blasdel went to his sanctum. King Kragen was close at hand; the scraping of his chitin armor sounded loud in Blasdel's listening device. Blasdel sounded his submarine horn; the scraping ceased, then began once more, increasing in intensity. King Kragen was approaching.

He appeared from the east, turret and massive torso riding above the surface, the great rectangular swimming platform gliding through the ocean on easy strokes of his vanes.

The forward eyes noted the offering. King Kragen approached casually, inspected the tray, began to scoop the sponges into his maw with his forward palps.

From the float folk watched in somber speculation mingled with awe. Barquan Blasdel came gingerly forth to stand on the edge of the pad, to gesticulate in approval as King Kragen ate.

The tray was empty. King Kragen made no motion to depart; Blasdel swung about, gestured to an understudy. "The sponges: how many were offered?"

"Seven bushels. King Kragen usually eats no more."

"Today he seems to hunger. Are others plucked?"

"Those for the market: another five bushels."

"They had best be tendered King Kragen; it is not well to stint." While King Kragen floated motionless, the coracles were pulled to the float, another five bushels were poured upon the tray, and the tray thrust back toward King Kragen. Again he ate, consuming all but a bushel or two. Then, replete, he submerged till only his turret remained above the water. And there he remained, moving sluggishly a few feet forward, a few feet backward.

Nine days later a haggard Denis Maible reported the capture of Henry Bastoff to the Seven. "On the following day King Kragen had not yet moved. It was clear that the new method of feeding had impressed him favorably. So at noon the tray was again filled, with at least ten bushels of sponge, and again King Kragen devoured the lot.

"During this time we learned that Henry Bastaff had been captured and condemned—indeed the news had gone out over the hoodwink towers—but we could not discover where he was imprisoned or what fate had been planned for him.

"On the third day Blasdel made an announcement, to the effect that the dissident spy had sinned against King Kragen and King Kragen had demanded the privilege of executing him.

"At noon the tray went out. At the very top was a wide board supporting a single great sponge; and below, the usual heap. King Kragen had not moved fifty yards for three days. He approached the tray, reached for the topmost sponge.It seemed fastened to the board. King Kragen jerked, and so decapitated Henry Bastaff, whose head had been stuffed into the sponge. It was a horrible sight, with the blood spouting upon the pile of sponges. King Kragen seemed to devour them with particular relish.

"With Henry Bastaff dead, we no longer had reason to delay—except for curiosity. King Kragen showed no signs of moving, of visiting the other floats. It was clear that he found the new feeding system to his liking. By then, Apprise Float was bereft of sponges.

"The Intercessors conferred by hoodwink and apparently

arrived at a means of dealing with the situation. King Kragen's meal on the fourth day was furnished by Granolt Float and ferried to Apprise by coracle. On the fifth day the sponges were brought from Sankeston. It appears that King Kragen is now a permanent guest at Apprise Float. . . . On the evening of the fifth day we launched our coracle and returned to New Float."

The Seven were silent. Phyral Berwick finally made a sound of nausea. "It is a repulsive situation. One which I would like to change."

Sklar Hast looked toward Meth Cagno. "There is the man who smelts metal."

Meth Cagno smiled wryly. "Our enterprises are multiplying. We have found a number of sources which when burned in sufficiently large quantities produce at least four different metals. None seem to be iron. We have bled everyone on the float, twice or three times: this blood has yielded several pounds of iron, which we have hammered and refined until now it is hard and keen beyond all belief. Our electrical device has produced twenty-four flasks of acid of salt, which we maintain in bottles blown by our glass shop, which is now an establishment completely separated from the smelting."

"This is encouraging and interesting," said Robin Magram, "but what will it avail against King Kragen?"

Meth Cagno pursed his lips. "I have not yet completed my experiments, and I am unable to make an unequivocal answer. But in due course our preparations will be complete."

# CHAPTER VII

Some two hundred days later, toward the end of the year, swindlers working the waters to the east of Tranque Float spied the armada from the east. There were two dozen canoes sheathed with a dull black membrane. Each canoe carried a crew of thirty, who wore helmets and corselets of the same black substance, and carried lances tipped with orange metal. They accompanied a strange craft, like none ever seen before along the floats. It was rectangular, and rode on four parallel pontoons. A bulwark of the black sheathing completely encircled the barge, to a height of five feet. Fore and aft rose stout platforms on which were mounted massive crossbowlike contrivances, the arms of which were laminated stalk and kragen chitin, and the string cables woven from strips of kragen leather. The hold of the barge contained two hundred glass vats, each of two quarts capacity, each two-thirds full of pale liquid. The barge was propelled by oars—a score on either side—and moved with not inconsiderable speed.

The swindlers paddled with all speed to Tranque Float and the hoodwink towers flickered an alarm: *The . . . dissidents . . . are . . . returning . . . in . . . force! They . . . come . . . in . . . strange . . . black . . . canoes . . . and . . . an . . . even . . . more . . . peculiar. . . black . . . barge. They . . . show . . . no . . . fear.*

The flotilla continued up the line of floats: Thrasneck, Bickle, Green Lamp, and at last Fay, Quatrefoil, and finally Apprise.

In the water before the lagoon lolled King Kragen—a bloated monstrous King Kragen, dwarfing the entire flotilla.

King Kragen swung about, the monstrous vanes sucking whirlpools into the ocean. The eyes with opalescent films shifting back and forth within, fixed upon the black sheathing of canoe, barge and armor, and he seemed to recognize the substance as kragen hide, for he emitted a snort of terrible displeasure, jerked his vanes, and the ocean sucked and swirled.

The barge swung sidewise to King Kragen. The two crossbows, each cocked and strung, each armed with an iron harpoon smelted from human blood, were aimed.

King Kragen sensed menace. Why otherwise should men be so bold? He twitched his vanes, inched forward—to within a hundred feet. Then he lunged. Vanes dug the water; with an ear-shattering shriek King Kragen charged, mandibles snapping.

The men at the crossbows were pale as sea-foam; their

fingers twitched. Sklar Hast turned to call, "Fire!" but his voice caught in his throat and what he intended for an incisive command sounded as a startled stammer. But the command was understood. The left crossbow thudded, snapped, sang: the harpoon, trailing a black cable sprang at King Kragen's turret, buried itself. King Kragen hissed.

The right crossbow fired; the second harpoon stabbed deep into the turret. Sklar Hast motioned with his hand to the men in the hold. "Connect." The men joined copper to copper. In the hold two hundred voltaic cells, each holding ten thin-leaved cathodes and ten thin-leaved anodes, connected first in four series of fifty, and these four series in parallel, poured a gush of electricity along the copper cables wrapped in varnished pad-skin, which led to the harpoons. Into King Kragen's turret poured the energy, and King Kragen went stiff. His vanes protruded at right angles to his body. Sklar Hast said to Meth Cagno, "Your experiments seem to be as valid as with the lesser kragen—luckily."

"I never doubted," said Meth Cagno.

Sklar Hast waved to the canoes. They swung toward King Kragen, beaching on the rigid subsurface platform. The men swarmed up the torso. With mallets and copper chisels they attacked the lining between dome and turret wall. There was thirty feet of seam, but many hands at work. The lining was broken; bars were inserted into the crack; all heaved. With a splitting sound the dome was dislodged. It slid over and into the water; the men leaped down into the knotted gray cords and nodes and began hacking.

On Apprise Float a great throng had gathered. One man, running back and forth, was Barquan Blasdel. Finally he persuaded several score of men to embark in coracles and attack the flotilla. Eight black canoes were on guard. Paddles dug the water, the canoes picked up momentum, crashed into the foremost coracles, crushing the fragile shells, throwing the men into the water. The canoes backed away, turned toward the other coracles, which retreated.

Out in the lagoon King Kragen's nerve nodes had been cast

into the sea. The harpoons were extracted, the flow of electricity extinguished.

King Kragen floated limp, a lifeless hulk. The men plunged into the sea to wash themselves, clambered back up on the dead swimming platform, boarded their canoes.

The barge now eased toward Apprise Float. Barquan Blasdel gesticulated to the folk like a crazy man. "To arms! Stakes, chisels, mallets, knives, bludgeons! Smite the miscreants!"

Sklar Hast called to the throng, "King Kragen is dead. What do you say to this?"

There was silence; then a faint cheer and a louder cheer, and finally uproarious celebration.

Sklar Hast pointed a finger at Barquan Blasdel. "That man must die. He murdered Henry Bastaff. He has fed your food to the vile King Kragen. He would have continued doing so until King Kragen overgrew the entire float."

Barquan Blasdel made the mistake of turning to flee—an act which triggered the counterimpulse to halt him. When he was touched, he smote, and again he erred, for the blow brought a counterblow and Barquan Blasdel was presently torn to pieces.

"What now?" called the crowd. "What now, Sklar Hast?"

"Nothing whatever, unless you choose to kill the other Intercessors. King Kragen is dethroned; our duty is done. We now return to the New Floats."

From the shore someone called out, "Come ashore, men of the New Floats, and share our great joy. Greet your old friends, who long have been saddened at your absence! Tonight the arrack will flow and we will play the pipes and dance in the light of our yellow lamps!"

Sklar Hast shook his head, waved his hand and called back: "Now we return to the New Floats. In a week certain of us will return, and the weeks after that will see constant traffic between Old and New Floats, and out to floats still unknown. King Kragen is dead, the lesser kragen are our prey, so who is there to stop us? Now that we know metal and glass and electricity, all things are possible. Rejoice with all our goodwill. For now, farewell."

The barge and the canoes swung about; oars and paddles dipped into the ocean, the black flotilla receded into the east, and disappeared.

# MERMAID

There was an old belief that every land animal had its counterpart in the sea. There's nothing to that, of course, but we still see traces of that legend in the names given some sea creatures. The "sea horse" is a tiny creature, but it does have a head reminiscent of that of a small, bony horse. Then there is the sea cow (manatee), the sea hog (porpoise), the sea lion and sea elephant (seals), the sea robin and sea wolf (certain fish), and so on.

It would be astonishing if, under these circumstances, people didn't decide the sea must also harbor the equivalent of human beings—sea people, in other words.

They did decide that, and legends are full of "mermen" and "mermaids." (The prefix is from an archaic English word "mere" meaning "sea" or "lake.")

There are many circumstantial tales of mariners having seen mermaids, but nevertheless they do not, in reality, exist. Some people suggest that sailors are fooled by the sight of manatees or dugongs (the "sea cows" referred to above). These have breasts in the human position, and a female manatee rising to the surface with one flipper clasping her young to her breast might, at a distance, and to a near-sighted sailor, suggest a mermaid.

Mermaids are sometimes viewed as malevolent creatures who deliberately lure ships onto reefs and rocks by exhibiting their beauty to sailors who have not seen a woman for a long time. In this way, mermaids resemble *the sirens of Greek legend, and the lorelei of Teutonic legend. All may be personifications of wind and storm.*

*In more modern times, however, mermaids tend to be portrayed as sweet and innocent, playful and alluring, and in the following story, this is done.*

# THE LITTLE MERMAID

*Hans Christian Andersen*

Far, far from land, where the waters are as blue as the petals of the cornflower and as clear as glass, there, where no anchor can reach the bottom, live the mer-people. So deep in this part of the sea that you would have to pile many church towers on top of each other before one of them emerged above the surface.

Now you must not think that at the bottom of the sea there is only white sand. No, here grow the strangest plants and trees; their stems and leaves are so subtle that the slightest current in the water makes them move, as if they were alive. Big and small fishes flit in and out among their branches, just as the birds do up on earth. At the very deepest place, the mer-king has built his castle. Its walls are made of coral and its long pointed windows of amber. The roof is oyster shells that are continually opening and closing. It looks very beautiful, for in each shell lies a pearl, so lustrous that it would be fit for a queen's crown.

The mer-king had been a widower for many years; his mother kept house for him. She was a very intelligent woman but a little too proud of her rank: she wore twelve oysters on her tail; the nobility were only allowed six. Otherwise, she was a most praiseworthy woman, and she took excellent care of her grandchildren, the little princesses. They were six lovely mermaids; the youngest was the most beautiful. Her complexion was as fine as the petal of a rose and her eyes as blue as the deepest lake but, just like everyone else down there, she had no feet; her body ended in a fishtail.

The mermaids were allowed to play all day in the great hall of the castle, where flowers grew on the walls. The big amber windows were kept open and the fishes swam in and out, just as the swallows up on earth fly in through our windows if they are open. But unlike the birds of the air, the fishes were not frightened, they swam right up to the little princesses and ate out of their hands and let themselves be petted.

Around the castle was a great park where there grew fiery-red and deep-blue trees. Their fruits shone as though they were the purest gold, their flowers were like flames, and their branches and leaves were ever in motion. The earth was the finest sand, not white but blue, the color of burning sulphur. There was a blue tinge to everything, down on the bottom of the sea. You could almost believe that you were suspended in midair and had the blue sky both above and below you. When the sea was calm, the sun appeared like a crimson flower, from which all light flowed.

Each little princess had her own garden, where she could plant the flowers she liked. One of them had shaped her flower bed so it resembled a whale; and another, as a mermaid. The youngest had planted red flowers in hers: she wanted it to look like the sun; it was round and the crimson flowers did glow as though they were so many little suns. She was a strange little child: quiet and thoughtful. Her sisters' gardens were filled with all sorts of things that they had collected from shipwrecks, but she had only a marble statue of a boy in hers. It had been cut out of stone that was almost transparently clear and had sunk to the bottom of the sea when the ship that had carried it was lost. Close to the statue she had planted a pink tree; it looked like a weeping willow. The tree was taller than the sculpture. Its long soft branches bent toward the sand; it looked as if the top of the tree and its root wanted to kiss each other.

The princesses liked nothing better than to listen to their old grandmother tell about the world above. She had to recount countless times all she knew about ships, towns, human beings, and the animals that lived up on land. The youngest of the mermaids thought it particularly wonderful that the flowers up there had fragrance, for that they did not have on the bottom of the sea. She also liked to hear about the green forest, where the fishes that swam among the branches could sing most beautifully. Grandmother called the birds "fishes"; otherwise, her little grandchildren would not have understood her, since they had never seen a bird.

"But when you are fifteen, then you will be allowed to swim to the surface," she promised. "Then you can climb up on a rock and sit and watch the big ships sail by. If you dare, you can swim close enough to the shore to see the towns and the forest."

The following year, the oldest of the princesses would be fifteen. From one sister to the next, there was a difference in age of about a year, which meant that the youngest would have to wait more than five whole years before she would be allowed to swim up from the bottom of the sea and take a look at us. But each promised the others that she would return after her first day above, and tell about the things she had seen and describe what she thought was loveliest of all. For the old grandmother could not satisfy their curiosity.

None of the sisters longed so much to see the world above as the youngest, the one who had to wait the longest before she could leave her home. Many a night this quiet, thoughtful little mermaid would stand by the open window, looking up through the dark blue waters where the fishes swam. She could see the moon and the stars; they looked paler but larger down here under the sea. Sometimes a great shadow passed by like a cloud and then she knew that it was either a whale or a ship, with its crew and passengers, that was sailing high above her. None on board could have imagined that a little beautiful mermaid stood in the depths below them and stretched her little white hands up toward the keel of their ship.

The oldest of the sisters had her fifteenth birthday and swam up to the surface of the sea. When she returned she had hundreds of things to tell. But of everything that had happened to her, the loveliest experience by far, she claimed, had been to lie on a sandbank, when the sea was calm and the moon was out, and look at a great city. The lights from the windows and streets had shone like hundreds of stars; and she had been able to hear the rumbling of the carriages and the voices of human beings and, best of all, the sound of music. She had seen all the church towers and steeples, and heard their bells ring. And just because she would never be able to enter the city, she longed to be able to do that more than anything else.

How carefully her youngest sister listened to every word and remembered everything that she had been told. When, late in the evening, the little mermaid would stand dreaming by the window and look up through the blue water, then she imagined that she could see the city and hear the bells of the churches ringing.

The next year the second of the sisters was allowed to swim away from home. Her little head had emerged above the water just at the moment when the sun was setting. This sight had been so beautiful that she could hardly describe it. The whole heaven had been covered in gold and the clouds that had sailed above her had been purple and crimson. A flight of wild swans, like a white veil just above the water, had flown by. She had swum toward the sun, but it had set, taking the colors of the clouds, sea, and sky with it.

The third of the sisters, who came of age the following year, was the most daring among them. She had swum way up a broad river! There she had seen green hills covered with vineyards, castles, and farms that peeped out through the great forests. She had heard the birds sing and the sun had been so hot that she had had to swim under the water, some of the time, just to cool off. In a little bay, she had come upon some naked children who were playing and splashing in the water. She had wanted to join them, but when they saw her they got frightened and ran away. A little black animal had come: it was a dog. But she had never seen one before. It had barked so loudly and fiercely that she became terrified and swam right back to the sea. What she never would forget as long as she lived were the beautiful forest, the green hills, and the sweet little children who had been able to swim even though they had no fishtails as she had.

The fourth of the sisters was timid. She stayed far away from shore, out in the middle of the ocean. But that was the most beautiful place of all, she asserted. You could see ever so far and the sky above was like a clear glass bell. The ships she had seen had been so far away that they had looked no bigger than gulls. But the little dolphins had turned somersaults for her and the great whales had sprayed water high up into the air, so that it looked as though there were more than a hundred fountains.

The fifth sister's birthday was in the winter and, therefore, she saw something none of her sisters had seen. The ocean had been green, and huge icebergs had been floating on it. Each of them had been as lovely as a pearl and yet larger than the church towers that human beings built. They had the most fantastic shapes and their surface glittered like diamonds. She had climbed up on the largest one of them all; the wind had played with her long hair, and all the ships had fearfully kept away. Toward evening a storm had begun to blow; dark clouds had gathered and bolts of lightning had flashed while the thunder rolled. The waves had lifted the iceberg high up on their shoulders, and the lightning had colored the ice red. The ships had taken down their sails; and on board, fear and terror had reigned. But the mermaid had just sat on her iceberg and watched the bolts of lightning zigzag across the sky.

The first time that any of the sisters had been allowed to swim to the surface, each had been delighted with her freedom and all she had seen. But now that they were grownups and could swim anywhere they wished, they lost interest in wandering far away; after a month or two the world above lost its attraction. When they were away, they longed for their home, declaring it the most beautiful place of all and the only spot where one really felt at home.

Still, many evenings the five sisters would take each other's hands and rise up through the waters. They had voices far lovelier than any human being. When a storm began to rage and a ship was in danger of being wrecked, then the five sisters would swim in front of it and sing about how beautiful it was down at the bottom of the sea. They begged the sailors not to be frightened but to come down to them. The men could not understand the mermaids' songs; they thought it was the wind that was singing. Besides, they would never see the beauty of the world below them, for if a ship sinks the

seamen drown, and when they arrive at the mer-king's castle
they are dead.

On such evenings, while her sisters swam, hand in hand,
up through the water, the youngest princess had to stay
below. She would look sadly up after them and feel like crying;
but mermaids can't weep and that makes their suffering even
deeper and greater.

"Oh, if only I were fifteen," she would sigh. "I know that
I shall love the world above, and the human beings who live
up there!"

At last she, too, was fifteen!

"Now you are off our hands," said the old dowager
queen. "Let me dress you, just as I dressed your sisters."
She put a wreath of white lilies around her hair; each of the
petals of every flower was half a pearl. She let eight oysters
clip themselves onto the little mermaid's tail, so that everyone could see that she was a princess.

"It hurts," said the little mermaid.

"One has to suffer for position," said her old grandmother. The little mermaid would gladly have exchanged her
heavy pearl wreath for one of the red flowers from her garden
(she thought they suited her much better) but she didn't dare.

"Farewell," she said and rose, light as a bubble, up
through the water.

The sun had just set when she lifted her head above the
surface. The clouds still had the color of roses and in the
horizon was a fine line of gold; in the pale pink sky the first
star of evening sparkled, clearly and beautifully. The air was
warm and the sea was calm. She saw a three-masted ship;
only one of its sails was unfurled, and it hung motionless in
the still air. Up on the yards the sailors sat, looking down
upon the deck from which music could be heard. As the
evening grew darker, hundreds of little colored lamps were
hung from the rigging; they looked like the flags of all the
nations of the world. The little mermaid swam close to a
porthole and the swells lifted her gently so that she could look
in through it. The great cabin was filled with gaily dressed
people; the handsomest among them was a young prince with
large, dark eyes. He looked no older than sixteen, and that

was, in truth, his age; that very day was his birthday. All the festivities were for him. The sailors danced on the deck, and as the young prince came up to watch them, a hundred rockets flew into the sky.

The night became as bright as day and the little mermaid got so frightened that she ducked down under the water. But she soon stuck her head up again; and then it looked as if all the stars of the heavens were falling down on top of her. She had never seen fireworks before. Pinwheels turned; rockets shot into the air, and their lights reflected in the dark mirror of the sea. The deck of the ship was so illuminated that every rope could clearly be seen. Oh, how handsome the young prince was! He laughed and smiled and shook hands with everyone, while music was played in the still night.

It grew late, but the little mermaid could not turn her eyes away from the ship and the handsome prince. The colored lamps were put out. No more rockets shot into the air and no more cannons were fired. From the depth of the ocean came a rumbling noise. The little mermaid let the waves be her rocking horse, and they lifted her so that she could look in through the porthole. The ship started to sail faster and faster, as one sail after another was unfurled. Now the waves grew in size and black clouds could be seen on the horizon and far away lightning flashed.

A storm was brewing. The sailors took down the sails. The great ship tossed and rolled in the huge waves that rose as though they were mountains that wanted to bury the ship and break its proud mast. But the ship, like a swan, rode on top of the waves and let them lift her high into the sky. The little mermaid thought it was very amusing to watch the ship sailing so fast, but the sailors didn't. The ship creaked and groaned; the great planks seemed to bulge as the waves hit them. Suddenly the mast snapped as if it were a reed. It tumbled into the water. The ship heeled over, and the sea broke over it.

Only now did the little mermaid understand that the ship was in danger. She had to be careful herself and keep away from the spars and broken pieces of timber that were being flung by the waves. For a moment it grew so dark that she could see nothing, then a bolt of lightning illuminated the sinking ship. She looked for the young prince among the terrified men on board who were trying to save themselves, but not until that very moment, when the ship finally sank, did she see him.

At first, she thought joyfully, "Now he will come down to me!" But then she remembered that man could not live in the sea and the young prince would be dead when he came to her father's castle.

"He must not die," she thought, and dived in among the wreckage, forgetting the danger that she herself was in, for any one of the great beams that were floating in the turbulent sea could have crushed her.

She found him! He was too tired to swim any farther; he had no more strength in his arms and legs to fight the storm-whipped waves. He closed his eyes, waiting for death, and he would have drowned, had the little mermaid not saved him. She held his head above water and let the waves carry them where they would.

By morning the storm was over. Of the wrecked ship not a splinter was to be found. The sun rose, glowing red, and its rays gave color to the young prince's cheeks but his eyes remained closed. The little mermaid kissed his forehead and stroked his wet hair. She thought that he looked like the statue in her garden. She kissed him again and wished passionately that he would live.

In the far distance she saw land; the mountains rose blue in the morning air. The snow on their peaks was as glittering white as swan's feathers. At the shore there was a great forest, and in its midst lay a cloister or a church, the little mermaid did not know which. Lemon and orange trees grew in the garden, and by the entrance gate stood a tall palm tree. There was a little bay nearby, where the water was calm and deep. The mermaid swam with her prince toward the beach. She laid him in the fine white sand, taking care to place his head in the warm sunshine far from the water.

In the big white buildings bells were ringing and a group of young girls was coming out to walk in the garden. The little mermaid swam out to some rocks and hid behind them. She covered her head with seaweed so that she could not be seen and then peeped toward land, to see who would find the poor prince.

Soon one of the young girls discovered him. At first she seemed frightened, and she called the others. A lot of people came. The prince opened his eyes and smiled up at those who stood around him—not out at the sea, where the little mermaid was hiding. But then he could not possibly have known that she was there and that it was she who had saved him. The little mermaid felt so terribly sad; the prince was carried into the big white building, and the little mermaid dived sorrowfully down into the sea and swam home to her father's castle.

She had always been quiet and thoughtful. Now she grew even more silent. Her sisters asked her what she had seen on her first visit up above, but she did not answer.

Many mornings and evenings she would swim back to the place where she had last seen the prince. She watched the fruits in the orchard ripen and be picked, and saw the snow on the high mountains melt, but she never saw the prince. She would return from each of these visits a little sadder. She would seek comfort by embracing the statue in her garden, which looked like the prince. She no longer tended her flowers, and they grew into a wilderness, covering the paths and weaving their long stalks and leaves into the branches of the trees, so that it became quite dark down in her garden.

At last she could bear her sorrow no longer and told one of her sisters about it; and almost at once the others knew as well. But no one else was told; that is, except for a couple of other mermaids, but they didn't tell it to anyone except their nearest and dearest friends. It was one of these friends who knew who the prince was. She, too, had seen the birthday party on the ship, and she could tell where he came from and where his kingdom was.

"Come, little sister," the other princesses called, and with their arms around each other's shoulders they swam.

All in a row they rose to the surface when they came to the shore where the prince's castle stood. It was built of glazed yellow stones and had many flights of marble stairs leading up to it. The steps of one of them went all the way down to the sea. Golden domes rose above the roofs, and pillars bore an arcade that went all the way around the palace. Between the pillars stood marble statues; they looked almost as if they were alive. Through the clear glass of the tall windows, one could look into the most beautiful chambers and halls, where silken curtains and tapestries hung on the walls; and there were large paintings that were a real pleasure to look at. In the largest hall was a fountain. The water shot high up toward the glass cupola in the roof, through which the sunbeams fell on the water and the beautiful flowers that grew in the basin of the fountain.

Now that she knew where the prince lived, the little mermaid spent many evenings and nights looking at the splendid palace. She swam nearer to the land than any of her sisters had ever dared. There was a marble balcony that cast its shadow across a narrow canal, and beneath it she hid and watched the young prince, who thought that he was all alone in the moonlight.

Many an evening she saw the prince sail with his musicians in his beautiful boat. She peeped from behind the tall reeds; and if someone noticed her silver-white veil, they probably thought that they had only seen a swan stretching its wings.

Many a night she heard the fishermen talking to each other and telling about how kind and good the prince was; and she was so glad that she had saved his life when she had found him, half dead, drifting on the waves. She remembered how his head had rested on her chest and with what passion she had kissed him. But he knew nothing about his rescue; he could not even dream about her.

More and more she grew to love human beings and wished that she could leave the sea and live among them. It seemed to her that their world was far larger than hers; on ships, they could sail across the oceans and they could climb the mountains high up above the clouds. Their countries seemed ever so large, covered with fields and forests; she knew that they stretched much farther than she could see. There was so much that she wanted to know; there were many questions that her sisters could not answer. Therefore she asked her old grandmother, since she knew much about the "higher world," as she called the lands above the sea.

"If men are not so unlucky as to drown," asked the little mermaid, "then do they live forever? Don't they die as we do, down here in the sea?"

"Yes, they do," answered her grandmother. "Men must also die and their life span is shorter than ours. We can live until we are three hundred years old; but when we die, we become the foam on the ocean. We cannot even bury our loved ones. We do not have immortal souls. When we die, we shall never rise again. We are like the green reeds: once they are cut they will never be green again. But men have souls that live eternally, even after their bodies have become dust. They rise high up into the clear sky where the stars are. As we rise up through the water to look at the world of man, they rise up to the unknown, the beautiful world, that we shall never see."

"Why do I not have an immortal soul!" sighed the little mermaid unhappily. "I would give all my three hundred years of life for only one day as a human being if, afterward, I should be allowed to live in the heavenly world."

"You shouldn't think about things like that," said her old grandmother. "We live far happier down here than man does up there."

"I am going to die, become foam on the ocean, and never hear the music of the waves or see the flowers and the burning red sun. Can't I do anything to win an immortal soul?"

"No," said the old merwoman. "Only if a man should fall so much in love with you that you were dearer to him than his mother and father; and he cared so much for you that all his thoughts were of his love for you; and he let a priest take his right hand and put it in yours, while he promised to be eternally true to you, then his soul would flow into your body and you would be able to partake of human happiness. He can give you a soul and yet keep his own. But it will never happen. For that which we consider beautiful down here in the ocean, your fishtail, they find ugly up above, on earth.

They have no sense; up there, you have to have two clumsy props, which they call legs, in order to be called beautiful."

The little mermaid sighed and glanced sadly down at her fishtail.

"Let us be happy," said her old grandmother. "We can swim and jump through the waves for three hundred years, that is time enough. Tonight we are going to give a court ball in the castle."

Such a splendor did not exist up above on the earth. The walls and the ceilings of the great hall were made of clear glass; four hundred giant green and pink oyster shells stood in rows along the walls. Blue flames rose from them and not only lighted the hall but also illuminated the sea outside. Number-less fishes—both big and small—swam close to the glass walls; some of them had purple scales, others seemed to be of silver and gold. Through the great hall flowed a swiftly moving current, and on that the mermen and mermaids danced, while they sang their own beautiful songs. Such lovely voices are never heard up on earth; and the little mermaid sang most beautifully of them all. The others clapped their hands when she had finished, and for a moment she felt happy, knowing that she had the most beautiful voice both on earth and in the sea.

But soon she started thinking again of the world above. She could not forget the handsome prince, and mourned because she did not have an immortal soul like his. She sneaked out of her father's palace, away from the ball, from the gaiety, down into her little garden.

From afar the sound of music, of horns being played, came down to her through the water; and she thought: "Now he is sailing up there, the prince whom I love more than I love my father and mother: he who is ever in my thoughts and in whose hands I would gladly place all my hope of happiness. I would dare to do anything to win him and an immortal soul! While my sisters are dancing in the palace, I will go to the sea witch, though I have always feared her, and ask her to help me."

The little mermaid swam toward the turbulent maelstrom; beyond it the sea witch lived. In this part of the great ocean the little mermaid had never been before; here no flowers or seaweeds grew, only the gray naked sea bed stretched toward the center of the maelstrom, that great whirlpool where the water, as if it had been set in motion by gigantic mill wheels, twisted and turned: grinding, tearing, and sucking anything that came within its reach down into its depths. Through this turbulence the little mermaid had to swim, for beyond it lay the bubbling mud flats that the sea witch called her bog and that had to be crossed to come to the place where she lived.

The sea witch's house was in the midst of the strangest forest. The bushes and trees were gigantic polyps that were half plant and half animal. They looked like snakes with hundreds of heads, but they grew out of the ground. Their branches were long slimy arms, and they had fingers as supple as worms; every limb was in constant motion from the root to the utmost point. Everything they could reach they grasped, and never let go of it again. With dread the little mermaid stood at the entrance to the forest; her heart was beating with fear, she almost turned back. But then she remembered her prince and the soul she wanted to gain and her courage returned.

She braided her long hair and bound it around her head, so the polyps could not catch her by it. She held her arms folded tightly across her breast and then she flew through the water as fast as the swiftest fish. The ugly polyps stretched out their arms and their fingers tried to grasp her. She noticed that every one of them was holding, as tightly as iron bands, onto something it had caught. Drowned human beings peeped out as white skeletons among the polpys' arms. There were sea chests, rudders of ships, skeletons of land animals; and then she saw a poor little mermaid who had been caught and strangled; and this sight was to her the most horrible.

At last she came to a great, slimy, open place in the middle of the forest. Big fat eels played in the mud, showing their ugly yellow stomachs. Here the witch had built her house out of the bones of drowned sailors, and there she sat letting a big ugly toad eat out of her mouth, as human beings sometimes let a canary eat sugar candy out of theirs. The ugly eels she called her little chickens, and held them close to her spongy chest.

"I know what you want," she cackled. "And it is stupid of you. But you shall have your wish, for it will bring you misery, little princess. You want to get rid of your fishtail, and instead have two stumps to walk on as human beings have, so that the prince will fall in love with you; and you will gain both him and an immortal soul." The witch laughed so loudly and evilly that the toad and eels she had had on her lap jumped down into the mud.

"You came at the right time," she said. "Tomorrow I could not have helped you; you would have had to wait a year. I will mix you a potion. Drink it tomorrow morning before the sun rises, while you are sitting on the beach. Your tail will divide and shrink, until it becomes what human beings call 'pretty legs.' It will hurt; it will feel as if a sword were going through your body. All who see you will say that you are the most beautiful human child they have ever seen. You will walk more gracefully than any dancer; but every time your foot touches the ground it will feel as though you were walking on knives so sharp that your blood must flow. If you are willing to suffer all this, then I can help you."

"I will," whispered the little mermaid, and thought of her prince and how she would win an immortal soul.

"But remember," screeched the witch, "that once you have a human body you can never become a mermaid again. Never again shall you swim through the waters with your sisters to your father's castle. If you cannot make the prince fall so much in love with you that he forgets both his father and mother, because his every thought concerns only you, and he orders the priest to take his right hand and place it in yours, so that you become man and wife; then, the first morning after he has married another, your heart will break and you will become foam on the ocean."

"I still want to try," said the little mermaid, and her face was as white as a corpse.

"But you will have to pay me, too," grinned the witch. "And I want no small payment. You have the most beautiful voice of all those who live in the ocean. I suppose you have thought of using that to charm your prince; but that voice you will have to give to me. I want the most precious thing you have to pay for my potion. It contains my own blood, so that it can be as sharp as a double-edged sword.''

"But if you take my voice," said the little mermaid, "what will I have left?"

"Your beautiful body," said the witch. "Your graceful walk and your lovely eyes. Speak with them and you will be able to capture a human heart. Have you lost your courage? Stick out your little tongue, and let me cut it off in payment, and you shall have the potion.''

"Let it happen," whispered the little mermaid.

The witch took out a caldron in which to make the magic potion. "Cleanliness is a virtue," she said. And before she put the pot over the fire, she scrubbed it with eels, which she had made into a whisk.

She cut her chest and let her blood drip into the vessel. The stream that rose became strange figures that were terrifying to see. Every minute, the witch put something different into the caldron. When the brew reached a rolling boil, it sounded as though a crocodile were crying. At last the potion was finished. It looked as clear and pure as water.

"Here it is," said the witch, and cut out the little mermaid's tongue. Now she was mute, she could neither speak nor sing.

"If any of the polyps should try to grab you, on your way back through my forest," said the witch, "you need only spill one drop of the potion on it and its arms and fingers will splinter into a thousand pieces.''

But the little mermaid didn't have to do that. Fearfully, the polpys drew away when they saw what she was carrying in her hands; the potion sparkled as though it were a star. Safely, she returned through the forest, the bog, and the maelstrom.

She could see her father's palace. The lights were extinguished in the great hall. Everyone was asleep; and yet she did not dare to seek out her sisters; now that she was mute and was going away from them forever. She felt as if her heart would break with sorrow. She sneaked down into the garden and picked a flower from each of her sisters' gardens; then she threw a thousand finger kisses toward the palace and swam upward through the deep blue sea.

The sun had not yet risen when she reached the prince's castle and sat down on the lowest step of the great marble stairs. The moon was still shining clearly. The little mermaid drank the potion and it felt as if a sword were piercing her little body. She fainted and lay as though she were dead.

When the sun's rays touched the sea she woke and felt a burning pain; but the young prince stood in front of her and looked at her with his coal-black eyes. She looked downward and saw then that she no longer had a fishtail but the most beautiful, little, slender legs that any girl could wish for. She was naked; and therefore she took her long hair and covered herself with it.

The prince asked her who she was and how she had got there. She looked gently and yet ever so sadly up at him with her deep blue eyes, for she could not speak. He took her by the hand and led her up to his castle. And just as the witch had warned, every step felt as though she were walking on sharp knives. But she suffered it gladly. Gracefully as a bubble rising in the water, she walked beside the prince; and everyone who saw her wondered how she could walk so lightly.

In the castle, she was clad in royal clothes of silk and muslin. She was the most beautiful of all, but she was mute and could neither sing nor speak. Beautiful slave girls, clad in silken clothes embroidered with gold, sang for the prince and his royal parents. One sang more beautifully than the rest, and the prince clapped his hands and smiled to her; then the little mermaid was filled with sorrow, for she knew that she had once sung far more beautifully. And she thought, "Oh, if he only knew that to be with him I have given away my voice for all eternity."

Now the slave girls danced, gracefully they moved to the beautiful music. Suddenly the little mermaid lifted her hands and rose on the tips of her toes. She floated more than danced across the floor. No one had ever seen anyone dance as she did. Her every movement revealed her loveliness and her eyes spoke far more eloquently than the slave's song.

Everyone was delighted, especially the prince. He called her his little foundling. She danced again and again, even though each time her little foot touched the floor she felt as if she had stepped on a knife. The prince declared that she should never leave him, and she was given permission to sleep in front of his door on a velvet pillow.

The prince had men's clothes made for her, so that she could accompany him when he went horseback riding. Through the sweet-smelling forest they rode, where green branches touched their shoulders and little birds sang among the leaves. Together they climbed the high mountains and her feet bled so much that others noticed it; but she smiled and followed her prince up ever higher until they could see the clouds sail below them, like flocks of birds migrating to foreign lands.

At night in the castle, while the others slept, she would walk down the broad marble stairs to the sea and cool her poor burning feet in the cold water. Then she would think of her sisters, down in the deep sea.

One night they came; arm in arm they rose above the surface of the water, singing ever so sadly. She waved to them, and they recognized her, and they told her how much sorrow she had brought them. After that they visited her every night; and once she saw, far out to sea, her old grandmother. It had been years since she had stuck her head up into the air; and there, too, was her father the mer-king with his crown on his head. They stretched their hands toward her but did not dare come as near to the land as her sisters.

Day by day the prince grew fonder and fonder of her; but he loved her as he would have loved a good child, and had no thought of making her his queen. And she had to become his wife or she would never have an immortal soul, but on the morning after his marriage would become foam on the great ocean.

"Don't you love me more than you do all others?" was the message in the little mermaid's eyes when the prince kissed her lovely forehead.

"Yes, you are the dearest to me," said the prince, "for

you have the kindest heart of them all. You are devoted to me
and you look like a young girl I once saw, and will probably
never see again. I was in a shipwreck. The waves carried me
ashore, where a holy temple lay. Many young girls were in
service there; one of them, the youngest of them all, found
me on the beach and saved my life. I saw her only twice, but
she is the only one I can love in this world; and you look like
her. You almost make her picture disappear from my soul.
She belongs to the holy temple and, therefore, good fortune
has sent you to me instead, and we shall never part.''

"Oh, he does not know that it was I who saved his life,''
thought the little mermaid. "I carried him across the sea to
the forest where the temple stood. I hid behind the rocks and
watched over him until he was found. I saw that beautiful girl
whom he loves more than me!'' And the little mermaid
sighed deeply, for cry she couldn't. "He has said that the girl
belongs to the holy temple and will never come out into the
world, and they will never meet again. But I am with him and
see him every day. I will take care of him, love him, and
devote my life to him.''

Everyone said that the young prince was to be married; he
was to have the neighboring king's daughter, a beautiful
princess. A magnificent ship was built and made ready. It
was announced that the prince was traveling to see the neighboring kingdom, but that no one believed. "It is not the
country but the princess he is to inspect,'' they all agreed.

The little mermaid shook her head and smiled; she knew
what the prince thought, and they didn't.

"I must go,'' he had told her, "I must look at the beautiful
princess, my parents demand it. But they won't force me to
carry her home as my bride. I can't love her. She does not
look like the girl from the temple as you do. If I ever marry, I
shall most likely choose you, my little fondling with the eloquent
eyes.'' And he kissed her on her red lips and played with her
long hair, and let his head rest so near her heart that it
dreamed of human happiness and an immortal soul.

"Are you afraid of the ocean, my little silent child?'' asked
the prince as they stood on the deck of the splendid ship that
was to sail them to the neighboring kingdom. He told the

little mermaid how the sea can be still or stormy, and about the fishes that live in it, and what the divers had seen underneath the water. She smiled as he talked, for who knew better than she about the world on the bottom of the ocean?

In the moonlit night, when everyone slept but the sailor at the rudder and the lookout in the bow, she sat on the bulwark and looked down into the clear water. She thought she saw her father's palace; and on the top of its tower her old grandmother was standing with her silver crown on her head, looking up through the currents of the sea, toward the keel of the ship. Her sisters came; they looked at her so sorrowfully and wrung their white hands in despair; she waved to them and smiled. She wanted them to know that she was happy, but just at that moment the little cabin boy came and her sisters dived down under the water; he saw nothing but some white foam on the ocean.

The next morning the ship sailed into the harbor of the great town that belonged to the neighboring king. All the church bells were ringing, and from the tall towers trumpets blew, while the soldiers stood at attention, with banners flying and bayonets on their rifles.

Every day another banquet was held, and balls and parties followed one after the other. But the princess attended none of them, for she did not live in the palace; she was being educated in the holy temple, where she was to learn all the royal virtues. But at last she came.

The little mermaid wanted ever so much to see her; and when she finally did, she had to admit that a more beautiful girl she had never seen before. Her skin was so delicate and fine, and beneath her long dark lashes smiled a pair of faithful, dark blue eyes.

"It is you!" exclaimed the prince. "You are the one who saved me, when I lay half dead on the beach!" And he embraced his blushing bride.

"Oh, now I am too happy," he said to the little mermaid. "That which I never dared hope has now happened! You will share my joy, for I know that you love me more than any of the others do."

The little mermaid kissed his hand; she felt as if her heart were breaking. His wedding morning would bring her death and she would be changed into foam of the ocean.

All the churchbells rang and heralds rode through the streets and announced the wedding to the people. On all the altars costly silver lamps burned with fragrant oils. The priests swung censers with burning incense in them, while the prince and the princess gave each other their hands, and the bishop blessed them. The little mermaid, dressed in silk and gold, held the train of the bride's dress, but her ears did not hear the music, nor did her eyes see the holy ceremony, for this night would bring her death, and she was thinking of all she had lost in this world.

The bride and bridegroom embarked upon the prince's ship; cannons saluted and banners flew. On the main deck, a tent of gold and scarlet cloth had been raised; there on the softest of pillows the bridal couple would sleep.

The sails were unfurled, and they swelled in the wind and the ship glided across the transparent sea.

When it darkened and evening came, colored lamps were lit and the sailors danced on the deck. The little mermaid could not help remembering the first time she had emerged above the waves, when she had seen the almost identical sight. She whirled in the dance, glided as the swallow does in the air when it is pursued. Everyone cheered and applauded her. Never had she danced so beautifully; the sharp knives cut her feet, but she did not feel it, for the pain in her heart was far greater. She knew that this was the last evening that she would see him for whose sake she had given away her lovely voice and left her home and her family; and he would never know of her sacrifice. It was the last night that she would breathe the same air as he, or look out over the deep sea and up into the star-blue heaven. A dreamless, eternal night awaited her, for she had no soul and had not been able to win one.

Until midnight all was gaiety aboard the ship, and the mermaid danced and laughed with the thought of death in her heart. Then the prince kissed his bride and she fondled his long black hair and, arm in arm, they walked into their splendorous tent, to sleep.

The ship grew quiet. Only the sailor at the helm and the

little mermaid were awake. She stood with her white arms resting on the railing and looked toward the east. She searched the horizon for the pink of dawn; she knew that the first sunbeams would kill her.

Out of the sea rose her sisters, but the wind could no longer play with their long beautiful hair, for their heads had been shorn.

"We have given our hair to the sea witch, so that she would help you and you would not have to die this night. Here is a knife that the witch has given us. Look how sharp it is! Before the sun rises, you must plunge it into the heart of the prince; when his warm blood sprays on your feet, they will turn into a fishtail and you will be a mermaid again. You will be able to live your three hundred years down in the sea with us, before you die and become foam on the ocean. Hurry! He or you must die before the sun rises. Our grandmother mourns; she, too, has no hair; hers has fallen out from grief. Kill the prince and come back to us! Hurry! See, there is a pink haze on the horizon. Soon the sun will rise and you will die."

The little mermaid heard the sound of her sisters' deep and strange sighing before they disappeared beneath the waves.

She pulled aside the crimson cloth of the tent and saw the beautiful bride sleeping peacefully, with her head resting on the prince's chest. The little mermaid bent down and kissed his handsome forehead. She turned and looked at the sky; more and more, it was turning red. She glanced at the sharp knife; and once more she looked down at the prince. He moved a little in his sleep and whispered the name of his bride. Only she was in his thoughts, in his dreams! The little mermaid's hand trembled as it squeezed the handle of the knife, then she threw the weapon out into the sea. The waves turned red where it fell, as if drops of blood were seeping up through the water.

Again she looked at the prince; her eyes were already glazed in death. She threw herself into the sea and felt her body changing into foam.

The sun rose out of the sea, its rays felt warm and soft on the deathly cold foam. But the little mermaid did not feel death, she saw the sun, and up above her floated hundreds of airy, transparent forms. She could see right through them, see the sails of the ship and the blood-red clouds. Their voices were melodious, so spiritual and tender that no human ear could hear them, just as their forms were so fragile and fine that no human eye could see them. So light were they that they glided through the air, though they had no wings. The little mermaid looked down and saw that she had an ethereal body like theirs.

"Where am I?" she asked; and her voice sounded like theirs—so lovely and so melodious that no human music could reproduce it.

"We are the daughters of the air," they answered. "Mermaids have no immortal souls and can never have one, unless they can obtain the love of a human being. Their chance of obtaining eternal life depends upon others. We, daughters of the air, have not received an eternal soul either; but we can win one by good deeds. We fly to the warm countries, where the heavy air of the plague rests, and blow cool winds to spread it. We carry the smell of flowers that refresh and heal the sick. If for three hundred years we earnestly try to do what is good, we obtain an immortal soul and can take part in the eternal happiness of man. You, little mermaid, have tried with all your heart to do the same. You have suffered and borne your suffering bravely; and that is why you are now among us, the spirits of the air. Do your good deeds and in three hundred years an immortal soul will be yours."

The little mermaid lifted her arms up toward God's sun, and for the first time she felt a tear.

She heard noise coming from the ship. She saw the prince and the princess searching for her. Sadly they looked at the sea, as if they knew that she had thrown herself into the waves. Without being seen, she kissed the bride's forehead and smiled at the prince; then she rose together with the other children of the air, up into a pink cloud that was sailing by.

"In three hundred years I shall rise like this into God's kingdom," she said.

"You may be able to go there before that," whispered one of the others to her. "Invisibly, we fly through the homes of human beings. They can't see us, so they don't know when we are there; but if we find a good child, who makes his parents happy and deserves their love, we smile and God takes a year away from the time of our trial. But if there is a naughty and mean child in the house we come to, we cry; and for every tear we shed, God adds a day to the three hundred years we already must serve.''

# MINOTAUR

A bull cult is not an uncommon thing among primitive agricultural peoples. The bull is a strong symbol of masculinity and it is through his matings with cows that generations of cattle to supply beef, milk, cream, cheese, butter, and leather can be maintained—to say nothing of the patient farm work performed by oxen.

The legend of the golden calf during the Exodus was an attempt to establish a bull cult by Israelites tired of dealing with an invisible God. When Israel broke away from the Davidic dynasty, it established a bull cult within its own borders to discourage its people from worshiping at Solomon's temple in Jerusalem.

The best-known bull cult of ancient times is that of early Crete, which has left us paintings of games and rituals involving bulls. While we don't know all the details of the Cretan cults, it would not be surprising if gods were sometimes portrayed as humans with the heads of bulls, and if human beings were sacrificed to the bull god.

The ancient Greeks, gathering some details of the Cretan civilization that had preceded theirs, added to it out of their own excellent imaginations. Minos, the king of Crete (Minos is a general title for the Cretan kings, like Pharaoh for the king of Egypt), was supposed to sacrifice a beautiful bull to Poseidon, god of the sea. He didn't want to and chose a less attractive bull instead. In punishment, Poseidon caused Minos' queen, Pasiphaë, to fall in love with the bull, and, in consequence, she gave birth to a bull-headed *monster, the Minotaur (from Greek words meaning "Minos bull").*

*Minos hid it in a labyrinth and, after a war with Athens, sent young Athenians into the labyrinth as food for the Minotaur. The Athenian prince Theseus came with the third group and killed the Minotaur. The following story is a modern reminiscence of the myth.*

# LETTERS FROM LAURA

*Mildred Clingerman*

Monday

Dear Mom:

Stop *worrying*. There isn't a bit of danger. Nobody ever dies or gets hurt like that while time-traveling. The young man at the Agency explained it all to me in detail, but I've forgotten most of it. His eyebrows move in the most fascinating way. So I'm going this weekend. I've already bought my ticket. I haven't the faintest idea where I'm going, but that's part of the fun. Grab Bag Tours, they call them. It costs $60 for one day and night, and the Agency supplies you with food concentrates and water capsules—a whole bag full of stuff they send right along with you. I certainly do *not* want Daddy to go with me. I'll tell him all about it when I get back, and then he can go himself, if he still wants to. The thing Daddy forgets is that all the history he reads is mostly just a pack of lies. Everybody says so nowadays, since time travel. He'd spoil everything arguing with the natives, telling them how they were supposed to act. I have to stop now, because the young man from the Agency is going to take me out to dinner and explain about insurance for the trip.

Love,<br>Laura

Tuesday

Dear Mom:

I can't *afford* to go first-class. The Grab Bag Tours are not the leavings. They're perfectly all right. It's just that you

230

sorta have to rough it. They've been thoroughly explored. I mean somebody has been there at least once before. I never heard of a native attacking a girl traveler. Just because I won't have a guide you start worrying about that. Believe me, some of those guides, from what I hear, wouldn't be very safe, either. Delbert explained it all to me. He's the boy from the Agency. Did you know that insurance is a very interesting subject?

Love,
Laura

Friday

Dear Mom:

Everything is set for tomorrow. I'm so excited. I spent three hours on the couch at the Agency's office—taking the hypno-course, you know, so I'll be able to speak the language. Later Delbert broke a rule and told me my destination, so I rushed over to the public library and read bits here and there. It's ancient Crete! Dad will be so pleased. I'm going to visit the Minotaur in the Labyrinth. Delbert says he is really off the beaten track of the tourists. I like unspoiled things, don't you? The Agency has a regular little room all fixed up right inside the cave, but hidden, so as not to disturb the regular business of the place. The Agency is very particular that way. Time travelers, Delbert says, have to agree to make themselves as inconspicuous as possible. Delbert says that will be very difficult for me to do. Don't you think *subtle* compliments are the nicest? I've made myself a darling costume—I sat up late to finish it. I don't know that it's exactly right, historically, but it doesn't really matter, since I'm not supposed to leave the cave. I have to stay close to my point of arrival, you understand. Delbert says I'm well covered now with insurance, so don't worry. I'll write the minute I get back.

Love,
Laura

Friday

Dear Prue:

Tomorrow I take my first time-travel tour. I wish you
could see my costume. Very fetching! It's cut so that my
breasts are displayed in the style of ancient Crete. A friend of
mine doubts the authenticity of the dress but says the charms it
shows off are *really* authentic! Next time I see you I'll lend
you the pattern for the dress. But I honestly think, darling,
you ought to get one of those Liff-Up operations first. I've
been meaning to tell you. Of course, I don't need it myself.
I'll tell you all about it (the trip I mean) when I get back.

Love,
Laura

Monday

Dear Prue:

I had the stinkiest time! I'll never know why I let that
character at the travel agency talk me into it. The accommo-
dations were lousy. If you want to know what I think, it's all
a gyp. These Grab Bag Tours, third-class, are just the *leavings,*
that they can't sell any other way. I hate salesmen. Whoever
heard of ancient Crete anyway? And the Minotaur. You
would certainly expect him to be a red-blooded he-man,
wouldn't you? He looked like one. Not cute, you know, but
built like a bull, practically. Prue, you just can't *tell* anymore. But I'm getting ahead of myself.

You've heard about that funny dizziness you feel for the
first few minutes on arrival? That part is true. Everything is
supposed to look black at first, but things kept on looking
black even after the dizziness wore off. Then I remembered it
was a cave I was in, but I did expect it to be lighted. I was
lying on one of those beastly little cots that wiggle every time
your heart beats, and mine was beating plenty fast. Then I
remembered the bag the Agency packs for you, and I sat up
and felt around till I found it. I got out a perma-light and
attached it to the solid rock wall and looked around. The floor
was just plain old dirty dirt. That Agency had me stuck off in
a little alcove, furnished with that sagging cot and a few coat
hangers. The air in the place was rather stale. Let's be

honest, it smelled. To console myself I expanded my wrist mirror and put on some more makeup. I was wearing my costume, but I had forgotten to bring a coat. I was freezing. I draped the blanket from the cot around me and went exploring. What a place! One huge room just outside my cubbyhole and corridors taking off in all directions, winding away into the dark. I had a perma-light with me, and naturally I couldn't get lost with my earrings tuned to point of arrival, but it was *weird* wandering around all by myself. I discovered that the corridor I was in curved downward. Later I found there were dozens of levels in the Labyrinth. Very confusing.

I was just turning to go back when something reached out and grabbed for me, from one of those alcoves. I was *thrilled*. I flicked off the light, dropped my blanket, and ran.

From behind I heard a man's voice. "All right, sis, we'll play games."

Well, Prue, I hadn't played hide-and-seek in years (except once or twice at office parties), but I was still pretty good at it. That part was fun. After a time my eyes adjusted to the dark so that I could see well enough to keep from banging into the walls. Sometimes I'd deliberately make a lot of noise to keep things interesting. But do you know what? That character would blunder right by me, and way down at the end of the corridor he'd make noises like "Oho" or "Aha." Frankly, I got discouraged. Finally I heard him grumbling his way back in my direction. I knew the dope would never catch me, so I just stepped out in front of him and said "Wellll?" You know, in that drawly sarcastic way I have.

He reached out and grabbed me, and then he staggered back—like you've seen actors do in those old, old movies. He kept pounding his forehead with his fist, and then he yelled, "Cheated! Cheated again!" I almost slapped him. Instead I snapped on my perma-light and let him look me over good.

"Well, Buster," I said very coldly, "what do you mean, cheated?"

He grinned at me and shaded his eyes from the light. "Darling," he said, "you look luscious, indeed, but what the hell are you doing here?"

"I'm sightseeing," I said. "Are you one of the sights?"

"Listen, baby, I *am* the sight. Meet the Minotaur." He stuck out his huge paw, and I shook it.

"Who did you think I was?" I asked him.

"Not *who*, but *what*," he said. "Baby, you ain't no virgin."

Well, Prue, really. How can you argue a thing like that? He was completely *wrong*, of course, but I simply refused to discuss it.

"I only gobble virgins," he said.

Then he led me down into his rooms, which were really quite comfortable. I couldn't forgive the Agency for that cot, so when I spied his lovely, soft couch draped in pale blue satin, I said, "I'll borrow that if you don't mind."

"It's all yours, kid," the Minotaur said. He meant it, too. You remember how pale blue is one of my best colors? There I was lolling on the couch, looking like the Queen of the Nile, flapping my eyelashes, and what does this churl want to do?

"I'm simply starved for talk," he says. And about what? Prue, when a working girl spends her hard-earned savings on time travel, she has a right to expect something besides *politics*. I've heard there are men, a few shy ones, who will talk very fast to you about science and all that highbrow stuff, hoping maybe you won't notice some of the things they're doing in the *meantime*. But not the Minotaur. Who cares about the government a room's length apart? Lying there, twiddling my fingers and yawning, I tried to remember if Daddy had ever mentioned anything about the Minotaur's being so persnickety. That's the trouble with books. They leave out all the important details.

For instance, did you know that at midnight every night the Minotaur makes a grand tour of the Labyrinth? He wouldn't let me go along. That's another thing. He just says "no" and grins and means it. Now isn't that a typical male trait? I thought so, and when he locked me in his rooms the evening looked like turning into fun. I waited for him to come back with bated breath. But you can't bate your breath forever, and he was gone hours. When he did come back I'd fallen asleep and he woke me up *belching*.

"Please," I said. "Do you have to do that?"

"Sorry, kid," he said. "It's these gaunt old maids. Awful souring to the stomach." It seems this windy diet was one of the things wrong with the government. He was very bitter about it all. Tender virgins, he said, had always been in short supply and now he was out of favor with the new regime. I rummaged around in my wrist bag and found an antacid pill. He was delighted. Can you imagine going into a transport over pills?"

"Any cute males ever find their way into this place?" I asked him. I got up and walked around. You can loll on a couch just so long, you know.

"No boys!" The Minotaur jumped up and shook his fist at me. I cowered behind some hangings, but I needn't have bothered. He didn't even jerk me out from behind them. Instead he paced up and down and raved about the lies told on him. He swore he'd never eaten boys—hadn't cared for them at all. That creep, Theseus, was trying to ruin him politically. "I've worn myself thin," he yelled, "in all these years of service—" At that point I walked over and poked him in his big, fat stomach. Then I gathered my things together and walked out.

He puffed along behind me wanting to know what was the matter. "Gee, kid," he kept saying, "don't go home mad." I didn't say goodbye to him at all. A spider fell on him and it threw him into a hissy. The last I saw of him he was cursing the government because they hadn't sent him an exterminator.

Well, Prue, so much for the bogey man. Time travel in the raw!

Love,
Laura

Monday

Dear Mom:

Ancient Crete was nothing but politics, not a bit exciting. You didn't have a single cause to worry. These people are just as particular about girls as you are.

Love,
Laura

Tuesday

Dear Mr. Delbert Barnes:

　Stop calling me or I will complain to your boss. You cad. I
see it all now. You and your fine talk about how your Agency
"fully protects its clients." That's a very high-sounding name
for it. Tell me, how many girls do you talk into going to
ancient Crete? And do you provide all of them with the same
kind of insurance? Mr. Barnes, I don't want any more insurance from you. But I'm going to send you a client for that
trip—the haggiest old maid I know. She has buck teeth and
whiskers. Insure *her*.

　　　　　　　　　　　　　　　　　　　　　　　　　Laura

P.S. Just in case you're feeling smug about me, put this in
your pipe and smoke it. The Minotaur *knew*, I can't imagine
how, but *you*, Mr. Barnes, *are no Minotaur*.

# PEGASUS

*One of the most enduring dreams of human beings is to fly. All sorts of spirits and monsters were pictured with wings, since flying seemed an obvious attribute of supernatural beings. In addition, there were various ways of enabling human beings to fly—flying carpets, for instance, are common in the stories included in* The Arabian Nights.''

*The ancient Greeks came up with the most attractive of all flying creatures—Pegasus, the divine and immortal winged horse. The thought of a flying horse may well have arisen from the wonder of horseless human beings at the speed with which a horseman could cover the ground. To a man going no faster than an oxcart will carry him, the racing horse might as well have been flying.*

*Pegasus was supposed to have been born of the blood of the severed head of Medusa, the gorgon killed by the Greek hero Perseus. Another Greek hero, Bellerophon, rode Pegasus during the task of killing the chimera, and later in wars against the Amazons. Still later, Bellerophon tried to use Pegasus to scale Olympus, the home of the gods, but was thrown and badly hurt as punishment for this blasphemous attempt.*

*In later myths, Pegasus was associated with poetic inspiration. After all, the poet's fancy lifts him to the skies (so to speak) as though he were riding a flying horse. Pegasus was supposed to have landed on Mount Helicon near Thebes, and his hoof dug out a hollow from which emerged a spring called the Hippocrene ("fountain of the horse"), which was a legendary source of poetic inspiration.*

*It's almost a shame to have to point out that muscle-powered wings could not support the weight of a man, let alone that of a horse. The following story, however, tackles that impossibility.*

# THE TRIUMPH OF PEGASUS

*F. A. Javor*

It was working out beautifully, just beautifully, and if Colin Hall had been a less dedicated young man he would have been rubbing his capable hands together and perhaps even pounding his equally young but no-so-sedate partner, Ed West, on his ample back.

Their entry in the jumper division of the horse show, Ato's Pride, so named from the initial letters of their fledgling company's name, Animals to Order, a gleaming black stallion with four perfectly matched white stockings and a diamond-shaped blaze on his forehead, was just being led to the edge of the obstacle-planted ring and the roar of the crowd's approval was hackle-raising.

Instinctively Colin's eyes flew to the six-inch screen he'd jerry-rigged to monitor a select few bits of the information being sent by the dozens of micro-transmitters implanted under the skin, adjoining the organs, the nerves, even sampling the bloodstream of the animal waiting to go through its paces below them.

Information being transmitted and recorded on the slowly turning tapes to be fed later into the University's computer if they, he and Ed, wanted a more complete analysis and, more to the point, if they could scrape together the necessary service fee.

But the complex and shifting pattern of light on the jerry-rigged screen, small though its sampling was, was enough to let Colin know how their animal was taking to what was by far the largest massing of people he'd ever been exposed to.

An emotional crowd that this, perhaps the greatest of the year's shows, never failed to attract.

*A little too much salivating . . . pain response a little high. I told that rider he had a tender mouth.* But all in all, Ato's Pride was taking this crowd's adulation as much in stride as he had that of the smaller shows around the country they'd had to enter him in to garner enough first ribbons to allow him to qualify for this particular show.

This show that he and Ed had finally decided to aim at in a mixture of hope and desperation. Then the grinding press of work and doing without, in which the gingerly placing into its embryo tank of the cell that was to grow into the magnificent animal below them was almost an anticlimax.

An anticlimax to the arduous task of mapping its gene pattern and to the planning and the tailoring of the solutions that were to be so delicately, so precisely metered to it, but only a beginning of their gamble to save Animals to Order, their two-man partnership that gave promise but only of dying in the womb.

He had plucked the salmon-colored bank notice from the pile of due-chits that had just fallen from the vac-tube beside their office door.

"A lethal gene," he said wryly to Ed, sitting at what they'd hoped would be the desk of the receptionist they'd never been able to afford, straightening and rebending a paper clip. "A lethal gene. A fatal deficiency in the customer-forming enzyme."

"I've been thinking about that," Ed said, his face deadly serious for once. "Animals to Order is basically a sound idea, but I think our trouble lies in the fact that nobody knows we're alive." He clenched his fist. "If we could only advertise."

The wryness in Colin's smile deepened. "It isn't ethical."

Ed flung down his paper clip. "It isn't ethical," he parroted. "So we sit around and wait for recognition to come to us, and meanwhile we starve."

His voice went up a notch. "Ten seconds. Ten lousy seconds in the middle of somebody else's vid-cast. Ten lousy seconds."

"Relax," Colin said. "We couldn't scrape together the cash now even if we could advertise. Our equipment . . ."

Ed waved a hand. "You don't have to tell me how much the rental on our equipment is costing us. I signed the papers with you, remember?"

He stopped short and rubbed the back of his neck with his palm. "I'm sorry, Colin," he said. "I don't mean to snarl at you but it riles me. We've got a potentially great service here and the rules of our game make it something dirty for professional people like us to go out and holler in the crossroads for people to come buy it."

Ed held up a finger and went on talking. "One order. One solitary order all the while we've been in business. It'd gripe anybody."

It was true. Although they'd been open for half a year, their business had produced little more than inquiries like the tentative one from a physician who was hoping they'd run across an enzyme, an acid, anything that might make the cells of an arm stump de-differentiate and then re-differentiate and grow to restore the amputated limb.

Sorrowfully, Colin had to tell him that, although they could grow an animal with short legs or long legs or even transplant a developing leg, their science could not yet do what he asked of it.

Then there was the usual scattering of requests from biology and genetics students for the results of their most recent work sent quickly, please, by return vac-tube because there was only this weekend coming up in which to get the papers completed and turned in.

And the one solid order Ed had mentioned. From a down-country milk manufacturer. Four heifers. All identical and matching perfectly their trademark. To be sent around to the various state and bureau food exhibits to promote the name of their company and product. It was not a particularly difficult assignment. A great deal of research and gene mapping had already been done by associations and others interested in food animals so that it was chiefly a case of bringing together what he and Ed needed, and filling in the gaps to produce the animal they wanted.

Matching an animal to one in the picture of a trademark was not difficult because you had only to look at it to know how well you'd succeeded. It was the intangible qualities that made for a challenge.

As for identical animals, nature had been producing them for centuries. It was simply a case of splitting the egg once, and then splitting each of the daughter halves again.

It was the heifer order that gave Colin his idea, and staring at the pile of due-chits on his desk made the tussle with his conscience a brief one. "Ed," he said, "we have to do something to call attention to ourselves."

"That's not hard. Let's go out and blow up the Sub-Capital building."

"I'm not joking. You remember the heifer people?"

"Of course. Our one solitary contact with that great world of commerce out there beyond the laboratory walls. We were going to sweep it off its collective feet with our brilliance. I remember."

"They paid us for four animals whose only purpose was to promote their company name and advance the sale of their product. Right?"

"Yes, but that money is long gone and the rent is due in . . ." Ed counted on his fingers. ". . . four days. What are you getting at?"

"Simply this," and now Colin spoke slowly, the excitement in him growing. "What we did for them, we can do for ourselves."

"Build four heifers . . . ?" Ed was patently puzzled.

"Of course not. I mean use our skills to build for ourselves an animal to do for us what the heifers are doing for the milk people. Call us to the attention of the public in general, and of our potential customers in particular."

Ed was pulling his lower lip. "An animal for the express purpose of getting publicity. . . ." And then his head came up. "Hey, TV coverage, wire services, the sport commentators . . . the Sport of . . ."

Colin finished it for him. "Exactly, the Sport of Kings. A horse."

And now Ed's eyes were shining. "Great! We'll build the greatest, the fastest racehorse to come down the pike since . . ."

"No," Colin shook his head. "Not a racing horse."

"Not a racehorse?" Ed looked puzzled again.

"No. The people we want to notice us don't have racing connections. Besides," and he smiled wryly again, "we can't ethically afford to be that obvious. This has got to look like a labor of love. We'll build a horse to enter in the next international showing at the New Arena."

"Wait a minute," Ed said. "Doesn't the Dean's brother raise horses?"

Colin shook his head. "Not Harrison Bullitt . . . his wife. But do you know who is honorary president of the horse show association?"

It was Ed's turn to shake his head. "No."

"Commodore Joshua E. Wall."

"Commodore Joshua E. . . . Not Commodore Wall of NavAir?"

Colin nodded, the smile on his face broad now. "That's right, Commodore Joshua E. Wall, Chief of Procurement for NavAir . . . and the man we've been trying to get in touch with since we first started."

"Don't keep the club so exclusive. He's only one of a long roster of people who haven't responded to our maidenlike overtures."

"True, but if we can get him to give us a contract, then we don't need to worry about many of the others."

Ed pushed back his chair and stood up. "What are we waiting for then, let's get started. . . . When is the next show scheduled for?" he added.

"Early November, but entries usually close in October."

"October! That's cutting it close for a full-grown animal."

"Closer than you think. We've got to get him out and picking up a fistful of first ribbons before that, else he won't be able to even qualify for the big show. But tell me, Ed, can we wait until next year?"

"My head can, but my stomach knows better. I repeat, what are we waiting for? There's only four days' rental left on the analyzer."

The electron analyser. The rental on the unit dug deep into their credit fund, but it was indispensable in their work. Offspring of the early instrument packets shot off to Earth's neighboring planets to analyze and report back by radio on their life forms, it had also done away with much of the time and tedious labor cost needed to map a gene pattern when all the researchers had to work with before its advent were bits of absorbent paper and a photographic plate exposed to a diffracted X-ray.

He and Ed might have used the University unit, but then its rigid rules would have compelled them to be researchers working for the University, and not the co-establishers of Animals to Order, their independent and commercial enterprise.

And now the months of work, of lost sleep, of going back to the making of tutor-tapes for the University to earn the money to live on, to keep open the skeleton of their office, to pay for the hauling of Ato's Pride from show to show around the country and the professional riders required, for fees; all of it looked now to have been worth it. From the sound of the Arena crowd's reaction to their first glimpse of the black stallion, it was plain that his snowballing reputation had reached here before him, and that their gamble was at long last about to pay off.

He felt Ed's elbow in his side, Ed's voice, over the sound of the crowd, excited in his ear. "The Commodore! Over there, on the other side of the ring. I think that's the Commodore coming toward us."

There were many figures in bright blue formal clothes below them across the arena, but Colin had no trouble making out the Commodore's white hair and beefy shoulders. And it *did* look as though he was working his way through the assembled officials and others in their direction. Well beyond the Commodore, Colin noticed another man, also white haired but built small, like a jockey, who looked to be following the Commodore toward them.

He called him to Ed's attention. "The little man, just coming around the left side of the judge's table. Do you know him?"

"No . . . ," Ed said after a moment, "but he seems

to be trying to give the Commodore a race. I hope it's a tie.''

"You hope it's a tie?"

"Right. If you've got something to sell, there's nothing wrong with having two bargainers on the grounds at the same time to sort of encourage each other to make you more and more extravagant offers. After all, who is the girl in town that everybody wants to date? Why the one who has the most boyfriends already, that's who."

The Commodore went out of Colin's line of sight, going underneath their overhang, and in a moment, the little man as well. If they really were coming to them then they'd be at the head of the ramp behind them in seconds. Colin forced himself to keep his eyes away from the spot.

And then the Commodore was bearing down on them. "Mr. Colin Hall?"

Colin turned his head toward the big, white-haired man. "I'm Colin Hall," he said and did not go on to introduce Ed, stopped by a strangeness in the the Commodore's manner. Somehow, the big man looked oddly embarrassed.

"Mr. Hall," the Commodore said, "there's been a question raised . . ."

"Hall? West?"

The voice, not loud, but penetrating, cut in on the Commodore. It was the small, white-haired man.

"Just a minute," Colin snapped, irked by the man's abrupt manner and anxious to hear what the Commodore had been about to say to him.

"You Hall or West?" the man said, still flatly.

Colin turned in his seat to look full at the little man. "I'm Hall," he said and wondered why, with all the noise of the crowd around them, he should suddenly get the feeling of being in the midst of an apprehensive silence.

"Mrs. Bullitt wants to see you. Now."

Annoyance flared inside Colin and he didn't try to hide it. "Friend," he said to the little man who might have once been a jockey, "I don't know who you are, but . . ." Colin stopped, suddenly rehearing what the man had said. "Did you say Mrs. Bullitt wanted to see me?"

The man nodded. "Now."

Colin was torn. The Commodore was important to him and Ed, and added to this was the fact that some question had been raised important enough for him to seek them out at what must be, for him, a busy moment. But Ed and he frankly needed their jobs at the University and the wife of the Dean's brother was known to be an impatient and irascible woman.

The Commodore settled Colin's quandary for him. He spoke to Colin, but his eyes were on the little man. "Mrs. Bullitt has raised a question about the validity of your entry's breeding qualifications. There will have to be a hearing, of course, but for now tell me this. Was your jumper a . . ." He groped for the expression. ". . . a test-tube animal all through his gestation period?"

"No," Colin said, puzzled. "He's a replant. Why?" There was certainly nothing new about the technique of removing a potential egg from the dam of a desired animal, starting its growth in an embryo tank and then replanting it in a mother animal to complete its development. He and Ed had used the technique with Ato's Pride for the one compelling reason of its economy. It would have cost a great deal for the battery of technicians and equipment needed if they'd used a full-span series of tanks to bring their stallion to borning size. But to feed and control one pregnant mare . . . ?

"In other words," the Commodore said, "your entry was natural-born."

"Yes," Colin nodded.

The Commodore spoke to the little man directly, his voice sounding to Colin unnecessarily defiant.

"Ato's Pride stays. And you can tell *that* to your employer."

The little man shrugged. "I'll pass the word, Commodore," he said, "but you'll forgive me if I remind you that it's the association's rules committee and not the president who must pass on a thing like this."

Colin thought he saw the Commodore's eyes on the little man's waver. "Wait a minute," he said, half wildly. Someone, and from the sound of things it was Harrison Bullitt's intransigent wife, was trying to keep his and Ed's one hope out of competition. "You can't pull our entry now. His event is about to start."

The Commodore turned away from the little man. "He's right, you know," he said to Colin. "I don't have the authority for this, but I can call together the rules committee and I will."

"But the event, it's starting."

"Not yet it isn't, and I'll have it held off for as long as the crowd will allow. Meanwhile," he indicated the small man with his head, "we'd better go along with him."

"Let's go," the little man said, not seeming to be the least bit abashed by the Commodore's obvious dislike of him.

And half seething, half numb, Colin let him lead them to the Owner's Suite four levels below the arena floor, and eight levels below the street.

The room he ushered them into was large and brightly lit. Neoplast walls niched and hung with award ribbons, platters, trophy cups. Antique photos of horses and behind the stylishly narrow afra-wood desk, a fleshly-faced man in the customary bright-blue formal jacket. Behind him a huge vistaphoto of open fields, fences, white clustered buildings, pasturing animals. ABBY BULLITT HORSE FARMS cut very large into the gateside panels. The size of the establishment startled Colin fleetingly. He had no idea that Mrs. Bullitt's interest, and investment, in horses was so great.

And standing beside the desk, thumping its top with a hard-sounding finger, a short woman, thick-bodied and dumpy-looking even in the smart green-and-white-striped riding coat and sleek boots of a Major Hunt.

Harrison Bullitt Colin knew from having seen him in the Dean's office at the University; the woman turning pale eyes and a querulous mouth toward them as they entered, he assumed to be Mrs. Bullitt.

"Why didn't you knock," she began without preamble. "Martin, you know I don't like people walking in on me without knocking."

The little man beside Colin made no answer, but Harrison Bullitt put a hand on his wife's pudgy arm. "We're not at home, dear. This is an office. It's all right for Martin to walk in here without knocking.''

Mrs. Bullitt shook off her husband's hand. "I don't like people to walk in on me without knocking. Martin?'' And there was venom in her look, all out of proportion to the incident that had sparked it.

"Yes ma'am,'' the little man said and his voice sounded sincere.

There was a long silence while Mrs. Bullitt continued to stare at her hireling, long enough for Colin to become conscious of his own heavy breathing. In a reflex of discomfort he cleared his throat and the woman's eyes snapped to his face.

"You,'' and again she spoke without preamble, "and you.'' And her eyes shifted to the space behind Colin where he knew Ed stood, and back to his with a darting motion of her head that somehow made him think of a lizard he'd once seen catching flies.

"You are the two young men who call yourselves Animals to Order?''

It was a question, but to Colin it somehow sounded like an accusation. "Yes, ma'am,'' he said.

"Speak up, speak up,'' she said. "I can't hear you. I like people to speak up when they talk to me.''

"Yes, Mrs. Bullitt, we are,'' Colin said, louder, more than a little annoyed with himself at the way her sharp tone had put him off balance. Angry also that she could bring disaster to his and Ed's long-held hopes if her objection to their entry in the arena above should stand.

"Good,'' the small woman in the striped riding jacket said.

The word of approval startled Colin. "Good? I . . . I don't understand.''

"What is there to understand?'' and her voice was impatient sounding. "You say you can make animals to order. Very well, I want you to make one for me. A horse . . . a special horse . . . and after you make it I want you to smash the mold or whatever it is you use. I want it to be unique . . . mine alone and no one else ever to have another like it.''

The light that had come into Mrs. Bullitt's eyes as she

spoke made Colin think shiveringly of medieval princelings who would have a craftsman's hands cut off after he'd provided a work of art for them so that he could not surpass it for another, of architects blinded and put to death so that they could not build for another prince, in another place, a palace, a castle greater, or even the match of, the one possessed by their executioner.

Ed's voice in his ear, low, urgent. "Hey, a contract for an exclusive animal with Bullitt Farms. It may not be NavAir, but from the look of that vistaphoto behind the old man, it's no small-stake operation either. Don't haggle, man. After all, it's quick money and we've already done a lot of the groundwork with Ato."

Harrison Bullitt leaned forward. Even sitting he was a big man, and, although he bore no apparent physical resemblance to his wife, there was a certain flatness about the expression in his eyes that made the thought skim the surface of Colin's mind that here, Harrison Bullitt and his wife Abby, were two of a very unpleasant kind.

"Animals to Order," Bullitt said. "What is it that you do?"

Colin had answered that question dozens of times. He did not need to grope for an analogy to tell of his and Ed's work with the living germ plasm of animals; of the fascination and the monotony of charting gene positions; of converting desired qualities into intricately interacting enzyme patterns; of eliminating genetic loads, the stores of harmful genes carried by all sexually reproducing species.

Of their bio-solutions and the organism growing in its succession of tanks, of the enjoyable tension of watching it until it could emerge and survive without their direction in the open world and be, if they were as lucky as they were entitled to be for their chosen profession was still as much an art as it was a science, be exactly as they had envisioned it at the start.

But Colin's analogy was simple. "Think of a chromosome as a microscopically tiny string of beads present in every plant and animal cell. Now each head is a gene that determines or helps to determine some characteristic of its own animal or plant, like the color of its eyes, the structure of its bones, the smoothness or roughness of its coat, everything about it.

"What we do is sort of rework the beads, repair any damaged ones, shape the string to grow into what we want it to be."

Harrison Bullitt shrugged his meaty shoulders. "Sounds cut and dried to me."

"I suppose it is, in theory. But we're dealing with a living organism. It can be killed, and quite easily . . . or just die. A temperature can get a shade too warm or a shade too cold . . . or a stray cosmic ray can strike it . . . and it turns out in a way we didn't predict. Just being alive, I guess, is enough for it to not always do what you expect it to."

"Sounds like pretty much of a slipshod operation to me," Harrison Bullitt said, and from his voice Colin didn't know if he was being talked to or if the big man was just thinking aloud and not particularly interested or caring if he was heard.

But Bullitt went on. "Can you switch parts around?"

Colin thought of fruit flies with misplaced wings, of experimental animals with third eyes, of two-headed dogs. The early researchers had produced all of these and more, and with modern pressor and laser beam techniques it would be even simpler to do. But it was one of those understandings that can exist between two men without ever having been mentioned or even thought of, that he and Ed would not debase their profession by peddling sideshow freaks.

"We can," Colin said aloud, "but we won't."

Mrs. Bullitt laughed shortly. "That's one of the stupidest expressions in the language. Young man, never say you won't do some particular thing. You'd be surprised at the things you'd do if the bind gets tight enough."

Colin had no answer for her except to hold his rising temper in check. What answer did anyone ever have for boors, particularly influential ones like these two?

Mrs. Bullitt dropped her heavy figure into the plastiform visitor's chair beside her husband's desk, letting her booted heels fly out in front of her as she did so.

Colin noticed roweled spurs and was surprised. He didn't think anyone wore the spiked discs anymore, particularly to ride valuable animals.

There were other chairs in the room, two long sofas along opposite walls, but Mrs. Bullitt did not wave them to a seat. Colin, Ed, and Martin off to one side of them now, remained standing. The Commodore settling deep in the chair dropped into when they came in.

"I want a horse," the sitting woman said matter-of-factly, "with wings."

"A horse," Colin started to say and then did a mental double-take. "A what?"

"A great idea, isn't it?" A horse that can fly. Nobody, but nobody in the association, in the world, will be able to top that."

Colin could only stare at the woman. She couldn't be serious, but from the set of her face it was plain that she was. "It's impossible," he managed to say. "It's a physical impossibility."

Annoyance flared in Mrs. Bullitt's pale eyes. She struck the arm of her chair sharply with the flat of her hand. "Don't use that word," she said. "I don't like it. Do you hear? I don't like it."

"But it is impossible," Colin said and he didn't know if he was pleading for her to understand or to hold on to his own sanity. He had never before in his life met people like this.

Beside him, Colin heard Ed whistle through his teeth, softly to himself. "A Pegasus she wants. A flying, neighing, flaming Greek legend she wants."

"A flying horse is a physical impossibility," Colin said.

Harrison Bullitt seemed amused. "Everything is impossible . . . until the price gets right. All right," and he sat up in his chair, "let's stop this nonsense. How much is it going to cost me?"

Colin felt like a man trying to keep his footing on a mound of slippery sand. "You don't understand. It's not a question of money. It's not money at all."

Bullitt seemed to be getting annoyed. "I don't see that you should have any particular problem. You said that you could switch parts around. What's so tough about grafting a pair of wings onto a horse?''

The feeling of floundering on shifting sand deepened in Colin. ''A wing isn't just something added onto the outside of an animal, and it's not an oversized shoulder blade. It's an integral part of the skeleton, it has a full system of muscles to support it, to move it. Look.''

He held up his arm, his fingers extended, his hand bent downward at the wrist. ''It's like an arm. The finger bones are long.'' He made the stretching gesture with his other hand, slapped his arm. ''These bones are there, holding, supporting the tissues of the wing itself . . .''

''I never noticed much of a skeleton in a fly wing,'' Harrison Bullitt interrupted, not bothering to hide the growing of his annoyance.

The sand was beginning to have a sucking feel to it. ''Yes, but a fly, any insect, has but the tiniest fraction of the weight of even a small bird. A bird,'' Colin said, grasping at a fact that would convince these two that he was not merely throwing up phony obstacles to milk them of their money. ''The largest bird. A condor. Ten feet across the wings. Weighs how much? Forty pounds.

''Now a horse. Even a lightly built saddle horse will weigh a thousand pounds, and you know better than I how large his muscles have to be just to move him around on the ground. Even if we did . . .'' he stopped himself. He was beginning to think like these people about the fantastic.

''Even if we *could*,'' he corrected himself and went on. ''Even if we could re-form his front legs into some semblance of wings, the muscle structures needed to lift half a ton into the air would be so huge that the poor beast probably couldn't even stand under their weight. Then to support all that weight we'd have to make the bones thicker and sturdier and that would add to the weight and . . . don't you see?'' he ended helplessly.

''Weight,'' Bullitt said. ''Don't prattle about weight. Only last night on TriV we saw a . . . some kind of a flying dinosaur. Weight.'' He snorted.

''A reptile,'' Colin said, and it was quicksand he felt the

suction of. "A pterodactyl. But even the largest of those had only a twenty-foot wing span."

Colin hadn't been watching Mrs. Bullitt particularly, but now she seemed to explode out of her chair. "You see," she flung at her husband. "I told you there was no point in trying to be nice to these people. They know only one kind of language. All right, if that's the way they want it."

Her eyes, flat and expressionless in spite of the anger in her voice, bored into Colin's. "Young man," she said, "I want a flying horse. Are . . . you . . . going . . . to . . . give . . . it . . . to . . . me? She spaced the words deliberately.

"I . . . I . . ." Colin floundered and then was amazed to hear Ed's voice.

Calmly, rationally, Ed was saying, "Now let me understand this clearly, Mrs. Bullitt. You want us to recreate for you the legendary flying horse Pegasus. Is that correct?"

Colin stared at Ed. *Recreate . . . legendary . . .* what had gotten into Ed?

And then he heard Mrs. Bullitt's voice. "Legendary. You mean someone has already had a flying horse?"

Colin's eyes snapped back to Mrs. Bullitt's face. Petulance seemed to be always in the set of her mouth, but was there something else there now? Did he see disappointment?

Hope flared up in Colin at the method he thought he saw in Ed's apparent madness. If Mrs. Bullitt became convinced that someone else had beaten her to the possession of a flying horse, even centuries removed in time, then maybe enough of the bloom would be rubbed off the idea of her to abandon it.

But he must have, couldn't have, but he must have misread Ed's intent because his partner's next words were, "Not exactly, perhaps, but I do believe that many legends, even the more fantastic, may well have a basis in fact."

Mrs. Bullitt took Ed's words for ammunition. "You see," she snapped at Colin. "Your partner admits that it can be done."

But Colin was staring at Ed. Unbelieving.

"What are you talking about?" he half shouted at Ed. "What legends and what facts?"

And Ed was looking him right in the eye and saying,

"Almost any legend . . . or folk saying. Like 'dumb blonde' for example. You know that every once in a great while someone comes up missing one of the pigment-forming enzymes. Naturally, they can't help but be blonde. But they are also mentally retarded, and seriously. Somebody noticed the two conditions, jumped to a vastly broader conclusion than the observation warranted, and there you are. But there was *some* basis in fact."

Colin could only stare at Ed. The enzyme was phenyla-laninase and the mental condition phenylpyruvic oligophrenia. But Ed couldn't be serious about a Pegasus.

Or could he? Ed was going on. "And you remember the zoo on the continent that was back-breeding legendary animals?"

"Backbreeding legendary animals? They took modern cattle and backbred them until they had a cow that looked like an extinct ancestor. Where," he demanded, "where are you going to get me the germ plasm of a demigod to repeat the feat for a flying horse?"

Taking firm hold of his voice because he didn't know whether to laugh or hit somebody or just bang his head on the paneled and trophy-hung walls, Colin said to the room in general, "Thank you very much for your confidence in our ability. It is very flattering, but very much misplaced. We cannot build a flying horse. Thank you again and goodbye."

And he put a hand under Ed's elbow and almost shoved him out of the room, and into the passageway, the angry voice of Mrs. Bullitt following them out.

"You'll be back, I promise you. You'll be back, and remember, I won't be as easy to get along with next time."

Controlling himself, Colin slid the door shut gently.

He turned to Ed. "What got into you? You know as well as I do that we can't give her what she wants. Nobody can."

"Of course I know it," Ed said. "But that woman isn't rational. I was hoping to at least gain us a little time to figure out something, anything. The way it is now, Lord knows what she'll do."

"I . . . I'm sorry, Ed," Colin started to say, but he was interrupted by the opening of the door they'd just come through. The Commodore emerged and slid it shut again. He stood rubbing the back of his white hair with the flat of one hand. "A flying horse," he said and shook his head. "A flying horse."

He looked at Colin. "I suppose it's impossible."

Colin didn't feel like going through that one again. He nodded.

"Are you sure?" the Commodore persisted. "I don't want to quote an old saw, but the one about doing the difficult right now and the impossible taking a little longer has a good deal to it, I think. We *are* doing things today as a matter of course that we used to *know* were impossible."

He smiled. "It used to be an obvious fact that what went up had to come down." He paused and looked from Colin to Ed and back to Colin again. "Have you checked any of our satellites lately?"

It struck Colin that the Commodore was beginning to sound like Harrison Bullitt. "I think I get your point, sir," he said, not because he did, but because the quicksand feeling was back and he wanted to get away from it and Abby Bullitt's office.

"No you don't," the Commodore said, suddenly blunt. "I thought of buying Ato's Pride, looked him over very carefully. Then I realized that if you can do for food animals what you did for him, then you've got something I can use. I could give you an initial contract and I could defend it, I'm sure. But with Abby throwing her weight around there's more to it than being willing to justify your actions to an investigating committee. She's thorough and she's fast. You'd probably get hung up because one of your hogs dribbled on the sidewalk."

He shook Colin's hand and then Ed's. "You think about it," he said. "And you look me up when you get Abby Bullitt off your back. Hear?"

And after the older man had left them to go back up the ramp, it was Ed who broke the gloomy silence that he'd left behind him. "You know," he said, "he might just be right."

"About getting Mrs. Bullitt off our backs? I'm convinced."

"No, about what we *know* is impossible. We know that a horse can't fly and we know why not. Maybe if we turn the whole thing upside down and start by assuming that a horse *can* fly. Now what can we come up with?''

But Colin's mind was numb. *A horse can fly*. Now the Bullitt virus was getting to Ed. *A horse can fly*. ''Forget it,'' he said aloud. ''Let's go secure Ato and then check out.''

Their stallion was already in his stall when they got to the animal-quarters level just below the arena proper.

Slatted concrete floors, cushioned, with lagoons below to catch the droppings. Lagoons constantly running with their odor-controlling washes. Show feeds, specially formulated to inhibit the action of gas-forming bacteria. Everything doing its job of holding down, of eliminating, the characteristic offal odor. Doing it well too, but when all was said and done, a stable still smelled like a stable.

More than once Colin had wondered why the whole problem couldn't be eliminated at the source, so to speak, by just not feeding the animals at shows in the usual way. Penetra-dermal units were standard items, available at any lab supply house. The concentrates were not expensive, and they need be used only during indoor shows and perhaps a short time before.

A unit to feed an animal the size and weight of a horse need use an area no larger than a man's palm. There was no pain reaction that he'd been able to detect; in fact, some of their lab animals even seemed to enjoy the warmed-air caress of a penetra-dermal feeding unit.

But, Colin supposed, a practice taken more or less for granted in one field was too startling a break with the traditions of another to be even talked about, much less adopted. Besides, from what he'd seen of horse fanciers in recent months, he was beginning to think they rather liked the smell of horses. He knew that for himself, he was beginning to find it not altogether unpleasant.

They rubbed their animal thoroughly behind his ears, accepted the condolences of the attendants for their hard luck at his not being able to compete, showed their pass-out badges at the Manager's window.

He was a balding man behind the grilled opening. He ran a

finger down the tally-board at his elbow, ticking off their badge numbers.

"Mr. Hall? Mr. West?" he said. And when Colin nodded, went on.

"Message for you to call this number." He passed a small folded slip through the bars of his grille.

"Thank you," Colin said and unfolded the paper. "It's the Dean," he said to Ed. "I wonder what he wants?"

"I can guess," Ed said, "and I don't think I'm going to like it."

Colin dialed the University and flipped the phone switch to multispeak so that Ed could hear.

The Dean sounded embarrassed and he talked a great deal of the fine work Colin and Ed were doing. He made a passing mention of a board of trustees. He assured Colin and Ed of the warm personal regard in which he held both of them. But when he was through talking and the phone was back on its cradle his message was clear.

The University no longer needed their unique talents in the making of its tutor-tapes. Not now, nor in the foreseeable future.

"She moves fast," Ed said. "Fast."

"She said we'd be back. I guess we could have more or less expected her to do something, but I never thought that this was the kind of pressure she had in mind. It . . . it doesn't seem civilized somehow."

"Breaking a man's rice bowl seldom is," Ed said. "But cheer up, we still have an office with our name on the door."

He laughed, and it was not a pleasant sound. "That is if the cleaning people haven't told the landlord we've been sleeping in it for the past three months."

The horse show ran from Tuesday of one week through Tuesday of the next and, surprisingly to Colin, Mrs. Bullitt did not appear to be put out when the rules committee found in their favor on the question of Ato's breeding raised by her.

"You know," Ed said, "I don't think she really wanted to win this one. After all, if she'd managed to get our entry disqualified this time around, then she couldn't very well have expected any animal we might build for her to be eligible, if she had in mind to enter it in the future."

"I think she might expect a special class, if not for her flying horse, then for her."

But Ed could be right. She meant only to keep their entry out, to give them a charge, to encourage them, she might say, to see things her way.

He and Ed had won in the committee room, but it turned out to be an academic victory. When they got down to the stable level they found the shield-shaped sheriff's notice taped to an upright of Ato's stall. Some confusion among their creditors, the bank being chiefest. Until it could be straightened out, their assets, Ato's Pride included, were being impounded.

Sudden, impotent, frustrated fury poured through Colin. It wasn't quicksand. It was a solid brick wall and he was backed against it. He clenched and unclenched his fists . . . and felt completely helpless.

Ato's Pride made a little dancing movement with his hoofs. He tossed his head, his nostrils flaring.

"I'm upsetting our horse," Colin said. "Let's get out of here."

"Yeah," Ed said. "Yeah." And Colin noticed that his face was white and he too was shaking.

It was after they'd checked out and were striding up the ramp to the street that the thought hit Colin.

He caught hold of Ed's arm and pulled him to a halt. "Ed," he said, "how do you know a horse is a horse?"

Ed pulled his arm away roughly. "I'm in no mood for jokes right now," he said, "so do me a favor and skip it."

"I'm not kidding. How do you know a horse is a horse?"

"All right, Mr. Interlocutor. How do I know a horse is a horse? Because it looks like a horse. That's how." Ed stopped. "You can't mean. . . ."

"That's exactly what I mean," Colin said. "Turn our problem inside out. Don't try to build a horse and make it fly, instead, take a creature that can fly already and make it look like a horse."

Ed was laughing. Colin thought he heard a hysterical note in the sound.

"A . . . a . . . thousand-pound bird."

"It wouldn't weigh a thousand pounds. Birds are built differently from horses. Hollow bones. . . . Are you listening?"

But Ed was still laughing. "A . . . a horse with feathers."

"What is a feather if not a modified hair . . . and vice versa."

Ed was wiping his eyes. "Hollow bones. Did you ever heft the bones of a thirty-pound turkey? You build an animal as big as a horse, it's going to weigh like a horse. You've still got half a ton to lift into the air, and it doesn't much matter whether it's a horse muscle or a bird muscle that tries to do it. It still is an impossible job."

Ed was right. To end up with what they wanted, they would have to start with something just as special. "I'm sorry," Colin said, "I . . . I'm just not thinking straight."

They made their way on up the ramp and walked the not-so-great distance to their office buildings. Colin laughed shortly when they came in sight of it. "It's a cold night. I hope Mrs. Bullitt hasn't managed to have us locked out."

Colin thought he was making a bitter joke, but when they reached the door of their office, a small green placard hung on its knob. The terms of their lease clearly prohibited the use of the premises as living quarters. Would they kindly be ready to vacate in the required three days.

"She is a witch," Ed said, his eyes staring.

But all Colin could do was pound his clenched hand against the wall of the passageway until the pain of it brought him to some semblance of calm.

"We're going back," he finally said. "We're going back and we'll sign her contract. We'll give her something. I don't know what, but believe me, it will look like a horse . . . and I promise you . . . it will fly."

At the Arena they found Mrs. Bullitt in the Manager's office rattling a fistful of papers under the balding man's nose while the handful of clerks in the room made it plain that they were too deep in their work to see . . . or hear . . .

what was going on. Fleetingly, Colin wondered if she wore those roweled spurs to bed.

She did not seem suprised to see them, nor did she seem inclined to take Colin and Ed to her own office. She half-turned away from the manager, the papers still clutched in a fist, to face them. "You're back," she snapped. "I told you you would be."

The waspish tone of her voice might have made Colin turn around and walk away from her only the day before. Now, in some perverse way, it made him stand his ground.

He was surprised at how quiet his voice sounded. "Yes, Mrs. Bullitt. I think we're ready to accept your assignment."

The woman in the striped coat and boots made an abrupt motion to one of the clerks and the girl came to her immediately. "There's a blue envelope on my desk. Get it," Mrs. Bullitt snapped. The girl scurried out the door.

"I knew you'd be back," she said to Colin and Ed. "You see, it's all a question of understanding people. It always is. People never know what they can really do until they absolutely have to do it or else."

She smiled and her face looked smug. "All I ever do is provide the 'or else.' "

Colin held his tongue, but beside him he could hear Ed breathing heavily.

The girl clerk came back and Abby Bullitt took the long blue envelope from her hand and dropped it on the Manager's counter in front of Colin.

"Sign it," she said, leaving it to him to take out and unfold the long shape of the contract for himself.

Colin ignored the slight, but at his first glimpse of the printed form he looked up at Mrs. Bullitt, puzzled. "This . . . this contract is with the University. I don't understand. Yesterday your husband . . ."

"Yesterday's contract was with me. Today's is with the University."

She smiled and now she seemed to be thoroughly enjoying herself. "I told you then that I wouldn't be as easy to get along with again."

And suddenly Colin was aghast as the full implication of

what she meant to do struck him. She meant to have her flying animal, and she meant to compel them to give it to her for nothing. Absolutely nothing . . . or else.

Under a University grant they could, of course, use its facilities, its equipment, but at no profit to themselves, not even a mention of their names if the University was not disposed to lift them from anonymity.

He ran his eyes down the page. It was the standard University form, printed, with the usual blank spaces for additional items left to be filled in.

But the items filled in were anything but usual.

"Sixty days," Colin gasped, his eyes, unbelieving and dazed, moving from the smiling woman, to Ed, and back again. "Sixty days?"

"A little added incentive to keep you from dawdling," she said. "I know how you people like to stretch things out when you think you have hold of someone you can take advantage of. Surely in sixty days you ought to have something to show me. Now sign."

Ed took the contract from Colin's nerveless fingers, it rustled loudly in his shaking hand as he glanced down it. "Sixty days and we guarantee results." He flung the contract on the counter. "The way that's phrased, we could go to jail for outright fraud if we don't deliver."

Abby Bullitt had her arms crossed in front of her, tight. She said nothing.

Silence hung in the room.

Abruptly Ed snatched the Manager's chained-down pen from its stand and scribbled his name across the bottom of the stiff paper. He shoved contract and pen at Colin. "Here, sign this and let's get out of here."

Through a haze that was red and gathering, Colin signed and flung down the pen. "Would you like your horse to be of any particular color?" he said bitterly, and was aghast to see that Mrs. Bullitt seemed to be taking the question seriously.

"Arnold," she said to the balding manager, "what is the name of that liqueur we had at the Hunt dinner last Wednesday?"

"Chartreuse, Mrs. Bullitt. Chartreuse."

"That's it," she said, and then to Colin. "Make it chartreuse."

And suddenly beside Colin, Ed was laughing and he didn't seem able to stop. "A chartreuse horse. A flying, flaming, chartreuse horse."

And in the open air of the street Ed was still gasping. "Oh, a chartreuse horse."

"Why not? A chartreuse horse is just as logical as a flying one."

Ed went off in another fit of laughter. "Logic. Oh, my aching . . . logic. He's talking about logic."

But logic was what they used at first. Logic and Colin's wild idea to start with a living animal that already flew. "It's a cosmetic problem now. Not engineering. It doesn't have to *be* a horse, it just has to *look* like a horse."

Weight against size. Colin thought of fish that could distend themselves with air. There was large size with small weight. He thought of a litter of fox terrier pups he'd once handled. All were solid, chunky, heavy in the hand. All but one. The same size, but lighter than the others, so much so that his hand had come up unexpectedly when he'd picked it up. It died, but it had been lighter.

They slept in the University dorm, ate in the cafeteria, and they worked. Together at first, then, as time pressed them and there was still not a glimmer of success, they worked separately to spread their investigations.

They worked with the cells of birds. Searching for size without weight. Speeding the development of their dividing cells as much as they dared, projecting the rest of the development by computer when they had even a tentative pattern to program, guessing at more than they should have.

Anything, anything at all, that was large and could lift itself from the ground. That to start and the hope of plastic surgery, transplants, for the rest.

Nothing. Not a thing.

Sixty days. Mrs. Bullitt. A reckoning . . . and a reprieve. Not of their asking, but of her brother-in-law's, the Dean's, pleading for them, for more time.

A reprieve. A reprieve and a new contract. A contract the Dean walked out of the room and would not watch them sign.

Sixty days. No more. And this time a cash penalty. Added. If they fail, they must reimburse the University in full for the loss.

They seldom saw each other now, Colin and Ed. They slept when they could, worked when they could, ate if they could. Ed was trying irradiated cells now. Gathering them from wherever he could.

"Sure it's as subtle as a shotgun," he'd said, "but nothing alive today is of any help to us. We've got to come up with something new."

"That is a typical panic response," Colin said.

"What else have we got left but panic?" Ed wanted to know.

And then one bleary afternoon Colin came awake in the dorm to Ed's shaking him. "Wake up," Ed was saying, excited. "I think I've got a lizard that's trying to make like a bird."

Colin tried to shake the weariness out of his eyes. "A lizard?"

"Yes, I got to thinking about how birds and reptiles are distantly related, so I went over to the reptile house, picked up what cells I could, brought them back and set them up to be bombarded. This one projected pretty light for its size so I let it develop. Just now it tried to attack me."

He held up a hand, the edge of it was bleeding. "It ran on its hind legs and took off right into the air at me, its front ones going like crazy. So help me, Colin, I think it was trying to fly."

It was a lizard all right, nondescript brown, the size of a small dog, sitting on its haunches. And Ed was right, it did look as though it was trying to fly when it leaped for their throats and struck its teeth at their padded arms instead.

They took what cells they might need from it and, because it was so patently vicious, they destroyed it.

Cells died. That was expected. Others went awry and were destroyed. But one. One cell developed well and its tapes projected well.

Sleek reptile head forming. Earless. No problem. Ears are easy to form and attach later. Front legs shaping up as true wings now, clawed toes long, well membraned. Transplant leg buds from another developing cell to chest of prime animal and hope musculature will develop enough to support them. Compatability of tissue no problem. After all, aren't they actually all from the same animal?

Coloring a bonus feature, though. They did not work for it, did not plan it, but their animal seemed to be developing a greenish, golden cast to its sleek skin. Ed laughed. "She might have her chartreuse horse after all."

And the tension. The unholy tension. Out of its tank for days now, still won't eat, but seems to be doing well on penetra-dermal regimen. And as light, beautifully light as the tapes had predicted.

University gym. Transmitting implants in position, tapes set up, monitoring screen ready. Long tether. Running, on hind legs like predecessor, wings spread. Glide, not true flight, a glide. Too weak yet, too undeveloped. More plastic work needed on that reptile head. Teeth also, still too carnivorous-looking for a horse. *Glad this one is docile, not like its pappy.* Tushes. Remember tushes. After all, he is supposed to be a male horse, you know. *Why won't it eat?*

They were working together now, but exhilarated. Intuition mostly, no mapping. Pointless. To map, you needed the developed animal to see what its genes would become. And if they did manage to develop one to suit Abby Bullitt, what was the need for a map?

More trials. Flying now. Really flying, no tether, comes when whistled for, obeys hand signals too. Open air, too large for gym now, needs open air. Try it tomorrow. Call Mrs. Bullitt.

University Field. Clear, beautiful day. They'd produced a magnificent animal.

Golden green in color. Its natural position at rest seemed to be sitting on its haunches, front feet resting on the ground; the claws had fused into very acceptable-looking hoofs. Its great wings not folded flat and down against the body, but carried high so that their tops, the leading bony edges curving gracefully behind its head and high arched neck, gave it a remotely haloed look.

The tail, although Colin could not see it from this angle, was not like a horse's, and not like a lizard's either, but flat and used like an airfoil. A handsome beast, and, holding it by the bridle it had learned to wear, Colin was at once proud yet fearful of it. Made uneasy by the look in its eyes of waiting, of a biding of time. *Where is that Bullitt woman?*

She came, and riding a horse, Ed swore and reached to help Colin hold their animal's bridle, but it did not shy. It had never seen any animal larger than a lab dog before, but it seemed no more than mildly interested and stayed sitting.

But not Abby Bullitt. She'd dismounted and stood in front of their animal now, hands clasped. "He's beautiful. He's beautiful," she repeated over and over, looking up at his great head towering above her.

Colin looked away from the light in her eyes. She looked hypnotized.

And now Colin felt his animal move. The biding eyes were looking down at Abby Bullitt, and slowly, magnificently, the great wings spread. Spread in a movement Colin had never seen before. Spread upward and outward until they seemed to blot out the whole of the morning's sun.

"Oh," the woman gasped. "Oh, I must ride him."

"No," Colin said. Something was going on here that he didn't understand and his feeling of uneasiness was deep. "No, he's never been ridden before. Never even mounted."

But Abby Bullitt had her hand on the bridle. "Let go," she said. "I must ride him."

"No," Colin said and then his hand was bloody where she'd cut it with her riding crop and snatched away the bridle.

She flung herself onto the animal's shoulders, into the hollow between the high-carried wings, her sharp spurs gouging.

It screamed and it ran. On its hind legs as Colin had so often seen it do, its grafted front ones tucked in, birdlike, and then it was in flight. Again it screamed and now Abby Bullitt's voice was blended in the sound. Was it delight . . . or terror? Colin could not tell.

The mount and its rider climbed higher. The screams were fainter now, but the terror in Abby Bullitt's was plain. Toward the river and the tall cliffs beyond it the animal flew. And then it and the screaming were gone. But, airborne, it had been seen and heard, and now the crowd was gathering.

On the rim of Colin's consciousness the voice of Ed was shouting.

"Now don't worry. We know exactly where they are. The transmitters, the police can home in on the data transmitters. . . ."

But Colin wasn't really hearing him. Colin was staring at his jerry-rigged monitoring screen. The pattern of light darting and swirling across its face was a strange one for this particular animal, but one not strange at all to Colin. He'd seen it before, many times, constantly almost, with Ato's Pride, and he recognized it now with a growing horror.

Somewhere, greedily, slaveringly, the Bullitt beast was at long last feeding.

Hunched, wrapped in blankets, holding steaming mugs, Colin and Ed, in the cockpit of the patrol boat that had pulled them out of the river. Ed still shaking his head.

"It went for us. Did you see how it went for us?"

Colin didn't answer him, knowing that Ed wasn't looking for him to. Remembering the two of them in the police copter, with the pilot and the man with the heavy carbine. Tracking their animal, homing in on the emitting signals of its data transmitters until, on the rocky face of the cliffs, halfway up, they caught the glint of the sun on its gold-green skin.

"There!" Ed shouted, pointing, and the copter hovered close.

Crouched it was, on the jutting shelf. The great wings half unfurled, opening, closing, twitching,

"Do you think she's still alive?" the man with the carbine said, then, "Forget it."

It rose to meet them. Hurling itself at them with a ferocity that brought to Colin's mind the vivid image of its dog-sized predecessor.

"Move!" the man with the carbine was shouting at the copter pilot. "Swing this thing around! Give me a clear shot!"

But the pilot had already swung his craft. Hanging on its screw, he'd turned it like a pendant bubble and the man was firing.

Again and again Colin saw him jerk with the recoil of his heavy weapon, but the great flying animal was still airborne.

Upon them now it was. Circling around them, great wings flailing. Lips drawn back from its bloodied teeth.

*Claws. It looks like it's got claws on those feet and not hooves.*

And then it struck. Like the huge beast of prey that it was. It struck, swooping down upon them from above and behind with a speed impossible to evade; with a whistling and a shrieking that Colin was sure he heard even above the clatter of their own copter blades.

And into those blades it plunged, and the impact was tremendous.

They hung there in the clear sky for a heart-stopping moment; the screaming animal and the maimed machine. Then they fell. Fell the few hundred feet to the river and into its chilling waters.

Beside Colin the copter pilot shivering in his blankets called out to the man at the patrol boat's wheel. "See it yet?"

"No," someone called back to him, and the man who had lost his carbine pulled his blankets closer and said, "Forget it. He's not floating with all the lead I put into him."

They were waiting for them on the jutting dock when the patrol boat swept close. On the dock and coming out to meet them in their hovering craft. The vidcasters, the reporters, the curious.

And after them the TriV coverage of the inquest, the investigations, the public's blatant, and their colleagues' more discreet, inquiries into how they produced their miracle, until at last even Ed turned to Colin in their office one morning and said in genuine dismay, "I know I wanted publicity to put us over the top, but enough is enough."

Colin smiled and waved the pale blue vac-tube message his secretary had just handed him.

"The Commodore says thank you but he doesn't think he ought to accept Ato's Pride from us, not as a gift anyway."

"Why not?" Ed said. "It's the least we can do to show him our appreciation for the contracts he's wangled for us."

Colin laughed. "Those he says he doesn't need to defend, not any more. But he doesn't want to get fouled up with any committee investigating expensive presents to government people."

"Tell him to take the horse and stop worrying," Ed said, and from his expression Colin could not tell if he was kidding or not. "If they fire him, a growing organization like ours can always use a good man who knows his way around Procurement."

# PHOENIX

*To early agricultural peoples, whose lives depended on the regular and reliable succession of seasons, it became clear that these in turn depended on the motion of the sun in the heavens. In the regions of the Middle East where agriculture and civilization first developed, the midday sun was always in the southern half of the sky. From noon to noon it rose higher and higher in the sky, but never reached the zenith. By the date we know as June 21, it got as high as it could and began to sink again.*

*For half a year it sank, until it reached its low point on December 21, and then began to rise again. As it sank the summer passed and ended and it grew colder and colder. It was clear that if the sun continued to sink indefinitely, all would freeze and life would come to an end. The time of the low point and the turnabout was therefore a time of rejoicing, so many cultures had a period of unrestrained celebration of the winter "solstice" ("sun standstill"). The modern version of this celebration is Christmas.*

*Naturally, this annual resurrection of the sun, with the promise of a coming spring and a new period of growth, gave rise to all sorts of death-and-resurrection cults. The Egyptians pictured a bird that died annually and was reborn out of its funeral pyre—an obvious sun-figure. The Greeks picked up the legend and visualized the bird as the size of an eagle, and as being gold, red, and purple in color. (These are the colors of the noonday sun, of the setting sun, and of the sky at twilight.) They called it the "phoenix"* from a Greek word for *"red-purple"* and had it die and be resurrected every five hundred years, rather than every year. Since the phoenix was its own parent, it needed no mate, and was pictured as one of a kind.

The following story gives us a very modern version of the myth.

# CAUTION! INFLAMMABLE!

*Thomas N. Scortia*

When the City Editor of the Gazette received word that a phoenix was building her nest on the very peak of the dome of the city hall, he naturally sent his best reporter speeding to the scene. The reporter, an intrepid young man known for his resourcefulness, decided that little was to be gained by observing the coming immolation from the pavement below and, after bribing a janitor, gained access to the ledge surrounding the base of the dome and climbed the narrow metal ladder to the peak where the bird was engaged in her labors.

"You realize," he said, accosting the phoenix, "that this is a very unorthodox place in which to build a nest, especially with the end you have in mind?"

"I do," the bird said, pausing in its work, "but there is no higher point in this area and I don't have enough strength remaining to make it west to some peak in the Rockies."

"Tell me," said the reporter, remembering his professional duties, "is it true that there is only one of your kind?"

"That's quite correct," said the phoenix, selecting a long shred of cellophane from a pile of debris balanced delicately on the slope of the dome. She began swiftly to weave it into the nest, following an intricately beautiful pattern.

"And when you become old, you build a nest and set fire to it while you are in it?"

"Yes," said the bird wearily.

"And arise reborn from the ashes?"

"Quite true."

"But," the reporter said, frowning, "I thought you were indigenous to the East."

"I was originally," the bird agreed. "However, since the phoenix is a symbol of ever-renewing youth, I decided to migrate to a more appropriate locale."

"Here in the Mississippi Valley?"

"Don't be silly," the bird said. "I was on my way to Hollywood, but I foresaw that I would die before I completed the flight."

"You can foresee your death, then?"

"Of course, as well as other events. I have precognition, you see."

"Precognition? That means you can predict coming events, doesn't it?"

"Yes," the phoenix said, beginning to weave a scrap of newspaper into the nest, which was nearly finished.

"Such as the outcome of the next election and who will win the World Series and . . ."

"Oh, that and much more," the bird said, settling itself into the completed nest. "But don't ask me to," she said. "Everyone's always asking for a free prediction. Very exasperating."

"I had no intention," protested the reporter.

"Yes, you did," contradicted the bird. "Anyway, there's only a few minutes left before twelve."

"Is that when . . . ?"

"Yes," said the phoenix. "Promptly at noon." The reporter paused and eyed the nest.

"That's not quite the nest I had expected," he remarked at last. "I thought you were supposed to use sandalwood and various other exotic plants."

"Now, tell me," the bird said impatiently, "where would I get sandalwood around here?"

"You do have a point," the reporter agreed. "I notice," he added with a small glow of pride, "that you have used my paper as part of your nest." He pointed to a large piece of newsprint bearing the masthead *The Gazette* and a black headline below.

"Yes. Not a very satisfactory texture, however." The

phoenix squirmed uncomfortably. "Do you have the correct time?" she said.

"It's one minute to twelve," the young man offered. "I suppose you ignite spontaneously?"

"I'm afraid that part of the legend isn't quite true," the phoenix sighed. "Usually in the past I've had help."

"Oh," said the reporter, "I didn't know. Can I offer you a match?"

The bird eyed the shred of newspaper whose black headlines said: "AEC to Test Nitrogen Super-Bomb Today Noon."

"That will not be necessary," she said.

# SPHINX

An obvious symbol of divine strength might be a human
body with a lion's head, or, in reverse, a lion's body with
a human head. The lion, after all, was a particularly
feared predator, and the "king of beasts."

The Greek griffins, as I explained earlier, were creatures with the torso of a lion and the head and wings of an
eagle. An only slightly different composite was one with
the torso of a lion, the wings of an eagle, and the head
and breasts of a woman.

Such a creature was pictured as a fearsome monster
from whose grasp no human being could escape. It was
called a "sphinx" from a Greek word meaning "to hold
tightly."

The most famous sphinx in the Greek myths was one that
existed just outside the city of Thebes and that stopped
travelers going to that city. It posed a problem to them:
"What goes on four legs in the morning, on two at noon,
and on three in the evening?" Failure to answer correctly
meant death. The Greek hero Oedipus, however, guessed
correctly that the answer was the human being, who crawled
on all fours in the morning of life, stood upright on two
legs in maturity, and needed a cane in old age. The sphinx
then killed itself in frustration.

The Egyptians would occasionally build lions with the
heads of reigning monarchs, simply to show the strength of
the monarch and, through him, of the nation. This was
sympathetic magic. Showing the nation to be strong would

*keep it strong in actuality. (We're familiar with that sort of thing today, too.) The most famous Egyptian sphinx is the very large Great Sphinx built in connection with the Great Pyramid.*

*This Egyptian sphinx is featured in the following story.*

# THE PYRAMID PROJECT

*Robert F. Young*

## THE SPHINX

Daniel Hall met the enemy in the blue skies of NRGC 984–D but it cannot be said that the enemy was his. Neither can it be said that he was the enemy's. In point of fact, about all that can be said about the encounter is that it never quite came off. One minute there were two trim scout ships, one Terran and the other Uvelian, arrowing toward each other, and the next minute there were two trim scout ships veering off at right angles to each other and dropping rapidly planetward. What happened to the Uvelian pilot will be touched upon later. Right now, the camera is focused on Daniel Hall.

He came down near the edge of a wide tableland and plowed a long furrow in a stretch of snow-white sand. The impact tore one of the viewscope brackets loose and sent it ricocheting from wall to wall. On the third ricochet it side-swiped Hall, ripping through both layers of his spacesuit and tearing open his left arm from elbow to shoulder. Still not satisfied, it struck the radio panel and smashed the transmitter. Then it gave up the ghost and dropped to the deck.

Hall hadn't meant to make such a hard landing. He hadn't meant to make any kind of landing. An invisible force had seized the controls and torn the ship out of the sky, and he hadn't been able to do a thing about it.

He tried the controls now. He tried them singly and in pairs. No matter how he tried them, they did not respond.

Next, he had a go at the radio. He knew even while he was beaming his S.O.S. that it would never get beyond the stratosphere and that all he would receive for his pains would be static. He was right. He turned the radio off.

Well anyway, NRGC 984-D had a reasonably amiable climate and a reasonably amiable atmosphere—his instruments told him that much. So he could stay alive for a little while at least.

Hall grinned. "A little while" was right. The Terran fleet's imminent engagement with the Uvelian wouldn't be postponed merely because an unimportant space scout, who had been sent on ahead to determine whether or not the planet in whose vicinity the engagement was to take place had intelligent inhabitants, failed to report back. The assignment had been no more than a token gesture in the first place—a gesture that would sound good on the flagship's log-tape when the war was over. Whether NRGC 984-D had intelligent inhabitants or not, the commander of the Terran fleet would carry out his original orders, and if a planet-wide tectonic upheaval resulted from the side effects of the battle— and only a miracle could avert such an eventuality—Terrankind would hold themselves no more responsible for it than they held themselves responsible for Carthage, Dresden, and Deimos.

According to Terran intelligence reports, the resemblance between Terrans and Uvelians was cultural as well as physical; hence, the odds had it that the Uvelian pilot had been on a similar token assignment and that if he, too, had been rendered helpless and incommunicado it would have a similar lack of effect on the commander of the Uvelian fleet. Anyway you looked at the situation NRGC 984-D was going to have to pay dearly for being in the wrong place at the wrong time—i.e., at a point in space equidistant from Earth and Uvel at the precise moment when the crucial battle of the Earth-Uvel war was going to take place.

Hall's arm was beginning to throb, and waves of weakness were washing over him. Breaking out a first-aid pac, he sterilized the wound and dressed it. The bleeding stopped, but he still felt weak and he knew that he should rest. However, he couldn't bring himself to do so. For one thing, he knew that regardless of what he did, he was doomed anyway, and for another, during his descent he had glimpsed a number of vaguely familiar structures in the distance. He hadn't been able to make them out clearly, but structures usually spelled intelligent beings, and he was eager to find out whether or not these structures were in keeping with the rule. It was silly of him, he supposed, to want to know what kind of beings, if any, he was going to share extinction with; but he wanted to know just the same.

So, after removing the cumbersome outer section of his spacesuit and taking off his helmet, he opened the scout ship's locks and stepped outside. NRGC 984 was well past meridian. Using it as a reference point, he oriented himself. To the north and to the east, the tableland dropped away into hazy foothills; far to the west, stalwart snow-crowned mountains rose sheerly into the sky. The structures which he had glimpsed lay to the south. There were four of them altogether, and three of them were pyramidal in shape. The fourth stood a little to the east of the others and was radically different from them. It looked like—it looked like—

Hall squinted his eyes against the glare of the sunlight. If he hadn't known that such a thing was impossible, he would have sworn that the fourth structure was a sphinx.

NRGC 984 was a KO star. However, if the rays which were raining down upon the tableland were a dependable criterion, it wasn't very far from attaining GO-hood. Hall felt dehydrated before he had gone half a mile. By the time a mile lay behind him, he was ready to drop.

He wet his mouth repeatedly from the vacuum container of ship's water which he had brought along, each time swallowing as much of the icy contents as he dared. He could see the pyramidal structures quite clearly now—clearly enough to know that in mentally referring to them as "pyramidal structures" instead of as "pyramids" he was only kidding himself. He could see the fourth structure quite clearly, too—clearly enough to know that in the strict sense of the word it wasn't a structure, but a huge statue, and to know that whether such a thing were possible or not, the statue was a statue of a sphinx.

As he progressed, reeling now and then from the heat and from his increasing weakness, he began to wonder whether he had somehow been catapulted back through space to Egypt—to the plateau of Gizeh, upon which the Great Sphinx Harmachis guarded the Great Pyramids of Cheops, Chephren, and Mykerinos, and at whose base the Terran capital of Kafr el Haram stood. And as he progressed still farther he began to wonder whether he had somehow been catapulted back through space *and* time to the Egypt of over five thousand years ago when the Great Pyramids and the Great Sphinx were new; for *these* pyramids and *this* sphinx were new—make no mistake about it. The pyramids looked as though they had been built yesterday, and as for the sphinx, its excellent condition lent it a realism so remarkable that Hall momentarily expected to see it rise up on its columnar legs and come thundering over the tableland to welcome him.

Or to annihilate him.

There was a third possibility, of course, and on the surface it made more sense than the other two: maybe his growing weakness and the merciless rays of the sun had combined forces and were causing him to hallucinate.

But if he *was* hallucinating, why hadn't he chosen a subject more in keeping with his character? Specifically, why hadn't he projected an image of a garish street lined with nepenthe nooks and fun bars, or an image of a blue mountain lake with a shack on its wooded shore and a canoe drawn up on its beach ready to take him gliding over the cool and limpid waters? Like many adventurers, Hall pursued both solitude and sin and found peace in neither; but they were at least a part of his makeup, and Egyptology was not. He had visited the plateau of Gizeh and seen the Great Pyramids and the Great Sphinx, and he had read about Cheops, Chephren, and Mykerinos in Herodotus' *History;* but the pharaohs and their sepulchers and their monuments were relatively unimportant items in the synthesis of real and vicarious experiences that constituted his character, and it was highly unlikely that he would be "seeing" a sphinx and three pyramids now.

He decided that the best way to find out whether or not he was imagining them would be try to walk right through them, and with this in mind, he forced himself to go on, even though he knew that he would do better to return to his ship and forget about the whole thing.

Gradually, the pyramids took on greater detail, particularly the largest of the trio. It stood in the foreground, and several hundred yards to the east of it stood the Sphinx. The Gizeh sphinx measured in the neighborhood of 189 feet in length, 70 in height, and 30 from forehead to chin. If anything, this one exceeded those dimensions. Lord, suppose it were to stand up, Hall thought. Why, it would tower almost a hundred feet above the ground!

Had the Sphinx read his mind? It would seem so. At any rate, the huge head had turned and the great golden eyes were fixed upon his face. As he watched in disbelieving fascination, it stood erect on its four legs and regarded him contemplatively across the half a hundred yards of tableland that separated them.

Everything caught up to Hall then—his weakness, the rays of NRGC 984, the heat rising from the white sand, the doubts that had been multiplying in his mind ever since he had participated in the destruction of the Deimos Dissenters—and he sagged to the ground. The ground, he discovered presently, was trembling. Well it might. The creature walking over it probably weighed several thousand tons.

He felt the coolness of shade. Looking up, he saw the massive humanoid face looming above him, the great golden eyes gazing down into his own. Slowly, the huge head began to lower; relentlessly, the gigantic jaws began to open. Belatedly, Hall tried to draw his laser pistol, only to discover that he no longer had charge of his right arm. He retreated way back into his mind then, found a deep dark cave, crawled into it, and closed his eyes.

## CHEOPS' DAUGHTER

Wherever else he might be, Hall decided some time later, he was no longer in the cave. Nor was he, apparently, in the belly of the Sphinx. There was the softness of eiderdown beneath his back and a pleasant perfume upon his nostrils. He was completely relaxed, and the throbbing in his arm had died away. Feeling fingers lightly touch his forehead, he opened his eyes.

There was a girl standing over him. Her face was narrow, the forehead high and rounded, the nose high-bridged and slender, the chin somewhat pointed. She had night-black hair, and her head was fitted with a ridiculous headdress that flared up into a flat crown. She was slim, but startlingly well-developed, and she was wearing a tight-fitting halter and a tight-fitting knee-length skirt. The headdress, the halter, and the skirt were golden in color, and, peering over the edge of the padded platform on which he lay, Hall saw that webbed sandals of similar hue encased her small feet. Her skin was the color of olives.

Despite her unusual attire and her equally unusual development, plus a queenly hauteur that somehow went well with both, her eyes still managed to be the most remarkable items in her feminine inventory. They were almond-shaped, slightly slanted, golden brown, and preternaturally large. In addition, there was a liquid quality about them that came close to devastating the defenses which Hall made haste to throw up around himself.

Well anyway, she made as much sense as the pyramids and the Sphinx did, he thought resignedly. As a matter of fact, she seemed to belong in such a setting. "I suppose you're going to tell me your name is Cleopatra," he said, even though he knew that the all-purpose English words were bound to be Greek to her.

She had withdrawn her hand from his forehead and had

stepped back from the platform the minute he opened his eyes. But she hadn't been in the least disconcerted, nor was she in the least disconcerted now. "Behold, I have dressed thy wound," she said. "Is it not enough that a pharaoh's daughter should have thus demeaned herself without her having to demean herself still further by giving thee her name?" Suddenly puzzlement crinkled her forehead, and she looked intently at his smartly tailored inner spacesuit. Actually, in combination with his snappy black spaceboots it constituted as sharp an outfit as the Terran Space Navy had ever come up with, but she certainly didn't seem to think so. "Where didst thou learn to speak the language of Egypt, slave from a far land?" she asked.

Clearly, NRGC 984-D was a planet of surprises, and by this time Hall should have been sufficiently acclimated to have been able to take each new development in his stride. He was not, though—not quite—and for a while he just lay there gaping at the girl. Then he propped himself up on one elbow, noting as he did so that she had indeed dressed his wound and noting simultaneously that in the process she had somehow eliminated its soreness and brought about at least a partial return of his strength. She had also, he reminded himself quickly, called him a slave. He said snidely, "I guess you might say that I learned to speak Egyptian in the same place you learned to speak APE."

She blinked, and it was obvious from the blank look she gave him that she had missed the point completely. He had the feeling that she was just dying to put him in his place with a few well-chosen epithets but that she wasn't quite sure enough of herself to risk doing so. "Great indeed must be my disfavor in the eyes of Amen-Ra," she said presently, "for me to have been afflicted by such circumstances and by such company."

Hall sat up on the platform, which, he saw now, was a bed of some kind. The room in which it stood was on the small side, and surprisingly pleasant. The ceilings and the walls had been carved out of pink granite, and the illumination was provided by candles burning in niches that looked a lot like light fixtures. Besides the bed, there were two marble benches, a marble table, and a slender diorite pedestal supporting a shallow diorite bowl that looked like a bird bath but which was probably a stone brazier. In the wall opposite the one against which the bed stood, a tapestry-hung doorway gave access to another room. The tapestry was heavily decorated with tiny humanoid figures with cowlike heads.

Hall had a hunch that he was inside the largest of the three pyramids—an upsetting enough possibility in itself without having a pharaoh's daughter to contend with too. "Which pharaoh are you the daughter of?" he asked.

She drew herself up as straight as could be and looked at him as though he were a chunk of mud that had just dropped from a chariot wheel. Nevertheless, the hauteur in her voice did not ring true, and he was certain that he detected a note of shame. "His Majesty King Khufu the blessed, slave! Dost thou dare profess ignorance of his reign?"

Khufu, he thought. That would be old Cheops himself. Which meant that the girl standing before him was in the neighborhood of fifty-two hundred years old. He sighed. "Well anyway, you dress a mean dressing," he said.

She just looked at him.

He regarded her shrewdly. "I take it we're in the neighborhood of Memphis," he said presently, "and that this pyramid we're in is the one your father took twenty years to build."

For the first time the underlying uncertainty which he had sensed in her from the start rose to the surface. Instead of bringing to mind a princess, she now brought to mind a little girl who had strayed out of her own back yard and become hopelessly lost in the next. "I—I know that what thou sayest must be true," she said, "but I know also that it cannot be true. Only the first mastaba of my father's sepulcher has been built, and it is to be the first sepulcher of its kind, yet here there are three of them, and each has been completed. I—I do not understand wherefore I am in this place, nor wherefore I am alone."

"But surely you must know how you got here."

She shook her head. "Behold, two nights ago I was sitting in the—" She paused, took a deep breath, and began all over again. "Behold, two nights ago I lay me to sleep, and when

Amen-Ra climbed upon his throne the morning after, here I lay in this strange place in this strange land. I do not know what to do.''

She looked as though she were going to cry. Hall would have felt sorry for her if the memory of her arrogance hadn't still been fresh in his mind. He didn't think much of people who went around calling other people slaves. Another reason he didn't feel sorry for her was that he couldn't bring himself to believe that she was on the level. How could she *possibly* be Cheops' daughter?

All right, who *could* she be then? A Uvelian Mata Hari? Nonsense! A Uvelian Mata Hari might try to pass herself off as a lot of things, but unless she was hopelessly out of her mind, she would never try to pass herself off as an Egyptian princess who had been dead for more than five millennia. Besides, what would a Uvelian spy be doing on a planet which, other than on an abstract level, neither the Terran nor the Uvelian empires had ever heard about until a few days ago and which they wouldn't have heard about even then if it hadn't been for the fact that NRGC 984–D was going to be occupying almost the same point in space that the major Uvelian and Terran forces, which were ineluctably drawing closer and closer together, would be occupying when they met in the crucial battle of the hundred-year galactic war—in the ultimate Armageddon that would decide whether the Uvelian demosocialistic ideology or the Terran sociocratic ideology was to endure?

"Tell me," Hall said presently, "is there really a monster the size of a young mountain hanging around these parts, or did I just imagine there was?"

He expected the question to disconcert her. It didn't in the least. "Oh yes," she said, as calmly as though a sphinx were no more awe-inspiring than a common alley cat, "She-who-builds-sepulchers is still with me. I feared at first that she, too, had deserted me, but she had not. But as she will not communicate with me, I have been unable to learn wherefore she interrupted her labors in my father's behalf to build these sepulchers in this strange land, or for whom she built them.''

A pyramid-building sphinx was all Hall needed. Lord knew,

the girl's story had been incredible enough before, but now it was fantastic. Sliding down from the platform-bed to the floor and noting to his satisfaction that his laser pistol was still in its holster at his hip, he said, "I can see that if I'm going to find out anything around here, I'm going to have to find it out for myself. So if you'll climb down off that high horse of yours long enough to tell me how to get out of this rock pile, Miss Whoever-you-are, I won't bother you any more!"

The girl gasped. She stamped her right foot. She stamped her left. She clenched her hands. "Hast thou the effrontery to imply that the noble daughter of His Majesty King Khufu the blessed is guilty of a falsehood, slave?"

Hall put his hands on his hips. "A falsehood! Why, you've been lying your head off."

He would have said more if tears hadn't come into her golden brown eyes. Turning, she pointed toward the doorway. "Beyond that portal thou wilt find another, slave," she said, "and beyond the second portal, yet another. Then thou wilt find thyself in the passage that leads to the portico. Go!"

Hall went.

## THE PYRAMID PROJECT

As he left the room, it occurred to him that he had forgotten to ask her how he happened to be inside the pyramid in the first place. It was just as well. She would only have told him another fib.

How did he happen to be inside it then?

Probably, after his sphinx hallucination, he had crawled the rest of the distance to his objective and the girl had found him and taken him in tow. For all he knew, she could very well have saved his life. He wished now that he hadn't been quite so rude to her.

As nearly as he could ascertain, the room that adjoined the one he had just left was a living room. It contained elaborately upholstered settees and chairs, and there were cushions scattered over the thickly carpeted floor. The next room was unquestionably a cooking room. Floor-to-ceiling shelves were lined with earthenware pots, and there was a brick oven large enough to roast an elephant in. In addition to the oven, there was a brazierlike affair on which less pachydermatous dishes could be prepared.

Passing through the third doorway, he found himself, not in the passage which the girl had mentioned, but in a spacious court. Stone columns gave the illusion of supporting the ceiling, and at the top of each, just beneath the capital, was the bas-relief of a cowlike face. Elaborate horns rising from the stone foreheads blended with the capitals and supplied their motifs. It finally dawned on Hall who this cowlike being was. It was Hathor, the Egyptian goddess of love.

He crossed the court without further delay and stepped through a wide doorway into a long corridor. At the end of the corridor, a dark, star-spangled rectangle showed. He made track for it, rejoicing in the cool night air that presently reached his nostrils. Obviously he had been unconscious longer than he had thought.

He could hardly wait to see the stars. He knew perfectly well that he couldn't possibly be in ancient Egypt, that there was another, far more practical, explanation for the presence of the Sphinx and the pyramids and the olive-skinned girl, but just the same it would be good to know for sure. The stars would tell him. Stars did not lie.

Stepping out of the passage, he looked up at them. The structure behind him and the roof of the portico had half of the heavens, but the half that was visible contained not a single familiar constellation. He gave a sigh of relief. A moment later, he wondered why. Wouldn't he be better off if he *were* in ancient Egypt? There, at least, he would have a chance to live out the rest of his natural life. Here, he would be dead before morning.

The portico was wide and lofty. Four columns, larger but similar in all other respects to the columns he had seen in the court, stood in a row along the marble apron, supporting the roof. Between the two center ones a short flight of wide marble steps descended to the ground. He crossed the apron and went down them.

All was silence. Above his head, a constellation suggestive of a huge crocodile sprawled across the heavens. The white sands of the tableland caught the starlight and shattered it into infinitesimal particles, and the particles glistened softly for miles around, seeming to emit a radiance of their own. Behind him, the Great Pyramid—he still thought of it as the "Great Pyramid" even though he knew that it wasn't—rose geometrically up into an apex that was nearly 500 feet above the ground. To his left, the lesser pyramids stood, and to his right crouched the Sphinx.

Despite himself, he was struck by her beauty—awed, almost. She had a silvery cast in the starlight. Her flanks rose up like smooth escarpments to the magnificent ridge of her back. Her noble head hid half a hundred stars. The cliff of her classic profile was a splendid silhouette against the sky.

Hall walked toward her in the starlight. He had been impressed by the Great Sphinx of the Gizeh Necropolis. Even in its state of disrepair there was a mysterious quality about it that he had found appealing, a massive grace that had intrigued him. But compared to *his* sphinx the one of the Gizeh Necropolis was nothing more than a crudely sculptured rocky promontory reinforced with masonry. Stone was all it had ever been and stone was all it could ever be. *This* sphinx was art apotheosized. No wonder in his dazed and weakened state of a few hours ago he had invested her with life. Even now, thinking clearly again, he felt that at any moment she would rise and walk beneath the stars.

What had happened to the race of people who had sculptured her? Hall wondered. To the race of people who had built the three pyramids over which she was standing guard? Did that same race of people have something to do with the building of the Egyptian pyramids? Did—

*Nothing happened to the race of people who built the pyramids, Daniel Hall. And nothing is going to happen to them if they can help it.*

As the words formed themselves in his mind, he saw that the Brobdingnagian head was turning toward him. Simultaneously he realized that, far from being inanimate, the massive leonine body was rampant with life. At length, the mysterious eyes met his and regarded him like a pair of intelligent golden suns. He stood stark still in the starlight, a statue now himself.

In the final analysis there was no reason why a sphinx couldn't be alive. Statues were sculptured of men, too, but this did not mean that men were made of stone.

*Even the poor Egyptian child who dressed your wound in the Temple of Hathor is less anthropocentric than you are, Daniel Hall. She realized I was alive the moment she saw me. And yet you allowed yourself to know resentment simply because her thought world ruled out the possibility of your being her equal, thereby forcing her to think of you as a slave. For shame, Daniel Hall!*

"And now what happens?" Hall asked, half in cynicism, half in fear. "Are you going to devour me?"

*There, your anthropocentric nature is influencing you again! You think that merely because a being is larger than you are, it must be evil. And the larger it is, the more evil it becomes in your mind, and the more partial to human flesh. No, I'm not going to devour you, Daniel Hall—it is you and your kind who are going to devour me and my sisters. That is, you would be going to devour us if we hadn't taken the necessary steps to prevent you from doing so, although the possibility exists that you may still succeed. You are on the verge of devouring us, not because you want to at the moment, but because you haven't bothered to find out whether or not we exist.*

"That's not true!" Hall objected. "I was sent here myself to find out!"

*And so was one of the members of the Uvelian forces. But even if either or both of you were able to report your respective findings to your respective headquarters the battle would still take place, and you know it. Incidentally, it's unnecessary for you to speak, to say nothing of shout. I can receive thoughts as well as send them.*

*It was you who seized our controls then—who—who caused us to crash.*

*It was I who seized your controls and caused you to crash, Daniel Hall. My sister in the neighboring demesne took care of your opponent. If our project is successful, we will need both of you. However, although I caused you to crash, Daniel Hall, I had no intention of causing you bodily injury. Small details are beyond the scope of our telekinesis. But I see that thanks to the skillful ministrations of Ahura, you've fully recovered.*

*Ahura?*

*The little Egyptian princess whom you were so rude to a few minutes ago in the Temple of Hathor.*

*She's no more of an Egyptian princess than you are!* Hall "said." *Egypt was consolidated with the Union of Terran States over a hundred years ago when the capital was built at Kafr el Haram, and couldn't recognize a princess even if she wanted to. Egyptian princesses were out of style long before that time anyway.*

*But millennia ago, they were not. Ahura wasn't lying to you—she really is Cheops' daughter.*

*But don't you see?—that's more incredible yet! Cheops' daughter has been dead for over five thousand years!*

*No,* said the Sphinx, *Cheops' daughter is very much alive. However, until yesterday she had been unaware of the fact for quite some time. Not long after I arrived on your planet some fifty-two hundred of your years ago and instituted the project my sisters and I had agreed upon, it came to my attention that in his zeal to see his sepulcher erected Cheops had placed her in the stews. Since I had told him that if he would put all of the resources of his kingdom at my disposal the first pyramid would be his, I felt responsible for his action; and, as I had intended to take back someone like Ahura anyway, I stole her from the stews, placed her in suspended animation, built a special capsule for her, and had one of my sisters come and get her. She was then entombed in a special vault on Pornos—NRGC 984-D to you, Daniel Hall—until such time as I should have need of her. Two days ago I brought her here, dressed her in clothing similar to what she was accustomed to, placed her in the Temple of Hathor, and revived her. Ahura is not her real name, incidentally. She thinks of her ordeal in the stews as having happened only a few days ago and has unconsciously taken the first step toward creating a new identity. I interceded in time, but the experience left its mark just the same.*

Drowning, Hall grabbed for the first straw he saw. *But according to Herodotus, she stayed in the stews for a long time, and also according to Herodotus, she made each of the patrons pay off with a building block for a small pyramid which she later built in front of her father's.*

*Come now, Daniel Hall, you aren't even convinced of that yourself. You simultaneously think of Herodotus as the "Father of History" and as the "Father of Lies." However, as his Egyptian history can't possibly be anything more than recorded hearsay, he can't have been deliberately lying in this case. Probably he merely repeated the myths which the generations that followed the fourth dynasty dreamed up to supplement their knowledge of Cheops, Chephren, and Mykerinos. In any event, what he wrote about Ahura is untrue.*

Hall had already forgotten Ahura. *You said you arrived on Earth fifty-two hundred years ago. That means you're over five thousand years old!*

*Right,* said the Sphinx. *Even older if you count my incubation period, which you really should in view of the fact that members of my race mature before they even see the light of day. Altogether, we have a longevity of some fifteen thousand years—your years, that is. So you see, I've still got quite a few to go—or will have if the preventive measures my sisters and I have taken succeed in averting the Armageddon which the Terran and Uvelian space navies are so determined to bring off in our skies.* Her golden eyes traversed the heavens, returned to Hall. *No Pleiades yet, I see. Well, there will be soon. Incidentally, I stole the expression from your mind, Daniel Hall.*

"Pleiades" was the term used by ground observers to describe a space fleet in planetary orbit. But at the moment Hall was concerned with more important matters than Terran war terminology. *You and your sisters—you're parthenogenetic, aren't you?* he said.

*Right again, Daniel Hall.*

*And does each of your sisters have a set of pyramids like these?*

*Not all of them, no—only those who have need for them at the moment.*

*Who built them for you?*

*We built them ourselves—not as a team, but as individuals. I myself built the set of Gizeh.*

*Come off it!* Hall said. *How could you build a pyramid?*

*I have spread my left forefoot. Look at it, Daniel Hall, and tell me what you see.*

Hall looked. *I—I see,* he said a long time later, *a set of five powerful appendages. Two of them—the ones which correspond to my thumb and forefinger—appear to be some manner of gripping tools. The next one appears to be a stone-cutting tool, and the last two appear to be tools that can be adapted for almost any kind of work.*

*Good. Basically, my sisters and I are equipped for quarrying and building, but through the ages our race extended its abilities to encompass innumerable other fields. The stone used in the set of pyramids behind you, I quarried in the mountains that form the western boundary of my dhen—or demesne; hence, transporation was no problem. Owing to the distribution of our dhens, it rarely is on our planet. However, the stone used in the Gizeh pyramids in many instances had to be quarried in neighboring countries; hence, transporation was a problem, and I had to enlist the aid of the reigning pharaohs. It's doubtful whether I could have succeeded without their cooperation in any case. The job took almost one hundred and fifty of their years—practically the whole of the fourth dynasty. It needn't have taken that long, but the timing had to be perfect, and besides, I wanted it to look as though mankind alone were responsible for it. The first pyramid became Cheops', the next, Chephren's, and the last, Mykerinos'.*

*But why did you build them on Earth?*

*My sisters and I have the ability to look into the future. It's a limited ability and functions only when we're enjoying complete freedom from fear and worry, but when we do foresee, we foresee quite well. Some fifty-two hundred of your years ago, Daniel Hall, one of my sisters foresaw the converging of the Terran and Uvelian fleets on Pornos and realized that our planet couldn't possibly survive the side effects of the battle that was bound to take place. She also foresaw the appearance of your scout ship and the almost simultaneous appearance of the Uvelian's. In keeping with our custom she convened an emergency council, and the situation was examined in detail. Finally the only possible solution was arrived at, and two of us were chosen, one to go to Earth and one to go to Uvel, there to take the necessary steps to save our civilization. I was the one who was chosen to go to Earth, and my sister in the neighboring dhen was the one who was chosen to go to Uvel. The strategic location of our dhens with respect to the predicted appearance of you and the Uvelian scout was partially responsible for the decision.*

*Well, you certainly put a stop to our hostilities in a hurry. How about the battle between the two fleets? Won't that come off either?*

*We hope it won't. In any case, all that could have been done to avert it has been done—short of stooping to genocide and short of prematurely interfering with the natural evolution of two civilizations.*

*But surely if this sister of yours could look fifty-two hundred years ahead one of the rest of you ought to have been able to look a little beyond that point and have found out whether or not you're going to succeed!*

*I told you, Daniel Hall, that we're capable of prescience only when we're enjoying complete freedom from fear and worry. We haven't been free from either for those same fifty-two hundred years.*

Hall was "silent" for some time. Then, *I'll overlook for the moment how a being of your size without any apparent means of space travel could have journeyed from here to Earth,* he said, *and I'll also overlook for the moment how your presence on our planet escaped being recorded in our history other than in legend form. But will you please explain to me how you expected to avert a battle in the vicinity of your own planet by building pyramids on another planet thousands of years before the battle was to begin?*

*Two other planets, Daniel Hall. While I was building the set on Earth, my sister in the neighboring dhen was building a corresponding set on Uvel.*

*All right, two other planets then. But that still doesn't answer my question. Does the shape and the size and the location of the Gizeh pyramids have anything to do with it? I mean, could they possibly be a focal point for some kind of fourth-dimensional weapon?*

The Sphinx laughed thunderously. *The shape and the size and the location of the pyramids have a great deal to do with it, Daniel Hall—but not in the way you suggest. The riddle will become clear to you before the night is over, I'm sure. The other two items that puzzle you may not, however, so I will clear them up for you now.*

*My sisters and I navigate space by teleporting ourselves through it. We do this by utilizing a paraspatial energy source which can be employed only when interstellar distances are involved. However, we can't teleport ourselves from point A to point B unless the cosmic variables pertinent to the two points are in appropriate relationship, and this severely limits our activities. And when the need arises, as it did in the case in question, for one of us to teleport herself from point A to point B and another of us to teleport herself from point A to point C within a single teleportative period, the cosmic variables are doubly limiting. Fifty-two hundred of your years ago, the cosmic variables with respect to Pornos-Earth and Pornos-Uvel limited us to a period of three hundred years. Following this three-hundred-year teleportative period was a twelve-hundred-year non-teleportative period, which in turn was followed by another three-hundred-year teleportative period, and so on. Ideally, one of the three-hundred-year teleportative periods should have partially coincided with the three centuries immediately preceding the battle we wished to avert; practically, however, none of them did, and as a result we had to pursue an indirect course in averting our planet's accidental annihilation. Fortunately, the first three-hundred-year teleportative period proved feasible for the plan which we presently devised.*

* * *

With respect to the second point that puzzles you, Daniel Hall, the reason my presence on your planet failed to find an authentic place for itself in your history books was that I took the necessary action to make sure that it didn't. My sisters and I simply couldn't allow you to know enough about us to take us seriously because if you had, you might have guessed our secret, and that would have meant the end of our plan— not to mention the end of us. So before I left your planet, I wiped all memory of my activities from the minds of men. This automatically gave Cheops, Chephren, and Mykerinos exclusive credit for the building of the three pyramids at Gizeh. However, memory eradication is only ninety-five percent effective, and while the pharaohs and the priests and the slaves and everybody else forgot about my activities, they didn't quite forget about me. I suspected as much but I wasn't sure until this afternoon when I read your mind while I was carrying you to Ahura. Fortunately, their memory of me was ambiguous at best, and although they associated me with the Gizeh pyramids, it simply didn't occur to them that I might have built them. So they adapted me to their religious needs of the moment and sculptured a statue of me in the Gizeh Necropolis, identifying me with the Harmachis version of their sun-god, Amen-Ra. Their other "sphinxes," as you call them, can undoubtedly be traced to me also, and the non-Gizeh pyramids with which Egypt abounds were undoubtedly modeled after mine, although before the reign of Cheops an architect named Imhotep had devised a "step pyramid" that may very well have resulted in similar structures. As for the non-Egyptian pyramids and "sphinxes" which are scattered over your planet, some of them can be traced to me also, but I daresay that in most cases they have religio-socio backgrounds of their own. In any event, the only pyramids I built on Earth are the ones on the Gizeh plateau. My sister, you see, foresaw not only the Terran-Uvelian Armageddon but also the future sites of the Terran and Uvelian capitals.

And your other sister, Hall said. The one who went to Uvel when you went to Earth. You say she built a set of pyramids too?

Exactly like my Gizeh set. In addition to looking and acting *alike, Terrans and Uvelians have almost parallel pasts. In a general sense, of course.*

The Sphinx had turned her head and was looking at a region of the heavens just above the eastern horizon. Following her gaze, Hall saw the first group of Pleiades rising into the sky. The distance was such that only the dreadnoughts attained the status of "stars." The thousands of smaller craft were invisible.

He counted six bright points of light, but the number told him nothing. Both the Terran and Uvelian fleets had six major vessels. Facing west, he was not surprised to see the second six climbing slowly above the mountains. *Looks like we're going to get a good view of the proceedings anyway,* he said. *Just the same, I wish they were meeting above the dayside. That way, we might stand a chance.*

*Not enough of a one to worry about. . . . You don't even know which fleet is yours, do you, Daniel Hall?*

*I'm better off not knowing.*

*Yes, I suppose you are.* The Sphinx was "silent" for a moment. Then, *Don't you think it would be a good idea if you went to Ahura and lent her one of your broad shoulders to lean on?* she asked. *She's going to need it. There's no terror that can compare to the fear of the unknown.*

Hall was annoyed. *Surely you could have briefed her on what's coming off!*

Again, the Sphinx laughed. *Tell me, Daniel Hall, how do you explain a battle between two huge space navies to a child who visualizes the creation of the universe as a trio of anthropomorphic deities in the midst of a fantastic hand-balancing act? As Shu the air supporting his sister, Nut the sky, with their brother, Keb the Earth, lying beneath them. I did well in the little time I had since reviving her to supplant her native tongue with yours.*

*I see your point,* Hall said. *Nevertheless, it can be done.*

*And it will be done. But not in hours, Daniel Hall, nor in days nor weeks nor months, and not by me, but by you. Ahura has an excellent mind, and given time she can learn all you can teach her, and then some. And with the aid of the special textbooks and other teaching aids contained in the first step of the smallest pyramid there's no limit to what you can teach her—nor to what you can teach yourself.*

Wait a minute, Hall objected. *Even assuming I decide to cooperate in this project of yours, how am I going to make use of textbooks I can't read and that are probably too big for me to open?*

*The textbooks are printed in APE and are no larger than those you are accustomed to. My sisters and I have had thousands of years to prepare for this crucial point in our history, Daniel Hall, and we've prepared for it well. However, at this juncture it's futile to discuss what you are or aren't going to do. The battle hasn't been averted yet, and there's a good chance that it may not be. If it is averted, come to me afterward. In the meantime, go to Ahura. You can take shelter in the Temple of Hathor if you wish, but I guess you know as well as I do that without a system of deflectors to protect you, the death rays of either fleet can reach you regardless of where you are.*

Hall looked up into the mysterious golden eyes. Was there sadness there? Concern? He could not tell. *And if the battle isn't averted?*

*Then this is goodbye. I have enjoyed knowing you, Daniel Hall. Basically, your race and mine are very much alike. Certainly, we share the same major character trait, and moreover we share it in common with the Uvelians. It's only in the matter of terminology that we differ. My sisters and I call the trait "selfishness," and your race and the Uvelian call it "patriotism." It's right for a man to love his country, but he should never forget that his country is only an extension of himself and that the intensity of his love for it is an infallible index of the intensity of his love for himself. We can't change the way we are, but it helps the cause of reason if we face the truth. Go now, Daniel Hall—Ahura awaits you.*

## AHURA'S TALE

Ahura was sitting on the bottom portico step. Hall sat down beside her. "Behold, I am here," he said.

She said, "Behold, I am aware of it."

Her almond eyes were fixed on the eastern Pleiades, which by now were quite high above the horizon. In the starlight, her classic face had a statuesque quality about it. At length, she lowered her gaze to his face. "I will prepare thee food if thou wish."

"Later on—I'm not hungry right now."

"I did not make thee the offer out of my heart. I made it because She-who-builds-sepulchers desired me to do this for you."

"That's all right," Hall said easily. "You probably can't even boil water anyway."

She looked at him. "Thou speakest in riddles, slave."

"The name is Daniel," Hall said, "and you'll do well to call me by it. A cog in one of the wheels of the Terran war machine I may be, but a slave I am not."

"Dan'el?"

"That's pretty close."

"I am Ahura—as no doubt She-who-builds-sepulchers hath told thee."

"Among other things. Incidentally, I've got a hunch she's tuned in on us now."

"She-who-builds-sepulchers is all-knowing," Ahura said. And then, "With thy strange garments and thy uncouth ways, from what far land dost thou come, Dan'el?"

"From a land you've never heard of, so the less said about it, the better." Noting that she had returned her gaze to the eastern Pleiades, he pointed to the sky above the mountains. "There's another swarm of them over there," he said.

She nodded. "I know. But the sky hath donned a strange dress. It is even stranger than the dress she wore last night."

Ahura raised her eyes to the crocodile constellation within whose confines, if the present trajectories of the two fleets remained unchanged, the encounter would take place. "Behold, Sebek hath left the river bottom and now rules the world. All is not well, Dan'el."

Hall remembered then that the ancient Egyptians had numbered a crocodile god among their many deities. Lowering his eyes, he saw that the girl's hands were tightly clasped together on her lap, and he realized that despite her deceptively calm demeanor she was terrified. Apparently in her primitive way she knew as well as he did that the hand of death was in the sky.

He tried to reassure her. "Sebek will be gone before morning, and Amen-Ra will rise in his glory. Relax, Ahura."

She shook her head. "All is not well, Dan'el," she repeated. "It is not the presence of Sebek alone from which I know this. All day, a tale about a prince which was told to me as a child hath been on my mind, and I cannot drive it away, and from this, too, I know that all is not well."

"The best way to get something off your mind is to tell it to someone, so why not tell the tale to me?"

She looked at him solemnly, as though trying to make up her mind. It dawned on him all of a sudden that in a way he had never quite figured on, she was the most beautiful girl he had ever seen. "Very well," she said presently, "I will tell thee. There was once a king to whom no son was born; and his heart was grieved, and he prayed for himself unto the gods around him for a child. They decreed that one should be born to him. And his wife, after her time was fulfilled, brought forth a son. Then came the Hathors to decree for him a desinty; they said, 'His death is to be by the crocodile, or by the serpent, or by the dog.' Then his Majesty's heart sickened very greatly. And his Majesty caused a house to be built upon the desert; it was furnished with people and with all good things of the royal house, that the child should not go abroad. And when the child was grown, he went up upon the roof, and he saw a dog; it was following a man who was walking on the road. He spoke to his page, who was with him, 'What is this that walks behind the man?' The page answered him, 'This is a dog.' The child said to him, 'Let there be brought to me one like it.' The page went to repeat it to his Majesty. And his Majesty said, 'Let there be brought to him a little pet dog, lest his heart be sad.' And behold they brought him a dog.''

"You see the significance there, don't you?" Hall interrupted. "By being indulgent in the seemingly most harmless aspect of his son's destiny, the father made him all the more vulnerable to the other two."

There was wonderment in Ahura's golden brown eyes as they touched his. "Thou art wise, Dan'el," she said. "I am sorry I called thee a slave. When the child became grown in all his limbs," she went on, "he sent a message to his father saying, 'Come, wherefore am I kept here? Inasmuch as I am fated to three evil fates, let me follow my desire.' They agreed to all he said, and gave him all sorts of arms, and also his dog to follow him, 'Behold, go thou whither thou wilt.' His dog was with him, and he went northward, following his heart in the desert, while he lived on all the best of the game of the desert. He went to the chief of Naharaina.

"And behold there had not been any born to the chief of Naharaina, except one daughter. Behold, there had been built for her a house; its seventy windows were seventy cubits from the ground. And the chief had caused to be brought all the sons of the chiefs of the land, and had said to them, 'He who reaches the window of my daughter, she shall be to him for a wife.'

"Seeing the youths climbing for the window, the young prince asked, 'What is it that ye do here?' They told him, and another day the sons of the chief came to climb, and the youth came to climb with them. He climbed, and he reached the window of the daughter of the chief of Naharaina. She kissed him, she embraced him in all his limbs. . . .''

Ahura's eyes had strayed to the sky again—to the western Pleiades this time. Their "rise" was slightly slower than that of the eastern Pleiades, owing perhaps to the fact that the former's course coincided with NRGC 984–D's rotational direction, or perhaps to their commander's disinclination to rush matters. Nevertheless, it was evident that the forthcoming battle would take place in the center of the NRGC 984–D's heavens—"in" the constellation of the crocodile.

Which were the good guys and which were the bad? Hall wondered. Certainly, their ideological differences weren't apparent at this distance. Would the differences be apparent to an objective observer such as the Sphinx from *any* distance?

Hall grinned wryly. Ahura was twining and untwining her fingers on her lap, and a barely perceptible quivering was going on in her lower lip. He moved a little closer to her, wanting to put his arm around her but not quite daring to. "Get on with your story," he said. "You left me hanging on a cliff seventy cubits high."

Her bewilderment would have been comical under less trying conditions. "Thou speakest in riddles, Dan'el. In many ways thou art like She-who-builds-sepulchers. But I will tell thee the rest of the tale.

"When the chief of Naharaina saw that the young prince had indeed reached the window of his daughter, he gave to him his daughter to wife; he gave also to him a house, and serfs, and fields, also cattle and all manner of good things. And after the days of these things were passed, the youth said to his wife, 'I am doomed to three fates—a crocodile, a serpent, and a dog.' She said to him, 'Let one kill the dog which belongs to thee.' He replied to her, 'I am not going to kill my dog, which I have brought up from when it was small.' And she feared greatly for her husband, and would not let him go alone abroad.

"And one went with the youth toward the land of Egypt, to travel in that country, and with him also went his dog. Behold the crocodile of the river, he came out by the town in which the youth was. And in that town was a mighty man. And the mighty man would not suffer the crocodile to escape. And when the crocodile was bound, the mighty man went out and walked abroad. And when the sun rose the mighty man went back to the house; and he did so every day, during two months of days.

"Now when the days passed after this, the youth sat making a good day in his house. And when the evening came, he lay down on his bed, sleep seized upon his limbs;

and his wife filled a bowl of milk, and placed it by his side. Behold the dog, it entereth into the house, and behind it came a serpent to bite the youth; behold his wife sitting by him, she lay not down. Thereupon the servants gave milk to the serpent, and he drank, and was drunk, and lay upside down. Then his wife made it to perish with the blows of her dagger. And they woke her husband, who was astonished; and she said unto him: 'Behold thy God has given one of thy dooms into thy hand; he will also give thee the others.' And he sacrificed to God, adoring him, and praising his spirits from day to day.

"And when the days were passed after these things, the youth went to walk in the fields of his domain. He went not alone, behold his dog was following him. And his dog ran aside after the wild game, and he followed the dog. He came to the river, and entered the river behind his dog. Then—"

Abruptly Ahura paused as a beam of blinding light leaped from the eastern to the western Pleiades, glanced from a deflector screen and lanced through NRGC 984–D's atmosphere, narrowly missing the mountains that formed the western boundary of the Sphinx's demesne. The Sphinx, silhouetted darkly against the eastern heavens, did not move.

Trembling, the girl raised her hands and pressed them tightly against her mouth. "It's all right," Hall said, "scream if you want to. No one éver had a better right to."

Another blinding beam—this one from the western Pleiades—speared the heavens, ricocheted from an enemy deflector, and arrowed off into deep space. The law of averages made it an even bet that the next one would strike NRGC 984–D dead center, gouge a crater two thousand miles deep, and precipitate a tectonic revolution. It was also an even bet that the tectonic revolution would give birth to a series of others and that the accompanying seismic and volcanic activity would alter every facet of NRGC 984–D's surface features and in the process destroy every living being on the planet.

"The object of the game," Hall went on, momentarily forgetting that his audience hailed from the twenty-ninth century B.C., "is for one fleet to penetrate the deflector sceens of the other. This isn't as impossible as it sounds. Deflector screens utilize a rhythmic frequency, and the trick is to hit them on the offbeat. Vulnerable as they are, though, they provide considerable protection, and I'd give my eyeteeth to have one over us right now. Well no, I'll qualify that: I'd give my eyeteeth to have one over us right now if it weren't for the fact that they won't function except in a vacuum.''

Ahura's hands were still pressed tightly against her mouth, and she was rocking gently back and forth. "I do not understand thee, Dan'el," she moaned. "I understand only that Sebek is greatly displeased and that Keb the Earth is in danger."

"You understand far more than that, Ahura. As a matter of fact, in your own way you know as much about what is happening as I do. You know that mankind is about to destroy himself because of his dog—his selfishness. That's why you can't get the story of the doomed prince out of your mind. The doomed prince is mankind, Ahura, only he isn't quite doomed. There's still hope for him. There's still hope for you and me—and She-who-builds-sepulchers. Tell me the rest of it, Ahura."

She had stopped rocking back and forth, and now she returned her hands to her lap. "There is but little left to tell thee, Dan'el. After the prince entered the river behind his dog there came out the crocodile, and took him to the place where the mighty man was. And the crocodile said to the prince, 'I am thy doom, following after thee.'* And there endeth the tale."

"So actually," Hall said, "we don't know for certain whether the crocodile got him or not. He may very well have escaped it in the end."

"Yes, but there is still the dog, Dan'el."

"There will always be the dog. But maybe by recognizing it for what it really is we can curtail its activities." He looked at the sky, gasped. "Ahura, look! they're going away!"

She, too, was staring at the Pleiades. They were rapidly fading from sight, one set of them into the eastern reaches of the heavens, the other set into the western reaches. Abruptly,

*Ahura's tale is an adaption of the Egyptian story "The Doomed Prince."

one set winked out as its hyperdrives went into effect. A moment later, the other followed suit. "Did—did we escape the crocodile, Dan'el?"

Hall hugged her. "We sure did, and all of a sudden I'm as hungry as a horse. Does that offer you made a little while ago still stand?"

She slipped free from his arms, not haughtily, but hesitantly, as though she weren't quite sure whether she wanted to be free or not. "I will prepare thee a feast fit for a king," she said. "Come."

## THE AMBASSADORS

*Well,* said the Sphinx, *it looks as though you two are going to live happily together ever after, after all, as they say in your planet's folklore. Where's Ahura now? I broke contact with you after you went into the Temple of Love.*

*She's tidying up the kitchen,* Hall answered, gazing up into the starlit Brobdingnagian face. *Incidentally, I was right when I told her that she probably could not even boil water. Would you believe it?—I had to show her how!*

*But she learned readily enough, did she not? You'll find her equally receptive when you begain teaching her full-time.*

*Who said I was going to teach her at all? And while we're on the subject, just what am I supposed to teach her, and why?*

*Everything you can. As to why, it would be rather impractical for you not to, don't you think, in view of the fact that you and she are going to be representing my sisters and myself on Earth in the negotiating of a million-year peace treaty between Pornos, Earth, and Uvel? Meanwhile, the Uvellian scout whom my sister in the neighboring dhen captured will be similarly engaged on Uvel.*

Hall was thunderstruck. *So that's what you've got up your*

*sleeve! But whatever gave you the idea that I'd make a good ambassador?*

*It was a gamble, Daniel Hall, but it paid off. You haven't a great deal of diplomacy, but I can teach you diplomacy. The really important attributes you already have. You have intelligence, and you are brave. Underneath your flippant exterior you are kind and gentle, but you can be firm when the occasion demands. Most important of all, you have motivation. Ever since you played a part in the destruction of the Deimos Dissenters you've hated war and everything it stands for. With someone like Ahura working at your side, there's no limit to what you can accomplish in the cause of peace, Daniel Hall. As man and wife, the two of you will—*

*Wait a minute!* Hall interrupted. *You're carrying this thing too far!*

*Come now, Daniel Hall, you're half in love with her already, and you know it. And you might as well know, too, that she's already half in love with you. I not only "heard" everything both of you said, I also experienced everything both of you felt. My sister in the next demesne "tells" me that her scout and her princess hit it off well, too.*

Her *princess?*

*She brought a princess back from Uvel just as I brought one back from Earth. We're going to arrange a double wedding ceremony that will comply with the customs of the four different religions which will be represented. I myself have been chosen to do the officiating. This will in no way conflict with the religions of the two princesses, and I'm sure that both you and the Uvelian scout are sufficiently sophisticated in such matters not to raise any objections. I've already built you and Ahura a love nest in my largest pyramid—not altogether authentic as regards her background, but authentic enough to satisfy her—and modern enough to satisfy you, as you will see presently when Ahura's education permits her to take such "miracles" as electricity and hot and cold running water in her stride.*

Hall threw up his hands. *All right, we'll let all that pass for the moment. Right now, suppose you drop that deep and mysterious mien of yours and break down and tell me how you managed to put a stop to the greatest space battle ever contemplated and to put two of the mightiest space armadas ever assembled to rout.*

The Sphinx laughed, softly this time. *You already know part of the answer, Daniel Hall. You know that we're parthenogenetic. You know that we build pyramids—or what you think of as pyramids. And you know that some of your legends depict us with wings. How do you account for that, Daniel Hall? Why should we be depicted with wings when we don't have any and never did?*

The truth dawned on Hall then. "You lay eggs!" he gasped.

*We do indeed. And we incubate them in inviolable capsules that lend the illusion of invisibility. These capsules are placed just beneath the apexes of the structures that you call "pyramids" but which we call "nests." Originally, we did this out of instinct alone; now, we do it out of knowledge as well. Owing to the length of the incubation period—some fifty-two hundred of your years—nests of this kind are ideal for the survival of our species. They provide protection, they provide warmth, they—*

*But no egg could possibly contain enough nutrients to nourish an embryo for fifty-two hundred years!* Hall objected.

*Of course it couldn't. My race obtains ninety-five percent of its nutrition from the sun, Daniel Hall, and your sun is an even better provider than ours is. I may seem to consist of flesh and blood, but I don't—at least not in the sense that you do.*

*And do you always build three nests of three different sizes?*

*Always. Our eggs are three in number and our offspring vary in size. Not very much, but enough to necessitate larger or smaller incubation areas. Now that the eggs which I incubated on the Gizeh plateau have hatched, I'm due to procreate again; consequently, I've built three new nests. When the time arrives, I'll remove the as-yet-unsealed apexes, place the eggs in the capsules, which are already in position, and seal the apexes over them.*

*I can anticipate your next question, Daniel Hall, so there's no need for you to ask it. Incubation time never varies, and*

*can be computed to the second, and the main reason I and my
sister in the neighboring dhen were chosen for the job was
that our procreation times were compatible with the Terran
and Uvelian time periods that had to be used. At the end of
the incubation period an adult rather than a child emerges
from the nest. Physically, she's only partially grown, but
mentally, she's completely mature, having inherited the parent's knowledge and abilities, plus a sizable quantity of the
parent's judgment. As a result, she's perfectly capable of
carrying out whatever commands the parent may have implanted in her embryo-mind at the beginning of incubation. In
the case of my Gizeh offspring, the commands which I implanted were three in number:* Take over the Terran capital of
Kafr el Haran, establish immediate contact with the Terran
Space Navy and order all of its units to return to base at once;
then retain control of the Terran government until otherwise
advised. *The commands which my sister implanted in her
offspring were basically the same, and her three offspring
carried out the Uvel end of the operation at roughly the same
time mine were carrying out the Terran end of it. Consequently, both governments are now under the dominion of
Pornos, and moreover they will remain under the dominion of
Pornos until such time as the million-year peace treaty is
signed. Since my sister just notified me that her scout has
already agreed to cooperate, the fate of the long-range aspect
of our plan is now in your hands, Daniel Hall.*

Hall sighed. *Oh, I'll go along with you, I suppose—I'd be
pretty much of a heel if I didn't. But before we get down to
brass tacks, how about relieving my mind on a certain little
matter? Granted, I'm half in love with Ahura, and maybe
she's half in love with me as you say, but there has to be
more to it than that for marriage to work. Now that the crisis
is past, how about taking a peek a little ways into the future
and finding out whether Ahura and I are going to hit it off the
way a married couple should?*

*I'll try, Daniel Hall,* said the Sphinx. She looked straight
ahead, and Hall could tell from the serious expression on her
face that she was concentrating with all her might. A few
minutes passed. Then the Sphinx turned to him and winked.

# UNICORN

The unicorn is a legendary one-horned creature. Almost all horned animals have two horns, one on each side of the head. An exception is the rhinoceros, which has a single horn on the nose, and there is some thought that the legend of the unicorn in the Middle East and in Europe originated with vague tales of rhinoceroses in India.

Much more likely is that it originated with Assyrian representations of wild bulls in profile. In profile, naturally, the two horns overlapped and only one was visible. Somehow this gave rise to the thought of one-horned bulls.

In the Bible, mention is made of a creature named re-em in Hebrew. The reference was to the wild bull (called an aurochs in Europe) which is the primitive ancestor of domestic cattle, and which is now extinct. It was described as immensely powerful.

In the Greek translation of the Bible, re-em was translated as monokeros ("one-horn"), the reference being to the Assyrian representations in profile. This became unicornis (also "one-horn") in Latin, and the legend was fixed.

Somehow, the unicorn tale became prettied up. Instead of a one-horned bull remarkable for its strength, it became a one-horned horse, or horselike antelope, remarkable for its beauty and swiftness. It began to symbolize purity and virginity; it could be caught only by a virgin woman.

Its horn is now pictured as a tight spiral, extending forward and slowly tapering. This is actually the "horn" *(really, the tooth) of the narwhal, a species of whale. The narwhal tooth was brought back by sailors and sold as a unicorn horn for large sums, since such a horn was considered a powerful aphrodisiac.*

*The following story deals with the unicorn at its prettiest.*

# THE SILKEN SWIFT

*Theodore Sturgeon*

There's a village by the Bogs, and in the village is a Great
House. In the Great House lived a squire who had land and
treasures and, for a daughter, Rita.

In the village lived Del, whose voice was a thunder in the
inn when he drank there; whose corded, cabled body was
golden-skinned, and whose hair flung challenges back to the
sun.

Deep in the Bogs, which were brackish, there was a pool
of purest water, shaded by willows and wide-wondering aspen, cupped by banks of a moss most marvelously blue. Here
grew mandrake, and there were strange pipings in midsummer.
No one ever heard them but a quiet girl whose beauty was so
very contained that none of it showed. Her name was Barbara.

There was a green evening, breathless with growth, when
Del took his usual way down the lane beside the manor and
saw a white shadow adrift inside the tall iron pickets. He
stopped, and the shadow approached, and became Rita. "Slip
around to the gate," she said, "and I'll open it for you."

She wore a gown like a cloud and a silver circlet round her
head. Night was caught in her hair, moonlight in her face,
and in her great eyes, secrets swam.

Del said, "I have no business with the squire."

"He's gone," she said. "I've sent the servants away.
Come to the gate."

"I need no gate." He leaped and caught the top bar of the
fence, and in a continuous fluid motion went high and across
and down beside her. She looked at his arms, one, the other;

309

then up at his hair. She pressed her small hands tight together
and made a little laugh, and then she was gone through the
tailored trees, lightly, swiftly, not looking back. He followed,
one step for three of hers, keeping pace with a new pounding
in the sides of his neck. They crossed a flower bed and a
wide marble terrace. There was an open door, and when he
passed through it he stopped, for she was nowhere in sight.
Then the door clicked shut behind him and he whirled. She
was there, her back to the panel, laughing up at him in the
dimness. He thought she would come to him then, but instead
she twisted by, close, her eyes on his. She smelt of violets
and sandalwood. He followed her into the great hall, quite
dark but full of the subdued lights of polished wood, cloisonné,
tooled leather and gold-threaded tapestry. She flung open
another door, and they were in a small room with a carpet
made of rosy silences, and a candle-lit table. Two places
were set, each with five different crystal glasses and old
silver as prodigally used as the iron pickets outside. Six
teakwood steps rose to a great oval window. "The moon,"
she said, "will rise for us there."

She motioned him to a chair and crossed to a sideboard,
where there was a rack of decanters—ruby wine and white;
one with a strange brown bead; pink, and amber. She took
down the first and poured. Then she lifted the silver domes
from the salvers on the table, and a magic of fragrance filled
the air. There were smoking sweets and savories, rare sea-
food and slivers of fowl, and morsels of strange meat wrapped
in flower petals, spitted with foreign fruits and tiny soft
seashells. All about were spices, each like a separate voice in
the distant murmur of a crowd: saffron and sesame, cumin
and marjoram and mace.

And all the while Del watched her in wonder, seeing how
the candles left the moonlight in her face, and how completely she trusted her hands, which did such deftness without
supervision—so composed she was, for all the silent secret
laughter that tugged at her lips, for all the bright dark myster-
ies that swirled and swam within her.

They ate, and the oval window yellowed and darkened
while the candlelight grew bright. She poured another wine,

and another, and with the courses of the meal they were as
May to the crocus and as frost to the apple.

Del knew it was alchemy and he yielded to it without
questions. That which was purposely oversweet would be
piquantly cut; this induced thirst would, with exquisite timing, be quenched. He knew she was watching him; he knew
she was aware of the heat in his cheeks and the tingle at his
fingertips. His wonder grew, but he was not afraid.

In all this time she spoke hardly a word; but at last the feast
was over and they rose. She touched a silken rope on the
wall, and paneling slid aside. The table rolled silently into
some ingenious recess and the panel returned. She waved him
to an L-shaped couch in one corner, and as he sat close to
her, she turned and took down the lute which hung on the
wall behind her. He had his moment of confusion; his arms
were ready for her, but not for the instrument as well. Her
eyes sparkled, but her composure was unshaken.

Now she spoke, while her fingers strolled and danced on
the lute, and her words marched and wandered in and about
the music. She had a thousand voices, so that he wondered
which of them was truly hers. Sometimes she sang; sometimes it was a wordless crooning. She seemed at times remote
from him, puzzled at the turn the music was taking, and at
other times she seemed to hear the pulsing roar in his ear-
drums, and she played laughing syncopations to it. She sang
words which he almost understood:

> "Bee to blossom, honey dew,
> Claw to mouse, and rain to tree,
> Moon to midnight, I to you;
> Sun to starlight, you to me . . ."

and she sang something wordless:

> "Ake ya rundefle, rundefle fye,
> Orel ya rundefle kown,
> En yea, en yea, ya bunderbee bye
> En sor, en see, en sown."

which he also almost understood.

In still another voice she told him the story of a great hairy spider and a little pink girl who found it between the leaves of a half-open book; and at first he was all fright and pity for the girl, but then she went on to tell of what the spider suffered, with his home disrupted by this yawping giant, and so vividly did she tell of it that at the end he was laughing at himself and all but crying for the poor spider.

So the hours slipped by, and suddenly, between songs, she was in his arms; and in the instant she had twisted up and away from him, leaving him gasping. She said, in still a new voice, sober and low, "No, Del. We must wait for the moon."

His thighs ached and he realized that he had half-risen, arms out, hands clutching and feeling the extraordinary fabric of her gown though it was gone from them; and he sank back to the couch with an odd, faint sound that was wrong for the room. He flexed his fingers and, reluctantly, the sensation of white gossamer left them. At last he looked across at her and she laughed and leapt high lightly, and it was as if she stopped in midair to stretch for a moment before she alighted beside him, bent and kissed his mouth, and leapt away.

The roaring in his ears was greater, and at this it seemed to acquire a tangible weight. His head bowed; he tucked his knuckles into the upper curve of his eye sockets and rested his elbows on his knees. He could hear the sweet susurrus of Rita's gown as she moved about the room; he could sense the violets and sandalwood. She was dancing, immersed in the joy of movement and of his nearness. She made her own music, humming, sometimes whispering to the melodies in her mind.

And at length he became aware that she had stopped; he could hear nothing, though he knew she was still near. Heavily he raised his head. She was in the center of the room, balanced like a huge white moth, her eyes quite dark now with their secrets quiet. She was staring at the window, poised, waiting.

He followed her gaze. The big oval was black no longer, but dusted over with silver light. Del rose slowly. The dust was a mist, a loom, and then, at one edge, there was a shard of the moon itself creeping and growing.

Because Del stopped breathing, he could hear her breathe; it was rapid and so deep it faintly strummed her versatile vocal cords.

"Rita . . ."

Without answering she ran to the sideboard and filled two small glasses. She gave him one, then, "Wait," she breathed, "oh, wait!"

Spellbound, he waited while the white stain crept across the window. He understood suddenly that he must be still until the great oval was completely filled with direct moonlight, and this helped him, because it set a foreseeable limit to his waiting; and it hurt him, because nothing in life, he thought, had ever moved so slowly. He had a moment of rebellion, in which he damned himself for falling in with her complex pacing; but with it he realized that now the darker silver was wasting away, now it was a finger's breadth, and now a thread, and now, and *now*—.

She made a brittle feline cry and sprang up the dark steps to the window. So bright was the light that her body was a jet cameo against it. So delicately wrought was her gown that he could see the epaulettes of silver light the moon gave her. She was so beautiful his eyes stung.

"Drink," she whispered. "Drink with me, darling, darling . . ."

For an instant he did not understand her at all, and only gradually did he become aware of the little glass he held. He raised it toward her and drank. And of all the twists and titillations of taste he had had this night, this was the most startling; for it had no taste at all, almost no substance, and a temperature almost exactly that of blood. He looked stupidly down at the glass and back up at the girl. He thought that she had turned about and was watching him, though he could not be sure, since her silhouette was the same.

And then he had his second of unbearable shock, for the light went out.

The moon was gone, the window, the room. Rita was gone.

For a stunned instant he stood tautly, stretching his eyes wide. He made a sound that was not a word. He dropped the glass and pressed his palms to his eyes, feeling them blink, feeling the stiff silk of his lashes against them. Then he snatched the hands away, and it was still dark, and more than dark; this was not a blackness. This was like trying to see with an elbow or with a tongue; it was not black; it was *Nothingness*.

He fell to his kness.

Rita laughed.

An odd, alert part of his mind seized on the laugh and understood it, and horror and fury spread through his whole being; for this was the laugh which had been tugging at her lips all evening, and it was a hard, cruel, self-assured laugh. And at the same time, because of the anger or in spite of it, desire exploded whitely within him. He moved toward the sound, groping, mouthing. There was a quick, faint series of rustling sounds from the steps, and then a light, strong web fell around him. He struck out at it, and recognized it for the unforgettable thing it was—her robe. He caught at it, ripped it, stamped upon it. He heard her bare feet run lightly down and past him, and lunged, and caught nothing. He stood, gasping painfully.

She laughed again.

"I'm blind," he said hoarsely. "Rita, I'm blind!"

"I know," she said coolly, close beside him. And again she laughed.

"What have you done to me?"

"I've watched you be a dirty animal of a man," she said.

He grunted and lunged again. His knees struck something—a chair, a cabinet—and he fell heavily. He thought he touched her foot.

"Here, lover, here!" she taunted.

He fumbled about for the thing which had tripped him, found it, used it to help him upright again. He peered uselessly about.

"Here, lover!"

He leaped, and crashed into the doorjamb: cheekbone,

collarbone, hipbone, ankle were one straight blaze of pain. He clung to the polished wood.

After a time he said, in agony, "Why?"

"No man has ever touched me and none ever will," she sang. Her breath was on his cheek. He reached and touched nothing, and then he heard her leap from her perch on a statue's pedestal by the door, where she had stood high and leaned over to speak.

No pain, no blindness, not even the understanding that it was her witch's brew working in him could quell the wild desire he felt at her nearness. Nothing could tame the fury that shook him as she laughed. He staggered after her, bellowing.

She danced around him, laughing. Once she pushed him into a clattering rack of fire-irons. Once she caught his elbow from behind and spun him. And once, incredibly, she sprang past him and, in midair, kissed him again on the mouth.

He descended into Hell, surrounded by the small, sure patter of bare feet and sweet cool laughter. He rushed and crashed, he crouched and bled and whimpered like a hound. His roaring and blundering took an echo, and that must have been the great hall. Then there were walls that seemed more than unyielding; they struck back. And there were panels to lean against, gasping, which became opening doors as he leaned. And always the black nothingness, the writhing temptation of the pat-pat of firm flesh on smooth stones, and the ravening fury.

It was cooler, and there was no echo. He became aware of the whisper of the wind through trees. The balcony, he thought; and then, right in his ear, so that he felt her warm breath, "Come, lover . . ." and he sprang. He sprang and missed, and instead of sprawling on the terrace, there was nothing, and nothing, and nothing, and then, when he least expected it, a shower of cruel thumps as he rolled down the marble steps.

He must have had a shred of consciousness left, for he was vaguely aware of the approach of her bare feet, and of the small, cautious hand that touched his shoulder and moved to

his mouth, and then his chest. Then it was withdrawn, and
either she laughed or the sound was still in his mind.

Deep in the Bogs, which were brackish, there was a pool
of purest water, shaded by willows and wide-wondering aspens, cupped by banks of a moss most marvelously blue.
Here grew mandrake, and there were strange pipings in midsummer. No one ever heard them but a quiet girl whose
beauty was so very contained that none of it showed. Her
name was Barbara.

No one noticed Barbara, no one lived with her, no one
cared. And Barbara's life was very full, for she was born to
receive. Others are born wishing to receive, so they wear
bright masks and make attractive sounds like cicadas and
operettas, so others will be forced, one way or another, to
give to them. But Barbara's receptors were wide open, and
always had been, so that she needed no substitute for sunlight
through a tulip petal, or the sound of morning glories climbing, or the tangy sweet smell of formic acid which is the only
death cry possible to an ant, or any other of the thousand
things overlooked by folk who can only wish to receive.
Barbara had a garden and an orchard, and took things in
to market when she cared to, and the rest of the time she spent
in taking what was given. Weeds grew in her garden, but
since they were welcomed, they grew only where they could
keep the watermelons from being sunburned. The rabbits
were welcome, so they kept to the two rows of carrots, the
one of lettuce, and the one of tomato vines which were planted
for them, and they left the rest alone. Goldenrod shot up
beside the bean hills to lend a hand upward, and the birds ate
only the figs and peaches from the waviest top branches, and
in return patrolled the lower ones for caterpillars and egg-
laying flies. And if a fruit stayed green for two weeks longer
until Barbara had time to go to market, or if a mole could
channel moisture to the roots of the corn, why it was the least
they could do.

For a brace of years Barbara had wandered more and more,
impelled by a thing she could not name—if indeed she was
aware of it at all. She knew only that over-the-rise was a
strange and friendly place, and that it was a fine thing on

arriving there to find another rise to go over. It may very well be that she now needed someone to love, for loving is a most receiving thing, as anyone can attest who has been loved without returning it. It is the one who is loved who must give and give. And she found her love, not in her wandering, but at the market. The shape of her love, his colors and sounds, were so much with her that when she saw him first it was without surprise; and thereafter, for a very long while, it was quite enough that he lived. He gave to her by being alive, by setting the air athrum with his mighty voice, by his stride, which was, for a man afoot, the exact analog of what the horseman calls a "perfect seat."

After seeing him, of course, she received twice and twice again as much as ever before. A tree was straight and tall for the magnificent sake of being straight and tall, but wasn't straightness a part of him, and being tall? The oriole gave more now than song, and the hawk more than walking the wind, for had they not hearts like his, warm blood and his same striving to keep it so for tomorrow? And more and more, over-the-rise was the place for her, for only there could there be more and still more things like him.

But when she found the pure pool in the brackish Bogs, there was no more over-the-rise for her. It was a place without hardness or hate, where the aspens trembled only for wonder, and where all contentment was rewarded. Every single rabbit there was *the* champion nose-twinkler, and every waterbird could stand on one leg the longest, and proud of it. Shelf-fungi hung to the willow-trunks, making that certain, single purple of which the sunset is incapable, and a tanager and a cardinal gravely granted one another his definition of "red."

Here Barbara brought a heart light with happiness, large with love, and set it down on the blue moss. And since the loving heart can receive more than anything else, so it is most needed, and Barbara took the best bird songs, and the richest colors, and the deepest peace, and all the other things which are most worth giving. The chipmunks brought her nuts when she was hungry and the prettiest stones when she was not. A green snake explained to her, in pantomime, how a river of jewels may flow uphill, and three mad otters described how a bundle of joy may slip and slide down and down and be all the more joyful for it. And there was the magic moment when a midge hovered, and then a honeybee, and then a bumblebee, and at last a hummingbird; and there they hung, playing a chord in A sharp minor.

Then one day the pool fell silent, and Barbara learned why the water was pure.

The aspens stopped trembling.

The rabbits all came out of the thicket and clustered on the blue bank, backs straight, ears up, and all their noses as still as coral.

The waterbirds stepped backwards, like courtiers, and stopped on the brink with their heads turned sidewise, one eye closed the better to see with the other.

The chipmunks respectfully emptied their cheek pouches, scrubbed their paws together and tucked them out of sight; then stood still as tent pegs.

The pressure of growth around the pool ceased: the very grass waited.

The last sound of all to be heard—and by then it was very quiet—was the soft *whick!* of an owl's eyelids as it awoke to watch.

*He* came like a cloud, the earth cupping itself to take each of his golden hooves. He stopped on the bank and lowered his head, and for a brief moment his eyes met Barbara's, and she looked into a second universe of wisdom and compassion. Then there was the arch of the magnificent neck, the blinding flash of his golden horn.

And he drank, and he was gone. Everyone knows the water is pure, where the unicorn drinks.

How long had he been there? How long gone? Did time wait too, like the grass?

"And couldn't he stay?" she wept. "Couldn't he stay?"

To have seen the unicorn is a sad thing; one might never see him more. But then—to have seen the unicorn!

She began to make a song.

It was late when Barbara came in from the Bogs, so late the moon was bleached with cold and fleeing to the horizon.

She struck the highroad just below the Great House and turned to pass it and go out to her garden house.

Near the locked main gate an animal was barking. A sick animal, a big animal . . .

Barbara could see in the dark better than most, and soon saw the creature clinging to the gate, climbing, uttering that coughing moan as it went. At the top it slipped, fell outward, dangled; then there was a ripping sound, and it fell heavily to the ground and lay still and quiet.

She ran to it, and it began to make the sound again. It was a man, and he was weeping.

It was her love, her love, who was tall and straight and so very alive—her love, battered and bleeding, puffy, broken, his clothes torn, crying.

Now of all times was the time for a lover to receive, to take from the loved one his pain, his trouble, his fear. "Oh, hush, hush," she whispered, her hands touching his bruised face like swift feathers. "It's all over now. It's all over."

She turned him over on his back and knelt to bring him up sitting. She lifted one of his thick arms around her shoulder. He was very heavy, but she was very strong. When he was upright, gasping weakly, she looked up and down the road in the waning moonlight. Nothing, no one. The Great House was dark. Across the road, though, was a meadow with high hedgerows which might break the wind a little.

"Come, my love, my dear love," she whispered. He trembled violently.

All but carrying him, she got him across the road, over the shallow ditch, and through a gap in the hedge. She almost fell with him there. She gritted her teeth and set him down gently. She let him lean against the hedge, and then ran and swept up great armfulls of sweet broom. She made a tight springy bundle of it and set it on the ground beside him, and put a corner of her cloak over it, and gently lowered his head until it was pillowed. She folded the rest of the cloak about him. He was very cold.

There was no water near, and she dared not leave him. With her kerchief she cleaned some of the blood from his face. He was still very cold. He said, "You devil. You rotten little devil."

"Shh." She crept in beside him and cradled his head. "You'll be warm in a minute."

"Stand still," he growled. "Keep running away."

"I won't run away," she whispered. "Oh, my darling, you've been hurt, so hurt. I won't leave you. I promise I won't leave you."

He lay very still. He made the growling sound again.

"I'll tell you a lovely thing," she said softly. "Listen to me, think about the lovely thing," she crooned.

"There's a place in the bog, a pool of pure water, where the trees live beautifully, willow and aspen and birch, where everything is peaceful, my darling, and the flowers grow without tearing their petals. The moss is blue and the water is like diamonds."

"You tell me stories in a thousand voices," he muttered.

"Shh. Listen, my darling. This isn't a story, it's a real place. Four miles north and a little west, and you can see the trees from the ridge with the two dwarf oaks. And I know why the water is pure!" she cried gladly. "I know why!"

He said nothing. He took a deep breath and it hurt him, for he shuddered painfully.

"The unicorn drinks there," she whispered. "I *saw* him!"

Still he said nothing. She said, "I made a song about it. Listen, this is the song I made:

> "*And He—suddenly gleamed! My dazzled eyes*
> *Coming from outer sunshine to this green*
> *And secret gloaming, met without surprise*
> *The vision. Only after, when the sheen*
> *And Splendor of his going fled away,*
> *I knew amazement, wonder and despair,*
> *That he should come—and pass—and would not stay,*
> *The Silken-swift—the gloriously Fair!*
> *That he should come—and pass—and would not stay,*
> *So that, forever after, I must go,*
> *Take the long road that mounts against the day,*
> *Traveling in the hope that I shall know*
> *Again that lifted moment, high and sweet,*
> *Somewhere—on purple moor or windy hill—*
> *Remembering still his wild and delicate feet,*
> *The magic and the dream—remembering still!*"

His breathing was more regular. She said, "I truly *saw* him!"

"I'm blind," he said. "Blind, I'm blind."

"Oh, my dear . . ."

He fumbled for her hand, found it. For a long moment he held it. Then, slowly, he brought up his other hand and with them both he felt her hand, turned it about, squeezed it. Suddenly he grunted, half sitting. "You're here."

"Of course, darling. Of course I'm here."

"Why?" he shouted. "Why? *Why?* Why all of this? Why blind me?" He sat up, mouthing, and put his great hand on her throat. "Why do all that if . . ." The words ran together into an animal noise. Wine and witchery, anger and agony boiled in his veins.

Once she cried out.

Once she sobbed.

"Now," he said, "you'll catch no unicorns. Get away from me." He cuffed her.

"You're mad. You're sick," she cried.

"Get away," he said ominously.

Terrified, she rose. He took the cloak and hurled it after her. It almost toppled her as she ran away, crying silently.

After a long time, from behind the hedge, the sick, coughing sobs began again.

Three weeks later Rita was in the market when a hard hand took her upper arm and pressed her into the angle of a cottage wall. She did not start. She flashed her eyes upward and recognized him, and then said composedly, "Don't touch me."

"I need you to tell me something," he said. "And tell me you *will!*" His voice was as hard as his hand.

"I'll tell you anything you like," she said. "But don't touch me."

He hesitated, then released her. She turned to him casually. "What is it?" Her gaze darted across his face and its almost-healed scars. The small smile tugged at one corner of her mouth.

His eyes were slits. "I have to know this: why did you

make up all that . . . prettiness, that food, that poison . . . just for me? You could have had me for less."

She smiled. "Just for you? It was your turn, that's all."

He was genuinely surprised. "It's happened before?"

She nodded. "Whenever it's the full of the moon—and the squire's away."

"You're lying!"

"You forget yourself!" she said sharply. Then, smiling, "It is the truth, though."

"I'd've heard talk—"

"Would you now? And tell me—how many of your friends know about your humiliating adventure?"

He hung his head.

She nodded. "You see? They go away until they're healed, and they come back and say nothing. And they always will."

"You're a devil . . . why do you do it? Why?"

"I told you," she said openly. "I'm a woman and I act like a woman in my own way. No man will ever touch me, though. I am virgin and shall remain so."

"You're *what?*" he roared.

She held up a restraining, ladylike glove. "Please," she said, pained.

"Listen," he said, quietly now, but with such intensity that for once she stepped back a pace. He closed his eyes, thinking hard: "You told me—the pool, the pool of the unicorn, and a song, wait. 'The Silken-swift, the gloriously Fair . . .' Remember? And then I—I saw to it that *you'd* never catch a unicorn!"

She shook her head, complete candor in her face. "I like that, 'the Silken-swift.' Pretty. But believe me—no! That isn't mine."

He put his face close to hers, and though it was barely a whisper, it came out like bullets. "Liar! Liar! I couldn't forget. I was sick, I was hurt, I was poisoned, but I know what I did!" He turned on his heel and strode away.

She put the thumb of her glove against her upper teeth for a second, then ran after him. "Del!"

He stopped but, rudely, would not turn. She rounded him,

faced him. "I'll not have you believing that of me—it's the one thing I have left," she said tremulously.

He made no attempt to conceal his surprise. She controlled her expression with a visible effort, and said, "Please. Tell me a little more—just about the pool, the song, whatever it was."

"You don't remember?"

"I don't *know!*" she flashed. She was deeply agitated.

He said with mock patience. "You told me of a unicorn pool out on the Bogs. You said you had seen *him* drink there. You made a song about it. And then I—"

"Where? Where was this?"

"You forget so soon?"

"Where? Where did it happen?"

"In the meadow, across the road from your gate, where you followed me," he said. "Where my sight came back to me, when the sun came up."

She looked at him blankly, and slowly her face changed. First the imprisoned smile struggling to be free, and then— she was herself again, and she laughed. She laughed a great ringing peal of the laughter that had plagued him so, and she did not stop until he put one hand behind his back, then the other, and she saw his shoulders swell with the effort to keep from striking her dead.

"You animal!" she said, good-humoredly. "Do you know what you've done? Oh, you . . . you *animal!*" She glanced around to see that there were no ears to hear her. "I left you at the foot of the terrace steps," she told him. Her eyes sparkled. "Inside the gates, you understand? And you . . ."

"Don't laugh," he said quietly.

She did not laugh. "That was someone else out there. Who, I can't imagine. But it wasn't I."

He paled. "You followed me out."

"On my soul I did not," she said soberly. Then she quelled another laugh.

"That can't be," he said. "I couldn't have . . ."

"But you were blind, blind and crazy, Del-my-lover!"

"Squire's daughter, take care," he hissed. Then he pulled

his big hand through his hair. "It can't be. It's three weeks; I'd have been accused . . ."

"There are those who wouldn't." She smiled "Or—perhaps she will, in time."

"There has never been a woman so foul," he said evenly, looking her straight in the eye. "You're lying—you know you're lying."

"What must I do to prove it—aside from that which I'll have no man do?"

His lip curled. "Catch the unicorn," he said.

"If I did, you'd believe I was a virgin?"

"I must," he admitted. He turned away, then said, over his shoulder. "But—*you?*"

She watched him thoughtfully until he left the marketplace. Her eyes sparkled; then she walked briskly to the goldsmith's, where she ordered a bridle of woven gold.

If the unicorn pool lay in the Bogs nearby, Rita reasoned, someone who was familiar with that brackish wasteland must know of it. And when she made a list in her mind of those few who traveled the Bogs, she knew whom to ask. With that, the other deduction came readily. Her laughter drew stares as she moved through the marketplace.

By the vegetable stall she stopped. The girl looked up patiently.

Rita stood swinging one expensive glove against the other wrist, half-smiling. "So you're the one." She studied the plain, inward-turning, peaceful face until Barbara had to turn her eyes away. Rita said, without further preamble, "I want you to show me the unicorn pool in two weeks."

Barbara looked up again, and now it was Rita who dropped her eyes. Rita said, "I can have someone else find it, of course. If you'd rather not." She spoke very clearly, and people turned to listen. They looked from Barbara to Rita and back again, and they waited.

"I don't mind," said Barbara faintly. As soon as Rita had left, smiling, she packed up her things and went silently back to her house.

\*    \*    \*

The goldsmith, of course, made no secret of such an extraordinary commission; and that, plus the gossips who had overheard Rita talking to Barbara, made the expedition into a cavalcade. The whole village turned out to see; the boys kept firmly in check so that Rita might lead the way; the young bloods ranged behind her (some a little less carefree than they might be) and others snickering behind their hands. Behind them the girls, one or two a little pale, others eager as cats to see the squire's daughter fail, and perhaps even . . . but then, only she had the golden bridle.

She carried it casually, but casualness could not hide it, for it was not wrapped, and it swung and blazed in the sun. She wore a flowing white robe, trimmed a little short so that she might negotiate the rough bogland; she had on a golden girdle and little gold sandals, and a gold chain bound her head and hair like a coronet.

Barbara walked quietly a little behind Rita, closed in with her own thoughts. Not once did she look at Del, who strode somberly by himself.

Rita halted a moment and let Barbara catch up, then walked beside her. "Tell me," she said quietly, "why did you come? It needn't have been you."

"I'm his friend," Barbara said. She quickly touched the bridle with her finger. "The unicorn."

"Oh," said Rita. "The unicorn." She looked archly at the other girl. "You wouldn't betray all your friends, would you?"

Barbara looked at her thoughtfully, without anger. "If— when you catch the unicorn," she said carefully, "what will do you with him?"

"What an amazing question! I shall keep him, of course!"

"I thought I might persuade you to let him go."

Rita smiled, and hung the bridle on the other arm. "You could never do that."

"I know," said Barbara. "But I thought I might, so that's why I came." And before Rita could answer, she dropped behind again.

The last ridge, the one which overlooked the unicorn pool,
saw a series of gasps as the ranks of villagers topped it, one
after the other, and saw what lay below; and it was indeed
beautiful.

Surprisingly, it was Del who took it upon himself to call
out, in his great voice, "Everyone wait here!" And everyone
did; the top of the ridge filled slowly, from one side to the
other, with craning, murmuring people. And then Del bounded
after Rita and Barbara.

Barbara said, "I'll stop here."

"Wait," said Rita, imperiously. Of Del she demanded,
"What are you coming for?"

"To see fair play," he growled. "The little I know of
witchcraft makes me like none of it."

"Very well," she said calmly. Then she smiled her very
own smile. "Since you insist, I'd rather enjoy Barbara's
company too."

Barbara hesitated. "Come, he won't hurt you, girl," said
Rita. "He doesn't know you exist."

"Oh," said Barbara, wonderingly.

Del said gruffly, "I do so. She has the vegetable
stall."

Rita smiled at Barbara, the secrets bright in her eyes.
Barbara said nothing, but came with them.

"You should go back, you know," Rita said silkily to
Del, when she could. "Haven't you been humiliated enough
yet?"

He did not answer.

She said, "Stubborn animal! Do you think I'd have come
this far if I weren't sure?"

"Yes," said Del, "I think perhaps you would."

They reached the blue moss. Rita shuffled it about with her
feet and then sank gracefully down to it. Barbara stood alone
in the shadows of the willow grove. Del thumped gently at an
aspen with his fist. Rita, smiling, arranged the bridle to cast,
and laid it across her lap.

The rabbits stayed hid. There was an uneasiness about the
grove. Barbara sank to her knees, and put out her hand. A
chipmunk ran to nestle in it.

This time there was a difference. This time it was not the slow silencing of living things that warned of his approach, but a sudden babble from the people on the ridge.

Rita gathered her legs under her like a sprinter, and held the bridle poised. Her eyes were round and bright, and the tip of her tongue showed between her white teeth. Barbara was a statue. Del put his back against his tree, and became as still as Barbara.

Then from the ridge came a single, simultaneous intake of breath, and silence. One knew without looking that some stared speechless, that some buried their faces or threw an arm over their eyes.

*He* came.

He came slowly this time, his golden hooves choosing his paces like so many embroidery needles. He held his splendid head high. He regarded the three on the bank gravely, and then turned to look at the ridge for a moment. At last he turned, and came round the pond by the willow grove. Just on the blue moss, he stopped to look down into the pond. It seemed that he drew one deep clear breath. He bent his head then, and drank, and lifted his head to shake away the shining drops.

He turned toward the three spellbound humans and looked at them each in turn. And it was not Rita he went to, at last, nor Barbara. He came to Del, and he drank of Del's eyes with his own just as he had partaken of the pool—deeply and at leisure. The beauty and wisdom were there, and the compassion, and what looked like a bright white point of anger. Del knew that the creature had read everything then, and that he knew all three of them in ways unknown to human beings.

There was a majestic sadness in the way he turned then, and dropped his shining head, and stepped daintily to Rita. She sighed, and rose up a little, lifting the bridle. The unicorn lowered his horn to receive it—

—and tossed his head, tore the bridle out of her grasp, sent the golden thing high in the air. It turned there in the sun, and fell into the pond.

And the instant it touched the water, the pond was a bog and the birds rose mourning from the trees. The unicorn looked up at them, and shook himself. Then he trotted to Barbara and knelt, and put his smooth, stainless head in her lap.

Barbara's hands stayed on the ground by her sides. Her gaze moved over the warm white beauty, up to the tip of the golden horn and back.

The scream was frightening. Rita's hands were up like claws, and she had bitten her tongue; there was blood on her mouth. She screamed again. She threw herself off the now withered moss toward the unicorn and Barbara. "She can't be!" Rita shrieked. She collided with Del's broad right hand. "It's wrong, I tell you, she, you, I . . ."

"I'm satisfied," said Del, low in his throat. "Keep away, squire's daughter."

She recoiled from him, made as if to try to circle him. He stepped forward. She ground her chin into one shoulder, then the other, in a gesture of sheer frustration, turned suddenly and ran toward the ridge. "It's mine, it's mine," she screamed. "I tell you it can't be hers, don't you understand? I never once, I never did, but she, but she—"

She slowed and stopped, then, and fell silent at the sound that rose from the ridge. It began like the first patter of rain on oak leaves, and it gathered voice until it was a rumble and then a roar. She stood looking up, her face working, the sound washing over her. She shrank from it.

It was laughter.

She turned once, a pleading just beginning to form on her face. Del regarded her stonily. She faced the ridge then, and squared her shoulders, and walked up the hill, to go into the laughter, to go through it, to have it follow her all the way home and all the days of her life.

Del turned to Barbara just as she bent over the beautiful head. She said, "Silken-swift . . . go free."

The unicorn raised its head and looked up at Del. Del's mouth opened. He took a clumsy step forward, stopped again. *"You!"*

Barbara's face was set. "You weren't to know," she choked. "You weren't ever to know . . . I was so glad you were blind, because I thought you'd never know."

He fell on his knees beside her. And when he did, the unicorn touched her face with his satin nose, and all the girl's pent-up beauty flooded outward. The unicorn rose from his kneeling, and whickered softly. Del looked at her, and only the unicorn was more beautiful. He put out his hand to the shining neck, and for a moment felt the incredible silk of the mane flowing across his fingers. The unicorn reared then, and wheeled, and in a great leap was across the bog, and in two more was on the crest of the farther ridge. He paused there briefly, with the sun on him, and then was gone.

Barbara said, "For us, he lost his pool, his beautiful pool."

And Del said, "He will get another. He must." With difficulty he added, "He couldn't be . . . punished . . . for being so gloriously Fair."

# WENDIGO

*There are many legends of human beings who, for one reason or another, become animallike in appearance and nature. This may have arisen perhaps because the quiet, settled farmers of agricultural areas may have been horrified (and justly so) at the wild barbarian nomads who occasionally struck at them from the surrounding wilderness. (Even today we hear expressions such as "They're animals" when people describe the criminal denizens of our urban environment.)*

*It may also be that in the primeval forests, especially at night, human beings, armed with only primitive weapons, ran peculiar dangers, so that exaggerated tales of fearsome and intelligent predators would naturally arise.*

*Of course, transformations of human beings into animals might be the result of charms or spells. The case of the handsome prince turned into a frog until he is kissed by a princess, or into a fearsome Beast until Beauty falls in love with him, are well known.*

*Much more frightening are transformations that take place spontaneously and even involuntarily. The best-known case in our own culture is that of the werewolf (actually "man-wolf," since "were" is an Old English term for "man"). The werewolf is only one variety of this sort of thing, and weretigers etc. are also spoken of. However, thanks to Hollywood, the werewolf ranks above them all.*

*Among the northeastern Indian tribes, it was thought that any hunter lost in the forest would gradually be forced by hunger to waylay some unwary human being and eat him. The hunter would then develop animal form and become an inveterate man-eater. He was then known as a wendigo, or, more correctly, windigo. It is a pity the following story was not named "Mood Windigo," for that would have been even better wordplay.*

# MOOD WENDIGO

## Thomas A. Easton

When did this story begin? It's hard for anyone here in town to say. It looped back on itself and tied its bit of time in a knot. No one is really sure just what happened, though we do know we lost a good boy.

Did it start when Lydia Seltzer told her high school biology class about the wendigo? She was talking about the world's mystery beasts, the Abominable Snowman, the Sasquatch, the Loch Ness Monster and its cousins in other lakes around the world. She told them about all the expeditions, the lack of results, the questions—are the searchers simply crackpots? Or do elusive things still exist in the hidden corners of the world? And then she mentioned the wendigo, a thing that had never been more than a story, a superstition, something no one had ever believed in enough to check it out. Its name was Indian, and it was known across the Northeast, from Maine to Ontario. It screamed in the night, and anyone who sought the screamer disappeared without a trace. If they ever returned, they were mad, too blown of mind even to say what had happened to them. There were no descriptions of the wendigo.

Or did it start the day our town acquired a second Lydia? Mad she was, and raving, but she was the same Lydia we had all known for a decade. The same wide mouth, the nose a little larger than she liked, the black hair worn short and curled over her collar. Neither was any beauty, but neither were they ugly, and it seemed surprising that she had never married. Or perhaps it was no surprise after all. She was tough-minded as only a woman can be, and she showed it at

332

an unusually young age. Most women wait till their forties
and later to show their steel. But not Lydia. She brooked no
nonsense, in class or out, and for as long as we had known
her she had been given to severely tailored pantsuits, wool for
work, denim for evenings and weekends.

When did it start? Who can say? The best I can do is tell
you where I came into it. That was some time after the
wendigo class. I was at home, sitting at the kitchen table,
going over the town budget for the fourth time. Sarah, my
wife, was in the living room, watching something inane on
TV. We didn't talk much anymore, not about her job at the
bank, not about mine. We had no kids.

When the buzzer sounded, I heard her chair creak as she
rose to answer the door. There was a murmur of voices, steps
in the hall, and "Harry? Miss Seltzer wants to see you."
There was a glare with the words. I ignored it, raised my
head from the papers and said, "Duty calls, then. Have a
seat, Lydia. Coffee, a drink?"

"Do you have any tea?" As Lydia pulled the other chair
out from the table, Sarah disappeared. A moment later, the
sound of the TV rose, as if to drown out anything that might
give my wife's fantasies the lie. But my attention was for
Lydia. She seemed more serious than usual, if possible, and
there was a folded paper jutting from her bag. I wondered
what was on her mind as I filled the kettle. I found out soon
enough.

She sat still, watching me as I moved about the room,
saying nothing until our tea was before us and I had sat down
again. Then she said, "Mayor, I need a leave of absence. A
short one."

She stirred her cup, squeezed the bag, and dumped it in the
ashtray half full of my pipe ashes. "Of course," I said. "But
shouldn't you be asking the superintendent about this?" I was
puzzled. It wasn't my chore to handle the teachers, thank
goodness. I was the town's unpaid mayor, and there were
professionals, paid ones, to handle day-to-day affairs.

"I will," she replied. She looked at me, her brown eyes
unblinking. I remember thinking that for all her mannishness
she would be worth shielding from all grief. Perhaps it was

the eyes. Maybe it was just Sarah. "But you can help," she said. "You know people, and . . ."

"But what do you need help with?"

She shrugged and took the paper from her bag. She unfolded it and handed it to me. "Look at this," she said. "It's French-Canadian, a rhyme, collected back in the thirties by the WPA people. I found it in the university library, buried in the folklore files."

The paper was covered with a pencilled scrawl, a copy of a poem that must have been set down by someone who wished to capture the flavor of a speech pattern:

> Ze Wendigo,
> Zat crazy beast,
> 'E never eats,
> But loves t'go.
>
> In darkest night,
> 'E runs and screams
> And stirs ze dreams
> Of second sight.
>
> But when you go
> To join ze run,
> 'E stays unknown,
> Ze Wendigo.

I packed and lit my pipe, studying the rhyme, before I spoke. "Interesting," I said. I sent a cloud of smoke toward the ceiling. "But what does it have to do with a leave of absence?"

Her fingers tensed around her teacup. She had come to me, but she seemed unwilling to reveal her problem. Could it be so rare or odd or shameful? Suppose it was, I told myself, and then I guessed the answer.

"You want to go wendigo hunting." I laughed.

Her lips tightened, and I was immediately sorry for the laughter. That was just the reaction she had feared. Of course. No one wants to be thought a nut, a crackpot, even if their ideas are a bit off the beaten track. "But go on," I said, trying to save the situation. "Maybe I can help. At least, I'm game to try."

She relaxed as if that was all she had wanted. I caught a faint whiff of perfume or cologne. And she began to talk. She told me of the wendigo class, of her own interest in the strange, of her sense of fairness that led her to the library, of her conviction that all the legends must reflect some grain of truth, of her wish to seek that truth. She had come to me for suggestions on where to seek, a guess at the chances of success, perhaps even a partner in the strange quest.

Why me? Well, I do have a reputation for imagination. Last year's ad program for my oil business certainly stirred folks up enough. And then there were the gimmicks I had come up with to get more tourists into the area. And then, too, there had been a few incidents now and again to connect me with the strange. Really, I should have been more surprised if Lydia had not come to me.

But what could I do? I wouldn't know a wendigo if I saw one. Or heard one, rather. She was silent while I relit my pipe and thought. She didn't fidget much, only turning her empty cup back and forth between her hands. Finally, I said, "There's at least one fellow in this town who could help. If you'll come to the town hall tomorrow after school, I'll ask him to meet us there."

She nodded and sighed. Her breath whistled as if she had been holding it. So I would help, after all. Her voice was softer when she spoke. "Do you really think we can . . . ?"

"How can we know?" I grimaced, sympathetically, I hoped. "We've no idea what it looks like or where to look. But we can try."

The fellow I wanted to talk to was Howie Wyman. Grizzled, always overalled and booted, he had been doing odd jobs as long as anyone cared to recall. He knew all the stories, too, though he didn't talk much. He seemed to prefer the woods and streams to human company, even his wife, but he was in town at the time, painting a house over on Water Street. I sent a secretary to ask him to come by a little after three.

I was still alone when he showed up, a motley collection of paint spatters, whiskers, and faded cloth completely alien to any civilized conception of a government office. My secretary showed him in, though, as if he were clad in a three-piece suit and fresh from the barber, which tells you something about our town. It's informal. Partly because it's small and partly because its people waste little energy on nonessential appearances. They dress up mostly for church and they try to keep their drinking private.

I said, "Thank you, Bonny," and waved Howie to a seat. He took it, looked for my wastebasket, and got rid of his wad of chewing tobacco. "You wanted me, Mayor."

"Ayuh," I said. "Lydia Seltzer dragged me in on a project of hers. I thought you might be able to tell us something helpful."

"Like what?" He looked doubtful. He knew Lydia was the science teacher, and he knew nothing about science. I doubted he'd ever gotten past the sixth grade. I was starting to tell him about the problem when Lydia walked in, Bonny holding the door until I waved at her. Her wool was pink today, and her face was flushed with eagerness. The combination wasn't attractive, but I didn't imagine it was anything but temporary. I hoped she wouldn't be disappointed.

I introduced Howie to Lydia. "This is the fellow I was talking about. I was just going to tell him the problem."

She took the other chair. "Shall I go on, then?" When I nodded, she produced that paper again and then handed it to Howie. While he read, she said what she wanted, flatly and directly. The nervousness I had seen last night was gone.

When she finished, Howie set the paper on the corner of my desk and said simply, "Pork Hill." I raised my eyebrows, and he went on. "My dad was up there once. Ayuh, huntin' deer in the dark of the moon. He heard that scream. Didn't see nothin', though."

"Where's Pork Hill?"

"North by west, 'bout ten miles."

And that was all he had for us.

We now had a place to look, and the next dark of the moon was just two weeks away, in case that mattered. Lydia could hardly wait. She insited on borrowing a tent, sleeping bags, a Coleman stove, all the gear anyone could want for a night camping on a lonely hilltop. She got most of it from two members of the school board. She got their sons, too. Keith Hutchison and Ronny Jackson were two of her best students, and she thought they deserved a field trip, a little hands-on research. They thought so too, especially since it meant a Friday away from school. I didn't argue, since I was sure we could meet no danger from a superstition.

I wish I had been right. Keith was a lanky boy, tall, a forward on the school basketball team. Ronny was shorter, sturdier, a soccer player. Both had family, friends, girlfriends, good prospects. Keith, in fact, already had a scholarship for college. They had a lot to lose, but they were eager. Danger was just a myth, and they wouldn't miss this trip for worlds.

They didn't, of course. I didn't believe in any danger myself, so I didn't try to talk them out of it, and Lydia made it sound like a lark. All the way up there, the four of us and the gear crowded into my old station wagon, she waved her camera and ran on about the splash a picture of a real, live wendigo would make.

We loaded the car on Thursday night and left town shortly after noon on Friday. When we met in the town hall lot, I was surprised to see Lydia in dungarees and a red-checked wool shirt. It was so unlike her that, even though the rest of us were dressed similarly, she seemed to stand out. But the clothes were suitable for the trip, and I soon stopped noticing them.

It took us half an hour to reach the foot of Pork Hill, and another two hours to hump the gear to the top. The hill wasn't big, no more than eight hundred feet high, but it was steep and wooded and there was no path. The going was slow until we reached the top, where the trees disappeared. Pork Hill was one of those rocky knobs scattered over the state of Maine, its top scraped clean by glaciers and still inhabited only by lichen, moss, blueberry bushes, and a few stunted birches.

We pitched the tent in a mossy hollow between boulders, and the boys went back down the hill to gather firewood.

There were plenty of fallen branches there, and though we had the stove, a fire was a comforting thing to have at night. Even small mountains can get chilly after dark.

By suppertime, the woodpile was large enough to last a week. We had all taken time to explore the hilltop, too, following Lydia as she sought some clue to what a wendigo might be, some trace of something strange. We found nothing but glacial scours and animal droppings and a few weathered shotgun shells, though Lydia was hardly discouraged. As she said when the boys were finally kindling their fire, "It is a traveler, they say. Maybe it never stops here."

I said something which I now wish I hadn't. Though it probably didn't change a thing. "Then you'll have to move quickly to get a picture of it. It won't be waiting for you."

"I suppose I will," she said, fingering the camera on its strap around her neck. She bent, then, to the totebag she had brought and extracted a flash, one of those electronic ones that don't need bulbs. "I'd better be ready."

We ate—hamburgers and potato salad and coffee and bakery pie—and sat around the fire staring, satisfied for the moment by the mystery of its flames. Only Lydia turned her head now and again to the darkness, straining to see what she waited for. But there was nothing but the odor of earth and growing things, the sight of stars like raindrops on a windshield. The air turned chill enough for sweaters, and we listened to the chirps and buzzes of insects, the lazy notes of sleepy birds, the small croaks of tree frogs, and the rare crackling of brush as some animal—deer, coon, rabbit, coyote, even a wild house cat—passed within hearing.

We talked, of what it meant to be a mayor or a teacher or a student, of sports and fishing and hunting, of politics and taxes. We told no ghost stories, though. I suppose that must have been because our mission was too much like such a tale. It would have been tempting fate to describe horrors and frights, and fate never needed tempting.

Eventually, we talked ourselves out and let the fire die. We were readying ourselves for the sleeping bags, washing up, brushing teeth, when it happened. We heard a moan at first, low as if far distant, swelling loud and clear and close. At its peak it sounded like a baby must when it is being dipped in boiling oil.

It was a little after midnight and as black as the inside of a closet. We had been using the light of an electric lantern as well as the glow of the coals. We had been contained in a small and cozy room, but that sound broke down the walls. I shuddered, and Lydia ran, the soap and water spilled on the moss, her camera ready in her hand, Keith hot on her heels. Ronny would have gone too, but I held him still with a hand on his shoulder. "Let go!" he cried. "I want to see it too!"

"Remember the stories," I said as softly as I could over the dying scream. "Someone should mind the camp." He subsided as I'd hoped he would. When the scream was gone and the night was again silent, I added, "Now. Now we can look for them."

We took our flashlights and tried to follow the marks Lydia and Keith had crushed into the moss as they ran. But the tracks soon disappeared in the tangled skein of prints we had made earlier that afternoon. We called and shouted. We covered every inch of that hilltop, again and again, shining our lights down cracks in the rock and under bushes, checking the bottom of every drop we came across, large or small. We searched until our batteries were exhausted, and then we huddled around a rebuilt fire, worrying, starting at every crackle of brush.

With the dawn, we searched and called again, but we had no better luck. Lydia and Keith had vanished without a trace, just as in the legends. I was closer than ever before to believing in the wendigo, and thus in ghosts, banshees, and all the rest of what I had once dismissed as so much claptrap.

Our second search soon ended in futility. We made a hasty breakfast, doused the fire, and broke camp. Then we lugged the gear back to the car. It took longer, since there were fewer of us now. I had plenty of time to berate myself, to think I should never have helped Lydia with her obsession, never have let the boys come along, never have come myself. But who could have expected a myth to be real? Who could have guessed it would cost us half our party? And what was the wendigo? What was it that made a sound that swelled and faded like a freight train's whistle, that screamed like a soul in torment? Like a god on a cosmic treadmill? If only I had known, I might have left the boys in town, but I would still have come with Lydia, hoping to protect her, shield her. I felt as I might for the child I didn't have, and I mourned.

Ronny was less thoughtful. He shivered when he thought of the night, and once he dropped his load with a clatter of pans. He had lost a teacher and a friend. He might have been lost himself. The horror of that scream had almost touched him, and he could barely control his thoughts. He stayed close to me, keeping a wary eye on the woods around us, talking endlessly, trying to imagine what had happened to the others. He failed to disrupt my thoughts only because I was as obsessed myself. There was no conversation. He talked on, while I muttered responsive noises, and we both scurried around our separate skulls, like rats seeking the way out of a trap.

By midmorning, we were back in town. I stopped the car in front of the town hall. The police station was across the street. We would have to go there first, of course. Missing persons, runaways, lost in the woods, carried off by a mythical beast, had to be reported, search parties organized, motions gone through even if they could do no good. Ronny was still talking, muttering, his skin a cold and clammy white, his eyes glazed. I helped him out of the car and steered him across the road. I remember being glad he hadn't collapsed while we had work to do. It would have been a shame to leave all that gear on top of Pork Hill.

Our town's Chief of Police was a heavy-bellied man whose moon face wore a thin mustache. He was young, about thirty, and as competent as we needed. Most of his energies were spent on rounding up drunks and vandals, occasional burglars, and the odd con man. He could do the work because the town was small and the crime rate low, but he could never hope to improve his lot. He would grow old in the job, the gut would sag, the cheeks jowl and the eyes go piggish. The tattoos on his forearms would fade, and somewhere along the line we would have to get rid of him. I wouldn't miss him; no one would. His sense of social class was far too keen.

When we entered his office, he rose and said, "G'morning, Mayor! I thought you were going wendigo hunting yesterday?"

"We did," I said shortly.

"Ah!" He grinned jovially, as if we shared some secret. "Stealing a march on your great white huntress, hey?"

"Whatever do you mean?" I asked. I was irritated by his tone, impatient with what had to be nothing but nonsense. But his next words sent me back.

"Lydia Seltzer. She didn't go with you."

It didn't sound like a question, but what else could it be? "Of course she did. That's why I'm here now. She disappeared last night. She and Keith Hutchison."

The Chief plopped his bulk back into his swivel chair. He looked startled. "But. . . ." Then he paused, looking at Ronny as if for the first time. "What's the matter with him?"

"Shock and exhaustion," I said. "We were up all night, searching for them. Maybe one of your men would get him over to the hospital and tell his parents where he is."

"Of course, Mayor." He pushed a button on his desk intercom. Then he said, "Maybe you'll tell me what happened when . . ." A patrolman entered, was given his instructions, and left with Ronny. The Chief turned back to me. "Now," he said.

I gave him the story. He nodded when I was done. "The shock I can understand," he said. "But why didn't you get here hours ago?"

"I didn't think it wise to go stumbling through the woods in the dark. Besides, I hoped we might find something in the morning."

"Not that it really makes a difference. A search party wouldn't do any good."

"Why not? They could still be there someplace! Maybe they fell in a hole we didn't see, or got lost in the woods."

"No." He shook his head and rose again. "C'mon, I'll show you."

He led me back to the small cell block. When we entered the narrow corridor, lined with steel bars, I could hear a noise, a jabbering sound, wordless, random. Or almost random. As he steered me toward the noise, I began to pick out shreds that might hold meaning: "fetal train," "stars and stars," "hopper freight," "take yon train," and more, though those were clearest. I wondered what madman he was holding here. And then we faced the last cell in the row. Through the bars, I made out a form strapped onto the narrow bunk, head tossing, face bruised and scratched, denim and wool clothes torn and soiled. It was Lydia.

The Chief spoke. "We picked her up like that yesterday afternoon. She walked into town, went straight to the school, and tried to get into her classroom, raving all the time, just like this. The substitute called the principal, and he called us. I'm waiting for the judge to sign the papers now, and then one of the men'll drive her to Augusta."

AMHI. The Augusta Mental Health Institute. Where they would try to bring her back, perhaps with drugs and electric shocks. But what else could anyone do? I turned away.

Back in the Chief's office, I remembered Lydia's camera. Did he have it? He did, along with everything that had been in her pockets. "Then perhaps," I said, "it might be a good idea to have the film developed. She could have got her pictures after all, and they could help the doctors understand what's wrong with her now."

"Of course," he said, and I left. I wanted sleep, but I should return the gear Lydia had borrowed first and tell Keith's family what had happened. Then, maybe, I could begin to puzzle over how Lydia had disappeared last night and reappeared yesterday. Time travel was impossible, wasn't it?

The Hutchisons and Jacksons were enraged. With me, with Lydia, with the town, with the school. One boy lost, another ill, but the lost one most on their minds. Jack Hutchison swore he would run against me come the next election, sue me for every penny I had, have Lydia fired if she ever regained her wits. But the prospect of no longer being mayor didn't bother me—after all, it didn't pay—and the trip had officially been a school field trip, and the school had insurance to cover lawsuits.

And then that fuss died down. The pictures came out.

Lydia had her wendigo, twice. One shot showed a line of shiny boxes stretched down a gleaming tunnel. The other showed Keith walking away from the camera, hand in hand with a figure that wasn't human, through a vast cavern of a room. The shiny boxes covered the floor of that room, and they were surrounded by machines that bore vague resemblances to freight dollies and forklift trucks.

I could guess what the wendigo really was. An interstellar freight train, its tracks looping close to Earth at certain times and places, a freight that could be hopped by anyone who got too close to its passing field. "Fetal"? Maybe "ftl," faster than light. By "take yon" had she meant "tachyon"? I read enough to know what that was, how it might fit, and Keith was alive and well, Earth's envoy to other worlds. Lydia, on the other hand, had been sent back on the next train, going faster than light, backward in time just enough to get her home a day before she left.

By the time Lydia stopped raving and returned to her job, Pork Hill could no longer be visited, either by deer poachers or by would-be interstellar hobos. The army had taken it over, and it was now ringed by wire fence and armed guards while the experts tried to find a way to flag some passing train down.

I don't know if they'll succeed. Lydia can't tell us anything, since she now seems to have no memory of her journey, and if it weren't for that last picture of Keith I'd be tempted to compare us to the moose. For years, the rutting bulls would answer train whistles by charging down the tracks into the engine. To the bull moose, it seems, the whistles sounded like the cry of a cow in heat, and they never learned the difference. The slaughter only stopped when the companies changed the note of the whistles.

But we can't be the equivalent of animals running head-on against an oblivious technology. After all, who among us would walk out of a railway station hand in hand—or hoof in hand—with a moose?